INTERNATIONAL PRAISE FOR
SILENT REACH

D1267934

SILENT REACH

OSMAR WHITE

Library of Congress Catalog Card Number: 79-10508

ISBN 0-345-29517-X

This edition published by arrangement with
Charles Scribner's Sons

Manufactured in the United States of America

First Ballantine Books Edition: August 1981

Cover photo by Anthony Loew

PROLOGUE

WHEN the sun dipped below the shattered battlements of Mount Featherstone, the east wind, fiery from its passage over a thousand miles of desert, died away. The cliffs of the Beechover Gorge changed color from crimson to purple and the wild creatures sheltering in their caverns and deep-scored ledges began to stir.

Nathan Ebbet stirred with them. He had learned from the euros, the small gray mountain kangaroos which had established colonies near the pools at the river source, never to travel in the heat of the day but to retreat into the rock piles and conserve body fluids. For more than four hours he had lain without moving at the back of the cave where the long-vanished Yilta people buried their dead. When the copper glare in the rag of sky framed by the entrance faded, he tucked his feet under him and stood up, fingering the fine sand from the corners of his eyes.

This, young Ebbet remembered disconsolately, was his last day on Featherstone. The chief geologist at Excon Four had been unmoved by his almost tearful plea for more time.

"Negative, Ebbet. You've had your three weeks. You're supposed to be a pro, not a rock hound. Bring in your notebooks written up and your samples properly labeled for a change. I want you and Jack Lightning on the mindrill team at Lake Triton on Monday morning. Report here Saturday. Over and out."

The bloody tinpot Hitler! The trouble with Margan was that he had no imagination. He'd rather trust a magnetometer than a man in the field. It was criminal negligence to pull him back to camp before he'd had a chance to prospect the pegmatites on the south buttress. And what the hell use would Jacky Lightning be

1

on a mindrill team anyway? He was a black, loafing bastard—work shy. He never tried. He spent his days tinkering with the clapped-out winch on the Bedford truck, fishing in the pools for yellowbellies, pottering about, and sleeping while the young-fella boss did the donkey work with hammer, gads, and specimen bags.

Ebbet bared his very white teeth in frustration and began stowing the day's harvest of rock samples in his rucksack. Only when he came to sorting and wrapping the stone artifacts gathered from the floor of the burial cave did the scowl fade from his face. The spearheads were particularly fine—symmetrical in a laurel-leaf pattern with razor-sharp, fluted edges. The vanished tribe which had brought its dead to this secret place had achieved rare skill in knapping quartzite. The *leilera* blades used for skinning and the *eloera* adze flakes for dressing wood were exquisitely fashioned. He'd be damned if he'd sell *this* stuff to old Westman at the going rate of ten dollars a pound. Not hammerstones, hand axes, and scrapers of this quality. Every single one of these pieces was worth that much—maybe double if he could flog them to the American technicians at Port Hedland.

So he wrapped each artifact separately in paperbark, stowed them in the side pockets of the rucksack where they would come to no harm, and dragged his burden from the cave mouth onto the wide ledge that sloped down to his ascent route a mile away.

It was not until he knelt down to slip the packstraps over his shoulders that he saw the *gimiri* stone half buried in the rubble underfoot. It must be a *gimiri* stone, he deduced subconsciously, because it was so unmistakably crystalline in form and therefore an erratic in this mass of sedimentary detritus. He prised it carefully out of the yellowish matrix in which it was embedded for half its length and hefted it. Twenty or thirty pennyweights. Hexagonal. Little if at all waterworn, but covered by a tough, fine-grained limey cement. It would clean up into an almost perfect rock crystal—probably clear but possibly smoky or purple.

Yes, it was certainly a *gimiri* stone because it must

have been brought here onto the ledge by the people who fashioned the spearheads and the knives. What a pity there was no market for *gimiri* stones. . . . Even the Americans were skeptical if you pulled one from your pocket and said, "This is one of the spirit stones, the lucky pieces, that the old aboriginal medicine men used to carry around in their amulet bags to make magic with."

Old Westman had made the point succinctly: "And you remember, Nathan my boy, it ain't no use bringing me artifac's that don't look like artifac's, see? I ain't in the science business like you. I sell genuine cheap Stone Age souvenirs. And they don't come off of native reserves, but off of stations and mining leases. You've got to be able to see they're handmade. Get the message?"

Well, with a bit of luck the stone would show color and be worth a few dollars in a rock shop. Ebbet slipped it into the pocket of his shorts, hoisted his pack, and set off down the inclined ledge pondering totally unrelated questions. Why would Wongai tribesmen want to haul the bodies of their dead up a vertical rock chimney to plant them in a burial cave? They'd have needed ropes—and old-time Wongais didn't know how to make ropes. There must be another way onto the roof of the tabletop. But where? Had a rockfall obliterated the easier route? Did one of the caverns in the walls of the gorge lead upward?

Damn Margan! In another week he'd have had the answers from the mountain. But now they must wait until he had the money to go it alone. That might take another year if he wanted proper equipment. What he needed was a stroke of luck—something impossible like a win in a lottery or an opalized human skull or a legacy from a rich uncle he'd never heard of. . . . But, shit, nobody in the Ebbet family ever got that sort of break! The sensible thing to do would be to ditch the girl friend, take a job on the crayfishing boats for the summer, save all his money, and buy equipment. Then he'd come back next year and clean out the floor of the cave thoroughly. If the sacred *gimiri* stone was any guide, there must be enough museum stuff lying around on it to stake him for six months on the opal fields at Andamooka.

Jacky Lightning was not in camp when young Ebbet, sweating heavily from the exertion of the descent with sixty pounds of specimen on his back, trudged down the donkey path that skirted the western margin of the big pool beside which they had camped and dumped his pack under the tailgate of the truck. The cooking fire in a trench beside the trailer van was dead. No wood had been gathered. The water bag hanging on a hook beside the door was almost empty and dirty dishes from the morning meal were still in the tin basin, buzzing with blowflies.

Nathan Ebbet felt the blood pounding in his temples. That loafing son of a bitch! God, Doc Margan was going to get an earful on the subject of Jacky Lightning!

"Jack!" he bellowed. "Coo-ee! Jack!"

A flock of galahs rose screeching out of the cabbage-tree palms and a flotilla of pelicans took off from the backwater, thumping frantically. Ebbet listened intently after the racket of echoes triggered by his shout subsided. Then he wrenched open the door of the truck cabin and pounded furiously on the horn. The metal bray bounced back and forth from the painted cliffs in ear-splitting cacophony. That ought to stir up the dopey sod, wherever he was. . . .

Fuming with anger at having been cheated of the day's end luxury of a warm shower from an oil drum and a quart pot of tea, Nathan Ebbet rummaged for sticks from the nearest deadfall, flung them on the ashes of the fire, and took a towel and a bar of soap down to the muddy bank of the pool. He stripped and bathed in the shallow water, lathering his curly black hair energetically and scooping up water in his hands to sluice his body. He took his time but Jack Lightning had still not returned when he finished. He sounded the horn again. There was still no answering shout.

Night had now overtaken the brief twilight and the darkness was full of muted sounds—the squeak of flying foxes leaving their camps to forage, the distant bellow of a scrubber bull, a susurration of small birds disturbed at their drinking by some predator. The frogs were tuning their orchestras and beetles began battering at the screen door.

Ebbet lit a gas lamp and brewed tea on a Coleman. Then he opened a can of beans, forked food into his mouth, and swallowed it without tasting. Apprehension was beginning to replace the indignation he had felt at Jack Lightning's absence. What on earth could have induced Jacky to wander so far from the van that he could not get back before dark? Could he have fallen somewhere and hurt himself—broken a leg or hit his head? Christ, it was too early to get in a panic yet! It was only a little after eight o'clock. Still, a lamp on the cab might be an idea. Relax. Be sensible. Soon enough to worry if the man wasn't back by morning. . . .

Meanwhile there was no point in sitting clucking like a broody hen. It made no odds that Excon camp was the best part of two hundred miles away. All he had to do if he needed help was to get on the emergency frequency and yell for it. If the trouble was serious they could have a chopper up here in hours. To kill time he'd have a shot at cleaning up the *gimiri* crystal and identifying it—not the sort of job he'd have undertaken if Jack Lightning was in camp because the silly black bugger was superstitious.

Young Ebbet lit the second lamp, stood it on the cab roof, and closed and locked the van door. He retrieved a battered copy of *Elements of Mineralogy* from the drawer under his bunk, pliers, emery paper, a magnifying glass, and a set of hardness pencils from his field kit, and set to work to clean one face of the stone. It was occluded by fine, baked mud, and an even more finely textured cement on which the emery paper made little impression. That might well indicate that the *gimiri* stone had lain on the floor of the ledge for centuries. But it had certainly been carried there by human agency. The cliff was weathered limestone, and the nearest pegmatites in which he had tried so hard to interest Doc Margan were a good three miles away.

A man really needed lab equipment for this job. He'd quit when he'd cleaned up enough of the surface to try for streak and get some idea of the color. . . .

In half an hour Nathan Ebbet had made enough progress to determine that a no. 8 pencil left no streak and that the luster of his stone was adamantine. Color was still indeterminate because he had removed the cement from only one face and it was impossible to tell if the crystal was entirely opaque or partly translucent. He began working on the adjacent face, but after ten minutes or so was interrupted by noises outside the van. He slipped the stone hastily into his pocket again, rose, and unlocked the door, throwing it wide. Just beyond the circle of light thrown by the beacon lamp, the sooty backdrop of night was studded with tiny, red reflectors. Then there was a soft, accelerating beat of hooves. . . .

Wild donkeys. A dozen or more. What the hell were they on about? Usually they stayed well clear of camp, watering at a downstream pool. Something had scared them off.

Ebbet sounded the horn again, took the beacon lamp, and started on the path to the deep hole where he knew Jack Lightning often set night fishing lines on springers. Every two or three hundred yards he stopped, put the light down, cupped his hands to his mouth, and shouted with all the power of his lungs, *"Jack! Whoo-ee! J-a-ack!"*

At the hole he found that Lightning had set a line at a favorite spot, a flat rock overlooking the deepest water. A fish had hooked itself. The springer pole was jerking.

Automatically, indifferently, Ebbet pulled it in, flipped it far back onto dry land, and stepped to the rim of the shelf. The stars had lost their hard glister as a crescent moon rose and swam on its back through a sky of deepest turquoise. Now he knew in his bones that Jack Lightning had come to grief somewhere in the gorge . . . somehow. He flung his head back and bellowed at the cliffs, "Whoo-ee! Jack-ee!"

While the echoes were answering "ee-ee-ee, ee-ee-ee" in diminuendo, death came silently and instantly to Emanuel Nathan Ebbet, cadet geologist, aged twenty years and four months.

CHAPTER 1

THE time of departure came and the loud-speaker in The Cockpit echoed a final call for all passengers on Flight 220 to Perth to board their plane loading through gate nine. George Galbraith was drunk—to his own satisfaction and the well-concealed embarrassment of the neat gray man sitting opposite him. They were an incongruous but not improbable pair. The neat gray man might well have been a housemaster in an unprogressive but expensive private school where the staff still wore neckties. And George might have been head prefect the year before last, elated by having passed his first-year university examinations with second-class honors.

When George Galbraith was drunk he was invariably cheerful—and garrulous, hyperbolic, and facetious. These foibles had irritated a succession of ambassadors and first secretaries, but since he was drunk only rarely, and never indiscreet in his flow of extravagant talk, they bore with him. There are diplomatic advantages in having on post a cultural—or commercial—attaché who seems so young that he cannot possibly have learned the uses of duplicity. George was in fact thirty-four years old and looked ten years younger. It gave him a head start in his line of business.

He raised his glass, examined the dregs of the sixth double martini he had consumed within the hour, and made to beckon a waiter.

"No," the neat gray man said firmly, "not now,

Galbraith. Finish the job later if you must. You'll miss your plane and that's something I couldn't grin and bear. Get moving, man. Get moving. Come along. Hup!"

George twitched his elbow away from the steadying hand beneath it and rose to his feet with a commendable imitation of sober dignity.

"Please, sir," he said reprovingly. "We are creating a disturbance. You will recall that we field agents are trained to assume a low profile at all times. Someone in this crowd of overfed displaced persons may see you manhandling me and remember us. That would never do. There must be no public notice of our parting. We must avoid emotion. Tears must wait, *da?*"

"Exactly," said the neat gray man. "Now come along like a good fellow."

George fell into step beside him, swaying slightly. Then a seraphic smile illuminated his fresh-complexioned face.

"Do you know, sir, I've just had a thought!"

"Congratulations. Keep moving."

"Seriously. I've just had the thought that I don't have to defer to you any more. If I choose to miss this flight, it would be entirely my own affair."

"Entirely. This way."

"At this moment I am my own man, constrained only by the provisions of the Official Secrets Act. True and correct?"

"True and correct."

"If I don't want to be hurtled across this godforsaken, desiccated, kangaroo-ridden, empty husk of a continent, I can opt out. I'm free and accountable to no one."

"Only to God and your bank manager. Watch it, Galbraith, it's an escalator."

"So it is. Silly of me. Thank you. Do you know something? Strong drink rageth. I am profoundly pissed."

"Quite."

"The drink has made me melancholy when I should be joyful in my freedom."

"Naturally. Gin is a depressing spirit."

George wagged his head. "It's all very well for you, Colonel Callaghan. You've made your distinguished career. You've left your mark. In two years' time—or is it three?—you will retire with honors from the Queen. You will enjoy the golden handshake, your stone cottage in Cornwall, your vintage Bentley, your armchair at your club, your still serviceable wife . . ."

"Watch the escalator, Galbraith!"

"Thank you. But do not deny me my civil liberties or my right of protest. Your world is secure and your future rosy. You have a son at Cambridge and a daughter married to a member of Parliament on his way up. Whereas I, at the peak of my powers and the prime of my youth . . ."

"Have a chance to step into a job which could carry twice your old salary and give you a freedom of action and conscience I've not had in thirty years. . . . No, Galbraith, you will *not* buy the evening papers. You'll be able to read them on the plane. Now you're being a bloody bore. Pull yourself together."

There was an edge to the gray man's tone that cut through the haze. George blinked and his gait steadied. After a moment he said: "I beg your pardon. If I'd known you were coming to the airport, Colonel, I wouldn't have got tight. I'm grateful for your courtesy. Can I ask a final question?"

"If you must."

"It was the Umbeni business that finally cooked my goose with the Executive, wasn't it?"

The gray man pursed his lips, then sighed.

"You could put it this way, Galbraith. The Executive badly needed a man in Umbeni. Now it hasn't got one. Professionally your lapse was inexcusable—though a lot of people thought it commendable personally. You must realize times have changed. Attempted rape of a British national no longer justifies a British diplomat, however junior, in assaulting the person of a Commonwealth head of state—even if the head of state is an illiterate savage and a syphilitic.

There's no room for moral sentimentality in resources diplomacy. You should have known that. Besides, it was an absolute miracle a Royal Navy corvette was in harbor and that you and the wretched girl managed to get to it without a gunfight. That would have been disastrous. However, it's all water under the bridge now. You can rest assured you've taken the sensible course. You're not leaving us under a moral cloud. Good luck, my dear chap, and good-bye. We'll miss your tomfoolery."

The handshake was cold, firm, and brief. The gray man turned and melted into a crowd of incoming passengers spilling out of an adjacent bay. Galbraith shook his head slightly and felt a sudden surge of distrust near to apprehension in his queasy belly. Momentarily he was sobered.

Rest assured! The cunning, half-invisible old bastard! If Colonel Neil Callaghan, formerly chairman of the Security Intelligence Executive assisting Her Majesty's Under-Secretary of State for Foreign Affairs, should ever elect to tell the world that it could rest assured the sun would rise tomorrow morning, wise men would do well to repent their sins, for doomsday would be at hand.

Why was he in Australia anyway? There was an angle to it. Callaghan had been at pains to make certain he caught this plane—and for some inscrutable reason had not passed the chore to an underling. But what angle?

He focused with great deliberation on the "Passengers Only" sign above the entrance passage to the plane and set a course. A trim hostess on gate-check duty glanced at his boarding pass and exclaimed: "You *are* cutting it fine! The team manager must be having kittens."

George looked startled—so startled that the girl examined the pass again, blushed faintly, and said: "I'm awfully sorry, sir. I thought you were with the rugby team. The first compartment please. . . ."

With Italianate finesse, George bestowed on her bottom the merest hint of a pinch, murmured:

"Really, my dear—rugby at my age?", and passed on into his new life.

He closed his eyes for takeoff from Melbourne and kept them closed. He still actively disliked flying although he had endured many hundreds of hours in these hurtling, pressurized, temperature-controlled drainpipes which gave spurious rationale to the term global village. Those last two martinis had been a mistake. He must conjure up the vision of an artificial horizon, keep it level, and on no account vomit. He must reflect on the reality of departure and make an intelligent assessment of what arrival might imply.

It was difficult to adjust to the idea that he was flying solo for the first time in twelve years. At the end of this journey there would be no languid second secretary waiting to greet the new commercial or cultural attaché, no well-polished limousine with a C.D. number plate parked obstructively and immunely at the concourse entrance. No accommodation would have been assigned in the chancellery or appointment made for a formal briefing by His Ex. No list of obligatory calls and cocktail parties. . . . For twelve years he had invariably operated from a base, access to which had been guaranteed by the production of a red passport. A red passport was a very present help in time of trouble—like God, only more reliable. From Ottawa to Osaka, Stockholm to Sydney, Dar es Salaam to Seoul or Samarkand, a red passport was the magic talisman that deflated bumptious policemen and enlivened comatose frontier functionaries. It certified membership in an elite that could command the subservience of all petty bureaucrats. It was a license to practice the arts of dissimulation and prevarication at an exalted level; to win respect, acclaim, and honors for the expertise with which you cooperated with your country's strong enemies and double-crossed its weak friends.

And now? Callaghan had hinted that he might safely ask for a salary of between twenty-five and thirty thousand dollars. It wasn't as much as he could earn if he went free-lance and worked for the Company, but there were uncertainties about the wisdom of that course ever since Nixon invited Kissinger to join him in prayer on the Oval Room floor. No, the money was adequate. It was Callaghan's angle that worried him. When an agent boobed, the Executive didn't sell him down the river to some scruffy provincial tycoon. It buried him urbanely in a sinkhole like Djakarta or Caracas where he could rot in dignified idleness, blow his stack and take to the bottle, or resign.

There must be an angle. Yet his recollection of Callaghan's summing up was crystal clear.

You can, of course, apply for a new foreign posting out of the mainstream, but I must warn you that there's nothing available at the moment likely to appeal to you in the least. You are under no compulsion to take leave and accept employment with the Wrightson organization. It's entirely up to you to decide after you have talked to the man. But I want to make one thing plain. If you do take the job you'll be responsible solely to your employer. You'll not be required or expected to provide information to the Executive or to any other agency. You've been recommended to Wrightson on the personal initiative of the high commissioner, with my concurrence, as possibly able to help him with certain problems of security.

You would be quite right to infer that Wrightson is *persona grata* with the high commissioner here but there are no political undertones or overtones in which the Executive has the faintest interest. They're exclusively domestic industrial and without international complications. . . .

One more thing, my dear chap. The man may strike you as naïve, and unsophisticated for one who has won great wealth and power quickly—but don't make the mistake of underestimating him.

Codswallop! There was an angle somewhere. George Galbraith's search for the elusive clue ended in a mental too-hard basket as he slid into shallow sleep.

". . . at thirty-two thousand feet. Our ground speed is four hundred and seventy knots and we should be on the ground at Perth airport at ten fifty-five, Western Australian time."

George surfaced reluctantly and glanced at his watch. Two hours to go. Then why were the seat-belt lights on? He pressed his nose against the window and squinted down. There were battlemented storm clouds maybe twenty thousand feet below. Summer lightning was raveling their edges. The stars were veiled by high stratus and the big Boeing was knifing through wisps of vapor and vibrating uneasily, nosing upward.

"Excuse me, sir, you'll be more comfortable with your belt fastened."

George groaned. "I was asleep," he croaked. "You woke me up with gongs and loudspeakers and flashing lights. I'm under sedation. There's been a death in the family. I know you're very beautiful, but please go away."

She leaned down, smiling. "I'm sorry to disturb you, sir. Your belt . . . Can I help you?"

"No one can help me. When are we due to crash?"

"Not for about five minutes," she said soothingly. "There . . . that's better. Would you like another pillow?"

"No. No, thank you. Just a double brandy if you can manage it before the moment of truth, dear girl."

In the midships galley she commented to the senior hostess, sotto voce, "That handsome hunk in J-1 has had an awful skinful. He was drunk as a skunk when he came aboard and passed out. Now he thinks he's Monty Python and wants a double brandy. Do you think it's okay?"

The senior hostess shrugged indifferently. "Make it a triple," she said. "When you've been rostered on wet runs as often as I have, Claire, you'll know that handsome hunks who think they're Monty Python are less trouble when they're unconscious."

So George slept again—this time deeply—through forty minutes of severe turbulence and subsequent excitements caused by a Chilean matron in the economy class. who went into premature labor and had to be accommodated behind a partition rigged to screen off the first row of seats facing the forward bulkhead.

His second awakening was even more painful than the first. A gang of pixie demolitionists was hard at work inside his skull and his tongue adhered tackily to the roof of his mouth. Out of the corner of one eye he saw someone sitting beside him in the aisle seat which had been vacant before. Cautiously he tilted his head and focused through slitted lids on a pair of hands in beige crocheted gloves rigidly grasping the handle of a large, clumsily fashioned satchel of crocodile hide. The incongruity was slow to register. Crocodile hide? But surely you didn't cobble up crocodile hide with waxed twine. Better look again. No, crocodile hide—without a shadow of a doubt.

George moved, winced, and raised the back of his seat gingerly. The girl was sitting bolt upright with the satchel across her knees. Seventeen—eighteen? Younger. Schoolgirl dowdy. Her camelhair coat, also genuine, was a size too large. She was wearing thick stockings and black lace-up shoes. Convent—or Salvation Army? Convent, of course, with a camel-hair coat . . . Big girl—heavy features with a southern European complexion, full lips, and a magnificent head of wavy, dark brown hair. Her mouth drooped a little at the corners and she sat unnaturally still.

"Hullo there," rasped George from his dry throat. "Where did you spring from? Don't tell me you've been there all the time."

She replied without moving her head: "They told me to sit here."

"Oh, I see."

After a pause she added: "It was when they changed people around to take the sick lady up to the front."

"The sick lady?" George shook his head and regretted it. "I must have been asleep."

She made no response. Queer kid. Scared stiff. Probably her first plane flight. If so, she wouldn't be scared much longer. The cabin lights dimmed. The landing lights blazed through the driving rain and the flaps came down with a grinding jolt.

George would have forgotten his companion completely if he had not seen, briefly but clearly as she unfastened her seat belt and stood up, that a fine metal chain linked her left wrist with the handle of the satchel of crocodile hide. Good God! A courier! But of what?

George was now wide awake but it was too late. Passengers were requested to disembark through the rear entrance. Ambulance men were busy up front. George lost sight of the camel-hair coat in the crowd scampering awkwardly under airline umbrellas across the puddled tarmac to the passenger lounge. Cyclone Christine, an unnaturally early arrival since it was still October, had turned back from the Indian Ocean to die untidily in flatulent thunderstorms on the seaward side of the Darling Ranges. The night smelled of flowering oleanders and aviation fuel. . . .

Would Mr. George Galbraith, a passenger from Canberra via Melbourne, please call at the information desk?

"Your transport, Mr. Galbraith," the desk clerk said, waving a weary hand at a small, wizened old man wearing a chauffeur's cap on the back of his bald head, dungarees, and a T-shirt with "Disneyland" stenciled across the chest.

"Callaghan, you shit!" George said under his breath.

"Your name Galbraith, mate?"

"Yes."

"Outside at the taxi rank. The blue Chevy. Gimme yer ticket and I'll get yer bags."

George watched the spry ancient dart like a terrier through the pack milling in front of the baggage-delivery bay. Then he drifted toward the exits. He spotted the girl with the camel-hair coat and satchel ahead of him. Curiouser and curiouser! She was walking sedately between two nuns in white habits and wimples.

The blue Chevrolet tourer parked in the first space at the taxi rank was not a taxi. Prudently George delayed getting into the back seat until the decrepit chauffeur reappeared with his suitcases and stowed them in the trunk.

An irate taximan banged on the roof, thrust his head in the driver's window, and yelled, "Get that bloody tank off this rank, Grandpa!"

"Get knotted—and wipe yer chin, bub," the old man snapped, and wound the window up violently. Then he leaned back.

"Yer must be a real V.I.P., sport. Ham Wrightson's girl said to tell you there was a mistake. You've been booked at the Golden Galleon. They canceled the Ascot."

"It sounds all right, but I wouldn't know."

"First trip to the West, eh?"

"Yes."

"Me name's Bob. I'm standing in for Ham's regular driver, Ted. Ted rolled the Mercedes on the way out. Fair bloody crash but he got off lucky. Thought I was goin' to miss yer, but yer plane was late. Lousy weather. Was it a rough trip?"

"No, just a rough send-off," said George. "You might be able to tell me something, Bob . . ."

"What?"

"Did you see those two nuns with a girl get into the taxi behind us?"

"Uh-huh."

"Would you happen to know what order the nuns belong to?"

"Order? Oh, I get you. Wouldn't have a clue, friend. I'm Presbyterian."

George sighed. "Not to worry," he said. "Only don't roll the Chevy. That would be too much in one day."

CHAPTER 2

HAMILTON WRIGHTSON looked the part, even though he had not shaved before coming to the office in a slightly soiled mesh shirt and unpressed gabardine trousers. His was the aura of a man with power. He was fifty-six years old. No one ever remarked that he looked either younger or older. He was of medium height, broadly built, heavily muscled, big bellied, and inclined to move clumsily. He had a large nose, prominent hazel eyes, and skin the color and texture of an old saddle. The preliminaries of the interview were offhandedly routine. Wrightson made it clear he was impatient of idle conversation.

"Very well. Let's get down to it. Tell me, Galbraith, did you enjoy the work you were doing for the . . . Board of Trade?"

George smiled gently, noting the calculated hesitation.

"On the whole, yes."

"Why?"

"Mainly because I was good at it, I suppose. Partly because the job carried with it what might be described as fringe benefits."

"Why did you resign?"

"I didn't." George looked straight into the prominent hazel eyes. "I was asked to take indefinite leave."

"Any reason given?"

"Necessary economies. Cutting down on intelligence personnel in areas where the British political influence, trade, and commerce are declining. The toothless bulldog regrets . . . That sort of thing."

Wrightson was not amused. "So you believe you were axed for reasons of economy?" he asked sharply.

Take care! That one was loaded in both barrels.

"Not for a moment, Mr. Wrightson."

17

"Then why?"

"Because you and the high commissioner—or interests he aims to protect—are concerned with some project on which I can't be employed officially because of what I imagine are political considerations. It would have been better if the high commissioner had seen fit to take me into his confidence. But then, of course, Sir Ambrose Fergusson is a career diplomat. The first rule of career diplomacy is never to take anyone into your confidence."

The cool impertinence of the reply caught Wrightson off balance. His bleached, shaggy eyebrows drew together and the leathery jowls darkened. But, after a silent half minute, he relaxed.

"Well," he said. "Fergusson and Callaghan warned me you were a smart bastard. I told them I needed one. Okay. Do you want this job with Conwright or don't you?"

"I can't answer that until I know what the job is."

"Fair enough. But if you use your skull and draw one set of conclusions from Fergusson's double-talk, you ought to be able to draw a second set."

"May I smoke?"

Wrightson blinked. "Sure. I don't, so I forget."

George lit a cigarette. "Since I've been employed by a British government agency in collecting and collating political and other information in various parts of the world," he said, "I assume you want me to collect political and other information of value to the industries in which you've got holdings. The high commissioner is sympathetic but can't risk being personally or officially involved."

Wrightson shook his head. "You don't score a bull for that, son," he said, "only an outer. The information I want isn't political—or at least I think not. We can look at that bit later. But there are one or two points not covered in this file about you." He tapped the closed manila folder on the desk in front of him. "Are you interested in money?"

"Comes the dawn," George said to himself. And aloud: "Of course. The alternative-society idea doesn't turn me on. But neither am I the kind of chap who could devote his whole life to making money. Let's say I'm interested to avoid being short of money when I see something I feel I need."

"No other ambition, eh?"

"I didn't say that I had no ambition. My career has had its long, dull spells, but you could put up with them because there were other times when the work was absorbing."

Wrightson appeared to be listening attentively, but he was looking past George now, rather than at him. "Suppose, Galbraith, you could use your know-how helping to build something really big, really important —would you reckon that was a career?"

"If I felt that I was using my know-how to help build something big and important by my own definition, I probably would."

The big man grunted, began to swivel his chair, but thought better of it and turned back.

"How long have you been in this country?"

"Ten weeks—waiting for reassignment. Or I believed so until four days ago."

"Do you like what you've seen of the place? The people?"

"I haven't seen anything of the place or the people. I was in Canberra the whole time."

Wrightson threw back his head and guffawed.

"Ten out of ten for that one, son," he chuckled. "You and I could even be on our way. Look, I'll show you something. . . ."

He heaved his bulk out of the chair, turned to the wall behind him, and rolled down a six-by-four map. It was a beautifully drafted projection of the administrative division of Western Australia lying north of the twenty-sixth parallel. Physical features, towns, roads, harbors, and airfields were boldly indicated in code colors.

"*That* territory," Hamilton Wrightson said, slapping an open hard hand into the center of the glazed buckram, "is bloody nearly ten times the size of Great Britain and Ireland. It's one of the most highly mineralized bits of dirt on the face of the earth and tens of thousands of square miles of it will grow crops and graze herds. And it's got a population of one person to every forty square miles. The fact that a handful of speculators in London and New York and Melbourne got taken to the cleaners by sharks in the mining boom —and a few Yanks lost their shirts in Ord River cotton and Kimberley beef—doesn't mean that country can't produce what the world needs and will be forced to buy one of these days. If you think I'm shoveling you prospectus bullshit, take a look at this. . . ."

He pulled down a transparent overlay sheet and fixed it to the map with paper clips. The clear plastic was pimpled with areas hatched in red, blue, and green. Wrightson jabbed at them with a thick, stubby forefinger.

"Twenty-three million acres. Freehold, pastoral leases, mining tenements, or live options which forty Conwright companies either own outright or hold through controlling interest. I own a majority of shares in the holding company. See here . . . Red's for mining, green for pastoral, blue for the odds and sods like prawning, culture pearl farms, processing plants, town developments, and so on. Last year we netted thirteen and a quarter million out of ore, salt, gypsum, cattle, wool, fish, and hides. Well, Galbraith?"

"It's a great deal of country and a great deal of money," George murmured.

Wrightson snorted. "Don't give me that. It's a great deal of country earning fuck-all money—and you know it. Nine out of ten Conwright shows lose money or just break even because they're still undeveloped. The tenth pays the bill for developing them—slowly but surely. I don't play tag with the money sharks and pay fourteen percent in the hope of making fifteen. I finance my own projects. I'm not in a hurry. Until I was forty years old all I owned was the leasehold of half a million acres of scrubland that carried two thousand head of merino sheep in a good season. And I owned a dirty big hole in the ground that produced about eight thousand dollars' worth of low-grade copper ore every year for use in fertilizers. The newspapers say I found Mount Millswyn in '63, and sold the property to the Japanese for a lump sum and royalties worth four million a year. Crap! I found Mount Millswyn when I was lugging a geiger counter through the gorges in '52 looking for uranium. I had the leases sewn up a year before Canberra lifted the embargo on iron-ore exports. For ten years I had the sense to keep my trap shut, my ear to the ground, and sweat it out until the time was ripe. Well?"

George, puzzled by the man's vehemence and apparent candor, was a little uneasy.

"It's the kind of success story you don't hear often these days, Mr. Wrightson," he said politely.

Wrightson's mouth curled. "What you really mean is —that's old hat. It happened more than ten years ago. Why keep blowing your own trumpet, Wrightson? It's rusty."

George lifted his eyebrows protestingly. "Why not blow your own trumpet? It was the start of a twenty-three-million-acre empire, wasn't it?"

Wrightson spun his chair and sat down again. "Yes. Twenty-three million acres of scrub and sand spinifex grass and rock, handpicked out of a quarter of a million square miles. Why would a man who'd already made his killing want to take on developing that?"

"I suppose," George said drily, "it would be one way of spending an income of four million a year. Plowing it back. With good luck and good management you get the snowball effect in the end. The rate of growth and profit accelerates."

Wrightson stared at him reflectively, then dropped his eyes to the manila folder, opened it, and flipped through the typewritten sheets.

"It says here you spent time on the Persian Gulf and in Saudi Arabia as well as Pakistan and East Africa."

"Yes."

"Did you always sit on your behind in the embassy or did you get out into the field?"

George's tone was cold. "I don't know what information about my previous employment you've got in that folder, Mr. Wrightson, but whatever it is I'm not prepared to elaborate on it."

Wrightson grinned. "Yeah. Fergusson said you

could be a proper prickly bastard. But do you know
what a population of one person to forty square miles
means?"

"Yes. It means your empire's in a howling wilder-
ness—in a country where people won't live unless
they're driven to it."

The grin relaxed into a smile—a smile with perhaps
a hint of contemptuous superiority. "That's right. Like
Siberia, or Alaska, or the western prairies in the States
a hundred years ago. Do you believe in free enterprise, Galbraith—or do you go along with the socialist
line?"

Oho! The thirty-thousand-dollar-a-year question. . . .
Callaghan had said naïve and Callaghan had been
right—but not so naïve that he'd fall for "I've always
voted Conservative, sir."

George took his time answering. "I don't believe the
labels manufacturers stick on soap powders, Mr.
Wrightson. They're designed to deceive, not describe.
Likewise I don't believe the labels politicians stick on
the theories and beliefs they claim to hold. So I can't
honestly say I believe in free enterprise—or in the socialist line. I'm an agnostic about 'isms.' The people
who preach them, don't practice them. They use them
as a smoke screen to cover their attempts to win or increase personal power."

Wrightson was sardonic. "And that's what your
work's taught you? Not to believe in anything?"

"You get me wrong. I said I don't believe in 'isms.'
Being a political agnostic has been useful. If you don't
lean yourself, then you're in a better position to judge
which way other people—particularly people on the
other side of the fence—do lean, or are likely to lean."

"What fence do you mean?"

"You could call it the fence that divides people of
different races, origins, environments, customs, reli-
gions. I'm interested in doings on the other side. But
when the stakes are down, my loyalties have their
roots in my own backyard."

Hamilton Wrightson rubbed the graying stubble on
his chin. "You're an offbeat young bugger, Galbraith,

but then you've followed an offbeat trade. Maybe we can get together. Maybe we can't. Now listen—"

An intercom buzzer sounded loudly on the desk. Wrightson started, glared at it disbelievingly for a second, snapped a switch, and bellowed, "What in the name of Christ has got into you, Weatherley? I thought I told you no calls!"

The tinnily distorted soprano at the other end of the line was agitated.

"I'm sorry, Mr. Wrightson, there's an emergency."

"An emergency? What sort of emergency? Where?"

"At Excon Four. Dr. Margan wants you to call him urgently."

"Why?"

"Nathan Ebbet is missing."

"Sweet Jesus!"

Hamilton Wrightson might give the impression of being clumsy, but he could move with startling rapidity. Before George could rise from his chair the man was out of the room.

Five minutes later a tiny woman, well in her forties, with an apple-shaped face and a withered little apple-blossom mouth came in, carrying a tea set on a teak-wood tray. She placed it on the desk and said, "I'm Hilda Weatherley, Mr. Galbraith—Mr. Wrightson's private secretary. Would you like a cup of tea?"

"That's very good of you, Miss Weatherley," George said with his brightest smile. "Will Mr. Wrightson be long?"

She made a helpless motion with her hands. "I honestly don't know, Mr. Galbraith. There has been an accident at one of the prospecting camps. He's in the communications room speaking to Dr. Margan on the radiotelephone now. He may decide to go straight on to the airport."

George consulted his wristwatch. "Well, Miss Weatherley, in that case I'll just drink my tea and see how things turn out, eh? Would you be terribly kind and call a taxi for me in . . . let's see . . . fifteen minutes?"

The apple-blossom mouth opened in surprise, even faint alarm, that this fresh-faced, unassuming young man should be so arrogant as to put a limit on the time he would wait for Mr. Wrightson.

"But Mr. Galbraith . . . I don't know for certain that he'll be going straight to the airport."

"Don't worry about it for a minute. He'll get in touch with me again and we'll fix a mutually convenient time to continue our talk. Oh, by the way, thank you for booking me into the Golden Galleon. It's very luxurious—and intriguing."

The smoothly careless change of subject seemed to reassure her. A twinkle came into the shrewd blue eyes behind the rimless spectacles.

"I'm so glad. Some people feel that the Golden Galleon is a little overdone."

He laughed heartily. "Of course, it's preposterously overdone. That's why it's intriguing. A by-product of the mining boom of a few years ago, I suppose? Does it pay?"

"It's a Conwright property," she said remotely. "You wished for the taxi in fifteen minutes, Mr. Galbraith?"

George was left to observe the office furniture in detail. No profit accrued. The exercise merely confirmed his impression that the man didn't give a damn about his image. Although grandly sited on the top of the twelve-story Conwright House, the boss's sanctum would have looked a trifle old-fashioned in 1930.

Three hours in the newspaper room of the state library on James Street yielded little more information about Wrightson than George had been able to glean from his crash homework sessions in Canberra. The daily and periodical press in 1964 had carried a number of ecstatic articles about the Mount Millswyn iron-ore find and the subsequent sale of the Wrightson leases to a Japanese–American consortium.

But for the newspaper biographers, Wrightson the discoverer had proved a dull subject. A profile in one Sunday paper described him as a simple, taciturn bushman whose domestic life-style in "a modest suburban bungalow" had been changed very little by his sudden acquisition of wealth. He had served in the Islands during the Second World War. He married Edith Macgregor, the daughter of the master of a pearling fleet in Broome, after his discharge from the army in 1946. There was one son of the marriage, John, born in 1947, who now had business interests in eastern Australia. The only bright spot in two soporific columns of stodge, headed "Croesus in Close Up," was Edith's confession that her greatest thrill from Hamilton's Millswyn windfall had been his gift of "an absolutely enormous automatic washing machine."

Maybe, George reflected, Callaghan had been wrong about the naïvety. In his experience there was no such beast in the financial jungle as a simple, taciturn bushman with the nous to create and hold together a pastoral and mining empire of twenty-three million acres. Who advised Hamilton Wrightson to affect soiled shirts and a three-day stubble—some extremely expensive firm of non-image makers?

George wondered if a few drinks in the pubs frequented by indigenous newspapermen might not serve his purpose better than honest library research, but there was no need for haste. Perth was a city that invited relaxation. He strolled west on St. George's Terrace, spent an hour in King's Park, distracted from his preoccupations by a brave show of late spring wildflowers, and made his way back to the Golden Galleon.

Hamilton Wrightson's preposterously overdone hotel might offend the aesthete but at least it pandered to the sybarite. For half an hour George took his ease on a double bed proportioned for gymnastics, thinking how vastly superior it was to the bed at the Canberra Regal where Juliette Fellini, cipher clerk at the Italian Embassy, had performed such skillful evolutions. Then he showered, changed into a safari jacket and slacks, and at eight thirty, the last lingering shadows of hangover dispelled, he went down to dinner in the Captain's Cabin, the least atmospheric of the Golden Galleon's three restaurants. There, fortune, which always favors the unworthy, smiled on him and solved the problem of what to do with one potentially unenchanted evening. She also was dining alone. Her au-

burn hair was done in ringlets and she wore a
Kashmiri sapphire of lima-bean size below her platinum wedding ring. Her figure was curvaceous and her
age might be only thirty-nine. Over coffee she confided that she was a refugee from one of the iron-ore
towns a thousand miles north, where ambitious hus-
bands worked a ninety-six-hour week.

There were no complications. At twenty to six the
next morning, George gently disengaged her fingers
from his pubic hair and left her in deep sleep, legs
opulently open. She was snoring, quietly and rather
charmingly.

What was the sailor's song?

> *She was a nice girl, a decent girl*
> *And her hair hung down in ringlets.*
> *A nice girl, a decent girl,*
> *But one of the roving kind.*

He saw the paper-wrapped half brick before he noticed the shattered plate glass of the French door
which opened onto his balcony. The message was in
headline type clipped from newspapers and held in
place by adhesive tape:

SPY
gO hOMe

CHAPTER 3

It was barely mid-afternoon but the Quarterdeck Bar at the Golden Galleon—seventeenth-century
Spanish naval décor with replicas of carronades and
ships' lanterns framed in cast aluminum—was well
patronized by American tool pushers and other oilmen
from the *Glamis* and *Miramar* rigs, laid off for the cyclone season after drilling dry holes on the North West
Shelf for seven months.

George Galbraith sipped at a vodka Collins alone at a side table, distastefully mulling over the wording and possible implication of two communications. The first was the message wrapped around the half brick. The second was exquisitely typed on heavy bond under an embossed Conwright Enterprises logo. It read:

CONFIDENTIAL

MEMORANDUM TO:	Mr. G. Galbraith
FROM:	H. Weatherley
DATE:	October 29th
SUBJECT:	*Your discussions with Mr. Wrightson*

I have transcribed the following message taped by Mr. Wrightson at the airport before his departure:

DEAR GALBRAITH, I HAVE BEEN CALLED AWAY UP THE BUSH ON URGENT BUSINESS AND I DON'T KNOW WHEN I'LL BE BACK. DIAGULSKI KNOWS THE SCORE AND WILL EXPLAIN. I TRUST CALLAGHAN'S JUDGMENT AND THINK WE CAN DO A DEAL. DIAGULSKI HAS MY AUTHORITY TO NEGOTIATE. I HOPE YOU AGREE TO HELP US. IN HASTE.

Mr. Wrightson was under pressure when he left, so I am taking the liberty of adding a few words of explanation as I understand you have not met Miss Diagulski. She has been with us for some years and is Mr. Wrightson's personal assistant. She had to accompany him on the aircraft but will return with it early tomorrow. I will telephone you at the hotel when she arrives and make an appointment for her to call at a convenient time.

Diagulski! To George's jaundiced mind the name conjured up visions of some Polish mare with gold-rimmed pince-nez and a mouth like a rattrap.

His anger had been steadily rising since he had been awakened at midday by Miss Weatherley's call. He'd been kept out of bed all morning by the "deep concern" of the management that a Golden Galleon guest should be subjected to the unpleasantness of

having a half brick thrown through his glass door by
vandals, by the pertinent questioning of the house detective, and the time taken to transfer his belongings
to another suite where the glaziers would not disturb
him.

When reception had not called him by the appointed hour of three o'clock to announce the arrival
of a visitor, he descended to the Quarterdeck, snarling
as he passed the desk, "If a woman comes looking for
me, tell her I'm in one of the bars. Don't page me."

But the indignant, terminal confrontation he had
been rehearsing in his mind did not follow the script.
He saw the stool-straddling drillers swivel their heads
and gape before he realized what had riveted their attention. A young woman wearing a superbly cut olive-
green pantsuit was threading her way between the
tables—a young woman who walked with such fluid,
aloof grace that he was immediately reminded of a
Siamese cat. She ran the gauntlet of twenty pairs of
avid eyes without either slowing or hurrying her gait.

Long conditioned to avoid solecism, George stopped
short of gaping, but his oblique examination took in
the perfection of her figure, the double cascade of ash-
blonde hair plunging to her shoulders, and the smooth,
deep-tan complexion that owed nothing to cosmetics.
She was one of the most strikingly beautiful women he
had seen in years. And to his consternation she walked
directly to his table, looked down, and said, "Are you
Mr. Galbraith? I'm Tamara Diagulski."

George rose with such startled haste that he overset
his glass.

"I . . . er . . . yes. Galbraith. How terribly clumsy of
me. I do apologize. How do you do?"

She smiled—a devastating smile that curved her
wide, softly contoured mouth a little awry and revealed white, even teeth. A drink waiter appeared like
a genie out of a bottle—a drink waiter in canvas cu-
lottes, striped skivvies, a bandana, and a false tarred
pigtail. The Golden Galleon was consistent in striving
for atmosphere. The small puddle of liquor on the tabletop and the glass vanished under the bewilderingly
expert flick of the waiter's napkin.

"Momento, signore. . . . Vodka Collins. Will the *signorina* order also?"

"Hullo, Mario," she said cheerfully. "It's nice to see you again. Yes, a vodka Collins as usual, please." And to George: "A good omen, I hope, Mr. Galbraith."

"Subito, signorina."

"And Mario—perhaps you could arrange for the tray to be sent to Mr. Galbraith's room?"

"Volentieri, signorina." Mario bowed low.

"Shall we go, Mr. Galbraith?"

"Apparently we are already on our way, Miss Diagulski," George said drily, following a pace behind her, acutely aware of his own embarrassment—and of twenty pairs of eyes that followed their retreat with lewd speculation.

"Gee-zuzz," exclaimed the Mississippian on the end stool very audibly, "that lucky bastard's gonna vanish without a trace!"

Mario put down the tray and withdrew, leaving the door open, for he was Swiss trained of the old school. Tamara Diagulski closed it, switched off the air conditioning, and opened the windows to the balcony. She stood there for a moment inhaling the warm, gum-scented air that flowed in. Then she turned. He saw that her eyes, merely large and dark in the carefully contrived gloom of the Quarterdeck, were an extraordinary shade of deep violet.

"I detest air conditioning unless it's absolutely necessary, Mr. Galbraith. Shall we sit down?"

"All that I have is yours, Miss Diagulski—and, in any case, I'm the guest of your company. Sit down wherever you prefer."

If she was aware of the irony she did not respond to it.

She went to the armchair beside the desk. He put her drink beside her, offered his cigarette case.

"No, thanks. Not never, but seldom."

He lit a cigarette for himself and waited. The lady had taken the ball with a show of authority. Now it would be interesting to see what she did with it.

After a long minute she said: "I was late because of

a delayed overseas telephone call. It was important
but I apologize."

"That's quite unnecessary. I've no other engage-
ments."

"And I think you owe *me* an apology, Mr. Galbraith. It was most discourteous to instruct the reception desk that you were not to be paged."

George was startled at the uncompromising direct-
ness of the reproach. "I beg your pardon most sincerely, Miss Diagulski. The discourtesy was uninten-
tional—and thoughtless."

"In that case we can forget it. But to clear the air
further, I should explain why Mr. Wrightson interrupted your talk so abruptly."

"I understand. There was an emergency."

"Yes—one with which he is involved personally. The
son of an old close friend is missing from one of our
prospecting camps in the Gibson Desert. It's very hot
up there now and there's very little hope that he will
be found alive."

George nodded gravely. "That's grim," he said. "I
can imagine how Mr. Wrightson must be feeling—and
his friend."

She shrugged, a small lifting of her shoulders. "It's a
bad country, Mr. Galbraith—unforgiving. You'll learn
that if—" she broke off and drank. "Can we start with
the assumption that, if we can agree on salary, you
will join Conwright?"

George was no longer quite so sure that he was going to enjoy himself, but it was too late to change tack.
Tamara Diagulski's physical beauty had thrown him
off balance, and the cool authority with which she had
administered her rebuke nettled him, but these things
had no relevance.

"I'm afraid we can't start with that assumption at
all, Miss Diagulski. I have already decided not to join
the Conwright organization."

She gave no visible reaction of surprise other than a
faint, puzzled frown. "May I ask why you've come to
that decision?"

"Of course. There are two unsatisfactory areas. The
first may or may not concern your—company or corpo-

ration or whatever you term it. But the other certainly does."

"Please go on."

"Mr. Wrightson sent me a message before he left the airport to the effect that you knew the score. I take it you know the full story behind his offer to employ me?"

"I think so. Yes."

"Then you have the advantage, Miss Diagulski. I don't by any means know the full story. To put it crudely, the whole business stinks."

"Stinks of what?"

"Duplicity—by which I am the party put at the disadvantage."

She frowned again. "Duplicity is an ugly word."

"It's not difficult. I'm fired from one job but firmly steered toward another by my former employers. The whole business is so hush-hush that nobody will even tell me what the job is. In government service it's sometimes necessary to accept a blind assignment in the line of duty, but then one has support and protection. As I am no longer in government service, it would be plain damn stupidity to take blind assignments."

"Aren't you jumping before you come to the fences? If news of that dreadful business at Excon camp hadn't interrupted Mr. Wrightson, he would have told you exactly what job he was offering. That's why I'm here now. The situation . . ."

George held up an admonitory finger. "No, stop. Whatever the situation, I'm not taking the job, so don't risk the possible indiscretion of describing it. I said two areas were unsatisfactory. We've covered the first, but the second is far more serious."

At last he had jolted her—and he took an ungenerous pleasure in it. When her frown deepened to a scowl, it made her look years older, heightened the outline of her cheek bones. He could sense as well as see her sudden tension and uncertainty. She wasn't calling the shots any more.

"Could you . . . say exactly what you mean, Mr. Galbraith?"

"I'll do better, Miss Diagulski. I'll show you exactly what I mean."

He took the wrapping-paper message from his wallet and handed it to her. "That not-very-original literary work was thrown through my balcony door last night, wrapped around a half brick. I'd say somebody has been awfully indiscreet at this end, wouldn't you? And someone else has been premature in assuming that I'd accepted the job."

She refolded the paper and put it, almost in slow motion, on the desk. Then she tossed her head to throw back the long, blonde hair.

"Could I have another drink, please?"

"Of course. Vodka Collins? I'm not exactly expert. . . . It's supposed to have fresh lemons, isn't it?" He went to the refrigerator. "Poor show. No fresh lemons. I'll call room service."

"No. The vodka's the thing. Squash will do."

He mixed two drinks.

"May I have a cigarette? This . . . this is one of the seldoms."

He saw, with interest and approval, that her fingers were quite steady. The lady was formidable. He decided not to interrupt her train of thought. She had the message.

She drew on the cigarette deeply, inhaled, expelled the smoke slowly through relaxed lips.

"Mr. Galbraith . . ."

"Yes?"

"What will you do now?"

He humped one shoulder. "What most people in my profession do when they're blown. Get out from under as fast as I can. What I mean is . . ."

"You don't need to explain. Before I took a job with Conwright, I was employed as confidential secretary to a senior minister of the Australian government. Did you know this?"

"No."

The smile was fleeting. "Fortunately," she said, "notoriety is short-lived if you don't cultivate it. That's unimportant. I just wanted to explain that I know the jargon and I take your point. You're blown. But perhaps this time the game isn't quite the same."

"Sorry, I'm not with you."

"You said someone had been indiscreet at this end. At this end three people and three people only knew who you were and why you were coming to Perth—Hamilton Wrightson, Hilda Weatherley, and myself."

"That simplifies the process of elimination, doesn't it? You'll hardly need a computer."

She tossed back her hair again and stood up abruptly.

"Does it occur to you that you might need a computer at your end?"

He shook his head vehemently. "I'll concede that some leaks are deliberately contrived but in this case there could be no possible reason for blowing me before I'd begun. The alternative explanation is that the leak was accidental—a failure of security. With all respect, I'm of the opinion that my former employers are more practiced in preserving security than the Conwright organization. But if I were you, Miss Diagulski, I wouldn't take all this too much to heart. After all, *this*," he tapped the paper on the table, "is pretty crude, isn't it? Cheapjack hoodlum stuff. It suggests your problem could well be solved by complaining to the police or hiring a firm of reliable private investigators."

"Your view isn't shared by Sir Ambrose Fergusson—or Colonel Callaghan."

George was not surprised. The lady was very much in the picture. But he raised an eyebrow.

"Surely that remark was hardly discreet, Miss Diagulski?"

Her face darkened in anger—an anger too sudden and hot to conceal. She drew a deep breath and stubbed out the remains of her cigarette savagely.

"I wonder," she said in a low voice, "if you are sophisticated enough to stop scoring debating points at my expense and make a generous gesture to the simpleminded peasantry who are scared of cheapjack hoodlums. Would you consider delaying your return east until Ham Wrightson gets back and can talk to

you again? . . . No. Don't answer now. Personally I
don't give a damn what you decide, but think it over.
If and when you want bookings and transport, ring
Miss Weatherley at the office. Good-bye, Mr. Galbraith."

George swallowed the last of his vodka and squash,
closed the window, and switched the air conditioning
on again. He felt ghastly—ragged from lack of sleep,
savagely irritated by the Conwright fiasco, and
wounded in pride that Callaghan should have involved
him in such an untidily amateurish business.

Then there was the complication of Tamara
Diagulski. He had been provoked by her cool air of
command, the incisive sharpness of her tongue, and
the complete absence of sexuality in her attitude toward him. What a bloody black joke by the malicious
little gods who mix the endocrine cocktail if she were
a lesbian!

Anyway he had muffled the chance of finding out
about Wrightson's job. It had been childish to cut
short her explanation and it would put him at a disadvantage in any future dealings with Callaghan—if
there were to be any future dealings.

Sleep on it. . . .

But sleep wouldn't come. He sat up and reached for
the Golden Galleon's service directory printed on fake
parchment and bound in fake green morocco. He
took up the bedside telephone and jabbed at the dial.

"Yes, Mr. Galbraith?"

"I see you don't list squash courts among this hotel's amenities."

"No, sir. But we have an arrangement with the
Macrombie Health Centre. If you care to make a reservation . . ."

"Never mind. Do I need a reservation to get into . . .
what-the-hell stupid name do you call it? . . . Sauna
Korna?"

"When did you wish to use it, sir?"

"Now."

"I'll inquire and ring you back, Mr. Galbraith."

"Make it half an hour. In the meantime, send up today's newspapers, will you?"

"Certainly."

Within five minutes a bellboy had arrived with eight morning newspapers from throughout the country and the early edition of the *Perth Daily News*. The pile was topped by a neat card which invited Golden Galleon guests to make use of the facilities of Sauna Korna on Floor B. Under the supervision of Nilsen Aagard. Hydrotherapy, chiropody, manicure, and Swedish massage by appointment. On the back a flowing hand recorded in violet ink that a reservation had been made for Mr. George Galbraith at five o'clock.

The headline of the front page of the *Daily News* was:

2 MISSING IN DESERT
BIG LAND-AIR SEARCH

He ran his eye down the column. Truck found bogged in sandhills. . . . Missing: Nathan Ebbet, 20, Colby Street, South Perth. Jack Lightning, 46, Meekatharra . . . employed by Conwright Exploration Pty. Ltd. . . . Returning to base camp on Lake Mullamurra from prospecting expedition. Mining magnate Hamilton Wrightson directing ground search personally. Missing youth the eldest son of retired doctor who had served . . . And so on.

George Galbraith grimaced. Tamara Diagulski had said: "It's very hot up there now." The newspaper claimed that Lake Mullamurra reported 129 degrees Fahrenheit at three o'clock the previous day. The retired doctor, poor old bugger, must have been whistling in the dark when he'd told "Our Special Reporter" that his son Nathan was an experienced bushman and that he had every confidence.

Lacking a brazier, birch twigs, and a bank of snow to roll in, Sauna Korna was not authentic, but it tried hard. On the other hand the masseuse in Booth 4— Helga, according to the plastic disk on her white cotton blouse—was entirely authentic.

"And now if you pliss, oops and ofer. . . ."

George accepted the cold towel across his eyes and the brisk tattoo on his pectorals and abdominals which preceded precise dissection.

"You are very strong, sir. Very fitted. It is a pleasure to do my vork vith a goot body. So many who comes here are fat bellies."

"Kind of you," George murmured. "You've a good body yourself, Helga."

"Ah, so? But now I tell you, you are very vite. You must go more to the sea bitch and bath in the sun."

"You're probably right."

"The talcum or the muscle oil. Then ve are done. Vitch?"

"Your department, my dear," George said dreamily.

She really *was* good. The staleness of insufficient sleep and the hangover of intense but unproductive thought had been reduced and confined to a small area somewhere behind his eyes. She really was *very* good.

George removed the cold towel and raised his head. She had unbuttoned the flimsy blouse. Big, firm, pink-nippled breasts were swinging rhythmically above his thighs. A dew of sweat gleamed on her forehead as she kneaded closer and closer to his crotch.

George let his head fall back and said firmly, "You can leave my cock alone, Helga. No special relief today, thanks. I'm saving myself for the army."

No precipitate, huffed haste. The kneading simply diminished—ending in a feather-light passage of her palms over the contours of his body. "So."

He sat up, swung his legs over the edge of the padded table, twitched the dislodged loin cloth across his belly to conceal an erect penis, and smiled at her. She had discarded her skirt. She was leaning against the door of the booth watching him, unresentful but baffled.

"I do not belief you are a sodom," she asserted. "You haf the horn for me, no? I do not belief the army. You choke."

"You're a smart girl, Helga. I joke. Thank you for the rest of the treatment, though. I feel marvelous."

She pouted, dropped long, bleached eyelashes against her cheeks, thrust her hips forward.

"If you do not tell," she whispered, "it is with compliments. No charge."

George advanced, took her firmly by the shoulders, spun the big body, and pinned her with her elbows. He hefted the slippery breasts in his palms and said against her ear: "Look, Helga, let's make a deal. If I'm still in Perth at the weekend, I'll book you for a private session on your day off. We'll go to the sea bitch and lie in the sun, then have a night on the town. What do you say?"

She stopped moaning and grinding her buttocks against his thigh. He released her. She stepped into her skirt, zipped the placket, and buttoned her blouse with practiced swiftness. She avoided his eyes.

"You are choking again," she said rather pathetically. "I know. Tomorrow you will go. But you say no so nice. . . . Ach, she is a locky vumman, that vun you are focking!"

In the anteroom he rested for the half hour recommended by Nilsen Aagard, drank a pint of tepid spa water, mused on Swedes and sex—and wondered if Hamilton Wrightson knew he owned a quick-service whorehouse. Men as rich as Wrightson often had only the vaguest idea of what they owned.

After the meal that night he went early to his room, listened to two movements of Mahler's Second Symphony on the radio before he was discouraged by the static and switched it off. The next hour he spent practicing Arabic script on the Golden Galleon's deckle-edged notepaper. He believed in keeping rare accomplishments furbished. They had a way of turning out to be marketable.

At ten thirty he went to the bar, chose a bottle of Carlsberg, and carried it out to a small wrought-iron table on the balcony. He sat sipping the beer, smoking a last cigarette, and watching the streaming headlights of the freeway traffic on Narrows Bridge. The breeze across Perth Water was perfumed, aromatic with gum smoke from innumerable backyard barbecues. Cicadas were drumming ecstatically, overlaying the noise of distant traffic. A charming little city with its meandering sidewalk crowds, its comic Olde English Tea Shoppe façades cheek by jowl with iron lace, corrugated-iron verandahs and fronts of mellow, handmade bricks. Some plagiarizing brochure bard called it the loneliest, loveliest city in the world—and quoted the air miles to Sydney, Johannesburg, Buenos Aires, and Singapore. And early astronauts, whose names he had forgotten, called it the City of Lights.

Well, the lights were starting to go out in suburbia across the river. At ten fifty George poured the last of the beer and replaced the empty bottle on the table. As he raised the glass to his lips the bottle exploded. The bullet that shattered it struck the ferroconcrete pillar of the window behind him and mewed away into the night.

CHAPTER 4

THE rattle of a passkey in the lock of the bedrom door and the muffled thump of its edge striking the safety chain jackknifed George Galbraith into raw-boned, instant wakefulness.

"Who is it?"

"The housemaid, sir. There's two messages from reception."

He hitched up his pajama pants, groped across the room, and slid the bolt back.

A tray, two envelopes, and a glass of orange juice over cracked ice.

George knuckled his eyes and glowered. He reached for the square envelope with a red "Urgent" sticker. It contained a telex:

CEXCAN 101A 29/10 GALBRAITH GOLGAL PERTH URGENT PERSONAL REGRET APOLOGIZE LEAKAGE

THIS END REPEAT THIS END. FAULTY CONNECTION STILL UNLOCATED BUT EMPLOYING BEST PLUMBERS. WILL ADVISE RESULT. DECISION REMAINS YOURS BUT PENDING CLARIFICATION SUGGEST PATIENCE FURTHER CONSULTATION. WATCH THE ESCALATOR. KINDEST REGARDS

CALLAGHAN

Watch the escalator. . . . Sarcastic, devious old bastard! So you did set me up for a patsy! Faulty connection . . . Like hell there was a faulty connection!

George was so swamped with indignation that he opened the second envelope unconsciously. It contained a single sheet of cheap writing pad on which was typed:

Final Notice. We hit what we aim at. We don't miss. Next time we won't waste good grog.

He gulped the orange juice and did his thinking under the shower. Then he dialed reception.

"This is Galbraith in M-4. You just sent up a telex message. What time did it arrive?"

"About two minutes before you received it, sir. It was marked urgent."

"Thank you. There was another message in a plain envelope. Do you know when that arrived?"

"It was left on the desk, sir. Probably early this morning after the night porter went off duty. Otherwise it would have been in your box."

"Thank you. Will you be kind enough to make a reservation for me with either airline for the first flight to Melbourne or Sydney which leaves after midday."

"There's a direct service to Sydney at eleven twenty-five."

"No. Not before midday. And ring me back when the booking's confirmed."

"Very good, sir."

"Now, can I have an outside line?"

"Certainly. Just dial 'O' and the number, sir."

George glanced at his watch. It was three minutes

past eight. He consulted the address book in his wallet and called the main number for Conwright.

"Can you tell me what time Mr. Wrightson's private secretary, Miss Weatherley, comes into the office? Miss Weatherley has already come in? Please put me through. My name is Galbraith."

Miss Weatherley was virtuously bright, like any secretary discovered at her desk at eight o'clock in the morning.

"Good morning, Mr. Galbraith. Can I help you?"

"Has Mr. Wrightson returned?"

"No, I'm afraid not. We're not expecting him in today."

"Very well. Two things. Could you please arrange for a car to pick me up at the hotel and take me to the airport in time to catch the first flight east after midday. I'll confirm the exact departure time later."

"But Mr. Galbraith, Miss Diagulski—"

"I'm coming to that. I need to speak to Miss Diagulski on a matter of the greatest urgency."

Miss Weatherley sounded affronted and defensive. "I can arrange for the car if you wish, Mr. Galbraith, but Miss Diagulski doesn't come in until nine thirty."

"Then telephone her at home and ask her if she'll call on me at the hotel on her way to work. Please stress the urgency."

"Perhaps, Mr. Galbraith—"

"Thank you for your help, Miss Weatherley."

By the time the room phone rang, George had shaved, dressed, transferred certain essentials including a compact .32 caliber automatic pistol and spare ammunition clips to an airline bag, and repacked his suitcase.

"Miss Diagulski? Please ask her to come up."

In silk shirt and business skirt, hair drawn back and coiled into a loose bun, Tamara Diagulski could still crick male necks, but George did not even smile when he opened the door and snapped: "Come in."

"Miss Weatherley gave me your message."

"Obviously."

"I expected that under the circumstances . . ."

"You can skip what you expected. Callaghan sent me a telex an hour ago admitting he'd set me up."

"You keep talking about being set up. I don't understand."

"Then come and take a look."

He jerked back the curtains and flung open the French windows. The heavy base of the Carlsberg bottle was still on the wrought-iron table. The terrazzo of the balcony was dusted with granules of shattered glass. He pointed to the pockmark left by the bullet in the pillar.

"If you take time to work it out you'll see it was a damned long shot in poor light—most likely from the bamboo clump on the embankment over there by the parking lot."

Her face was crumpled, slack with bewilderment.

"What . . . what do you mean?"

"Mean? I mean some bright-eyed bully boy shot a beer bottle out of my hand when I was sitting here last night."

"Shot?"

"Well, you can be bloody sure he didn't break that bottle with his beautiful tenor voice, *macushla,* or take a chip out of concrete with a catapult. Come in."

He slammed the doors. She sat down abruptly on the edge of the bed. "Furthermore, I got another love letter."

She read the typescript, handed it back to him, and shook her head. "I don't understand that . . . I . . ."

"I do. Where's Wrightson now?"

"At Braund outstation, I think."

"Where's that?"

"Sixty or seventy miles northwest of our camp on the lake."

"How far from here—in traveling time, I mean?"

"Four hours in a light plane."

"I want to talk to Wrightson."

"On the radio?"

"No. Not on the radio. I want to talk eyeball to eyeball. I'm tired of all this fan dancing and newspeak."

"But Weatherley said . . ."

"She said I wanted a car to take me to the airport by midday in time to catch a flight east. I still want it —and you can come and kiss me good-bye if you like. But if you think you can cooperate in a more practical way, I won't be on the flight east. I'll be on a company plane or a charter flight to wherever Wrightson is."

She caught on so fast that George felt, for the moment, almost reassured. "Yes," she said. "I'm reading you. It'll be . . . pretty tight on time. How elaborate do you want to make it?"

"Make what? How do you mean elaborate?"

"Do you want someone to travel on the plane under your name—make a switch with him in the check-in line at the airport?"

George's eyes widened. The lady was even faster at catching on than he'd thought.

"Could you organize that? It might put the opposition off the scent if the switch here isn't noticed and if they send someone to check at point of arrival. How could you arrange it?"

"We retain a private investigation agency for credit work and occasional security jobs in the city. Conwright's a pretty big account. I could lean on them, I think. But I don't know if they'd be able to assign anyone roughly your age and build at short notice."

He stared hard at her. "I wouldn't worry too much if it comes unstuck," he said. "We're up against amateurs. Or else someone is playing games."

"Why amateurs?"

"In a pro game the baddies don't fire warning shots and send comic-strip letters. They play for keeps. If you lose you either get knocked off tidily or flung into a high-security prison for twenty years—after they've made you talk. Which reminds me—was it you or Wrightson who spoke to Callaghan in Canberra yesterday?"

"I did."

"And you asked him to convince me that there hadn't been a leak at this end?"

"It amounts to that, I suppose."

George looked at her reproachfully. "My dear girl,

don't try to con me. I've worked under Callaghan for twelve years. And I've never known him to accept anybody's personal assurance for anything—at any time or under any circumstances. He checks and double-checks. And he didn't have time to check even once before he signaled me."

"Perhaps he already knew that the leak must be at his end."

George's repressed indignation exploded. "You can bet your last pantyhose on that, darling! The treacherous bugger drilled the hole himself and I'm going to find out why. Don't waste time feeding me pap-crap about mutual trust and confidence and expect me to wag my ass like a tin duck in a shooting gallery. Callaghan sold me down the river to you colonials and we both know it. Who pays your rent, anyway? The Australian Security Intelligence Organization?"

To his amazement she burst out laughing.

Excon Four—base camp of the division of Conwright Exploration Pty. Ltd. operating in the Madison Basin —was sited on the eastern shores of Lake Mullamurra, twenty-eight thousand acres of glittering gypsum and salt pan which last held surface water in the autumn of 1958. The camp was comprised of a dozen or more enormous, aluminum trailer vans drawn up in a semicircle around a vehicle and equipment pool of assorted prime movers, desert trucks, tractors, bulldozers, four-wheel-drive runabouts, motorcycles, light drilling rigs, generators, and compressors. It accommodated thirty-eight geologists, technicians, and subordinate staffers. A makeshift airstrip was marked by lines of oil drums painted in yellow and black stripes, a wind sock set on two lengths of jointed drill stem, and a steel hangar frame thatched with spinifex grass held by chicken wire. It had been graded and oiled in compacted sand between the van park and the blinding white margin of the lake.

Chasser Fitzpatrick—whose record as a crop duster and survey pilot in the Kimberley irrigation lands four hundred miles to the north had been so spotless for three seasons that Conair Services Pty. Ltd. (a wholly

owned subsidiary of Conwright Enterprises) promoted
him to chief pilot—had difficulty putting the Beechcraft down. The temperature in the slatted met box
beside the hangar was 124 degrees Fahrenheit, and
Chasser made three passes before making contact
with the ground half a mile beyond the limp wind
sock.

"Shit and derision!" he cursed as he pulled the little
plane out of a ground loop twenty yards from a sand
drift at the end of the strip. "Anybody who works for
this outfit ought to get a brain transplant."

"Ar," said George huskily, opening his eyes. He
had been acutely uncomfortable for more than three
hours. The landing climaxed his misgiving.

Chasser taxied to the hangar in angry spurts, nosed
into its inky shadow, and switched off. A rake-thin
man, burned almost black by the sun and naked except for a ragged pair of khaki shorts, a slouch hat,
and scuffed army boots, opened the passenger door
and said, "Good day. Good day, Chasser. How did it
go?"

"Like a fuckin' roller coaster with square wheels,"
said the pilot disgustedly.

"You should have left it for a couple of hours. You
know what it's like in the middle of the day."

"Tell Diagulski that. She scrambled me out of bed
even when I told her I was sixteen hours over my time
this month. Some sort of panic again. Ours not to
reason why."

"What sort of panic again?"

"Ask my friend here. What did you say your other
name was, George?"

"Sinclair," said George—truthfully in part because
he had been christened George Algernon Sinclair
Galbraith.

"George Sinclair. This is our head geologist, Dick
Margan, better known as Doc."

The rake-thin man's hand was dry and hard as
horn. "Well, Mr. Sinclair," he said, "if you're bringing
a message to Ham Wrightson you might just as well
have spent the afternoon in the bar and then had a

comfortable trip this evening. The boss flew back to
Braund in a chopper a couple of hours ago."

George was beyond reacting.

"Miss Diagulski said she'd spoken to him on the
radiophone and told him I was coming," he said dully.

Margan shrugged. "Something's cropped up about
the search, I suppose."

"Do you think they could've found them, Doc?"
Chasser asked.

"Wouldn't make any damned difference if they
have." Margan's voice was grimly indifferent. "They've
been out three days now. You'd better come up to the
van."

"Wait," Chasser said. "I've got four cartons of
Swan in the back. They were cold but they'll be boiling by now. I'd better get them before they bloody
explode."

He and the thin man tucked a beer carton under
each arm.

"Is this all your gear, Mr. Sinclair?" Margan asked,
jerking his head at George's airline bag.

"That's all."

"You want to look out you don't get your knees
sunburnt in those shorts. If you're going to chase after
Ham Wrightson up the track, we could fix you up
with a pair of dungarees. English, aren't you, Mr. Sinclair?"

"Thanks," George replied. "And George or Sinclair
will do. It isn't mister country. Yes, I'm English and
lily white. You answer to Doc, do you?"

"Right."

"I'm not going to chase Wrightson up the track if I
can help it."

The thin man laughed.

George was to remember the five-hundred-yard
walk to Margan's van for a long time. The blood hammered in his head and his tongue was tacky before he
had taken a dozen steps. Sweat spurted from every
pore and dried before it had time to run. Myriads of
tiny black bush flies assailed every square inch of ex-
posed skin and gathered in festoons about his eyes
and nose the instant he stopped swatting them. Once

in the line of duty George had spent July in the tents
of a desert tribe in Trucial Oman but he had never
experienced heat as stunning as the afternoon heat on
the shore of Lake Mullamurra late in October.

Doc Margan's van was refrigerated to a glacial 86
degrees Fahrenheit. It was twenty-eight feet long and
divided into three compartments, each filled with rock
specimens, drill cores, and magnetic and seismic records—all apparently in chaotic confusion. The walls
were papered with 1:250,000 survey maps attached
to the metal with tape and scribbled over with grease-
pencil hieroglyphics.

Chasser dumped his beer cartons on the floor.
Margan stacked his on the corner of a work bench
and shrugged his leathery shoulders into a loud Ha-
waiian shirt.

"Pull up a pew if you can find one, George," he
said, vaguely waving a hand. "What brings you to this
out-of-the-way little holiday resort? You a mining
man?"

"No. I'm a money man. I look after the financial
end of feasibility studies."

"Ah?" George felt he had scored. There were times
when double-talk came in handy. Margan looked puzzled and doubtful.

"George was telling me he's been around the Middle East for a while," Chasser interposed. "On the
Gulf and all. Knows a couple of the oil sheiks."

"Oh? You're interested in oil?"

"Not in oil. Only in the price."

They laughed politely. The pilot mopped vigorously
at his receding hairline and his sideburns with a blue-
and-white-spotted handkerchief.

"All this yak dries me out, man. Swap you eight
hot cans for six cold ones, Doc."

Margan gestured. "You know where it lives."
Chasser hefted the beer cartons through the foil-strip
curtain that partitioned the center compartment.

"Did the boss say when he was likely to get back
here—or am I really supposed to chase him?" George
asked.

Margan shook his head. "No orders. He was on the

radio with the police party at Braund. Something up-set him and he took off like a bat out of hell. If I were you I'd just relax until you hear from him. Could be he'll be back tonight. The old boy's pretty stirred up about young Ebbet. The kid was the son of a friend of his from way back—one of the flying doctors who worked out of Hedland in the days before Ham got his break at Mount Millswyn. Young Nat was a bush boy. The half-blood aboriginal I sent with him, Jack Lightning, worked in Pilbara mines all his life. That's why I can't understand it. Something's bloody screwy about the whole business."

"What actually happened? All I know is what I read in the newspapers."

"I don't actually know what happened myself. Ebbet was with a ground party I sent into the Mount Featherstone area last year to check gravity anoma-lies . . ."

"Sorry," George interrupted. "I don't know the coun-try and I'm not a mining man. You'll have to spell that out for me."

Margan grunted impatiently. "Mount Featherstone is a hundred and fifty miles north from here—where the Beechover River comes to the surface out of the West Madison Desert catchment. The rivers up here mostly run underground. Last year we made air surveys of the section—with instruments to measure minute variations of gravity and magnetism. Do you follow that much?"

"Yes."

"When the results were processed, I thought there were one or two anomalies—indications—that war-ranted sending in a team to take shallow drill sam-ples."

"What are you looking for—oil?"

"No. Not here. This is not oil-bearing country. We are prospecting for base metals—copper, nickel, man-ganese, tin, whatever."

"Go on."

"Ebbet went with the drillers. He was a keen young-ster just out of the School of Mines and he'd got a thing about the area. This year he kept pestering me to let him go back and poke around the rock heaps on his own, because he had a feeling we'd overlooked something. I know the feeling. I used to get it myself when I was a kid in the game and sometimes the hunches paid off. So when I had a truck to spare, I told him to take a chain man, Jack Lightning, and three weeks' grub and get it out of his system. Now I wish to Christ I hadn't."

"They lost themselves coming back?"

"Lost! Holy cow, man, how in the hell could they get lost on a graded track with a compass on the dash and maps and a radio transceiver? No. Whoever was driving the truck bogged it down to the axles in a sand drift—fifty miles this side of Beechover River. That could happen—through carelessness or belting it out too fast. But I can't understand why they didn't use their radio to call for help, and, above all, why they left the vehicle. It's the first rule if you break down in country like that—don't leave your vehicle."

"When did you find the truck?"

"Sunday night. I told Ebbet to be back here by Saturday. When he hadn't shown up by nightfall on Sunday and there was nothing on the radio, I sent out a couple of men in a Land Rover. They picked up the truck in their headlights about midnight and scouted around until dawn, blowing their horn, but they found nothing—not even tracks. We got going with a full-scale search on Monday. Ham even called in the choppers from the Canning prospect, but it was too late even if they had spotted them."

"You're dead right, Doc," Chasser said, juggling six frosted cans of beer into spaces on the cluttered work bench. "I was down on Lake Wells once with a busted fuel line. I was out for two days. I had a gallon of water and I didn't move twenty feet from the aircraft, but by the time they found me I hadn't got enough piss in me to fill an acorn. Here, George, get one into you before it bloody evaporates."

It was the smallest can of beer George had ever drunk. His throat was still swallowing convulsively five seconds after he had emptied it. Chasser watched him with a grin.

"How do you reckon this climate compares with the Persian Gulf, George?"

George reached for the second can, ripped out the tab, drank, and said, "Wouldn't have a clue, chum—not until I knew how hot it gets here in summer."

Chasser guffawed, but Margan seemed not to have heard. Perhaps his mind was on something else—like a double line of footprints in the rippled, burnt-orange sand that the ground and air searchers hadn't seen.

Maybe, George thought, it hasn't been such a smart wisecrack after all.

When night fell Hamilton Wrightson had not returned to Excon Four, although several trucks roared in from the north after the sun dipped behind a bank of high cloud and the heat slackened.

When only three cold cans were left in Margan's freezer, Chasser Fitzpatrick said, "I'd better take George over to the mess or he'll miss out on a feed. Where will he bed down for the night, Doc?"

"Fred Zercho and his sidekicks won't be back so there'll be spare bunks in Rickety Kate. It's not as plush as Yarralumla but if Ham does come in late, the superintendent will probably be with him. I'd better not hire out the honeymoon suite."

"No. How's it for a shower?"

"Not on. The tanker isn't due in until tomorrow night. The search has ballsed up all the vehicle schedules. Wing Foon will make an ablutions issue of two gallons a man a half hour before tea."

Chasser groaned and then suddenly laughed.

"Zercho . . . ah yes! It's been going around the head office that Zercho tried to rape Diagulski and she laid him out with a kick in the nuts. What's the true story?"

Margan grimaced sourly. "Head office is like a bloody hen coop for cackle. Rape? Bullshit! The true story is that Zercho goosed her and she clouted him on the side of the head with a tire lever. Four stitches. That little bitch has got a temper. The super asked her what happened and she said: 'When that ape comes to, ask *him* what happened—and warn him that if he ever tries to put his hand up my pants again I'll finish the job.'"

On the way to the mess trailer, Chasser, whose prodigious beer consumption in the previous two hours was betrayed only by a slight exaggeration of gesture, pointed out what he described as "our interesting and historic buildings"—the dormitory vans, each named with heavy whimsy, the mobile laboratory and machine shop, the medical office and sick bay, the diesel power plant, the ablutions trailer and cement-block latrines that were cleared twice weekly, Chasser explained pridefully, with a flame thrower from army surplus.

The handful of crew in the mess trailer showed no interest in George. They acknowledged Chasser's in-introduction with a muttered "good day" or "how are you going" and went back to their listless card playing or magazine reading. They had a common physical denominator—desiccation. They were baked dry. Their gauntness was emphasized by red-rimmed eyes and the trick of slow, deliberate movement they had acquired to cope with the exertions of work in extreme heat. Most of them were old hands who had spent three or more seasons in Excon desert camps. They went south every November layoff, swearing never to work north of the twenty-sixth parallel again—but the lure of big money always brought them back in April.

Only one man, the geochemist Tommy Maloney, a wisp of a man with enormous eyebrows and a simian face, bothered to make any show of cordiality. When Chasser Fitzpatrick left to supervise the refueling of the plane, Maloney moved a large can of beer to the table where George was sitting, fetched an extra glass from the galley hatch, poured two drinks, pushed one across the Formica top without comment, and asked, "Would it be the search that's brought you this way, Mr. Sinclair?"

"No," George said, "just a bit of business with the boss that couldn't wait."

"Ah. Yes, he's an impatient man is Ham Wrightson. More crockery in the air all at once than a Chinese juggler. Maloney's the name—Tommy to me mates."

"George," said George. They shook hands.

"It'll be your first time in the North West, George?"

"Yes."

"And a hell of a welcome you've had today, by God! You came up from Perth with Chasser Fitzpatrick, did you now?"

"That's right."

"Do you know something?" The little man leaned forward eagerly. "The Madison Basin is the hottest place on the face of the terrestrial globe. Did you know that?"

"No, but you don't surprise me."

"I keep the weather records in this camp. It's a hobby. November to March inclusive the mean daily maximum exceeds 113 degrees Fahrenheit and I've seen 131 degrees under the screen twice in three years. Could you beat that in the Rub' al Khali or the Mourdi Depression or Death Valley, could you now?"

"Probably not," George said somberly, "probably not. I won't be recommending the shareholders to develop it as a health resort."

"But, ah, that's where you'd be wrong, man! From May through August it's a dream of paradise. When the showers come south, it's guinea flowers and everlastings and Sturt's pea and Star of Bethlehem as far as the eye can see—and budgerigar birds as bright as jewels in their millions . . . and the little racehorse lizards skittering away through the spinifex with their tails up. A terrible, beautiful, capricious country it is. In June it kisses you and you fall in love with it but by December it's burned you to a frazzled husk."

"You're a poet, Tommy," George said. "Can I buy you a beer at the canteen?"

"After dinner. Best draw your water now if you want to wash."

"How do I go about that?"

"With the yellow plastic pail by your bunk. The cook, Wing Foon, or his sidekick will fill it from the tank by the galley door. They've billeted you in Rickety Kate, have they?"

"I believe so."

"You'll find clean sheets and blankets in the locker."

"Blankets?" George raised an eyebrow—then remembered the nights he had edged closer to the dung fires in the black tents of Qardam. "Thanks. I'll see you later."

"Why don't you eat with me here if you haven't a mind to be solitary? And there'll be a movie outside tonight."

"Thanks again, Tommy. Very good of you. Everything's up to date in Excon City."

But George didn't make it for dinner or the movie. Rickety Kate was cool and empty. He found a yellow plastic pail and drew his water ration, sponged the incrustations of dried sweat and fine red dust from his body, ran a comb through his hair, and pulled on a clean shirt. Then he sat down on a bunk, blearily pondering the vicissitudes which had transported him from the fleshpots of the Golden Galleon to the austerities of Excon Four in a single day.

The clatter of Hamilton Wrightson's helicopter dropping down to land an hour after dawn awakened him, chilled to the bone and with a throbbing headache. He could not remember undressing.

CHAPTER 5

THE summons came as George was half through breakfast—alone in the mess because the men in the field started their day at first light and returned to refuge before the sun reached the meridian.

Chasser Fitzpatrick, ruffled, came into the van and slammed the door violently behind him.

"Cap'n Bligh's compliments," he said loudly, "and will Mr. Christian join him right away in the captain's cabin—otherwise known as Yarralumla—our big tin Government House on wheels just across campus. Top priority. Immediate, urgent, and all that horseshit."

George laid down his knife and fork, reached for another slice of toast, and said, "Mr. Christian's compliments to Captain Bligh and Mr. Christian will join him when Mr. Christian's good and ready. Can I pour you a spot of tea, old boy? There's no hurry."

Chasser's jaw dropped.

"Look, mate," he protested, "you'd better get over there. The old sod is as mad as a cut snake about something."

"That makes two of us," George said, buttering the toast. "Tell me, Chasser, do you remember *exactly* what Wrightson said when he told you to call me? The actual words he used, I mean."

The pilot looked puzzled, then embarrassed. "Yes," he said. "If you've got to know—'Tell Sinclair to get off his pink ass and come over here on the double!' "

Sinclair. Good. Diagulski hadn't slipped up on essential details. He wondered just how she could have communicated that particular item of her briefing on an open radiotelephone channel. Or perhaps they ran to a scrambler between Excon Four and the head office.

"Don't fuss, Chasser. If you think the old man really is going to have kittens, go back and tell him I'll be over when I've finished breakfast. Don't worry. I'm not working for him."

"Lucky you," Chasser muttered sourly. "But you want to look out he doesn't bloody well make you walk home."

Hamilton Wrightson, wearing a filthy shirt and shorts, was sitting with his chin in his hands at a metal drop-leaf table scattered with dog-eared survey maps. A massive, black-bearded man in immaculate khaki drill rose from a stool opposite him when George entered.

Wrightson moved one hand from under his chin in a gesture of dismissal. "Okay, Milt, do what you can, but you'll need luck to get anywhere. This is George

Sinclair. Doing a feasibility study for me on Barrington Bar project. This is the camp super here, Milt Broderick."

George smiled and nodded. Broderick merely nodded.

"I'll see you before you leave, Ham," he said. "I'll get out there again as soon as I can travel and check those points. We could move a party up to the Beechover crossing tomorrow."

When Broderick had gone, Wrightson straightened and ran his hands through his stubble of graying hair.

"So you take your time, son? A hearty breakfast man?"

"Runs in the family. It never worries me when it's in my time. Now that I'm here, we might save everybody's time if you stopped playing tag and told me what your trouble is."

The prominent hazel eyes, dull with fatigue, studied him almost apprehensively, George thought. The man was under heavy strain and too tired to conceal it.

"So they warned you off?" he asked.

George shrugged.

"But you got your dander up."

"Look, Mr. Wrightson, I didn't get my dander up, as you put it, because I was warned off. I got my dander up because they knew *who* to warn off. If I'm set up as a patsy, I want to know about it first—and why. But I believe you had no part in that so we can skip it."

"They shot at you, Diagulski says."

"They shot at a bottle a foot away from me—at night and at a range of more than seventy yards."

Wrightson nodded. "You did the right thing to make them think they'd scared you off."

"We'll see. I'm going to ask some plain questions, Mr. Wrightson, and I want plain answers. For a start you'd better tell me who *they* are."

Hamilton Wrightson shook his head slowly from side to side, then to George's surprise, rose, opened the locker above the bench on which he had been sitting, and took down a bottle of whisky and two glasses.

"Do you drink whisky, Galbraith?"

"Not at this hour of the morning."

"I do—when I've had a rough enough night." He poured a generous three fingers of spirit and swallowed it straight, replaced the bottle and glasses, and sat down again.

"You asked me one plain question and here's your plain answer. I don't know who *they* are. I'm hiring you to find out." He made no effort to elaborate.

George said, "You misunderstand me. I wasn't asking for names and addresses. I want you to define the opposition. Who are you up against—business competitors, political extremists, labor unions, common or garden nuts, gangsters, blackmailers, or what? Exactly what are they doing to you and why? If you can't or won't answer all of that, then you can be bloody sure you're *not* hiring me."

Wrightson's face flushed, but he kept his voice at low pitch. "You may be a shit-hot expert on subversion, sabotage, and terrorism as Fergusson claims you are. But don't try bullyragging me, Galbraith. Get the chip off your shoulder. I'm up against organized sabotage and murder. I asked Fergusson for help and he sent you, God help me."

George grinned faintly. "We're making progress, Mr. Wrightson. Don't be impatient. You're up against sabotage but what sort of sabotage? Why don't you begin at the beginning?"

For the next half hour Hamilton Wrightson told his story—simply and without apparent emotion. George listened with complete concentration, interrupting only once or twice to ask about unfamiliar technical or slang terms. It was a puzzling recital of apparently haphazard harassment, extending for more than two years, of Conwright properties all over the North West. The acts of destruction had sometimes been trivial, sometimes crude, and sometimes subtle. Fences had been cut and stock shot. Windmills had been wrecked, bores choked with rubble. Rations stored in boundary huts for the use of station hands had been wantonly spoiled. Wild bulls—scrubbers—had been turned into stud paddocks. A drum of poisonous-spray concentrate had been emptied into a storage tank used to water valuable bloodstock. Three widely separated outstation cottages had been fired in the absence of their occupants. Iron filings had been put in lubricating oil, and sugar in gasoline drums.

At small, isolated mining and prospecting camps, explosives had been stolen, winding gear damaged, and valuable instruments smashed. Rafts had been cut adrift at an oyster farm on Beagle Bay and the seacocks of two prawning trawlers opened while they were lying at anchor in Maude Inlet.

Only when Wrightson came to the disappearance of Nathan Ebbet and Jacky Lightning did he become confused and incoherent.

George held up a hand to stop him. "Leave that for the time being. It's part of the general pattern and the worst thing that's happened yet. We'll get back to details later. But first there are other points I want to clear up. Are you positive that none of these incidents, these hits against you, has either been preceded or followed by warnings, threats, or demands of any kind?"

The big man shook his head distractedly. "None. None at all. That's the bloody baffling, maddening part of it!"

"And you say the sabotage has been confined to Conwright properties? Other station owners and miners haven't been hit?"

"I can't swear to that. These days most station owners have trouble of some sort with tourists—city vandals who buy themselves a set of wheels and a gun and start off to drive around Australia, taking casual work and bumming when they run out of money."

"My God," George said, half to himself, "tourists—city vandals out in that!"

"They travel in the winter mostly, and they don't get far off the highways. They do a lot of damage. But as far as I know nobody in the North West has suffered to anything like the extent that I have."

"What have you done to protect yourself?"

"Protect myself! Christ, man, how can I protect myself when I never know where or when I'm going to be hit next? How can I protect myself against bastards too cunning to leave a single track or trace behind them? Nobody's ever got close enough even to sight their dust."

"I presume all these incidents were reported to the police?"

"Of course they've been reported to the police!"

"And with absolutely no result?"

Wrightson grimaced bitterly. "You don't know the new breed of bush cop, son. They turn up on the scene days after the event—with or without a couple of fly-blown trackers in tow. They poke about and ask bloody silly stock questions and get bloody silly stock answers. Then they drive back in their flashy government station wagons to the nearest bar and wash down the dead flies. The only job bush coppers are fit for these days is breaking up bar brawls or maybe pulling in some wretched aboriginal woman for letting her baby die of starvation while she's on a wine jag with her child-endowment money."

George swallowed and started again.

"A man in your position ought to be able to exercise some influence with the police department other than at the local station level."

Wrightson snorted. "I exercised enough influence with the police department to get a couple of plain-clothes clowns posted to Port Hedland after the water tank at Tregarth Downs was poisoned and Arrowlea homestead was burned down. They spent three months buying beer for every bum between Wyndham and Meekatharra and all they found out was that they were a laughingstock. They tried to pass themselves off as itinerant workers blowing their paychecks. Itinerant workers! They didn't even have dirt under their finger-nails!"

George clasped his hands behind his neck, leaned back, and stared at the roof of the van. Wrightson got up and opened the locker again.

"Are you sure you don't want a whisky?"

"As a matter of fact," George said hoarsely, "I'll bend the rules. I'm getting a dreadful cold in the head. I went to sleep last night without a blanket."

"Tcha!" Wrightson pushed the bottle and an extra glass across the table.

George looked at the label somberly and observed, "Glenlivet. I see you're a whisky man. Thank you. Yes. You've certainly got a problem. And frankly I must know a great deal more before I can decide if I'm going to be able to help you. Look at it my way. I know nothing about this country—less than nothing. What I've seen from the air frightens the living daylights out of me. I can't think of any place in the world I'd sooner *not* be." He lifted his glass and sipped attentively.

"Fergusson said—"

"Hold on. For the time being, I can't get any picture in my mind of what sort of people are sabotaging you —and without leaving a trace. I can't visualize these acts of sabotage or imagine how they are carried out— physically, I mean. By your own account, local policemen can't get the picture either. Your own employees can't protect themselves or you from these attacks—or claim they can't. So what the devil do you think *I* can do? Well, certainly, I can use my brains—and my experience in a very different field—to put known facts together and make a pattern with meaning out of this series of crimes. Or at least I hope so. But first you must be really reckless and have a shot at suggesting a motive."

"I swear I don't know any motive, Galbraith. If I did—"

"Or you won't admit to knowing a motive."

"Just what the hell do you mean by that?"

"You know damned well what I mean. Nobody can get to own or control twenty-three million acres of land anywhere on God's earth without making enemies— personal enemies, business enemies, political enemies. Nobody gets as near the top without tramping on a lot of faces and provoking a lot of jealousies and grievances. Some of those enemies want to get their own back. They want to slow you down or put you out of business altogether. You're the victim of a vendetta which has now heated up so much that you're starting to run scared."

Wrightson's heavy face darkened. "That's a bloody libel. I've never run scared."

"The more fool you," George said. "You must know a score or more people who'd like nothing better than to break you and your empire up into little bits and bury them in one of your sandhills. Your problem is that you can't be certain which one—or which group —is now actively trying to do just that. In such a situation, only a man completely devoid of imagination *wouldn't* be running scared—particularly with so much more hanging on it than meets the eye."

"So much more what?" The question cracked like a whiplash.

"Oh, something out there in the hard, red yonder." George waved a hand vaguely. "Something that intrigues the interest of His Excellency the British high commissioner. I hope you both realize that in the long run I'm bound to find out what. It's the sort of thing I've been trained to do and I'm good at it. But to come back to your own problems, Mr. Wrightson— leaving 'His Ex' to worry about his—I'm afraid you'll have to give me information in sensitive areas, and it may go against the grain."

"What sort of information?"

"A list of individuals and concerns who might be regarded as in competition with Conwright or hostile to it. Some might feel aggrieved because you've outsmarted them in past deals. Similarly I want a list of people or concerns who've successfully resisted take-over bids by Conwright, who've refused to be bought. In particular I want a list of people and concerns you've leaned on heavily to get your way—and politicians or pressure groups who have been critical of your methods or your operations. It doesn't matter whether you think them important or not. List them. Oh, and I want a duplicate of that map you have on the wall of your office in Perth."

"That map is confidential."

"If it's so confidential, don't leave it hanging where any shutterbug can walk in and take a shot of it with his little Instamatic," George snapped. "I want the duplicate tagged with additional information—the location of all properties where there's been sabotage and the dates when the hits were made. I want photocopies of all reports and correspondence on the hits. The sooner I get the stuff, the sooner I can start work."

"Then you agree to start work?"

Unbidden, George poured himself more whisky. "If you guarantee me complete cooperation in obtaining information and meet my other terms, yes."

"What other terms?"

"A fee of fifty thousand Australian dollars, one half payable in advance, and the balance on receipt of a report from me which enables you to take effective action to protect yourself. Living, traveling, and out-of-pocket expenses are additional. My status is to be that of a consultant, not an employee. The terms are not negotiable."

When Wrightson, stony faced again, had said nothing for a full minute, George swallowed the whisky and stood up. "I'm sorry. I'm going to have to excuse myself, Mr. Wrightson. To tell you the truth I feel bloody awful—and you don't look much better yourself. We'd both better go to bed. Let me know."

Wrightson's lips moved, but George could not read them through a sudden mist of tears. He sneezed violently and plunged out into the glare of the morning, groping for a handkerchief.

"Ham Wrightson told me to give you this when you woke up."

George Galbraith groaned, rolled over in the bunk, and peered blearily at the geologist, Margan, silhouetted in the doorway.

"Come in," he whispered. "What did you say?"

"I thought I'd better give you a call if you want to eat. . . . Jesus, man, what's wrong? You look like something the cat did. You're really sick!"

"Yes, I know. Slept raw without a blanket last night. Caught the great-grandfather of all colds."

"Hell's bells, somebody ought to have warned you!"

"My own fault. Skinful of beer and passed out. What does Wrightson want?"

"He said to give you this. He took off for Perth with Chasser half an hour ago."

George groaned again, took the envelope, ripped it open, and read:

Sinclair: Agreed. Material you want will take time to get together but I've briefed Diagulski. She will bring it by safe hand soonest and make any arrangements you want. $25,000 to your credit National Bank, Perth, tomorrow. Forwarding letter of intent. Please acknowledge.

H. Wrightson

"Has the old man cut your movement orders? You can't travel in your condition."

George shook his head. "No, it's all right. I've got to wait for Miss Diagulski. A day or two, maybe. Have you got any aspirin in the sick wagon?"

"Yes. I'll bring it over."

"Good. Thanks."

"If it goes to your chest you'd better get some penicillin into you."

"Yes."

"Do you want anything to eat?"

George grimaced. "No. Just something to cut the taste of the stuff you use for water out here."

"Wing Foon should have canned fruit juice. Pineapple or orange?"

"No preference. Thanks. I'll come with you." George started to sit up.

"Don't be a bloody nitwit," Margan said gruffly. "Wing Foon can easily send his sidekick across with it. Stay where you are, man. There's no point moving you to the sick wagon because the pill roller is up the track with the search parties."

"Pill roller?"

"A young bloke named Taggert. Pharmacist's mate, ex-Yank navy. A real wiz with the rubbing alcohol. He can make it taste like the best London Dry. See you later, George."

During the night Milton Broderick drove the Bedford truck into camp after it had been pulled out of the sand drift by a tractor. He backed it into a space beside Margan's van and the roar of the big motor and the glare of the headlights aroused George from a shallow, feverish sleep. When Broderick switched off, his talk with Margan was clearly audible.

". . . I don't know what the old man's on about. He was making enough fuss about the kid's rock samples to make you think the poor young bugger had turned up a new Kambalda. Do you want the stuff unloaded now?"

"No," Margan answered. "The morning will do. I won't find anything—nothing of importance, anyway. Featherstone is a geological garbage heap."

"Ham's got a bee in his bonnet that Nat wasn't driving the truck when it bogged."

"I don't believe he was."

"You go for the notion that he and Jack Lightning had a fight and that Jack clobbered him and then faked the whole business to cover up?"

"No. I don't think Jacky was driving the truck either."

"Why not?"

"If he'd wanted to fake getting stuck in the sand, he'd have been smarter. He'd have revved in reverse as if he'd tried to back out. The truck was driven into the sand deliberately in low gear. Finish. Whoever was driving made no effort to get it out."

"What about the radio?"

"It could have been damaged by being dropped accidentally. A corner of the chassis was buckled. Have the police trackers picked up any signs on the dunes?"

"The police trackers *say* they haven't picked up any signs on the dunes. Christ, you should have heard Wrightson's performance, roaring round the place like a scrubber bull with its pizzle in a dog trap. This business has got under his skin. He's close to panicking."

"Yes," said the thin man drily. "So am I. We're having trouble too often, Broderick—far too often."

CHAPTER 6

SEVENTY-TWO hours later a Conair Cessna 210, northbound to Port Hedland on the mid-week milk-run flight, offloaded Tamara Diagulski and her luggage at the Excon strip without shutting down its motors. It immediately took off, chasing the sunset. Milton Broderick hefted three large duralumin-jacketed suitcases into the back of a jeep and drove to Yarralumla.

George Galbraith was playing solitaire on one corner of Doc Margan's laboratory bench while the geologist ticketed and cataloged soil samples from the costeans being scooped by a bulldozer working on the lake's northwestern shore. He watched the arrival closely but decided to await a visit rather than pay a call. The most distressing of his symptoms had abated, but he was weak and irritable after three days of confinement in the humming gloom of Rickety Kate. With the exception of Margan and the geochemist, Maloney, who were friendly enough to visit two or three times a day and inquire about his needs, the Excon Four crew continued to ignore him. They were not interested in money men, with or without head colds.

When the door of Yarralumla had closed and the camp superintendent had driven his jeep back to the pool, George gathered up his cards and said disingenuously, "The boss man's girl Friday is quite a dish, isn't she?"

Margan merely grunted.

"Tell me something, Doc . . ."

"Like what?"

"Why does everybody call her Diagulski—I mean, not Miss Diagulski or Tamara or Tammy, or some nickname?"

Margan laughed. "Do you know," he said, "I'd forgotten her name was Tamara. Ham always calls her Diagulski. We all do."

George shook his head. "Doesn't make sense. Not with those statistics and that coloring."

Margan laughed again. "Tell you what, mate. Next time you get into position, try squeezing her statistics. Then you'll understand why we call her Diagulski."

"Ah," said George. "Butch, do you think?"

The geologist examined a fragment of rock thoughtfully, put it on one side for further attention, and rubbed his nose.

"I doubt it. Somehow I don't get that feeling. Maybe she's just got a hang-up. Or maybe she's got an energetic boyfriend. Anyway I'm too bloody dried out to care."

George was displeased with himself. The notion of Diagulski with an accommodating boyfriend twisted a little knife in the pit of his stomach—a little knife that, in all the circumstances, should not be there.

"Are showers on tonight, do you know?" he asked morosely.

"Yes. The tanker made it."

"Then I'll see you at dinner."

Tamara Diagulski appeared in the mess van halfway through the meal. She wore fresh khaki overalls and her hair was plaited and coiled with unbecoming severity on top of her head. George rose when she came in and moved his chair to make room at the table where he was eating with Margan and Maloney. They greeted her with "Good day, Diagulski, how are you going?" in duet. The diners at the other tables, unenthusiastically shoveling Wing Foon's excellent roast beef, Yorkshire pudding, and four vegetables into their mouths, acknowledged her arrival only by nods or perfunctory waves with their forks. Wing Foon, who cooked for the camp on contract and bore an amazing resemblance to Chairman Mao in his heyday, knew better than to court industrial strife by serving Excon crews anything other than a "roast dinner" in any season—joint of beef, mutton, or lamb on weekdays and pork or poultry on Sundays. Any departure from this main meal diet—or failure to provide a choice between steak and chops and sausages with the breakfast eggs—would have been regarded by the workers as a ploy by the management to undermine their conditions.

Nevertheless Wing retained some personal interest in his customers. When Diagulski came into the mess van he thrust his head through the serving hatch and called raucously, "Diagulski, yer little bewdy! It's real grouse to see yer—and that's fair dinkum. Plant yer fanny and I'll be right out!"

He was a fourth-generation Australian whose great-grandfather had been lynched on the Victorian goldfields for the alleged rape of an Irish prostitute and he spoke the native language with excruciating purity. A Chinese who worked at being more Australian than most Australians—no less incredible for being real.

Diagulski took her seat and inquired after George's health politely but, he feared, indifferently. To Margan's "What's the bad news, darling?", she replied that the boss had at last conceded that there was no point in continuing the air search for the missing men. A police party had left Braund for the Beechover to see if they could find anything at Nathan Ebbet's campsite which might throw light on the mystery. Margan said contemptuously, "If *we* couldn't, there's bugger-all hope that the wallopers will."

A beaming Wing arrived with a large plate of cold ham and potato salad. "Thought yer might be comin' up, love," he said, "so I put it by. How's tricks? Are yer gettin' plenty?"

With gravity, Diagulski assured him she was. George managed to address himself to his food with a straight face.

The talk turned on the problems of pulling out the plant to a summer layoff site near Wiluna. Only when they had finished eating did Diagulski again address him directly.

"Mr. Wrightson sent the records you wanted, Mr. Sinclair. I warn you there's an awful lot of paper to check out. I've arranged with Mr. Broderick for us to use Yarralumla, but now that you've had a chance to see conditions here for yourself, I think we ought to consider moving on to either Broome or Port Epsom. If you need a detailed breakdown on the operational cost of running this sort of camp, Mr. Broderick will be able to help."

"Good," George said, putting on his keen-and-earnest face. "I need work to do."

There was an enigmatic spark in Maloney's eye. His tone was studiously casual. "Now I'd have sworn Ham had made up his mind to give Barrington Bar away altogether. It's to hell and gone and nowhere for underground mining."

Margan flicked an impatient hand. "If he's hiring Sinclair to check the estimates he must have changed his mind, mustn't he?"

"Indeed he must," Maloney said. "Ham moves in most mysterious ways his wonders to perform. But mining finance is beyond a simple fellow like me."

Diagulski stood up. "If you'd care to come over with me now, Mr. Sinclair, I'll show you the catalog of estimates on Phase One—unless you want to watch the movie."

"No, no," he said hastily. "I'm not a movie man, thanks. Lead on. I'm with you."

Maloney's grin was thoughtful as he watched them go. "Our Diagulski cracks a mean stockwhip," he said. "That boyo has really taken the knock. He looks as if he ought to be in a convalescent home. I wonder what he's really doing out here. He's no more a money man than I'm Nelson Rockefeller."

"Coffee?"

"Thank you."

He watched her take jars and mugs from the locker and plug in an electric jug. While the water was heating she unpinned the heavy plaits of ash-blonde hair and let them fall on her shoulders. Then she opened a briefcase, took out a long envelope, and slid it across the table to him.

"Letter of intent, deposit slip, and a form of acknowledgement. Mr. Wrightson said you charge like a wounded bull but he seems satisfied. Congratulations, Mr. . . . Sinclair."

"Thank you. No other developments, I suppose?"

"Nothing. Macready—the private detective who substituted for you—came back the following day. Someone did ring the airline in Melbourne asking if a Mr. George Galbraith was on the flight, but Macready couldn't spot anyone at the terminal who might have been there to check the arrival. He had no trouble."

"Good."

"I'm afraid your cover isn't holding up very well here. Milton Broderick is suspicious. He asked straight out if Mr. Wrightson or I had checked your credentials thoroughly. When I told him we had, he was rather unpleasant—hinted that undercover surveillance by management would be resented if it came to the notice of the men."

"The sad fate of the spy who came down with a cold," George murmured. "I rather suspected Mr. Broderick didn't like me. It doesn't matter what he thinks I am as long as he doesn't know who I am."

He eyed the ranks of portable file folders she had unpacked from the suitcases and placed on the bench along one wall of the van. "You've been very busy, I see."

"Yes. Ham said you wanted everything. We're working on it. Here's the first part of the catalog. Do you take sugar?"

"No, thank you."

He took the metal-clipped folder she held out, opened it, and ran his eyes down the columns of typescript. There were seventeen pages listing one hundred and seventy-three instances of malicious damage done to Conwright properties over a period of thirty-two months. The record was compiled chronologically with an estimate of monetary loss for each item. George's lips pursed in a soundless whistle when he saw the total—a little less than one and three-quarter million dollars.

"In the genteel language of my late masters in diplomacy," he said, "I can appreciate Mr. Wrightson's concern. I hadn't realized he was bleeding quite so badly. Did he give you the map I asked for?"

"Yes. I didn't try to transfer the damage information to it because of the loss of legibility. It's small-scale. I brought lands and survey sheets instead. They show a great deal more."

He nodded approval. "Good thinking, Miss Diagulski. You've made a flying start."

"The damage information was simple enough to assemble, but there were problems getting the reports and correspondence Xeroxed. Mr. Wrightson said you also want details of acquisitions, offers made, negotiations entered into, and disputes which have arisen since the formation of the holding company. That's a devil of a job because we now own or control more than forty individual concerns. In many cases their management is practically autonomous, subject only to policy directives. They keep their own records. The only papers we hold at head office are their annual reports and semiannual accounts. However, we've made a beginning and Mr. Wrighston has made a list from memory of certain . . . situations, I suppose you could call them that . . . that he thinks you could find interesting. Miss Weatherley remembered that there were a number of references to Conwright projects in state parliamentary proceedings—references not reported in the newspapers. She's having Hansard extracts made. They and the press clippings will arrive tomorrow or the next day."

George studied her over the rim of the coffee mug. Her face was composed, even serene, but there were lines and dark shadows under her eyes. Her mouth drooped a little. Wrightson's girl Friday was tired—very tired indeed.

"Your minister must have missed you when you came to this job," he said.

"I beg your pardon?"

"You told me you once worked as confidential secretary to a cabinet minister. That's demanding."

"Yes."

"What was his portfolio?"

"Defense," she replied curtly after a split second of hesitation.

"Don't get uptight," he said. "I'm not being nosy beyond my brief. I just wondered if you were ever required in the line of duty to sit in on an intelligence analysis."

"No. But sometimes I had to make a précis of findings or recommendations by the Joint Chiefs."

"Which your minister ignored for the most part, I imagine?"

"No. My minister was an intelligent man. He studied them carefully and then consigned them to the 'No Action' basket. He was also an intelligent politician."

George emitted a hoot of delighted laughter, but it petered out in a convulsive wheeze. He mopped his eyes, blew his nose violently, and gasped, "God rot your desert pestilences! I only hope my brains are in better condition than my tubes. How long are you staying here?"

"That's up to you. Mr. Wrightson has instructed me to give you as much help as you require with this material."

"Good. I'm grateful. But you're going to end up hating me."

"Why should I hate you?"

"Because, my dear girl," he said, "you and I are going to do a good, old-fashioned, precomputer intelligence analysis of that little lot. Without clerical help we're going to end up exhausted, exasperated, and bored rigid, but I can't see any other way to make a start. Somewhere or other in that horrible heap of papers there are concealed facts which, if isolated and examined in relation to one another, will point to certain places and certain people worth investigating in depth."

She looked puzzled. "But why not move out and get what help we need? We could get computer time. Wouldn't that be quicker, more efficient?"

George shook his head. "Not on. No way. Not yet. There's a long way to go before a computer can help and there's a very real advantage in staying out of sight until I know in what direction I should be looking to avoid personal trouble. If we turn up in Perth again—or in any center of population in Conwright country—I'll bet you it's only a matter of days before someone puts . . . sugar in my gas tank or more lead in my beer."

"I don't think that's a joking matter, Mr. Galbraith," she said almost angrily.

"Neither do I—which is why I'm resigned to life in Rickety Kate for a few more days. You know, the Canberra-Perth connection is the thing that bugs me. It suggests two things. The people who are pricking Conwright out here to the tune of nearly ten thousand dollars a pinprick have a pretty efficient spy system. That means they've got resources of money and manpower and they're coordinated well enough to start harassing me within a few hours of my arrival in Perth. From the start we must home in on *who* might command such resources and *why* they could be employing them in the way they do. The answers are somewhere in those files but how long it will take us to find them is anybody's guess."

"I'll do what I can to help, Mr. Galbraith."

"Bless you," said George, "I know that. Look, since we're going to fight on the same side, why don't you observe the customs of the country and call me George?"

The smile took his breath away.

"I'm terribly sorry, but no. I'm going to call you Sinclair. I don't much care for your first two given names."

George winced. "Oh?"

"And you can observe the customs of the country and call me Diagulski. Everyone does. It's a . . . sort of term of endearment."

"As you like," he said, and changed the subject. "Would Diagulski, used as a term of endearment, happen to know anything about statistical method?"

"Once—a long time ago—I attended a seminar at summer school. Not much has stuck, I'm afraid."

"What did will help. Excuse me if my gallantry is showing, but you look bushed. I think I'd better get back to my own life-support unit and let you have a night's sleep. First thing in the morning we'll start getting that . . . what did you call it? . . . catalog of estimates onto graph paper. Thanks for the coffee. Good night, colleague Diagulski."

"Good night, colleague Sinclair. I . . . I think you're right maybe. I am a bit bushed."

At the door he paused and turned. "By the way, do they really use catalogs of estimates in feasibility studies?"

Again the smile that riffled his heart. "Not that I know of. But it sounds as if they ought to, don't you agree?"

By midnight the trailer vans of Excon Four, gleaming in the starlight, and the baked red earth on which they stood, had once more rid themselves of the intolerable burden of the day's heat. But George couldn't sleep. He sat on Rickety Kate's rear step with a blanket draped over his shoulders, deep in meditation. The ambivalence of his attitude toward Tamara Diagulski alarmed him. It was logical enough that a beautiful young woman in her situation should build up the iron-maiden image as a defense against lecherous dolts and pests, and that the defense should be powerfully reinforced by her cool competence in the sort of work usually done by men with horn-rimmed spectacles, ulcers, and ambitions. What was illogical was that he, the incorruptible realist, should continue to respond to the stimulus of her physical presence in the way he did.

But if George feared that teaming with Tamara Diagulski would impair his concentration on the job at hand, the fear was unfounded. She grasped his exposition of the principles of intelligence analysis so quickly that he was inclined to doubt her denial of previous experience. When he explained that he wanted to reduce the information contained in the list of hits against Conwright properties to graphic form, she summed up crisply: "You want statistical graphs which show variations of occurrence, intensity, and target location. There are one hundred and seventy-three events recorded in a period of thirty-two months, so I'll have to work on a fairly large scale. Do you need any special equipment for the work you'll be doing?"

George blinked and swallowed.

"Only a pocket calculator," he said. "If you can take over the graphs, I'll make a start with Wrightson's map and the lands and survey sheets. I'll have a shot at building up the sort of operations map the opposition would use—if they've used an operations map. It'll be a slow process."

But in the event, the process was finished much more quickly than he expected. Hamilton Wrightson's personal assistant worked with an intense single-mindedness that shamed him into emulation. Not once in three fourteen-hour days did she address any remark to him—barring the brief courtesies of arrival or leave-taking—that was unrelated to the task at hand. Her exclusive concentration at first made him uncomfortable, but soon he was able to immerse himself in maps and distance tabulations even more completely than if he had been working alone.

At ten o'clock on the evening of the third day she pinned the last of six graph sheets on a particle-board mounting and announced: "Mission completed, sir. Permission to take a coffee break?"

George surfaced from his own calculations with a start. "Permission granted, staff—with pleasure and relief. You set a cracking pace. I've still got thirty or forty items to break down before I can start to get the time-distance picture. That is, if I ever do."

She shook her head. "Time-distance picture? Sorry. Too technical."

"Not at all. I'm simply making crude estimates of the distance between the localities where sabotage has occurred and the nearest public road."

"Why?"

"Item one: the distance between the geographical extremities of the strikes is about three hundred miles on the north–south axis and over four hundred miles on the east-west axis. Therefore the strike force, if it were operating from a central base, would make an *average* return journey of three hundred and fifty miles to hit the most distant targets and retire.

"Item two: the strike force has never yet left any evidence to indicate its approach or retreat routes. That suggests to me that the final approach to the target is made on foot, because it would be virtually impossible to obliterate tracks made by a wheeled vehicle or by a mounted party anywhere near the target. Travelers on foot can avoid leaving tracks by keeping to hard ground wherever possible and erasing them from unavoidable soft ground.

"Take item one and item two and you get at least an indication of probability that the raiders travel on public roads by motor vehicle to a point near the target. They cover the last few miles on foot, make the hit, and retreat under cover of darkness. Their vehicle picks them up again and drives off, leaving behind only tire marks of the sort left by random and perfectly legitimate passing traffic. At least this is the hypothesis I'm putting to the test of time and distance calculations."

She frowned in concentration. "Ingenious," she said, "but it'd be hard to prove on paper."

George waved a disclaiming hand. "I'm not fool enough to try to prove anything on paper, Diagulski. All I'm trying to do is to limit future field investigations to the areas of probability. Take your own work. I've learned a great deal from it already."

Her smile was very faint. "I knew before I started that the frequency is increasing, and so is the amount of damage done in a single strike."

"And the graphs don't reveal anything more than that?"

"Nothing of much significance that I can recognize."

"Have a look at the acceleration curve again."

She sat down beside him at the table and cupped her chin in her hands, studying the chart. "The rate of acceleration is fairly constant over the last two years."

"Exactly. And the curve is not much deformed—

flattened out—by the hot season in the arid or semi-
arid areas or by the wet season in the areas which receive heavy monsoonal rain. The raider's mobility
and activity is not seriously affected by weather—or
not at least by the sort of weather experienced in Conwright country over the last two summers. Later we'll
get around to analyzing the meteorological records
and find out if any raids were actually made in the
Kimberley country at times when ordinary road
traffic was interrupted by flooded rivers, washaways,
or violent storms. Maloney tells me that it is not unusual for sections of the main roads in the Kimberley
to be impassable for days or weeks during an ordinary
wet season."

"Yes," she said dubiously. "I can see the drift of
your theory."

"At this stage, there's not much more than a drift to
see. But take something else clearly indicated on
your graphs. Some of the larger pastoral properties
have been raided as many as seven times. Each raid is
made on a single limited objective. Look at Arrowlea
as an example. A seven-hundred-thousand-acre
property. It has been hit four times. First hit in June
—a windmill and troughs wrecked. Second hit in October. The manager and his wife are in Perth on
leave and the stockmen are mustering back paddocks
thirty miles or more from the homestead. The house is
burned to the ground and the police find evidence that
kerosene was used to start the fire. Third hit in Janu-
ary the following year. Fences are cut and scrubber
bulls driven into a paddock where breeding cows are
being grazed. Fourth hit in September. Lubricating
oil stored in a dump near a boundary hut is contaminated with iron filings and serious damage done to a
bulldozer and a Fordson tractor before the sabotage
is detected. Remember what I said and check it on
the charts. *One raid, one limited objective.*"

"Why do you stress that?"

"Because it is a principle of scientifically waged
guerilla warfare not to be tempted by targets of opportunity. To hit targets of opportunity slows down
the operations, increases the chances of being ob-

served either coming in or going out, tends inevitably to leave a trail from which deductions can be made. The brain behind this campaign is a very bright tactician indeed. His intelligence system is excellent because he knows precisely when and where to strike, and his field force is made up of physically tough, disciplined men. In the long term they're infinitely more destructive than vandals on a series of random rampages.

"Then again, here's your frequency graph from another angle. There were two hits in the first calendar month of the campaign. Last month there were eight. The average number of hits per month over the whole period is five and a half—or more than one a week. To me that suggests at least two and possibly three raiding parties made up of a driver who may be doubling as a lookout man and two operatives who can travel fast and wreck a particular type of target effectively. It takes a different kind of know-how to cut oyster rafts adrift or board and sink pearling luggers lying at anchor off a tropical coast from the know-how needed to dynamite windmills, wells, or mine workings in dry, open country. Arson, sabotage of machinery, interference with livestock, all require different skills too. I'm inclined to think that the person or persons out to smash Wrightson's empire are using small task forces of specialists, teams of not more than three or four men. Possibly fewer."

She dug her chin even more firmly into her palms. "You sound very sure, Sinclair."

"Larger teams are not needed. All these hits could have been made by two men with transport support. But it would be very nearly a physical impossibility to step up the hit rate to two a week with only two active groups. Three or even four groups would be kept busy enough."

"You're taking it for granted that the operation is controlled from the outside. Couldn't it be conducted from inside the Conwright organization—by a fifth column?"

George shook his head vehemently. "Supported possibly—particularly on the intelligence side. But conducted? No. For a start, what you call the Con-wright organization is only a financial interlocking of enterprises separately staffed and managed as far as day-to-day operations are concerned. The only thing they have in common is that they exist in this part of the world and are wholly owned or financially controlled by Wrightson. Systematic infiltration would be complicated and extremely difficult. Complete security would be almost impossible. Remember that there has been no leak, no defection from the opposition in thirty-two months, despite the fact that Wrightson and the police have offered substantial rewards for information leading to the conviction of those responsible for the Arrowlea sabotage, the Three Bamboos mine explosion, and the Beagle Bay sinkings. In addition, your own graphs give no indication of randomness. That would be implicit if the strikes were made by insider saboteurs who would be able to do their damage only as opportunity offered."

Tamara Diagulski covered her eyes with her fingers and said, "Too hard, too fast, Sinclair. You've left me behind. I'll have to look again and think."

"You're dog-tired." His voice was suddenly concerned, sympathetic. "You've been beating your brains out on exacting work without enough rest. You were exhausted when you arrived here. Why don't you take a few days off? Fly out to Perth and lie in a cold bath—sleep for eighteen hours straight?"

"Milton Broderick says he'll have to pull this camp back to Wiluna as soon as the vehicles used for the search have been checked and serviced. You'll have to decide where you want to work. Arrangements will have to be made. Soon."

"Yes. I've been thinking about it. Would it be possible to find me accommodation on one of the more remote sheep or cattle stations for a few weeks?"

She thought for a moment. Then, "Yes, it could be arranged, although not easily at this time of the year. You won't be very comfortable. The climate from now until the end of March is pretty beastly. You'd be better off at Broome or Port Epsom or Hedland where there are decent hotels. It could be arranged, say, for a marine biologist, Dr. Sinclair, no connection with Conwright mentioned, to arrive quietly and retire to his room to complete his thesis on the breeding habits of penaeus esculentis, the tiger prawn."

George chuckled. The girl had gallantry as well as brains. She could make a joke when every nerve in her body was ragged with fatigue.

"You've got a delightful imagination, Diagulski," he said. "The trouble with your suggestion is that Dr. Sinclair needs the help of an amanuensis to record his observations on passionate prawns. In a town you'd be recognized immediately and the cover wouldn't hold up for an hour if it were known we were working together. It might hold up for weeks if we could use one of the more remote station homesteads."

"Weeks?" The dismay was unconcealed.

"I'm sorry. But it's the name of the game, Diagulski. Unless we are lucky enough to make an early breakthrough, processing those files completely will almost certainly take weeks. Which reminds me—I need some additional information. Conwright runs a library and research section, doesn't it?"

"Yes. What do you want researched?"

"I want a list of all aboriginal reserves and settlements within or abutting on Conwright country— their enumerated or estimated population."

She stared at him with curious intensity. "Yes. Very well. When did it occur to you that natives might be involved? Did you deduce that from the graphs, too?"

"Good Lord, no. It was apparent to me that natives must be involved from the moment Wrightson finished telling me his troubles. What puzzles me is that he—and you—have studiously avoided mention of something so obvious."

Her voice held an edge of resentment. "Obvious? No raider has ever been sighted or tracked. What justification is there in the blind assumption that from the outset natives are responsible?"

"The justification of common sense," he snapped. "For God's sake, Diagulski, you're an intelligent woman! Both you and Wrightson know very well that these raids can be carried out only by people with an intimate knowledge of the terrain and the physical ability to move freely in it in all seasons. Who else but natives? Why the hell be coy about it?"

She made no reply and he went on, "What you and I have to do is to discover areas—areas in both the literal and figurative sense—where further investigation may lead us to the person or persons planning and directing the campaign. I doubt that the general officer commanding will turn out to be quite as aboriginal as his troops."

CHAPTER 7

ON first perusal, Hamilton Wrightson's list of "interesting situations" that had arisen in the acquisition of Conwright's subsidiary companies yielded little information to suggest to George Galbraith's mind a valid motive for such revenge—a campaign of diversified but systematic sabotage. There had been disputes in the courts about mining tenements but they seemed minor matters. There had been half a dozen confrontations with station labor about accommodations on East Kimberley properties, mostly resolved when management made concessions. A bookkeeper on a cattle run had been prosecuted for fiddling store accounts and had pleaded guilty in the Supreme Court. A prawn processing plant on Danger Bay had been closed down and its hands dismissed for striking in support of a trawler skipper suspended for running his boat aground while drunk and incapable. There were a score of even less portentous incidents.

Trivia. If Hamilton Wrightson ranked such petty affairs as the most memorable examples of conflicts incidental to his rise, then he had won his empire virtually by default. George was not prepared to believe that. The key to the riddle would be found in broader issues. It must lie in the potential of his properties rather than in their performance or any frictions during their acquisition.

In two days of stubborn plodding through a morass of inconsequential paper, he found only one item of possible significance—a Hansard extract covering a portion of a debate on North West development in the Legislative Assembly. An opposition member referred to "the Conwright octopus" in a fiery condemnation of the exploitation of aboriginal labor on pastoral properties in the Pilbara and Kimberly divisions.

Diagulski's comment was curt. "Nonsense. Ham Wrightson pays his natives exactly the same wages as he pays his white workers. They have exactly the same housing and conditions. It's always been his policy, even before he found Mount Millswyn, and that was long before the new awards were handed down. He's known among aborigines as a fair employer."

George scrubbed his chin and read the extract a second time.

"Do you know how many natives the Conwright group employs?"

"No. They're hired or fired on the same basis as the Europeans."

"Would that imply that roughly half the Conwright workforce in the North West is aboriginal?"

She looked hard at him. "Why do you ask that?"

"Because, according to the statistics, roughly half the population of the country where he holds interests is aboriginal. Therefore, if Conwright employs a much larger proportion of whites than blacks, the blacks are economically disadvantaged."

"Yes."

"Just yes? No more than that?"

"What more is there? If the blacks are disadvantaged, it is not because Ham Wrightson discriminates against them because of color. It is because they either don't want the sort of work he has to offer or because many of them who are employed don't earn their pay."

"Pragmatism," said George, "is a doctrine that measures any assertion solely by its practical bearing upon human interests. But whose human interests? Oh, leave it, Diagulski. I'm turning nasty. For two days, ever since you finished those so-beautiful graphs, I've been beating my head against a brick wall. It's damned nearly midnight. I'm going for a long walk in the fresh air. Do you want to come—or do you just want me out of your sight?"

No wind stirred. The stars blazed so fiercely that the salt pan glowed like a fluorescent silver plaque. The encircling sand ridges had yielded up their store of heat and the night air was perfumed by spinifex resin and dew-moistened dust.

They walked briskly, side by side, following the cincture of hard red earth between the pan and the surrounding dunes behind which the lights of Excon Four were finally obscured.

After a mile or two, the beat of the big diesel generator faded. There was no sound but the muted shuffle of their footsteps.

Diagulski stopped suddenly, laid a hand on his arm, and spoke for the first time since they had left the camp's perimeter. "Wait a while now. Get your breath."

He looked out over the glowing lake and at the slow, curving mingling of the wind-sculptured sands, dappled and tinseled in the light of galaxies.

"Did you watch the moon landing, Diagulski?"

Her fingers tightened on his arm. "Hush! Listen."

He listened. But the silence was absolute—the silence of a deep, dry cave. He leaned toward her. "What can you hear, Diagulski?"

"Don't talk. Listen again. They're there. . . ."

He tensed and drew back. *"They? Who?"*

The fingers gripping his arm relaxed and fell away. She laughed and murmured. "Don't worry, Sinclair. You haven't been working me quite as hard as that. But I *am* hearing voices. In time you'll hear them yourself if you listen hard enough."

"I'm sorry. You'll have to explain. . . ."

"The little things that live in the ground under the spinifex clumps and among the dead mulga roots. Tiny marsupial moles and thorny lizards and blind snakes and waterbag frogs. Armies of insects. They come out to hunt and drink the dew on a still night. If you listen hard enough you can hear them. Honestly. But you've got to learn to tune your ears in to the sound. Let's sit down and try listening again."

"Of course, if you want to."

She sat, elbows on knees, chin propped in cupped hands—the posture, mannerism, that was peculiarly hers—Diagulski concentrating, in deep thought. He squatted on his heels for a while, then relaxed and lay back on the ground, looking at the sky, tracing the swirling drifts in the blizzard of stars.

You've got to learn to tune your ears in to the sound. . . .

Imagination? Romantic fantasy? He held his breath, but could only hear the pulse in his temples.

Five minutes, or ten. A meditation? She made no movement. At length he turned his head toward her and asked: "Do you spend much time in these desert camps, Diagulski?"

She stirred. "No. Never long enough."

"You love the desert, don't you?"

"Yes."

"Why?"

"I think it's because it . . . it seems to restore my sense of perspective. That's a cliché, I know. But clichés can be the simple truth, can't they?"

"Probably. In any case I agree with you. In the desert the dimensions of living and dying, of succeeding and failing, are clearly defined. Tell me something. Why in the normal line of duty as Wrightson's personal assistant would you have reason to visit a camp like Excon Four at all?"

"Detail work," she replied indifferently. "It's a very expensive and complicated operation, this minerals survey of the Madison Basin. There are inquiries to be made, facts to be checked, which the radiophone can't deal with. But most field errands I do for Ham are on the pastoral side—checking that station improvement programs are really being carried out, that bookkeepers are really keeping the books, that company equipment is being properly maintained and not left out in the bush to rot, that fencing and bore-sinking contractors don't cheat."

"It sounds as if the job demands a pretty extensive range of technical knowledge."

"No. Not really. All you need is a natural skepticism and common sense. The sad fact is that the people who settle the Australian outback these days aren't very bright. Or, if they are, they're eccentric, temperamentally unstable. They're unproductive misfits. Ham Wrightson wants to change that by creating conditions and incentives that will attract first-rate people to the North West. Above all, he sees what he's doing as a project in reclamation—an attempt to regenerate at least some of the land ruined by the ignorance and greed of early settlers and absentee landlords. He's a man of broad vision and terrific energy. He believes in his country and its future."

George retrieved a cigarette from a crumpled packet in his trousers pocket and lit it.

"How did you get your job with Ham Wrightson, Diagulski?" When she made no answer he added: "If it's none of my business, I withdraw and apologize."

"No. I was just wondering how to cut a long, rather grubby story short. I met Ham Wrightson when I was working in Canberra five years ago. He had business with my boss. They got on well together. I saw a good deal of him while the complications were being sorted out. But before they were in order, a political dogfight broke out because my boss wouldn't toe the party line on the American extraterritoriality issue at North West Cape and Maralinga. In the end he got mauled to death—and I got badly bitten."

"For God's sake! How were you mixed up in it? You were simply his secretary, weren't you?"

"The newspapers mixed me up in it. One political writer whose paper backed the opposition was so grossly unfair that I was fool enough to lose my temper and call him a liar publicly. After that he saw to it that I made front-page headlines every day. The electorate got the message."

George snorted disbelievingly. "The message that a

cabinet minister was sleeping with his private secretary, do you mean? Was that the innuendo? Do you mean to say the Australian electorate was wet enough to be influenced by that sort of muck peddling?"

"No. The Australian electorate was influenced by the innuendo that I not only shared my minister's bed but carried his portfolio for him when he was on one of his periodical drinking bouts. Half of his cabinet colleagues were drunks of one kind or another, but my man's weakness was the fatal kind. You see, when he was in his cups he told the truth."

"I understand," George said at last. "A fatal weakness indeed! So when the blood stopped dripping, Wrightson offered you a job."

"Yes." She stood up. "We'd better get back. Soon it'll be cold. You don't want to risk another chill."

He took her hand and she made no effort to draw it away. It was soft and dry and oddly lifeless—one small, inert hand that pulled more heavily on his cloak of self-sufficiency than all the failures and the petty humiliations of rejections past and remembered only in half sleep. He wanted to take her in his arms to warm and comfort her, but her hand warned that they were not of one world.

The lights of the camp were in sight again before he spoke.

"I'm afraid I spoiled it by raking over old embers, Diagulski-as-a-term-of-endearment," he said quietly. "I could say I asked how you got your job out of idle conversational curiosity, but it wouldn't be true. We've worked together—close together and in difficult conditions—for more than a week now, but we've stayed strangers until tonight. That's worried me because Wrightson's problem is going to take a long while to solve. I need the help of someone I can trust and who can trust me. My curiosity wasn't idle, but I'm deeply sorry it hurt you. A lot of things have happened in my own life that I prefer not to remember—not because I was honest and innocent in a failure like you, but because I wasn't."

"There's no need to be sorry, Sinclair. Remembering doesn't hurt me any more—unless being angry

again is a sort of hurt. It's long over. Five years and
forgotten. It's sad how people when they're young believe in Nemesis."

Nemesis. The Goddess of Retribution. No—of ret-
ributive justice. Ill served by her self-appointed aco-
lytes. . . .

Her pace had quickened, almost to a run. He could
smell his own sweat and hers. Then, in half a pace,
she stopped dead, pulled her hand free, and pointed
east.

"Look!"

"What is it?"

"There—between the dunes. Watch!"

Three grotesque, humped bodies traversed the sky-
line of a saddle between two sand ridges a quarter
mile away—matt, soot-black silhouettes bobbing in
ungainly rhythm like inexpertly manipulated puppets.
They were visible for no more than a minute before
the folds of the desert from which they had emerged
swallowed them up again.

George expelled his breath slowly. "Well, I'll be
damned! Camels. A bull and two cows. Tommy Maloney was telling me only yesterday how the old-time
Afghan drivers used to turn their teams loose along
the Canning stock route rather than destroy them
when motor trucks took over hauling supplies for the
stations. It must be a hard life out there, even for
wild camels."

"Did you see them—clearly?" The question held an
urgency that surprised him.

"Very clearly. Why? What's wrong?"

"Did you notice anything strange?"

He laughed. "Only them. What else?"

"Nothing. Come on." She took his hand again and
pulled impatiently.

Under the awning at the entrance to Yarralumla
she turned and asked: "Do you want something to
drink—coffee, beer?"

"No thanks, Diagulski," he said gently. "You need
sleep. Go to bed now. Don't dream."

To his utter astonishment she leaned forward and
kissed him, very lightly and fleetingly—but on the

lips. "Thank you for walking me in the starlight and not spoiling it," she said. "Good night, colleague Sinclair. Sleep deep, too."

At ten after five in the morning, a charge of not less than twenty pounds of gelignite exploded under the generator van, overturning it and setting alight a small fuel tanker coupled to it.

The concussion hit Rickety Kate so violently that George was flung out of his bunk and slammed headfirst against the wall. Dazed, disoriented in pitch darkness, he groped on hands and knees for the door, found it, flung it open, and catapulted himself into the yellow dawn over Mullamurra.

The generator van, no more than a heap of deformed metal, was already the source of a fountain of bright orange flame and black smoke spurting fifty feet into the air and climbing higher.

CHAPTER 8

GEORGE GALBRAITH's recollection of events in the hour that followed the dynamiting of the power plant at Excon Four was never to be quite clear. He could remember scrambling to his feet, staring blankly at the blazing tanker and the pool of burning oil spreading toward the mess trailer. A nearby dormitory trailer, Fanny Adams, capsized by the blast, had a gaping hole in its roof torn by flying metal. George ran, hell for leather, in the direction of Yarralumla. Other men were spilling out of their sleeping quarters, shouting questions.

Someone bellowed, "Get your extinguishers. All hands. Get foam on it! Get the extinguishers."

He collided headlong with Diagulski, standing barefoot in pajamas in front of the big trailer.

"Thank Christ!" he panted. "Are you all right?"

"Yes. What was it?"

"I don't know. Gelignite by the stink of it."

"Sinclair! You're hurt! You're bleeding."

"Bloody nose. Bashed my face. Nothing. Where's Broderick?"

"I don't know."

"He'd better call off the damned fools trying to get foam on that blaze with hand-held extinguishers. They'll fry!"

The roar of the burning oil was drowning the shouts of the crew men, now dancing like dervishes around the spreading base of the flames. A minute later Broderick's voice, monstrously magnified and distorted by a bullhorn turned up to full volume, brayed through the din.

"Dozer drivers! All dozer drivers stand to the crawlers! Get sand to that fire. You men with extinguishers—stand back! Get back there! Back!"

Diagulski's fingers bit hard into his arm. *"Fanny Adams!* There were four men sleeping there."

"All right. Put some clothes on—your boots. I'm getting mine. Find that medical type, Taggert. Get over to the sick bay. He might want help. I'll take a look."

But he was forestalled. The three surviving occupants of the overturned dormitory van had already dragged the body of their companion into the open by the time George arrived. The dead man was a surveyor's chainman named Rowlands. His skull had been smashed by a fragment of engine casing. His mates were unhurt.

George helped them carry the body, swathed in blood-soaked blankets, to the dispensary trailer. The survivors, glassy eyed with shock, babbled obscenities and wild theories about the cause of the explosion. He wondered dimly why no one suggested that it had been deliberately set off.

By now three D8 bulldozers, thundering at full power, squealing, clanking, and bucking, were ripping trenches in the earth at the perimeter of the oil spill, first containing and finally smothering it under tons of spoil. The drovers had moved fast—but not fast enough to save the mess and galley annex. Both were blazing fiercely.

George watched until it was clear the fire could spread no further through the camp. He walked back to Rickety Kate and crammed his belongings into his airline bag. There was nothing he could do—except maybe stow the maps and records that cluttered Yarralumla's benches, ready for a quick move.

Halfway back to the big van he stopped short, rubbing his eyes in exasperation as he looked up at the eastern sky. There was something wrong with his vision. Three-quarters of an hour had passed since the explosion. Daylight should be brightening, not fading —even under the pall of greasy smoke which hung above the camp and was continually renewed from smoldering heaps of oil-drenched earth. But Mullamurra and its shattered camp were cowering under an eerie, deepening twilight. The sunrise was quenched by vast, columnar clouds—pillars of sand marching on the desert's horizon. The salt of the lake no longer glittered, it glowered like billet steel squeezed from a rolling mill.

Then the first of the storm wind came—a zephyr which unraveled coils of dust from the parched ground and, as it strengthened, tossed them up in erratic, choking puffs. George put his head down and ran.

Broderick's bullhorn blared again as George was cramming the last papers into Diagulski's cases.

"All hands muster at the vehicle pool! Muster at the vehicle pool! All hands muster! Hurry it, hurry it!"

The camp super had climbed onto the hood of the biggest tractor to bellow his orders. The wind, now blowing spates of sand with gale-force gusts, forced him to crouch as he shouted. "Hurry it up! Hurry it up and hear this! Get a move on!"

George felt a tug at his shirt-sleeve and turned.

Diagulski. Her face was bloodless and her eyes red rimmed. He steadied her against an eddy.

"Casualties. What's the score, Diagulski?"

"Rowlands is dead and three burned. Thorley, one of the drillers, is bad. His face . . . oh, my God, Sinclair . . . his face . . ."

The bullhorn bawled metallically.

"All personnel! Repeat, all personnel. Hear this! We are evacuating this camp. Do you hear me? We are evacuating this camp. We are pulling out to Braund homestead. We are pulling out to Braund. Regular drivers stand to their vehicles and check. Report to me when you're ready to roll. Report to me in Yarralumla. Report to me for dispatch, do you hear? Now get going!"

Broderick climbed down from his perch and shouldered his way through a press of smoke-blackened, half-naked men jabbering incoherent questions.

"Get your stuff together and stand by, Diagulski. I'm sending you out with Taggert and the casualties in the Range Rover. You'll be first off. You've got ten minutes."

"Wouldn't those men be better off here until we can get an air ambulance in?"

Broderick bared his teeth, savagely white in his matted beard.

"For the love of Jesus, Diagulski, don't you realize a sandstorm like this could last a week? We haven't even got a radio. There's a total blackout. The Range Rover's air-conditioned. In a van without power those men couldn't last until sundown. We'll have heat-stroke cases as it is."

Someone said: "You've got a lot of vehicles with power takeoff, Milt—and a couple of compressors not far out. You could run the fans in Yarralumla and the lab van on an emergency power rig."

George looked over his shoulder. It was Margan, with a blood-sodden strapping above his left eye.

Broderick's voice was gravelly, unsteady with tension. "Stay on your own pad, Margan. I'm evacuating to Braund."

The thin man shrugged. The camp superintendent turned on his heel. Diagulski called after him: "What do you want me to tell them at Braund? What do you want them to do?"

"Keep all down traffic off the track. I don't want a head-on collision. Tell them to do what they can to get the men under cover as they arrive. I'll try to send a couple of vans out last, behind a prime mover. But if the drifts build up they might have to uncouple."

George seized Diagulski's wrist and, bent against the wind, hauled her back to Yarralumla. He hoisted her roughly up the steps and across the sill, kicked the door shut, and groped for a battery lamp. Yarralumla's small, double-glazed windows, glowing eerily red, gave no more than darkroom illumination. Diagulski put her hands flat on the bench and leaned forward, shoulders heaving and tears streaming in muddy rivulets down her cheeks.

"That hairy half-wit's flipped his mind," George spat out. "He *can't* send trucks out in this! It's bloody murder!"

Her lips moved in reply.

"What did you say?"

"I said the gusts will drop . . . when the storm front moves through. The drivers are good. They know the track and their job."

"I wish to God," George muttered savagely, "I could be sure that Broderick knew his."

Twenty minutes later Diagulski, draped in a burnoose improvised from one of her bed sheets, climbed into the front seat of Excon Four's Range Rover beside a young driver wearing a cowboy hat pulled forward over his eyes and a bandana over his nose. As she had predicted, the gusts moderated but the gale was blowing at a steady fifty knots, veering gradually to the north. Visibility was no more than fifty yards. The car's taillights bounced erratically as the driver headed for the track that circled the airstrip and then were swallowed up in the dust clouds rolling down from the dunes.

Margan had rigged a pressure lamp in the laboratory van and he and Maloney were stowing equipment and records when George burst through the rear entrance, his head and shoulders swathed in the second sheet from Diagulski's bunk. The thin man's smile was sour and fleeting.

"Where's the rest of your thieving mob, Ali?" he drawled. "Not coming in one at a time, I hope. Close the door."

George unwound the sheet. "You ought to learn from your betters, Doc. The Saudis have forgotten more about kitting up for sandstorms than you'll ever know. Breathe in through your mouth and out through your nose. You ought to try it. Well, I've got bad news."

"Then for the love of God," Maloney groaned, "keep it to yourself."

"Black Broderick tells me I'm to travel with you in the Thorneycroft. Sorry, you're landed with a Jonah."

Margan grunted. "You'd be sorrier if he'd told you to ride in the work bus, chum. The Thorny's got a cooler. I'll let you sit in the middle if you can keep your feet off the clutch."

"Now black for Broderick is good—very good," Maloney said. "You were right about making shift with power takeoff from the heavies, Doc—at least until the worst of it lets up. The man's panicked. He's got no right to put vehicles on the track in what's blowing up."

"Maybe not. But then maybe the fan motors wouldn't take the overload when the intakes get dusted up. It's Broderick's responsibility. Belt up, Tommy. Yours not to reason why. Help me get the stuff lashed down."

The thermometer clipped to the sun visor in the Thorneycroft's cabin registered 126 degrees Fahrenheit at ten o'clock, two hours out. The odometer read twenty miles. Margan slapped the gear lever into neutral and let the big truck roll to a standstill.

"Smoke-oh," he announced. "Give the blowers another burst, Tommy. Not too long."

Maloney eased the ventilator levers under the dash onto cold and full. The thermometer needle began to sag. When it had fallen below 120 degrees, Margan said: "Okay, Tom. Cut it—or George here'll catch cold again. Enjoying your pioneer tour of Death Valley down under, George?"

George scrubbed a handful of sheet across his caked lips. "Scenery's fantastic—but fantastic," he croaked. "When do they serve refreshments? Didn't you bring any beer?"

The thin man grinned. He reached down and took a felt-coverered army water bottle from beneath the seat. "Here, take a swig. But go easy."

George's throat contracted painfully. The blood was pounding in his temples and every cell in his body was crying out for fluid. He forced himself to unscrew the cap slowly. The lukewarm water cut the tacky mucus in his mouth—but it was salted. He gulped and then gagged.

"Swallow it, chum, if you want to dodge the cramps. Take another mouthful, and *swallow it!*"

Margan took back the bottle, tipped a couple of ounces of weak brine into his mouth, and passed it to Maloney.

"Will you take her for a spell, Tommy? Unless George wants to have a go. Want to have a go, George?"

"Have a go at what?"

"Driving."

George felt a surge of hot resentment. "One thing they don't teach the chaps at English public schools, Margan," he said bitingly, "is how to fly a twenty-five-ton truck blind through a sandstorm. If you're stuck with such a useless bastard for a passenger, blame Broderick. I didn't book the berth."

Margan's teeth flashed again. "Good for you, George! A bit of temper helps. If you can keep your British prick as stiff as you keep your upper lip, you'll have a happy honeymoon. It was only a joke. I was having you on. Change seats with Maloney. Then he and I can shuffle."

When George had resettled himself, Maloney said, peering at the odometer, "Twenty point two, Doc. To my memory, the cutline turns east-west about four miles from here. Will you check on the map?"

"You worry about the feel of your ass, Tommy. You'll know if she runs over the cutline. Ease back out of it when she tilts. I'll keep an eye on the compass."

"Teach your grandmother, Margan."

The little Irishman engaged gears. Gradually the

deep growl of the motor again drowned out the wail of the wind and the rhythmic squeal of the wipers making egg-timer avalanches on the windscreen.

Forward visibility zero. Side visibility four feet, five . . . as far as the ground. Scuds and whorls of driven sand. Sometimes a shadow passed and melted in the maelstrom before its shape could be registered on the brain.

Maloney's small, oddly frail-looking hands rested delicately on the knurled rim of the steering wheel, coaxing it with a gentle patience whenever the truck lurched on its lateral axis. Not once did he seem to look ahead.

Margan said against George's ear: "Driving blind on a graded sand track isn't as hard as it looks. When they cut a line through here, the dozers scooped out side ridges four or five feet high and half a chain apart so tankers and low loaders could pass. The trick is to correct your steering when the front end tilts—ease back down into the big groove. If you had the nerve you could drive from the lake to the fifty-mile peg with your head in a bag and save the eye strain. But it gets harder when you hit the stonefields this side of Wurl Creek."

"Then?"

Margan twisted, fumbled in the hip pocket of his shorts, retrieved a flattened hand-rolled cigarette, reshaped it fastidiously between forefinger and thumb, and hung it between his lips. "You fly on a compass bearing. It would be a piece of cake if you had a gyro. But you haven't. These bloody magnetic things give a man Saint Vitus' dance. All the night drivers have really got going for them in bad weather is a white-painted tire on a cairn every half mile."

"Tell me when we get there and I'll rub my worry stone for you," George said in a hoarse whisper. "I only hope that hairless cowboy driving the Range Rover knows his folklore, too."

"They'll be okay. Young Andy McGill's driven the Braund track twice a week since the camp was set up in April—and he's got a spare air filter, which we haven't."

George adjusted the sheet over his mouth and closed his eyes. The needle of the thermometer had started to creep up again and the reek of hot engine oil was thickening. A time to meditate . . .

At noon, with forty miles behind them and twenty-seven to go, Maloney switched off. The truck bucked once and settled. The loud, continuous noise of the motor was taken over by the loud, continuous noise of the wind.

George straightened, stretched his legs, and winced at a stab of cramp.

"What's wrong?" He heard his own voice as if from a distance, distorted by his swollen tongue and agonizingly sore throat.

Margan replied: "Nothing. We're stopping to give the old bull a drink, that's all. Only a degree off boiling. And talking of drink, please pass the other canteen, Tommy."

With a supreme effort of will, George raised the canteen to his lips slowly and deliberately. His hands were shaking. Margan took the canteen away from him before, it seemed, the blood-warm liquid could reach his gullet.

"Steady on, Georgie boy."

"Christ! Is our water as low as that?"

"Don't be a bloody twit, man. Do you want the colic? That's what you'll get if you start sweating again. Besides I need a hand."

"Doing what?"

"Getting water into this mechanical camel before it blows a head gasket."

Somewhere in the suppressed turmoil of George Galbraith's forebrain a nerve impulse jumped and completed a thought pattern.

"Margan," he said, sitting bolt upright. "Camels . . . how would camel teamsters survive a sandstorm like this?"

"What?"

"I said how do camel teamsters survive a sandstorm?"

"There aren't any camel teamsters. There haven't been any camel teams in this country for fifty years."

"Then wild camels? I'm serious. I haven't blown my mind."

They stared at him. Then the alarm in their blood-shot eyes died. Maloney's gnome face creased into a broad grin.

"For sure it's a wonder of nature you're talking about, George. It's this way. When a sandstorm comes they form a circle. Then every camel sticks its nose up the fundamental orifice of the camel in front of it and they all breathe in and out together, synchronous!"

For one terrible moment George thought he was going to burst into tears. "You bloody bog comedian!" he rasped. "I'm trying to tell you something. Last night Diagulski and I sighted three wild camels in the dunes at the back of the camp."

Two pairs of red-rimmed eyes bored into him again, hard with disbelief. Margan spoke first.

"You say Diagulski saw them too?"

"She saw them first. Three camels. A bull and two cows."

"You were both sure of it? You couldn't have been mistaken?"

George could barely trust himself to speak. Then: "I've ridden camels in Saudi Arabia, Doc—to go places. I wasn't mistaken."

After a long interval of silence, Margan said: "They weren't wild camels. No wild camel would come within ten miles of that camp—or this track with the amount of traffic it's been carrying. But for Christ's sake, man, why didn't you—" He broke off.

"Why didn't I what?"

"When did you say you saw them?"

"Last night . . . this morning about one o'clock. In the dunes at the end of the strip."

"Yes. I see."

"Why didn't I do what?"

"Take it easy, George. Nothing. There was nothing you could have done at one o'clock this morning."

The remainder of the journey to Braund was a disconnected nightmare to George Galbraith. Margan took almost three hours to drive the last twenty miles.

Burning in a private hell of thirst and heat exhaustion, George was beyond all response, beyond caring whether he lived or died, stretched out on the rack of time until the thin man braked the truck to a halt under the lattice tower of the windmill at the site of the groundwater well from which the old stone-walled homestead drew its stubborn life.

"George! George, wake up, mate! We're there!"

There? He should look. . . . He *must* look. . . .

There. . . . A dark, spinning, wavering disk streaming pennants of sand across the tarnished copper bowl of the sky. And under it, a building with blind, boarded windows, crouched in the torrent of the traveling desert.

"Get someone to lend a hand, Tommy. The poor bugger's passed out."

CHAPTER 9

FIVE days grounded in Port Hedland waiting for flying weather had left their mark on Hamilton Wrightson. Perth newspapers described the sand and dust storms which smothered the northwestern quarter of the Australian continent as the worst in living memory. They precipitated red rain on seaboard cities fifteen hundred miles away and brought sunsets of improbable brilliance to the islands of the South Pacific.

When Chasser Fitzpatrick put the Beechcraft down on the Braund strip and taxied up to the knot of people beside the hangar and fuel pumps, Wrightson climbed out of the plane stiffly and walked slowly as if he were uncertain of his balance. His protuberant eyes seemed to have receded in their sockets and the pouches under them looked bruised. He shook hands with Broderick and Margan, then took Diagulski's shoulders between his hands and said gruffly: "I'm sorry you had to get caught up in it, young 'un. Are you really all right?"

"Yes, Ham, really all right." Her smile was affectionate, almost tender.

Wrightson turned to George. "You had a pretty rough time, too, Sinclair. How are you now?"

"Back in the saddle, thanks. I'll do better next round."

Their eyes met. Wrightson said: "Give me an hour. I must get a few things moving. Broderick!"

"Yes, Mr. Wrightson?"

"Those men who were hurt. Have you got them out?"

"The air ambulance came in just after daylight. They should be in Broome hospital by now. Taggert advised that two of the mindrill team ought to be checked, too. Heatstroke. I sent them out as well."

"Rowlands?"

"Taken care of as best we could, sir."

"Right. What about accommodation here?"

"It's tight. We got Yarralumla out behind the big crawler, but the other vans are still on site. We've had fifteen men sleeping in the old woolshed, seven in the store, and eight in the stockmen's quarters. Not so good until the wind dropped."

"No. Well, we'll clear out the hands we don't need. There'll be a chartered Westair Dakota in this afternoon. Do you think it'll be able to take off from this paddock in its present condition, Fitzpatrick?"

"Piece of cake if he restricts his load to thirty-eight hundred, skipper," said the little pilot confidently.

"You ought to know. All right, Broderick. You'd better put me in the Coolgardie room."

"We've got power on to Yarralumla, sir. Taggert set it up as a sick bay."

"I said the Coolgardie room, Broderick. Unlike a lot of people I'm not sick. I can survive outside a test tube." Wrightson's tone had a raw edge.

Broderick did not reply. He walked to the Range Rover, opened the passenger doors, and took his seat behind the steering wheel.

The Coolgardie room at the old Braund homestead—

once the living heart of a million-acre sheep run until the desert swallowed up the last of its eastern pastures in the great drought of the 1940s—was a lean-to built against the stone-walled main building. It was enclosed by a double frame of cyclone wire and angle iron into which dry spinifex grass had been rammed. A small pump circulated bore water through pipes drilled to leak onto the fibrous packing at ceiling level. Continuous evaporation by this method—first used at Coolgardie, a town on the Western Australian goldfields—kept the room temperature ten degrees cooler than the open shade on the verandah.

When George entered he found Wrightson sitting at an ancient, scrubbed pine table carried over from the kitchen block. Diagulski's graph sheets were in front of him. He motioned George to sit, reached into an opened beer carton, extracted two cans, and pulled the tabs.

"You had a rugged trip out, Margan tells me."

"No more rugged than the others," George said in a flat voice.

Wrightson grunted, shuffled the graph sheets, frowning down at them. George kept silent.

"You've seen for yourself now what a hit means."

"Yes."

"Do you know how they brought it off?"

"I've a good idea."

"Yes. Diagulski told me. Hard to believe, but there's no other explanation. It's too late to do anything about it now—a week too late."

"Yes."

"Have you formed any ideas?"

George pointed to the papers on the table. "Judge for yourself."

"Does this stuff help? Diagulski says it does. I haven't had time to study it."

"It has helped me find out that the wreckers are gangs of aborigines. I can't understand why you didn't tell me in the first place."

"There's no proof of that—not even now. Not a shred of proof!"

George's indignation was almost explosive. "You

mean nobody has caught Jacky with a stick of dynamite or a firestick in his hot little black hand. Holy
cow, Wrightson, don't tell me you don't believe in
atoms because you've never seen one!"

The big man's face darkened. "Keep your voice
down, Galbraith."

"Then stop duck shoving and remember to call me
Sinclair. Also remember you're not hiring me—you're
consulting me. It's up to you whether you act on my
advice. It's expensive, don't forget."

Wrightson had become accustomed to deference
since the terms of the Millswyn sale were made public
more than ten years before. People who argued with
him didn't shout. He controlled his anger with visible
effort.

"You'd better start giving me some of your expensive advice, don't you think—Mr. *Sinclair?*"

"What have you done about this bombing? Reported it to the authorities, I presume?"

"Police are due from Hedland on the Dakota this
afternoon. Two arson squad detectives from Perth will
come in by helicopter tomorrow morning."

"And the Hedland policemen will be the same men
who investigated Nathan Ebbet's disappearance, I suppose?"

Wrightson's eyes were miserable.

"I don't know. I suppose so."

"Very well. Here's my advice. Have those graphs
and our précis of Conwright dealings copied and take
them to Canberra. You've got political pull. You've
had dealings with cabinet ministers. I wouldn't be
here if you didn't have political pull. Get those papers
put on the desk of the highest-ranking public servant
you can reach—preferably in some department which
has links with service intelligence because the civilian
agencies are a dead loss. Last time we talked, I said
you were the victim of a vendetta. I'll correct that remark—you're the first target in a guerilla campaign
that's only just beginning. Give it three or four months
and you'll have company. Pretty soon you won't be the
lonely only, not by a long shot."

Hamilton Wrightson shook his head. He looked like

an old, tired bull fidgeting at his guard station on the outskirts of the herd. George, for the first time, felt pity for the man. What had Callaghan said? "Naive, uncomplicated . . ." He might have added: "A most improbable tycoon." But no longer confident of the power that he had come to take for granted. Well, tycoons come in all shapes and sizes.

"You don't know these aborigines, these kooris, Sinclair. I'll grant what you say. There's circumstantial evidence that Conwright is being sabotaged with the help of bush blackfellows. Christ knows we're being hurt enough—but to blow the whole thing up to the proportions of a race war is plain bloody ridiculous. God Almighty, man, there aren't a hundred and fifty thousand full bloods and part-blood aborigines in the whole of Australia!"

"Those one hundred and fifty thousand full bloods and part bloods are so distributed," George said acidly, "that they constitute a majority of the population in more than two-thirds of the continent's total area. At a rough estimate I'd say that in Conwright country, whites are outnumbered by blacks and part bloods by at least four to one."

"Lies, damned lies and statistics," Wrightson growled. "I know kooris. I've lived and worked in this country all my life. I like them, by and large, and I'm sorry that nature—or history if you like—has handed them the dirty end of the stick. I give them a fair go. I always have. They've got nothing against me. All the same, there's not one out of a thousand of them that I'd make foreman of a gang digging a bush shit house —for the simple reason that as soon as my back was turned he'd get on the booze or wander off—go walkabout. Don't tell me, Sinclair, that the poor bloody kooris have declared war on Australia. I can't swallow that. They're just not that sort of people."

George studied the legend on his beer can with every appearance of deep concentration, drained the last of its contents, and set it down.

"Look, Mr. Wrightson," he said levelly, "I've told you what I think you should do—put the facts before the people who are responsible for internal security in

this country. Let them judge whether it's a provincial
grudge fight against your organization or the beginning
of a terrorist campaign that could damage every industry in northern Australia. A task force of not more
than a dozen men—poor bloody kooris—has cost Conwright nearly two million dollars in less than three
years, not counting this present business. I wonder
what a comparably efficient team of poor bloody
kooris could do if they decided to sabotage the rail-
ways that carry iron ore from the mines at Tom Price
and Newman and Goldsworthy to the ports of shipment at Hedland and Dampier? Or to the unguarded
coaxial cables and lines of microwave relay towers you
depend on for your telecommunications. For every one
point of vulnerability I can name, you could name a
dozen out of your local knowledge—and they're points
of vulnerability that have their parallel outside Western Australia. In the stations and mines of the Northern Territory, Queensland, and South Australia.
Particularly the mines. I tell you a Black September
movement or its equivalent here could bring this country to its knees economically inside a year."

The old bull shook his head again. "No," he said, "I
don't believe that."

"You don't believe it," George said, fighting nausea
that had come on him again without warning, "on the
ground that it couldn't happen here and they're not
that sort of people! Jesus God, that girl who does half
your thinking for you said you were a man of broad
vision! You blasted, smug, fuck-you-Jack-I'm-all-right
Australians! What makes you think . . . ? You're living
in the nineteenth century—on another planet!"

Wrightson's face, suffused with surprised indignation
at the outburst, advanced and retreated . . . random
in a pinkish haze . . . wavering, bleaching . . .
distorted . . .

George made to stand up, lurched forward across
the table, cradled his head in his hands.

"Galbraith! Galbraith . . . what's wrong, man?"

George raised his head slowly, straightened his back.
The spate of pain behind his eyes receded to a dull
throbbing. "Sinclair!" he gasped. "A dose of boiled

brains is what's wrong with me. Don't worry. I'll live if I'm unlucky. Is there any Scotch in your ditty bag?"

"Look, with heatstroke, do you think . . . ?"

"That I ought to booze? No. I ought to take a couple of weeks' holiday at a sanatorium. Take a water cure at a ski resort. Not on. I've got other fish to fry."

The big man, who had risen when George fell forward, walked to the decrepit kerosene refrigerator against the Coolgardie room's stone wall, took out bottles and glasses, and brought them back to the table.

"You'd better fly out with Fitzpatrick and get a medical checkup," he growled. "You're a damned fool if you try to ignore heatstroke on top of flu."

George sipped his whisky.

"If you're concerned about the health of your staff, Mr. Wrightson, you'd better get Diagulski to fly out with Fitzpatrick. That woman's had about as much as she can take. I can get by without her help for a while. If you'll free her to do research jobs and answer questions for me, she'll be as much use to me in Perth as here. But I'll miss her. She's magnificent."

"Yes," Hamilton Wrightson said, "she's magnificent. You're right—she does do half my thinking for me. She'd better go south before she cracks up. What do *you* want to do? Where do you go from here?"

"I'm going to bet a little time on investigating what that geologist of yours, Margan, would call an anomaly. It's a long shot, but it could pay."

"What anomaly?"

George opened his mouth to speak and closed it again. He pointed to the graph sheets.

"Anomaly—here?"

"Yes. How long can you talk to me, Mr. Wrightson?"

"As long as you need."

George shook his head. "No, not that much time. But study what's in front of you. If you don't spot the anomaly yourself, then ask me. That way we'll both save time. Meanwhile I need a little more help from Diagulski—not much, but it'll get me moving."

"What sort of help?"

"You own or control a cattle run on the beef road

running east from Port Epsom. The lease is held in the name of Mrs. Patricia Mountfort, the majority shareholder in the Wandonning Downs Pastoral Company."

Wrightson looked mildly surprised. "Wandonning Downs? Patty Mountfort holds the lease. I control it to the extent that Conwright holds the mortgages. What about it?"

"Can you fill me in on the background of that property?"

"Sure. It's one of the oldest established runs in the Kimberley—but pretty remote. The original lease of about seven hundred thousand acres was taken up by an old-timer, Randolph Mountfort, in the 1880s. He and his son, Archie the first, grazed the guts out of the place and it was practically derelict between the wars. Then Archie the second, old Randolph's grandson, inherited a bit of money from his mother's side of the family and moved in just after the second war. He was an air-force type and completely sold on the air-beef scheme—the idea of killing and dressing prime beasts in abattoirs on the big runs and airfreighting the beef out to market. It was a smart notion when the prices were sky-high and a bloody disaster when they nosedived. To cut a long story short, Archie the second came to grief. He wasn't a bad sort of bugger, but his lah-de-dah ideas came too expensive—his and his wife Patty's."

"How did Conwright get an interest in the property?"

"Finance," the big man replied curtly. "Archie crashed the station airplane two or three years ago and broke his neck. He was in pretty deep. I took over the bank and agency loans and let Patty carry on under direction."

George raised an eyebrow. "On her own?"

"Not entirely. She's got a manager—a character named Carlin who worked for Archie as an overseer. Some sort of remittance man but okay for a caretaker's job. The place makes just enough money to give Patty a living and pay wages, but not enough to pay off its debts. Conwright carries the baby as an investment in pasture reclamation. It'll come good in time. I see that Carlin toes the line in keeping the vermin down and culling the scrubber cattle—turning them off for sale. Maybe in ten years—or twenty—I'll get my money back. That's the story. Why did you ask? What help do you want?"

"I want," said George, "some sort of excuse cooked up for me to visit Wandonning—to stay there for a few days and study the lie of the land."

Wrightson frowned. His puzzlement seemed genuine, colored by the merest hint of uneasiness.

"The lie of the land?" he repeated. "I don't follow that."

George ignored it. "What's equally important," he ran on, "I want you to put me in touch with someone in your own camp with an intimate knowledge of that particular part of the country who'll be willing to give me information and answer personal questions about people."

Wrightson thought for a moment, snorted at some private thought, and said: "Oscar Salinger, I suppose. The King of Port Epsom. If I cleared you, he'd probably unbutton. He'd be the man. He owns the damn town."

But Conwright holds the mortgages, George thought. He said: "Betts and Salinger. Yes, I remember. General merchants. Stock and station agents. Transport."

"You learn quick, don't you?" The ghost of a grin was approving. "Diagulski can lay it on with a couple of letters and a radio message or two. I'll fix it with her. Do you want to keep traveling as Sinclair?"

"Since it was Galbraith who got the bullet and the billets doux in Perth—yes. People who use their own names are easy to trace. But if you're sending me to this man Salinger, I think he'll have to know what I'm doing."

Wrightson nodded. "All right. If the police dig deep enough and get sticky . . . well, handle that in your own way. Do you want to talk to Salinger first, or Patty Mountfort?"

"Salinger."

"Okay. But how the hell Wandonning or Patty can

possibly have any tie-up with what you tell me is a black terror gang is beyond me."

Now? Why not? Wrightson had relaxed.

George's voice was elaborately flat. "I'm not particularly interested in the Mountfort property, Mr. Wrightson—except for its geographical location. It abuts on a much larger property owned by a man named Maxwell Burnie who on three occasions during the last five years has turned down offers of purchase made by Conwright interests."

Hamilton Wrightson was, all of a sudden, sitting very still. Beyond the total immobility, George could observe no reaction. The man's face was devoid of all expression—the face of a crack poker player who has bought one card to ace openers. Then his shoulders lifted and he put his hands, palms down, on the table.

"You've lost me, Galbraith. But play it your way. Tell Diagulski what you want. She'll fix it."

The uniformed constable looked up from his notebook, cleared his throat, and asked: "Is that statement correct, Mr. Sinclair?"

"It is," said George.

"You've nothing to add?"

"No."

"Very well. You're going up to Port Epsom?"

"Yes. I understand I'm to fly out sometime tomorrow or the next day."

"What will be your address?"

"I don't know. Accommodation is being arranged by Conwright."

"It won't be hard to find you—not in Port Epsom. The C.I.D. man may want to question you."

"Good Lord," George said in his most English voice. "Detectives? Do you mean there's something fishy about it—the explosion, I mean?"

The young policeman's look was not encouraging.

"That's for the detectives to investigate. Thank you, Mr. Sinclair. I've got to get statements from everyone, you know. There was a fatality."

Silly bloody stock questions—silly bloody stock answers. George perceived that more than mere testiness lay behind old Ham's summing up of the present breed of bush coppers.

He spent most of the afternoon dozing in Yarralumla, thankful for the privacy and silence now that the burn cases had been evacuated. When his headache and cramp had been severe, any noise and movement—even Diagulski's voice and presence— had been hard to endure. He didn't want to recall those days of squalid, miserable confinement . . . the stink of sweat and antiseptic and human waste, the bitterness of quinine tablets and strong tea, the fluting and whining of that damnable, strangling wind.

After the Dakota had taken off, standing on its tail with motors at full bore but barely clearing the low sand ridge behind the homestead, George wandered across to the stock trough into which the windmill was pumping irregular spurts of milky, brackish water. He stripped, sluiced his head and body, and sat on the edge of the trough until he had dried off. The water was warm and unrefreshing, but he felt more comfortable. He pulled on his shirt and shorts and headed for the house.

The door of the Coolgardie room was open. Diagulski was sitting at one end of the requisitioned kitchen table, alternately blowing through pursed lips and poking with a pencil at the vitals of a portable typewriter.

"Bloody, bloody dust," she said without looking up. "Nothing works."

George could see the price she was paying for dedication to the job. Huge eyes, hanks of untended hair, hollowed cheeks, lips puffed and colorless. All that was left of the magic of Diagulski in the Quarterdeck Bar was a smile. Tenderness moved him again. He bent down, put an arm around her shoulders, and said: "Don't you ever let up? Give that damned machine to me. I'm good with typewriters. If you don't ease up on this superwoman act pretty soon, Diagulski, you'll spin and crash."

"Ham says you don't need me any more, Sinclair. I'm relieved of duty."

"Ham's a liar. You've been redeployed to Perth, and you'll have plenty to do. I need research done on race relations in the North West—a rundown on strikes by natives, disorders, arguments, allegations and counter-allegations, personalities, the lot. I must have an over-all picture of the situation. The sooner I get it, the sooner I'll know where I ought to be looking."

"I hope so."

"Yes," he said. "Hope was the only gift that didn't escape from Pandora's box, wasn't it? Oh, I'm a great hoper."

She sighed, tapped her teeth with the end of the pencil, then laughed.

"You're an odd man, Sinclair. You're in this whole wretched business up to your eyes, struggling to make sense of situations that are nonsense to a stranger in this strange country that's already come close to kill-ing you. You don't give a damn for what it's all about, or for Ham Wrightson and what he's trying to achieve, or for aboriginal activists and what they might be trying to achieve. What is it that makes you tick—professional pride?"

George looked at her in surprise. "I suppose so," he said. "I'm a very reliable mercenary, you know—the soul of honor when it comes to earning what I'm paid. But I'm partisan to the extent that I never fight on the side of people who use dynamite and firesticks, or terror and blackmail, to get what they think they're entitled to. Where's Wrightson, anyway?"

"He flew down to the lake with Milton Broderick and Doc to try to sort out the mess."

"When will he be back—before dark?"

"Chasser couldn't land here at night. Ham may come back in one of the trucks that took the salvage men down the track. He'll kill himself just trying to save a few hours. He isn't a young man any more."

George leaned forward and took the upended type-writer.

"That's something else you needn't worry about, dear colleague. He's a very tough old soldier and not nearly so close to the end of his tether as you are.

Look, I'll take this infernal machine down to the engine shed and get some air blown through it."

When he returned she was deeply asleep, sprawled across the table, head on forearms. She did not stir even when he lifted her out of the chair, carried her into the homestead's littered living room, and put her down gently on an old horsehair sofa still coated with an inch of dust.

Wing Foon was joyfully pounding beef steaks in the kitchen, caroling in a cracked and tuneless tenor:

> *I'm forever blowing bubbles*
> *Pretty bubbles in the air*
> *They fly so high*
> *Nearly reach the sky*
> *Then . . .*

When George came in, he broke off, cleaver in midair, and said: "Station-killed meat, mate. We're set for a decent feed tonight. A four-year barren cow —what's wrong?"

"Who's quartered in the house tonight, Wing, now that the crowd's moved out?"

"How would I know? The boss, I suppose. Margan and Broderick. Why?"

"Your girl friend, Diagulski, went to sleep in the Coolgardie room. I've put her on the sofa inside. Do you think you could fix her up with a clean pillow and a sheet? I don't know my way about in the house."

Wing Foon wiped his hands on his singlet. "No worries, sport. No worries at all. Fix her up in a brace of shakes. Went to sleep, did she?"

"Dead to the world," said George.

"And about bloody time. Yous bludgers over in Yarralumla have a lot to thank her for. She's a bloody little bottler is that girl, that sheila—a bloody little bottler. A fair fuckin' Florence Nightingale."

The voice was blurred and pitched low, but Hamilton Wrightson's words carried clearly through the flimsy wire-and-fiber wall as the big man walked into the homestead's living room.

"You can't convince me of that, Margan. There's no connection between old Max Burnie and Frenchman's Bay and no connection between Frenchman's Bay and the murderous bastards who are out to do us. Frenchman's Bay has been a dead duck for more than five years. It was dead even before the bubble burst. The chrome that showed up in the assays saw to that."

"You're wrong, you know, Ham," Margan said. "There *is* a connection between Max Burnie and Frenchman's Bay—and it's the drift."

"Tcha! Smart-ass theory, Margan! Find me a reef and the ground, and I'll believe you know how the drift runs."

"You reckon?" Margan laughed. "I suppose you think it's only smart-ass theory that's made Sinclair curious about Silent Reach, do you?"

"I don't know what's made him curious about Silent Reach. The bugger's as smart as they said he was. Diagulski's sold on him and you don't sell her if you haven't got the goods. But even if he's on to something, I still don't believe Max Burnie's mixed up in it."

"How long is it since you talked to Max, Ham?"

"The best part of fifteen years, I suppose."

"That's a long time. A man can change in fifteen years."

"I still don't believe it."

Margan laughed again. "The trouble about you, big boss, is that you're a pigheaded sod who only believes what he wants to believe. I'm going to bed. Do you want the light or should I turn the engine off?"

Wrightson's reply was inaudible, but five minutes later the popping of the little engine that drove the homestead's lighting plant stopped.

George Galbraith, who had dropped off to sleep after dinner in the tattered canvas deck chair on the verandah behind the Coolgardie room and had been awakened only by the sound of voices a few feet away from him, waited for another five minutes.

Then he lowered himself quietly from the deck to the ground and made his way back to Yarralumla, gleaming in the moonlight like a gargantuan cigar tube.

Frenchman's Bay!

The name Frenchman's Bay was not included in Diagulski's meticulous list of properties under Conwright control. Nor was it shown on Hamilton Wrightson's master map.

CHAPTER 10

NEVER in eighty years of precarious existence beside the mud flats at the head of Beaurepaire Inlet has Port Epsom been described as an attractive, picturesque, or progressive little town.

The settlement has grown, of course, in phase with the slow and sporadic exploitation of the Kimberley coast and hinterland, always managing somehow to survive the long spells of depression that followed booms in pearling, beef cattle, mining, and iron quarrying on offshore islands. It began as a collection of slab shanties built by pearlers for a shore base from which they could recruit aboriginal women as skin divers and bed companions, and where they could shelter from early or late cyclones. It grew as a port of shipment and a service center for the great cattle runs of the interior. Now it luxuriates in amenities that came its way in the euphoric 1960s when the Australian government was pressed by the northern development lobby into building the Ord River dam for speculator cotton farmers, and "beef roads" to give access to grazing lands already ruined by overstocking and plague numbers of kangaroos and wild donkeys.

Today Port Epsom's three principal streets, surveyed in times when practical planners provided for camel and bullock dray drivers to make a turnaround without unyoking their animals, have a strip of bitumen down the middle to abate the dust and are bordered at fifty-yard intervals by wire cylinders in which exotic trees such as poincianas, jacarandas, and tamarinds are fighting at long odds against the onslaught of unwinking winter sun and the battering downpours of the wet season.

One welcome by-product of the short-lived upsurge of economic optimism was the construction of Bauhinia Lodge Motor Hotel which featured air-conditioned units, a lounge bar, and two dining rooms —one for patrons who wore shirts and shoes to meals and the other, less glamorously lighted, for those who didn't.

Mr. G. Sinclair, a Conwright management consultant inspecting company enterprises in the Kimberley, was bespoken to the lodge by no less a personage than Mr. Wrightson's personal assistant, Miss Diagulski, who had called on the radiotelephone to make a priority reservation and ask that a taxi be ordered to meet Mr. Sinclair at the airstrip.

George was therefore received personally by the sad-eyed hotelier, Mario Codligoni, and was ushered into his suite with deference. The airline agent had notified that two suitcases consigned from Perth to Mr. Sinclair had arrived on the midday plane and were awaiting collection at the depot. Did Mr. Sinclair wish them brought to the hotel? George, acutely conscious of his filthy khakis and the smell of his armpits, so wished. And he added that he would appreciate prompt service in this department.

The flight from Braund he had found disturbing— even more disturbing than that nerve-racking flight from Perth to Excon Four in the heat of the day. Chasser Fitzpatrick, animated and garrulous, had been at pains to show him points of topographical note from crop-dusting altitude. They had flown for more than an hour over a great tongue of sand-ridge desert before sighting ahead the Kimberley massif with its towering hogback ranges and purple-shadowed mesas. At rare and unpredictable intervals the iron roofs of homesteads and mining camps reflected sunlight so brightly that they hurt his eyes. Dry watercourses, marked out by thin fringes of dun scrub, appeared, meandered for a while like idle scribblings on stained and ancient parchment, and disappeared into the lion-colored nothingness from which they had come. As the mountains loomed larger, long, straight lines of station track and fence slit the skin of the plain. But again they led nowhere, had no conceivable purpose.

Looking down through sand-blasted perspex on this land of fierce loneliness, George realized how abysmally he had failed to visualize the physical realities of Hamilton Wrightson's empire. How could any six-by-four diagram, however liberally labeled and speckled with colored pins, give any credible representation of its barrenness and dispersion?

Diagulski had left Braund for Broome the previous day to catch a scheduled airline flight south. George found that he missed her, and was annoyed by the discovery. She moved him to compassion, provoked in him an absurd, reasonless, protective urge, a hunger to make her a part of his life. He had, in fact, fallen in love but was unprepared to admit it because in his experience love was an emotional disorder that rendered the strong vulnerable and the weak importunate.

The office of Betts and Salinger Pty. Ltd. adjoined the Port Epsom Emporium and Supermarket, a raffish structure of weatherboard and corrugated iron partly shaded from the afternoon sun by an ancient sidewalk verandah and a line of scrawny peppercorn trees. George walked along the half mile of Beaurepaire Street which separated Bauhinia Lodge from this hub of commerce at a leisurely pace. The November heat, though its intensity did not nearly match that of Braund or the furnace hollow of Mullamurra, was oppressive. The residue of the dust storms lay thickly on the little town.

It was pension day and groups of aboriginal women in bright-patterned mother hubbards were sitting in the shadows cast by the grotesquely bloated trunks of two gigantic boab trees in front of the Shire offices, waiting patiently for their men to be ejected from the public bar of the Commercial Hotel (Salinger Enterprises Ltd. Prop., Dennis A. Ryan, Nominee) across

the road. On pension day the pub cashed Commonwealth Social Security checks to the unemployed, de-
serted and de facto wives, supporting mothers, the
aged, and the physically disabled.

So, on pension day most of the three hundred in-
habitants of the Port Epsom Native Reserve, a collection of reeking-bag and black-iron lean-tos screened
by a belt of mangroves from the view of winter tourists traveling on the coastal highway, made the three-
mile journey to town to enjoy the pleasures of urban
life. Men of mature years gravitated immediately to
Ryan's pub to lay the foundations for a night of up-
roarious jollity to come. At sunset, flagons of port and
sweet sherry would be borne unsteadily back to the
reserve and the serious drinking would begin. In the
meantime the men foregathered to gossip and quench
their thirst.

Women flocked to the emporium and supermarket,
which did brisk business in ice cream, confectionery,
Coca-Cola, and potato chips and somewhat less brisk
business in unexciting staples such as flour, tea, canned
fish, sugar, and syrup.

Minnow shoals of children with rheumy, brown eyes
and noses streaming yellow mucus darted in the side
streets and vacant lots, deep in their fantasies of pur-
suit and battle. Adolescents—the boys in cowboy
hats, skintight trousers, tooled leather belts, checked
shirts, and high-heeled riding boots, and girls in trendy
muslin nightgowns or sweat shirts and miniskirts—
performed the rituals of their mating display, parading
in groups that swaggered or tittered according to sex.
The aged and infirm squatted on the curb under the
peppercorns, smoking, hawking, and spitting.

George, trim in mesh sport shirt and linen slacks,
ran the gauntlet of a dozen critical yet curiously indifferent eyes as he passed the storefront. His first sight
of the enemy in numbers was anti-climactic. Wrightson
insisted that they weren't *that sort of people*. George
had to admit that they didn't look that sort of people.
They seemed on the verge of self-extermination, not
revolt.

The head office of Betts and Salinger Pty. Ltd. was

a large, drab, dimly lit chamber furnished with an antique counter, equally antique tables, and much more antique filing cabinets and shelves crammed with tape-bound bundles and folders of yellowing paper. A lantern-jawed European woman of indeterminate age was hunt-and-peck typing at a table set against the rear wall. She ignored George's entrance until he rapped sharply on the counter. She then rose, slouched forward, and said "Yeah?" without troubling to look at the caller.

"I want to see Mr. Oscar Salinger if he's in," George said. "My name's Sinclair. I've got a letter of introduction from Mr. Hamilton Wrightson."

At last she raised her eyes. "What name did you say?"

"Sinclair."

"We're closed. But wait till I see."

She retreated through a side door masked by a plywood screen, leaving George to reflect that the man who owned Port Epsom deserved it. He could not have spent a penny on furnishing or equipping his office for thirty years.

Oscar Salinger was an enormously fat man in his mid-sixties. He had a thin stubble of white hair, pendulous cheeks, a pitted nose finely netted with heliotrope blood vessels, and a tiny, infantile mouth which drooped in permanent pique. He wore a collarless striped shirt with a neckband that was fastened by a large brass stud and constricted the rolls of blubber on his throat.

When George came in Salinger leaned back in his bow-backed office chair and clasped his hands across his paunch.

"He says he's got a letter from Mr. Wrightson, Mr. Salinger."

"All right. You can shut up shop, Eileen. I won't be wanting you no more tonight." The voice was high, soft, almost inaudible—the voice of a eunuch.

The woman went silently. Salinger unclasped his fingers and put one hand, palm up, on the desk in front of him. George interpreted the gesture correctly, took Wrightson's letter from his hip pocket and dropped it where the fat man had to heave himself out of his chair to reach it. He glared. George hooked a bent-wood chair up to the desk with his foot and sat down. Salinger ripped the envelope open, set a pair of steel-framed spectacles on his nose, and read. Slowly. Then he sighed.

"Sinclair, eh?"

"Correct," said George.

"Private eye, eh?" The fat man tittered.

"Started off as an investigator for Inland Revenue," George said solemnly. "Catching tax cheats. And worked my way down."

"Funny man." The piggy, pale gray eyes glittered. "In a hurry, too?"

"Not 'specially. Why?"

"You only got in this afternoon."

"So?"

Salinger sighed again. "What are you sniffing out, son?"

"Rotten apples."

"Quit horseshitting, son. What do you want?"

"As the man said in the letter, grandpa—I'm after facts, information, maybe about the kooris."

Salinger was staring at him with reptilian intensity. "Ham's hired you to look into his troubles, eh?"

"Not hired—consulted."

"What makes you think I know anything that'll help you?"

"Ham thought so. He thought you'd be interested because his troubles today are your troubles tomorrow."

"Like what sort of troubles?"

George waved an airy hand. "Oh, you know—like a couple of Molotov cocktails through the windows next door. Or a handful of iron filings in the oil down at the bus depot. Or a stick of dynamite or a loop of wire where it'll cost you plenty. Those are only for openers. Take in blowing culverts and wrecking road trains and planting bombs on airplanes."

Salinger's eyes moved. His jowls quivered as he shook his head. "Then it's not kooris, son. They haven't got the guts for that sort of caper."

George cleared his throat, dropped the stub of his cigarette on the floor, and ground it out.

"I see by the badge on your jacket you're a member of the Returned Servicemen's League, Mr. Salinger. Did you fight in the Middle East?"

"Syria. What's that got to do with it?"

"When you kicked the asses out of those gillie-gillie men in Suez, did you ever think their sons would have the guts to knock off the Israeli athletes at Munich?"

Salinger sat without speaking for a long while, looking at Hamilton Wrightson's letter. Then he said: "I always have my tea at half past six because I get a sour guts if I wait. I've got to think this one out. Come back at eight o'clock in the morning."

George stood up. "See you on the dot of nine," he said. "I always eat my breakfast at eight. Good night, Mr. Salinger. Good thinking."

On the way back to Bauhinia Lodge he stopped for a few minutes to watch two of Port Epsom's police doing their pension-day chores in front of Ryan's pub—dragging paralytically drunk black men out of the gutter and loading them into a paddy wagon.

Night comes fast in low latitudes. By the time George reached the lodge, the neons had flittered on in front of the supermarket and the Hellenic Café and Milk Bar. The Shell sign above the service station rivaled the rising moon. The windows of the dwelling houses were bright rectangles, ranging the length of the wide streets. A breeze from the inlet mingled the odors of mangrove flats and seaweed with those of cooking food, town garbage, outhouses, and frangipani blossoms.

George was depressed, although he knew he had scored with Oscar Salinger. He had frightened the fat man, or brought to the surface of consciousness the fear that already lurked in him—fear of the shambling, degraded black people he exploited. In the end, he would talk.

CHAPTER 11

OSCAR SALINGER was in a more agreeable mood when George arrived at his office the next morning. Eileen, now reinforced in her dismal workplace by two hardly more prepossessing women and a youth with spots and an incipient beard, actually wished him good morning. Mr. Salinger would see him right away.

The fat man made a symbolic effort ro rise in greeting, waved toward a chair, and told Eileen to hold calls and callers until Mr. Sinclair left—and to close the door.

George deduced that his bona fides had been established. Salinger said: "Sit down. Could you do with a beer?"

George replied that it was a bit early. The fat man nodded agreement and pulled the tab from a can. "Got the highest beer consumption in Australia, this town has," he said, wiping froth from his chin with his shirt sleeve. "Bloody terrible climate. How yer doing at the lodge?"

"Fine. It's a change after Mullamurra."

"Yeah. I reckon. So that wop Mario's looking after yer all right then?"

"Like a godfather."

Salinger tittered. "Heh! Heh-heh! Godfather. Yeah, that's good. . . . Well, I got Ham Wrightson on the blower last night."

"I thought you might have done that," George said. "Eileen gave me the eye."

"Heh! That'll be the day. Yeah. Ham ought to 've spoke to me in the first place. I'm buggered if I know what I can tell you. Ham says he goes along with your ideas that kooris are behind this trouble. He reckons you've turned up proof."

George shook his head. "Not exactly proof. And I

don't claim that natives are *behind* what's happening, only that they're making the actual hits. It could be they're hired for the job by white men."

"Ham says you reckon it could be Black Power stuff, like the niggers in the States."

"It could be. There's been Black Power talk in Canberra."

Salinger's tiny mouth writhed. "That mob of shit stirrers! They're no more aborigines than I'm a fuckin' Hun because I had a German great-grandfather. They're commies, jailbirds, lazy bums makin' capital out of having a dab of the tar brush—jumpin' on the land-rights bandwagon because the Gurinji tribe got away with it at Wave Hill. God Almighty, Sinclair, those cadging cunts would claim they were hairy ainus if they thought they could blackmail a few extra bob out of this gutless government."

"Maybe," George said. "I wouldn't know. I've got no idea of the rights and wrongs of it. All I want to do is put the finger on the people who've been hammering Wrightson. But I'll say this—if it does turn out they're Black Power, it won't be long before they're hammering a lot of other people."

"Ah. Yeah. You said that. If." Salinger grunted, shifted his bulk in his chair, fished a box of matches out of his trousers pocket, split a stick lengthwise with his thumbnail, and began picking invisible teeth. Finally he spat the accumulated detritus of food sideways and went on: "What's this about old Max Burnie?"

"I'm interested in his background and his property, Silent Reach."

"Why?"

"For a number of reasons, Mr. Salinger. First, according to my information he's the only substantial white leaseholder currently in the Kimberley who has gone native—as they used to say. Second, he employs native labor exclusively. Third, Silent Reach adjoins one of the largest native reserves in the state, administered by the missionary order of St. Gregory at Barramundi Bay. Finally, Burnie has refused financially attractive offers made by Conwright or its agents to purchase his holding. Those factors suggest that it could be worth my while to run a check on Burnie."

The fat man did not seem impressed. "That don't stack up to much, Sinclair. Why would old Max want to take after Ham? Or why would them monks down at Barramundi Bay? What would they get out of it?"

"You're the man with the local knowledge, Mr. Salinger," George said patiently, "and I'm asking you. Is it *possible* that Burnie would sympathize with aboriginal activists—as Donald McLeod did down Port Hedland way? Is it *possible* that Black Power types could be recruited on that mission reserve—or that either the missionaries or Burnie could be harboring them, knowingly or unknowingly?"

Salinger split another match. George did not interrupt his dental hygiene or his train of thought.

"The missionaries wouldn't be in it. They cop it much too sweet. The last thing they'd want is for the blacks to get on top. Those holy hypocrites live on the fat of the land if anybody does. Never do a hand's turn but preach and pray. Plenty of prime beef and fish. Plenty of fruit and vegetables off of the farm worked by school-kid labor. Plenty of black velvet, too, when they feel like it. But they know if the blacks got on top there wouldn't be nothing of Barramundi Bay Mission left inside a year. As far as old Max goes, well, I suppose it's just possible. Yes. You see, he church married a woman from the Nijama tribe when he got discharged out of the army in 1946 and went back on his place after a spell in the hospital at Broome. Had five kids out of her and sent the whole bunch of them to fancy Catholic boarding schools down near Perth when they got old enough. Only two of them ever come back to stay—the eldest boy, Ben, and one of the girls, Allie. Yeah. I suppose you could say it's just possible."

"Why only just?"

"Because Max is an old Nor' Wester. He might reckon black is beautiful but his heart don't bleed for it. He knows what'd happen if he let kooris take over on his place just as well as them missionaries do. But to put up against that he's been going round the bend further and further for years. As far as I know, he hasn't set foot off Silent Reach since 1964 when he flew south from here because one of the kids took sick at school."

As the fat man talked in his soft, fluting voice, a likeness of Max Burnie slowly formed and focused in Galbraith's mind. It was the likeness of an embittered recluse, a mad hatter who isolated himself from his own breed as completely as possible. He carried rejection of the white man's world even to the length of refusing to install a radio transceiver, electric lighting, or refrigeration at the Silent Reach homestead. To discourage idle or curious visitors, the seventeen miles of access road from the station's boundaries on the public highway remained ungraded, and passable in the wet season only by four-wheel-drive vehicles. Gates were chained and padlocked. To avoid direct contact with Port Epsom, Burnie had an arrangement with the mission, one hundred and fifty miles farther north on the seacoast, to overland his musters of cattle with the heads that the mission had turned off for market. The beasts were driven to road-train pickup points on the Wyndham highway. He bought his station stores by the same long and expensive route.

"Yeah," said Oscar Salinger, nodding so emphatically that his jowls quivered, "Max is a raving bloody madman, however you look at it." He had become almost animated in reciting Burnie's eccentricities, not the least of which was refusal to do business of any kind with the house of Betts and Salinger.

"Go back to the very beginning," George urged. "How did the man get a start on Silent Reach in the first place?"

"Bought it for a song in 1935 or 1936 with money he came into from his old man who owned trade stores in Onslow and Roebourne and a spinifex sheep run in the Hamersleys."

"Did Burnie actually work Silent Reach—live on the property—before the war?"

"No. He put in a manager. He never went out

there to live until he married this black gin when he come back from the war."

"You said he was in the army. Do you know where he served?"

"He got took prisoner by the Japs at Singapore in 1942."

"Did Wrightson and Burnie know one another in the old days before the war?"

Salinger hesitated, appearing to search his memory. Finally he said: "Not that I know of, but they could've. There weren't too many whites running their own places in the Pilbara—or the Kimberleys for that matter—in them days. The Depression was still on."

"And after the war, when Burnie came back from the prisoner-of-war camp, do you think they first met then?"

The fat man shifted restlessly. "For Christ's sake," he protested, "how would I remember a thing like when they met? That's thirty years ago, before you was born. What're you trying to get at anyway?"

"Were Wrightson and Burnie ever business partners or competitors? Do you know if they ever quarreled?"

The pendulous cheeks quivered again. "Look, son, break it down! I tell you it was before you was born. Ham's a bloody sight more likely to remember if they quarreled than I am. Ask him. I don't know."

A lie, or an evasion? George sensed that Salinger was uneasy, that the interrogation had somehow taken a turn that embarrassed him. Better not press too hard.

"Fair enough," he said indifferently. "If there was anything important you'd probably remember. Now about those offers to buy Silent Reach. Did you have any part in that—acting on Mr. Wrightson's behalf?"

"Of course I did. I'm a stock-and-station agent, ain't I? Max knocked all the offers back—said he wasn't interested in selling at any price. It was his country and he meant to stay with it as long as he lived and he didn't give a stuff about money." Salinger sniffed with indignation at the memory. "And I'll tell you what—the cunning old bugger don't give a stuff about money, neither."

"How do you mean?"

There was a sly glint in the fat man's eye. He leaned forward and wagged a pudgy forefinger. "You're smart at askin' questions, Sinclair, but I'll tell you one you never knew to ask. Where did Burnie get the cash a couple of years back when the Pastoral Appraisement Board upped his rent seven cents and leaned on him about his fencing and his vermin?"

George blinked. "That's new to me. You'll have to spell it out."

The sniff was contemptuous. "I mean that when the Crown lease on Silent Reach came up for review, old Max had to cough up the best part of three hundred thousand dollars for new fencing and water points. And clear out the donkeys and the dogs. If he hadn't he could have had his lease canceled for not keeping the covenants. He could've appealed for relief under war service, but he never. *He found the money inside eighteen months. And where did he get it from?*"

"Borrowed it," George suggested, "from the bank or some other lending agency? Landowners can get finance for improvements, can't they?"

Salinger made a hawking noise. "Like bloody hell he borrowed it from a bank or agency! He might get his labor for nothing, but the profit he makes on the beef he turns off of that place wouldn't pay interest on a three-percent loan—not these days with the Yanks and Japs out of the market."

"But if the property's so unprofitable, why did Wrightson want to buy it?"

"Because he's got the money to hang on, boy, that's why! Managed right, Silent Reach could treble its cattle turnoff inside four years. This slump won't last forever."

"It looks," said George thoughtfully, "as if Max Burnie has got the money to hang on, too—even if nobody knows where it comes from. What other interests has he got besides his cattle run?"

"Fuck-all. Years ago he done a bit of sluicing for alluvial tin along the Beechover and done all right for a while. But the claims would be forfeited by now —and worked out. The only tin that comes out of that country is what the gins dry blow by hand out of a dozen dry creek beds. We buy a bit of it at the store. They flog it to buy rotgut. But altogether it wouldn't amount to more than a few hundredweight a year."

When George left Oscar Salinger's office an hour later he had gathered very little additional information, but on the whole he was well satisfied. Silent Reach was worth investigating. Max Burnie had formidable financial resources of unknown origin. So had the saboteurs. Max Burnie's property was so incredibly remote—even in this country where everything was incredibly remote—that it would be impossible to put it under any form of surveillance without the move being immediately obvious. Max Burnie had spent thirty years perfecting the isolation and security of his domain.

How could the security be breached? In most other parts of the world, George thought bitterly, he could have set up in the business of buying information—but how the devil could you buy information in a town like Port Epsom? In any case the revolting Oscar Salinger probably knew as much about Silent Reach and its owner as any outsider.

Thinking over the session George decided that the fat man had been deliberately evasive in only one area—Wrightson's early association with Burnie. Wrightson himself had been uneasy when Burnie's name had been mentioned so the evasion was possibly significant. Embarrassed recollection of collusion in some shady deal? Complicity in some crime long since forgotten by everyone but its perpetrators and its victims?

On his way back to the lodge, George decided to call on the Betts and Salinger Motor Works and Service Station—Crash Repairs, Windshields, Retreads. The office, displaying on its dusty shelves the standard collection of flashlight batteries, motoring accessories, and sun-stained advertising brochures, was empty. George rang a bicycle bell clamped to the counter several times and without result. Then he heard a metallic clang from somewhere at the rear of the building and a voice raised in furious abuse. He stepped out of the office and almost collided with a young aboriginal running at full pelt, pursued by a European clad in grease-smothered overalls, brandishing a tire lever.

"Cheat, you cheeky black bastard!" he bellowed. "I'll give yer cheat! Put yer snotty black nose inside here again and I'll do yer—so help me Christ I will!"

Then he stopped, flung the tire lever down on the concrete apron, and walked back toward George, panting. "Them fuckin' Wongais! One of these days I'll do me block proper. The bloody hide of him!"

"Trouble," George said, nodding. "Do they worry you often?"

The man's eyes were bloodshot. He stank of anger, diesel distillate, and stale beer. He was middle-aged, unshaven, bowlegged, and going bald.

"Too often, sport. Their business ain't worth it."

"Just a dissatisfied customer, eh?"

"Dissatisfied? Jesus! They come in here cashed up from a poker game at the camp and want to be put on wheels for a couple of hundred. A couple of hundred, Christ! Then when the heap breaks down because they've forgot to put oil in it, or run it on a flat, they come back and complain."

"Ah," said George, deadpan. "You're probably right. The business isn't worth it."

The man glared at him suspiciously. "What's *your* trouble, mate?"

"None. I understand you've got a set of wheels for me. The name's Sinclair."

"Sinclair. Yeah. That's right. How long for?"

"For as long as it takes. I'll be moving around a bit."

"Yer workin' for Oscar Salinger, are yer?"

"Not exactly. Just do a bit of business with him now and then. I plan to look in on a few stations."

"You'll want a four-wheel drive then. The tracks

round here get pretty bad after an inch of rain. The wet'll break early this year, I reckon. Any day now."

"Could be, could be," said George, looking wise. "How's the new road out to the Beechover?"

"Pretty good in the day as far as the Bondy crossing, real boggy after that. If you're goin' east of the Bondy you'll need a four-wheel drive, that's for sure. There was a couple of Main Roads dozers and graders out there last season and surveyors ran a line of pegs through the Ferdinand Range. Lots of yak about the government puttin' a beef road through to Wyndham —waste of bloody money even if the market had held up. A man 'ud have to be raving mad to take on a run out there."

"Blackfellows' country?" George suggested disingenuously.

"Yer dead right. No white man would work on a run in the Ferdinands. You'd have to stuff a string of gins and breed yer own stockmen. When did yer want the truck, mate?"

"Tomorrow."

The manager of the Betts and Salinger Motor Works shook his head dolefully and beckoned. George followed him to the yard behind the building, a half acre of rutted red earth strewn with rusty junk, a graveyard of cars, trucks, and tractors that had met their ends through every cause from rust to collision or capsize.

"That short-wheel-base Landy over there any good to you?"

George looked and shrugged. The short-wheel-base Land Rover didn't look as if it would be any good to anybody. "If it goes—and keeps on going," he replied. "But Oscar said to leave it to you."

"She needs the points doin' up and a new generator. When did you want her?"

"Tomorrow."

"I'm flat out on a valve grind, mate. Rush job for a good customer. Can't make it tomorrow."

George's smile was benign. "Not to worry, sport," he said cheerfully. "Just give Oscar a ring and explain the delay. It's all the same to me. Oscar's the one who wants to get me on the road quickly. By the way, what's your name, mate?"

"Arthur," the bald-headed man said sullenly. "Christ, I've only got one pair of hands!"

"Yes, we're all human," George said cryptically. "I'm at the lodge. Let me know."

Port Epsom, George discovered during the next three days, was not a town that lavished hospitality or social encouragement on itinerant strangers. The only information of potential value he managed to pick up came from the saturnine headmaster of the state primary school who sought solace from the tensions of a job he clearly detested in the saloon bar of the Bauhinia Lodge between the hours of five and six every weekday afternoon, and from four to ten on Saturday. He was apparently unpopular with regular patrons because he spent most of his drinking time alone, staring critically at his whisky glass and occasionally bestowing on it a faint and presumably ironic smile.

His name was Ronald Saxeby, his age was forty-one years, he was a New Zealander who disliked Australians, and he was resolved to resign employment with the education department if he did not receive a transfer from Port Epsom's cultural desert by the start of next term. These basic facts he communicated to George within twenty minutes of having accepted the offer of a predinner drink. By the time he left to eat his evening meal at the Hellenic Café—he did not, he explained with gratuitous sarcasm, have the advantage of an expense account—he had confided that his wife had left him, that he did not propose to give her the satisfaction of filing for divorce, that he suffered from duodenal ulcers, and that he was working on a book that would expose the greed, corruption, and effrontery of the Australian "mining fraternity," who fleeced pensioners and widows of their paltry savings and ruthlessly exploited its illiterate migrant labor force.

His social conscience, the schoolmaster averred, had been outraged by the utter cynicism with which unscrupulous promoters and share pushers milked the

credulous during the mining boom by floating wildcat
companies on the strength of false or misleading geological reports and assays. He could, and did, name a
score of fly-by-night concerns which claimed to have
located in the Kimberley fabulously rich deposits of
every mineral known to man. Gold, silver, lead, zinc,
platinum, copper, tungsten. Chrome, manganese, co-
balt, tin. Bauxite, asbestos, beryllium. Bismuth, uranium, nickel, diamonds, mica, antimony, and
tantalum.

In the spate of fly-by-nights, only one name registered with George—Frenchman's Bay. He waited patiently until Saxeby had run out of breath and whisky,
signaled the barman for refills, and said: "I'm not a
mining man, you know, but . . . let me see . . . Frenchman's Bay does seem to ring a bell. Nickel, wasn't it?"

"Frenchman's Bay, bah!" the schoolmaster spat.
"Not nickel. Beach sands. Ilmenite. Pipe dreams.
Some crazy scheme for off-shore dredging that would
have cost millions. They raised a million in ten-cent
shares that went to a dollar thirty before the bubble
burst. Sucker money."

"Why did the bubble burst?"

"Chrome content. Impossibly expensive to produce
titanium from ilmenite sands contaminated with chro-
mium."

"I see," George lied. "And where is Frenchman's
Bay, anyhow?"

"Boyd Gulf—eighty miles out there at the mouth of
the Beechover on a coast where the tides run thirty-
eight feet. My God, the gullibility of some people!"

"Greed," George murmured. "Unadulterated greed.
But I suppose Frenchman's Bay could be a producer
one of these days. New metallurgical processes could
be discovered—that sort of thing?"

"If you're a gambling man," Saxeby said with a
sneer, "you could always pick up a few thousand
shares at half a cent. They're still listed. Half-a-cent
sellers. No buyers."

"Extraordinary," George said. "Fascinating. I'll certainly read your book with great interest."

Cogitating on Frenchman's Bay, and Wrightson's

mysterious interest in it, George strolled to the end of Port Epsom's decrepit jetty and inspected a two-thousand-ton coastal freighter sitting sedately high and dry on mud, yet flying the Blue Peter. When he returned to the lodge at twilight, he showered, changed, and dined by invitation at the managerial table.

Mario Codligoni ordered a bottle of wine for his influentially recommended guest but he drank mineral water himself, explaining that he suffered from high blood pressure, a condition aggravated by staff problems. The chef, a perfidious Greek, and three of the five waitresses he had trained so patiently since May, had given notice. They were going south for the wet season. He had even been obliged to employ black gins as housemaids. He, Mario Codligoni, had managed first-class hotels in Nairobi, Alexandria, Manila, Suva, and Colombo, but never yet had he had to contend with native domestics so abysmally stupid, lazy, and slovenly as black gins!

George expressed sympathy, but as soon as courtesy permitted he left the lugubrious hotelier and retired to his room where some stupid, lazy, and slovenly housemaid had folded his soiled clothes neatly, set out fresh towels, emptied the wastepaper basket and the ashtrays, and turned back the candlewick coverlet on the bed.

He sat for a while at the writing desk, staring moodily at the sheaf of survey maps on which he had been sporadically working. Obviously the next step was to put to the test of reconnaissance his theory that Silent Reach could be the saboteurs' headquarters.

But Diagulski had received his proposal to set up a forward base at Wandonning Downs without enthusiasm. She had pointed out rather drily that some eighty miles of rugged country separated the two homesteads and that Mrs. Mountfort had never mentioned the name of her "neighbor" to the east. That suggested there was little or no personal contact between them.

George had argued that Wandonning Downs and a smaller cattle station in the Conwright stable bordering Silent Reach to the north shared a zone of immunity from the harassment suffered by most other Wrightson enterprises. This was significant because the raiders, if they worked or were controlled from a single base, would probably consider it prudent not to strike too close to home. Diagulski had merely commented: "You're a devious man, colleague Sinclair, but the high and mighty are convinced you know your job."

But *did* he know his job? His sojourn in the wilted squalor of Port Epsom had produced some information but no dramatic results. A visit to Wandonning Downs might prove more rewarding, and in any case he must sooner or later confront the enigmatic recluse of Silent Reach in person.

George poured himself a generous three fingers of whisky as a nightcap, put the glass on his bedside table with a jug of iced water, took his small automatic pistol from the airline bag, checked it, and laid it beside the jug.

Then he sat down on the bed—decisively, as befits a man intending to remove his shoes and socks. There was a powerful, convulsive movement under his buttocks, a movement which triggered a reflex that sent him halfway across the room with a muffled yell before his forebrain had time to function. He whirled round and saw the flattened, ovate head of a large, gray snake lance angrily from between the sheets. Six feet of shining, sinuous, gray-brown body flowed to the floor and gathered itself to strike. When he later recalled those few seconds of galvanic shock and terror, George fancied that Warrant Officer Rumbold, the dedicated sadist who had schooled him in the dirty tricks which all well-educated intelligence agents must perfect, would have approved his reaction times. The second slug from his pistol disintegrated the snake's head, and its body looped backward across the bed, writhed violently, and spattered the coverlet and pillows with droplets of pale blood.

In less than two minutes, Mario Codligoni, followed by agitated occupants from nearby rooms, hammered on the locked door calling: "Mr. Sinclair, are you there? Mr. Sinclair, are you all right?"

George drew a deep breath. The palms of his hands were filmed with cold sweat and his fingers were trembling. "All right, all right," he cried testily, "don't break the bloody thing down! I'm coming!" and opened up.

Codligoni's swarthy complexion paled to a muddy gray when he saw the lashing body of the snake. *"Mamma mia!"* he breathed. *"Mamma mia!"*

This struck George as hilariously funny, but his laughter was drowned by the piercing shrieks of a young woman in the crowd of curious guests milling in the corridor. She created the diversion which allowed George to pull the agitated manager into the room and to explain loudly to those with the wits to listen that everything was under control. A snake had come up the drainpipe in the bathroom and he had shot it. That was all. He slammed the door.

Codligoni, still staring disbelievingly, mopped his forehead. "I do not believe it," he said. "I cannot believe it."

"Well, I bloody well do!" George snapped. "Pull yourself together, man! Get on the phone and have someone clean this mess up. What sort of zoo do you run here?"

In due course, one of the two ancient yardmen employed at the lodge arrived with a loop of fencing wire demanding "Where's that snake?" and, clearly peeved to have been deprived of a heroic role, identified the still-lively corpse as that of a mulga snake. "Yer gotter flucky, mate," he told George hoarsely, shaking his head. "If that bugger'd took a nip of yer, yer'd be playin' a harp by now! How'd he get in here?"

George opened his mouth to tell the truth, but closed it again when two aboriginal housemaids arrived, goggle-eyed and seeking instructions.

"You tell me," George said coldly. "Up the plug hole or the loo maybe. How would I know?"

"Impossible!" Codligoni exclaimed—then to the slack-jawed girls, "Bring clean things, you fools. Change the sheets, the pillows—all! *Subito!*"

"He never came up no plug hole," said the yardman, feeding the body into a pillowcase, "but we better take a look, boss."

The elder housemaid went for linen while the

younger began stripping the bed. George lit a cigarette, chagrined to discover that his fingers were still
unsteady.

"What's your name, love?" he asked the girl.

"Rosie, sir," she answered, looking up at him with
frightened eyes.

"Would you do something for me, Rosie?"

"Yes, sir."

"Give *that* back," George said, slowly and clearly,
pointing to the jouncing bag, "to the man or the girl
who brought it here. Say I said to cook it for dinner.
I'm told snake is very good chow. Say not to waste it."

Rosie's eyes were enormous. She clapped a hand to
her mouth.

"It is impossible, impossible!" declared Codligoni,
bursting out of the bathroom.

"Not impossible," George said oracularly. "Nothing
is impossible. It just takes a little longer. Now, if you
please, I'd like a whisky on the house—and tell the
desk to cancel that phone call to Perth in the morning.
I'll be leaving early."

CHAPTER 12

WANDONNING DOWNS homestead stood on
gently rising ground in the lowest foothills of the Ferdinand Range, one hundred and seventeen miles
northeast of Port Epsom. A beef road into the Ferdinands had been formed and graded only as far as the
ford over the Bondy River, a tributary of the Beechover, whose seasonal flooding over the millennia had
cut deep gorges in the massif of the Kimberley coast.
The station turnoff was five miles beyond the crossing
and the homestead stood a further ten miles along a
metaled track. Behind it, stony ridges carried a sparse
vegetation of stringybark trees and in front lay what
had been, at the turn of the century, five thousand
acres of lush home paddock. But sheet erosion had

stripped the topsoil from the underlying clay and degraded the rich pastures of Mitchell and kangaroo grass to bare pans dusted with salt and ringed by yellow samphire. The illusion of limitless space in this small, man-made desert was at once fascinating and daunting.

George Galbraith had driven Arthur's beaten-up Land Rover at a snail's pace to study the country and the road. The terrain was more varied than he had expected. The low-tree savannah was split here and there by bars of weathered red granite, spiked with acacias and tussock. Then the wooded land gave place to gibber plains and the gibber to levees of long-vanished rivers traversed by dry creek beds beside which coolibahs and casuarinas grew. Over one ten-mile stretch, a tumble of basalt hillocks carried stands of gray box, bloodwood, and messmate.

The weather was fiercely hot. The thermometer above the windshield read 120 degrees, a stifling, blinding heat. Several times he pulled off the road into the shade of casuarina clumps and sat, looking, listening, and thinking, trying to attune himself to the mood of the region. The only living creatures he saw in more than five hours' driving were a pair of hunting eagle hawks, soaring, dipping, and wheeling above the expanse of bleached buffel grass, and a flight of screeching white cockatoos rising from the undergrowth beside a dry billabong.

Wandonning swam up out of the mirage of the samphire flats like a Camelot from a quicksilver lake, its windmill towers trembling and distorted, its crouched outbuildings awry and on the point of vanishing in torrential emptiness. But, the desolate home paddock traversed, the oasis acquired substance and reality. The house stood solidly in a grove of peppercorns and coral trees now in clamant scarlet blossom.

George parked the Land Rover beside the garden gate and walked slowly up an immaculately raked pebble path to the porch. Whoever designed Wandonning homestead had ignored the traditional architecture of the Australian bush and drawn inspiration from the colonial Dutch and Portuguese. The outer walls were of lime-washed adobe, two feet thick, set under wide eaves and windowless. The front door, of adzed, oiled planks, stood open. Through its wire screen he could see a flooring of terracotta tiles and the cool green of a courtyard garden in which a sprinkler was playing lazily. The bellpull was stiff, but at a second tug the bell responded distantly and musically.

It was a little odd, George thought, that the oasis should appear as lifeless as the surrounding desert—and he was startled when a low, slightly husky voice behind him said: "Hullo! Were you looking for someone? What do you want?"

"Mrs. Mountfort? I'm George Sinclair . . ." He found himself looking into a pair of placid, strangely luminous brown eyes. The woman was young, probably in her mid-twenties, almost six feet tall, with a long, lumpish body and a long, lumpish face. She wore a faded housecoat with a frayed, stained hem and her bare feet were spattered with mud.

"I'm not Mrs. Mountfort. She isn't here. I'm Mary Dalziel. I've been in the garden."

"How do you do, Miss Dalziel. I must apologize if Mrs. Mountfort wasn't expecting me today. Some breakdown in communications, I suppose. I have a letter of introduction from Mr. Hamilton Wrightson."

"Oh? Yes. Aunt Patty did say something. Yes, I remember. I got your room ready. Aunt Patty and David flew to Kununurra this morning. I suppose they'll be back soon, but I forget if they told me when."

"I'm terribly sorry if I'm inconveniencing you."

"You don't look sorry. I suppose you want to come in? There's no one here but me. The men are away mustering or something."

"I assure you I'm harmless," George said with a touch of asperity.

The luminous brown eyes were quite without expression. "Did you drive from Port Epsom?"

"Yes."

"Then you'll be thirsty. You'd better come in."

"You're very kind, Miss Dalziel."

He followed her down the corridor to a deep gallery which ran around three sides of the courtyard and

gave access to rooms facing what was, in effect, a con-
servatory open to the sky but screened by nylon mesh
to exclude insects. Clearly the Mountfort ménage
spent its leisure in the tempered outdoors, cloistered
within a house fastidiously turned in on itself like the
walled palace of some Indian prince in an ocean of
slums.

Mary Dalziel waved vaguely without turning and
said: "Sit down where you like. Will beer be all right?
We can't have spirits until David and Aunt Patty get
back. The cellar's locked."

"Of course," said George. "I prefer beer. What a
charming and unusual house."

"Do you think so?" She spoke indifferently and
padded away down the narrower verandah on the
eastern side of the court.

George sat on the end of a cane chaise longue until
she returned, carrying two bottles of Pilsner and two
glasses on a chipped lacquer tray. She set the tray
down on a side table so clumsily that one bottle overturned.

"Fuck!" Mary Dalziel exclaimed without raising her
voice. "I've got the shakes today. Have you a cigarette
on you?"

George blinked, reached hastily into his shirt pocket
for a pack.

"Thanks. I've given them up, you see." She accepted a light and inhaled greedily, closing her eyes
and holding the smoke in her lungs until she coughed
explosively. "I used to smoke eighty a day until the
headshrinker made me give them up. You'd better not
let Aunt Patty catch you giving me one."

"Eighty does seem rather steep," George said helplessly.

"I used to drink a bottle of whisky a day, too.
That's why David and Aunt Patty padlock the cellar.
You wouldn't carry a flask, would you?"

"I'm sorry. No."

She sighed, poured the beer, and drained her glass
without pausing. "I suppose you've twigged it by
now."

"Twigged it? I . . . I'm afraid I don't quite follow, Miss Dalziel."

"I'm batty," she said. "Bonkers. But I wasn't once. I was quite smart. I used to be in advertising in Sydney, you know, before I went round the bend."

"Advertising drives a lot of people round the bend," George observed, pulling himself together. "But it doesn't show, Miss Dalziel. I shouldn't worry if I were you."

"I don't mind being batty at all. It's much simpler than being all there. People don't expect anything. But I'm an awfully good worker. That's why Aunt Patty has me as a companion. I like gardening. I do the cooking when the cook goes on the piss. I'm an awfully good cook. Do you like fishing?"

"When I . . er . . . get the time, yes, I do rather."

"I wonder"—wistfully—"if they'll let me take you fishing at the Bunyip Pool. It's where the river goes underground again—except in the wet season, of course. Sometimes you catch sawfish and barramundi there. They come up the river when the Beechover floods and get left behind when the water goes down."

"It sounds fun," George said.

"I'll get your bags out of the car and show you where your room is."

"Please!" George protested, jumping up. "I'm perfectly capable of doing that myself."

"Oh, do shut up," she said wearily. "The rouseabout's out with the stockmen, branding scrubbers, and we don't run to a houseman any more. You look as if you want to go to the loo. It's down at the end there, on the left. Your room's this way. I won't be long."

A single-engined Cessna passed low over the house just before five o'clock. George rose from a long but rather restless siesta, washed his face and hands, and ran a comb through his hair.

At five thirty there was a tap on the door. Mary Dalziel said Mrs. Mountfort was having tea on the verandah. Did he want some too?

Mrs. Mountfort was dressed for the outdoors in exquisitely cut cream-cord jodhpurs, elastic-sided riding boots, and a scarlet silk shirt. She was a dark-haired, strikingly handsome woman about forty years old. Her figure was only slightly coarsened by the passing of the years. Her features were patrician and regular. Her complexion and deep-set greenish eyes had recently been made up with skill and restraint.

"My dear Mr. Sinclair, I really can't think how to apologize. I was sure Miss Diagulski said that you'd call me on the radiophone before you left Port Epsom." A clear, projected drawl, unaccented.

The stage, was George's instant judgment. He took her slim, cool hand and pressed it gently.

"My own stupidity, Mrs. Mountfort," he assured her. "I must have misunderstood. I thought the date was firm. It's extremely kind of you to allow me to impose on you at all."

Patty Mountfort regarded him with approval. She could deal confidently with urbanity. Whatever his importance in the Wrightson organization might be, George behaved as Patty Mountfort believed gentlemen ought to behave.

"We won't wait for David," she announced. "The tiresome man is fiddling with that wretched airplane. Bring the tray now, Mary."

"Yessum," said Mary Dalziel, bobbing a curtsy.

Patty frowned. "Poor dear," she said when the girl had gone. "I'm afraid she's having one of her difficult days. Such a tragedy. I do hope she hasn't been embarrassing you, Mr. Sinclair? Sometimes—on her difficult days—she comes out with the most appalling things."

"Good grief, no," he said, laughing. "Many of my mother's friends are much, much more eccentric. She's been charming."

Over tea poured from a Queen Anne silver pot into Doulton cups, George learned that Patty Mountfort was struck with horror and terror at the thought of spending the forthcoming wet season at Wandonning —something which she had never previously done. But because of the directors paying no dividend this year and the staff situation being so catastrophic, what alternative was there? He also learned about Arch, her late husband—who had been the dearest, noblest man. Poor Arch—how utterly absurd that a famous fighter pilot in Spitfires with a bar to his DFC should be killed crash landing a tiny station airplane with a blocked fuel line!

George ventured that it must be extremely difficult for a widow to carry on in a locality so remote from civilization.

Patty seemed encouraged by sympathy and explained that she would never have entertained the idea for a moment if she had not been convinced that Arch would have wished it, so that their son Peter might have the option of remaining on the land. Peter was finishing his education at university. He was at a difficult age in difficult times, poor lad—unsettled and so questioning of established values. She hoped that he would mature quickly and give up the absurd idea of a scientific career when he found it so hard to pass examinations. However, she must stop being a bore about her family troubles. She promised to be much more socially acceptable at dinner. It was just this oppressive weather which afflicted one before the rain came. David and she took a glass of sherry about seven thirty and sat down at eight. Quite informal, just a tie. Jackets were barbarous at this time of the year.

George was mildly amused by Patty Mountfort's affectations. She enjoyed her role of indomitable widow enormously. George rarely failed to respond to good performances, and Patty's was first-rate.

As leading man in the continuing drama of Wandonning Downs Besieged, the Honorable David Carlin had presence but was less convincing. The station manager was tall, lean, slightly bowlegged, deeply tanned, and moved as if he had taken literally to heart the exhortation of Henry V to imitate the action of a tiger. The Honorable David never walked; he paced. Unfortunately for the effect, his eyes were a warm ginger and his smile revealed tobacco-stained, ill-fitting dentures.

In her introductions Patty was punctilious with honorifics.

"Delighted, Mr. Sinclair, delighted," the Honorable

David declared, leaping forward with paw out-stretched. "Fresh from the old country, I believe. Must be having an absolute ball, eh?"

"Rather. Quite fascinating," George agreed. "Carlin, what? Not the Milton Burbage Carlins, by any chance—Berkshire?"

The ginger eyes flickered and the dentures were immediately concealed. "Actually, yes. But no one . . . er . . . mentions it any more. Been out here since '54 actually, and have lost touch, you know. Marvelous country, marvelous life. Tell me, Sinclair, are you visiting or emigrating?"

"Reconnoitering," George said.

"For Hamilton Wrightson, I believe."

"At the moment, yes."

"Any particular interests?"

"Oh, for heaven's sake, don't be so quizzy, David," Patty interposed. "Mr. Sinclair needs a drink, not a cross-examination. We can talk after dinner if he wants to discuss business. Sherry, whisky, or gin, Mr. Sinclair?"

"Sherry, please. It's perfectly all right, Mrs. Mountfort. I'm visiting to ask a favor on behalf of Mr. Wrightson. No heavy business or anything like that —simply advice and some information if you can give it. But it's all rather complicated so it's probably better to talk after dinner."

Patty flashed him a scintillating smile. Carlin scowled and poured the sherry. "Tell me, Sinclair," he asked, "do you ride?"

"Quiet horses and low-powered motorcycles," said George. "I'm the complete tourist."

"Um," said the Honorable David. "Well, if you want to see something of Wandonning and don't mind a couple of long days on a stock horse, we could ride out to the Stinson Creek yards for the last of the branding. Bit of shooting, too. With a rifle, of course. Barrett, our head stockman, will probably be organizing a donkey drive in one of the gorges on the way back."

Patty shuddered delicately and said that she was sure Mr. Sinclair wouldn't think shooting wild donkeys was sport. Personally, she felt that the need to shoot donkeys was scarcely less revolting than the need to slaughter the brumby, the wild horse, population on the Beechover every few years.

"Facts of frontier life," declared the Honorable David hardily. He added that the Kimberley was no country for the queasy. A lot of the time it was positively damned crude. Always had been, always would be.

Mary Dalziel, wearing a voluminous blue caftan and embroidered sandals, served dinner on a solid-teak table furnished with ivory lace placemats, Thai bronze cutlery, Swedish crystal, and a flower arrangement of allamanda and white hibiscus in an embossed copper bowl. To confirm her status as a relation, she sat down to the main course—a roast crown of mutton, instant mashed potatoes, and canned peas—but took no part in the conversation. She ate hastily and hungrily and retired again to the kitchen without excusing herself. Patty discoursed with gallant wit on the frailties of Wandonning's regular cook, Clarice, a massive, but massive, treasure who disappeared twice yearly to Ryan's pub where she stayed ecstatically drunk and available to itinerant males for periods of up to three weeks. David Carlin poured claret and expounded the technique of lot feeding, the disadvantage of the fashionable Brahmin breed of cattle, the villainies of bookmakers at picnic race meetings, and the bureaucratic stupidities of the authorities.

After Mary Dalziel had served coffee in the gallery and departed, the Honorable David poured brandy and Patty introduced the subject of George's visit with admirable delicacy.

"When Tamara Diagulski called us on the radio with the delightful news that you'd be coming to Wandonning to stay for a few days, Mr. Sinclair," she said, "the dear girl was positively mysterious. She gave me not the slightest inkling of your business, except that Mr. Wrightson had retained you to give advice on matters affecting his pastoral interests. But if you're not a cattleman and are quite unfamiliar with conditions in the Kimberley . . . well, I'm sure you'll excuse my curiosity."

George chuckled.

"Miss Diagulski is always a paragon of discretion," he said. "It's true that I'm retained by Mr. Wrightson to advise him on a specific matter affecting his pastoral interests. But the heart of the matter is that I'm to advise him whether or not a neighbor of yours, the owner of the Silent Reach station, would be prepared to consider an offer of purchase by a consortium of investors not connected . . . er . . . overtly with Conwright Holdings."

There was a prolonged silence broken at last by David Carlin's contemptuous snort. "Good God!" he exclaimed. "Old Max would smell that breed of rat a mile off. You wouldn't have a chance of a snowball in hell, old boy."

"I'm interested in that verdict," George said smoothly, "because you obviously know Burnie and what attitude he would take to offers of purchase. But why should he be prejudiced against an offer by a group he suspected of being associates of Hamilton Wrightson?"

The Honorable David's tone was indulgent. "My dear chap," he said, "it's difficult to explain when you've no background in the local folklore, so to speak. Burnie went native thirty or more years ago and took himself off to the wilds to found his own little dynasty with half-caste offspring. In the days when he took up the lease of Silent Reach, the place was really cut off from the world. The big English pastoral companies had burned their fingers in the Kimberley and simply weren't interested in extending their holdings—not until the federal government came to the party with the beef-roads program in the mid-sixties. Max did as he pleased because there was no one to lean on him. For all anybody cared he could have lived in a bark *wurli* and eaten snake and goannas, the monitor lizards, for the rest of his days.

"But now it's a different story. The present slump is temporary. People who can afford to hold on to range land will prosper in the end. But Burnie, poor old bugger, is beyond wanting to cash in on his property, either now or in the future, so he keeps on playing King Canute by padlocking his gates and letting his station roads wash out every wet season."

George, as if thinking aloud, murmured: "You're a damned shrewd observer, Carlin. But what puzzles me is the specific hostility that seems to exist between Wrightson and Burnie."

"Who gave you the idea that there is specific hostility? Wrightson?"

"Indirectly—yes. What is it? An old rivalry—a grudge?"

Carlin's shrug was almost audible. "It's simply that they're two entirely different species of animal, old man. There's not an earthly chance of peaceful coexistence, my dear fellow—not a chance!"

George made a gesture of rueful despair. "Well," he said, "one can but try. I'll have to see him, even if it is a waste of time."

Carlin laughed. "You won't see him, old boy. It's simply not possible. The only people who can get as far as the homestead these days are the police—or Native Welfare and Pasture Protection types. They've got the legal right of entry. If you were to enter that property without Burnie's permission you'd be putting yourself in the awkward position of trespassing. And you'd be subject to forcible eviction—probably at the end of a shotgun."

"Suppose," George said, after a pregnant pause, "that you, as manager of Wandonning Downs, were to have urgent business to discuss with Burnie—some problem with boundary fencing or straying stock, shall we say, how would you go about it?"

"I'd send him a letter setting out the circumstances, care of the Gregorian missionaries at Barramundi Bay. He dispatches his stock and gets his supplies through them. He's paranoiac about not dealing with Port Epsom."

"But if it were extremely urgent you'd want to make direct contact, wouldn't you?"

"Probably. But I'd take the precaution of buzzing the homestead first—dropping him a note from the air. It would save a lot of unpleasantness with his stockmen."

"Good God! As fanatical about his privacy as that, is he? I wonder what he has to conceal."

Patty Mountfort said, "It's not a matter of concealing anything. The poor old man is just insane. I know it's quite incredible, but David is right. There's no way we can help you, Mr. Sinclair. We have no contact with Silent Reach, none whatsoever. I do hope Ham Wrightson will understand. Of course we'd like to help . . ."

George's tone was soothing. "Don't think of it, Mrs. Mountfort. I'm sure Mr. Wrightson will understand. Also he'll approve me bringing pressure to bear on Burnie to make him adopt a more reasonable attitude."

"Pressure?" Carlin asked sharply. "What do you mean by pressure?"

The idea that Max Burnie might not be untouchable had disconcerted the Honorable David. He was suddenly tense—no longer patronizing but uncertain of himself.

George decided that if he was going to fly a kite at all, now was the time. He lit a cigarette with deliberate care.

"I take it," he said, "that this conversation is completely confidential. Our interests and those of Mr. Wrightson are identical."

"Certainly."

"Of course."

"Very well. As practical people, skilled in station management, you must be aware that Silent Reach is an unprofitable property. By all normal accounting standards, it is run at a loss."

"A paper loss," Carlin objected. "Burnie runs the place as a subsistence proposition. He lives like a damned native. He doesn't raise beef, he just hunts wild cattle. His total operating costs wouldn't meet half our wages bill at Wandonning."

"Nevertheless," George persisted, "when his lease came up for review a couple of years ago, he was able to find more than a quarter of a million dollars for the improvements required by the covenants. Where did he get the money from?"

There were ragged edges in Patty Mountfort's voice. "Where we all get our money from, Mr. Sinclair," she said. "From moneylenders. We station people don't own our properties any more. We just work like slaves on them to pay our interest bills to the banks and loan companies—to backers like Ham Wrightson. Oh, the moneylenders do very well when times are bad!"

The Honorable David cleared his throat nervously. "Come now, Patty. Don't you think that's a little ungenerous?"

"You're in a position to be generous, David. You're on a salary."

"Which *you* don't pay, my dear," he retorted.

The kite was flying in the wrong direction. George applied a hasty twitch. "Suppose," he said, leaning forward to give the words emphasis, "your uncooperative neighbor were faced with foreclosure or—to be more precise—had to face up to the fact that the source of the funds which subsidize his unprofitable operations was about to dry up? Do you think that he would still refuse to discuss his situation? Mr. Wrightson doesn't have that impression."

Silence.

The Honorable David made to put his empty coffee cup on the table in front of him, but unaccountably misjudged the distance. The cup dropped from his fingers and shattered on the tiled floor.

Patty Mountfort gasped: "You . . . you clumsy ox! Why can't you watch what you're doing, you idiot! That was my Meissen!"

The Honorable David himself broke.

"Oh, shove your Meissen, you stupid bitch!" he shouted, leaping to his feet. "I'm fed up with your silly bloody playacting—fed to the back teeth! Who do you think you're fooling—Wrightson's hatchet man? I'm getting out!"

As he went—the tiger stride at least was no affectation—Patty burst into tears. George made soothing noises, gave her his handkerchief, and dropped to his knees to gather up the fragments of porcelain.

"My dear Mrs. Mountfort," he murmured when her sobs subsided to sniffs, "I'm most terribly sorry. I hadn't the faintest intention of upsetting the chap. I'd no idea he was involved in Max Burnie's affairs."

"But he isn't," she protested brokenly. "He can't be. We haven't seen the wretched old man in years."

George patted her hand reassuringly. "There, there, dear lady! Carlin probably has worries you don't know anything about. He's made an ass of himself—and he'll regret it in the morning."

She grasped his hand with alarming intensity and raised a tear-stained face to his, eyes closed. "Oh *God,* Mr. Sinclair, I wish I could make you understand—make Hamilton Wrightson understand! I *had* to defer his salary check because I had to pay my apprentice stockmen—the jackeroos—before they went on holiday. And I had to pay Oscar Salinger for the aviation fuel. I know we can't afford to run the Cessna, but *God,* I'd go mad if I didn't have some way of getting off this place! That beastly David can afford to wait for his money until we get paid for our last shipment of cattle."

The revelation that Patty's distress stemmed from an overdraft limit and not from any threat to the enigmatic Max Burnie's independence depressed George momentarily, until he recalled the Honorable David's frozen silence before dropping the coffee cup. It had been a reaction to shock—and the shock had come from George's bluff that the secret of Burnie's financial backing was known to Hamilton Wrightson.

He disengaged his fingers gently from Patty's dramatic clutch. "I think I can help you, Mrs. Mountfort," he said, "if you feel you can trust me enough to take me into your confidence. But we shouldn't talk any more now. You're upset and I think that I should make myself scarce. Things will seem much more manageable in the morning. Now I prescribe a small brandy and a night's sleep."

He poured the drink and put it down beside her carefully. For the first time the brave widow of Wandonning Downs stepped out of character. She swallowed the brandy at a single gulp.

"I hate the perverted animal," she said harshly. "I hate his rotten guts. I wish to Christ I never had to set eyes on him again!"

George lay for a long time on his guest-room bed, sweating gently, admiring the technique and palpitating intestines of a pallid gecko hunting gnats on the ceiling, and letting his recollection of the day's events flow through his mind without trying to analyze them. He was tired but, on the whole, well satisfied. Wandonning Downs was closer to Silent Reach than the maps and his informants indicated. It also had the advantage of lying within his estimated zone of immunity. He put the pistol, concealed under a handkerchief, on the floor where his hand would fall on it naturally if he dived.

CHAPTER 13

"AUNT PATTY has a migraine," Mary Dalziel declared, "and David's gone off somewhere in the plane. Here's your tea. Do you want eggs for breakfast? It's seven o'clock."

George struggled to surface out of sleep that had been deep and dreamless when it came. He was holding a glazed earthenware mug.

"Hullo, Miss Dalziel. Oh, tea. Thanks."

"Mechanical cow. If you don't want it, I'll bring a black one. Here's two sugar lumps."

"Eh? Oh, no, no, no. It's all right. What did you say?"

"Eggs."

"Yes, eggs . . . eggs will do splendidly, thank you. What else did you say?"

"Aunt Patty has a migraine—one of her headaches. She looks awful."

"Poor lady."

"It isn't a put-on migraine. I know. I used to get migraines. Sometimes they last two or three days. It isn't put-on."

George shook his head solemnly. "I'm sure it isn't."

"There'll just be me at breakfast. David's gone off somewhere."

"That's all right. I'll enjoy that."

"You don't like him, either?"

He laughed a little hollowly. "I didn't mean that. I meant that it would be nice to have breakfast just with you. Don't tangle me up. It's too early in the day. How long will the eggs take?"

"Till you've had your shower. You'll have to have an omelet. They're frozen. You'd better have a shower or you'll stink by lunchtime. Sometimes David doesn't and he always stinks. If you find toads in the bathroom, don't worry. They're harmless. At this time of the year they come up the water drain."

"Up the water drain, do they?" said George thoughtfully. "Thanks for the warning. I'll watch out."

In the harsh light of morning, the revelations of the previous evening seemed less pregnant. Patty Mountfort had a migraine. The Honorable David had departed for an unknown destination. The station hands were mustering. The jackeroos were on holiday. The cook was on a drinking bout. That left Mary Dalziel. What did she know about Silent Reach?

George examined his face in the bathroom mirror. He decided to postpone shaving, affected an expression of amiable vacuity, and went to breakfast.

Mary Dalziel was wearing yesterday's housecoat and her bare feet were muddy again. But the omelet was excellent, the pineapple juice chilled, and the coffee scalding.

"You must be an early riser," he said. "You've been gardening, haven't you?"

"I like gardening. I'm good at gardening."

"You are a very good cook, too. Do you like cooking?"

"Not much, but I've got to when Clarice goes into town and gets on the piss. When the jackeroos are here and the stockmen have to be fed as well, I get tired."

"Is Clarice a good cook?"

"She lets the bread rise too long and the dough goes sour, but she does good roast dinners and spotted dog. What do you do for a living?"

George cleared his throat and sipped at the coffee. "You could call me a sort of money man."

"An accountant, do you mean?"

"Well . . . not exactly."

"Then what?"

"I'm an . . . er . . . economic consultant."

"Why didn't you say so? I'm bonkers, not ignorant. Before I had my breakdown I was in advertising. I told you."

George stared hard at the lumpish, expressionless face framed in lank hair and at the vague, unnaturally shining eyes.

"That's right. I wear contact lenses."

"I think, Miss Dalziel," he said, addressing himself to the last of the omelet, "that you play up that bonkers bit too hard."

"Aunt Patty says I'm lucky to have her to live with. If I didn't, I'd have to go to a home."

"I think Patty's lucky to have you. I don't believe it about a home for one minute. You could easily get a job."

"Do you think so?"

"I'm sure of it."

"Do you want to go fishing at the Bunyip Pool today? The men won't be back till tomorrow or the day after. There won't be anything else to do."

"But what about Patty? It wouldn't be right to leave her alone when she's sick."

"It's best to. She won't let anybody in her room when she's got a migraine. She looks too awful. I'm supposed to show you around if you want to."

"That would be nice, but how far is the Bunyip Pool?"

"Two hours if we ride. A Land Rover can't get there."

Well, what the hell else was there to do? Mary

Dalziel was slightly alarming but he did not find her embarrassing. He would probably have been more uncomfortable in the company of a precocious nine-year-old child. She was friendly and placidly, devastatingly unself-conscious.

"All right," he said, "if you're certain Mrs. Mountfort won't mind."

"She won't. She doesn't want you to see her. You can look at the garden if you like. Don't eat the beans. I've just poisoned the bugs on them."

"Eh? Oh, no, certainly not."

"I've got to fix our lunch and catch the horses and saddle up."

"Can I help?"

"No. You wouldn't know what to do. Look at the garden if you like. You'd better not play a record. Aunt Patty might hear."

"No, I'll look at the garden."

Once clear of the homestead yards, they rode in complete silence. Mary Dalziel, who had changed the housecoat for jeans and a khaki shirt, watched his brief tussle with a stock horse that had been in the paddock for a month and resented strangers, and thereafter paid him no attention. She led, riding with long stirrup leathers and loose reins, ignoring her mount. The route among the stringybarks was faintly defined, an old cattle path which climbed to the crest of a ridge overlooking the river valley.

Beyond the crest the terrain changed dramatically. The sides of the gorge had collapsed into a tumble of enormous rock slabs and boulders. These stone heaps, some piled to a height of more than a hundred feet and pyramidal in form, were vividly colored—chrome yellow, ocher, burnt umber, gray, magenta, and dark chocolate. The track zigzagged down through rubble that glittered with mica and pulverized feldspar. It finally lost itself in a broad spit of shingle and mud-crusted sand where old river gums along the margin brandished their twisted, creamy arms in protest at the fierce sky of mid-morning. Behind them the cabbage palms and the she-oaks drooped in gloomy files.

This reach of the Bondy, now shrunken to a width of twenty or thirty yards, was deep green. It was bounded on the north and east by a bank of scoured shingle in which deep bays had been cut by summer floods. The backwaters were covered by lily pads coming into full flower, laying out free-form tapestries of mauve and ivory and suffused pink. In the setting of tumultuous, polychromatic rocks this was, George thought, one of the most strikingly dramatic stretches of water he had ever seen.

Mary Dalziel pulled up her horse in the shade of a gnarled casuarina and dismounted. "We can leave the horses here," she announced. "It's not far. There's green feed. They won't stray." She twitched the reins over the horse's head, unbuckled them, and shouldered the duffel bag she had carried across the pommel.

"Shall I take the gear?" asked George.

"No. I can."

"Is it far?"

"No. But you can't see it from here. It's hidden. A sort of spring. Keep close. You can take your boots and pants off if you don't want to get them wet. I don't bother."

George grinned. "Then I won't either."

"Come on then. Keep close."

He was surprised by the coldness and transparency of the water which reached his waist at its deepest. Mary Dalziel held the duffel bag above her head but she crossed so swiftly that George had difficulty keeping a footing behind her on the bar of loose, slippery pebbles.

The obliquely set entrance to the amphitheater of quartzite that contained the Bunyip Pool was choked by a dense, overhanging thicket of applethorn in flower. Its cloying perfume was almost overpowering. The tiny white petals showered on his face and shoulders, and a cloud of pollen made him sneeze violently. The girl, brushing the sticky debris from her face and chest, turned and held out a hand to guide him.

"It doesn't give me hay fever," she said. "I like it."

"You're lucky," George gasped. "Wait." He crouched and scooped water over his head. "All right. Lead on."

"We're here."

"Oh." He blinked and stared. The Bunyip Pool was a sheet of still, emerald water almost completely encircled by overhanging cliffs so high that they cut off all direct sunlight except at noon. Its diameter was not more than a hundred feet. A ledge of water-polished rock extended halfway round the pool on the easterly aspect.

Mary Dalziel threw down the duffel bag, pressed water out of her jeans and looked about her.

"Do you like it?"

"It's beautiful. Why is it called the Bunyip Pool?"

"Because a bunyip lives here."

"What's a bunyip?"

She looked at him with a slight, puzzled frown. "Don't you really know?"

"No. Truly."

"It's a thing that lives in the water. It only comes out at night."

"Have you ever seen it?"

She ignored that. "It lives down at the bottom in the deep with the sawfish and the crocodiles."

"Crocodiles!" He stiffened. "Here?"

"Didn't you see them when we came in? There were two lying on the bank. They slid in when they heard us coming."

"My God!" George exclaimed. "Did they? You might have told me to watch out."

"They don't hurt you. They only eat fish. They're not the salt-water sort."

George bent down, removed his desert boots and emptied out the water. "Thanks for telling me. What do bunyips eat?"

"Ghosts," she replied flatly. "Bunyips don't hurt real people. You wait here and I'll go back and get some grubs for bait. I forgot."

George waited, studying the intricate patterns of shadow on the cliff face across the pool where banks of moss and maidenhair fern were rooted in small recesses and fissures. There was no wind, but now and then gentle ripples spread from centers of disturbance beneath the silky surface of the water. Fish? Maybe. How reliable was the testimony of Mary Dalziel on the dietary preference of freshwater crocodiles? Or of bunyips, for that matter?

The absurdity of this bizarre excursion suddenly struck him. It could profit him nothing. When the opposition was committed to a campaign of sabotage that did not baulk at murder, what was George Galbraith, professional intelligence agent, doing in enemy territory blundering about, blind?

He looked up to the rim of the amphitheater—and felt a small, cold finger of fear run down his spine.

We hit what we aim at. . . .

'The fish won't bite yet. The sun's still on the water." Mary Dalziel was wedging the hand lines on their corks carefully into a rock crevice.

"Oh, well, you're the expert."

"We'll catch yellowbellies a bit later. They're good eating. Catfish bite best at night."

"I see. How long have you been living with your aunt at Wandonning?"

Her forehead puckered. "Three years, I think. I was about twenty when I had my operation."

"Your operation?"

"Here," she said, pushing her hair back to reveal small, white scars above her temples.

George felt his heart contract. Christ! Lobotomy, of course!

"You don't see the scars under your hair," he said inanely.

"The operation was successful. The doctor said so. Anyway I don't worry any more—about being bonkers, I mean."

"Is Patty your only family?"

"My dad ran away, I think. Mum died. I don't want to talk about Aunt Patty."

"Then we won't. They call this Bunyip Pool. Why do they call Mr. Burnie's place Silent Reach?"

"There's a big pool there—seven miles long. But

the birds and animals never come to drink at it, so it's always silent."

"Why?"

"Nobody knows. I don't want to talk about Silent Reach."

"But why not?"

"It's creepy."

"Have you ever been there?"

"No."

"Then how do you know it's creepy?"

"Peter told me."

"Peter? Patty's son, your cousin? You mean Peter's been to Silent Reach?"

"Yes. Do you want to eat your lunch now?"

"It's early. But I will if you're hungry."

"I want to go for a swim first."

"Here? What about the crocodiles?"

"I told you. They don't bite humans. They only eat fish."

"What makes you so sure?"

"The blackfellows. They know things like that."

"I haven't seen any blackfellows, even near the homestead. Are they all away mustering cattle?"

"No. We haven't got native stockmen any more. They used to live with their families in the cottages by the three-mile yard, but David wouldn't hire them back after the last time they went walkabout. He chased them all away. We've got a German and two Chileans now—Willy, and Felipe and Joe."

George had been idly interested in the girl's responses to his questions. But now he was alert, wholly attentive. But he was careful not to change his casual tone.

"That was a bit hard, wasn't it? Chasing the blackfellows away. Wherever did they go to live?"

"I don't know. I suppose they went over to Mr. Burnie's place. His wife's a black gin."

"Is Mr. Burnie quite a nice old boy?"

"I don't know. I've never seen him—only Ben."

"Is Ben all right?"

"I suppose so. Aren't you coming for a swim?"

George morosely watched a ripple widening on the

water. Mary Dalziel started to undo the buttons on her shirt.

"I'll leave it a while," he said, "but you go in if you want to." He wondered how she came to know Max Burnie's son, Ben—and how to phrase a question. Better leave it for the time being . . . maybe until they were fishing.

Without turning away, the girl removed her shirt and bra, stripped down her jeans and briefs, and stood naked, vigorously massaging her breasts.

"I only wear a bra when I go riding," she explained. "I don't like to, but my tits flop about too much."

George expelled his breath gently. "Don't they flop about in the water, too?" he asked.

"No. They float."

Stripped, Mary Dalziel looked younger, less lumpish. Her body was well proportioned, firm, almost powerfully muscled, with wide hips and a flat belly and thighs. It suggested the vigor of youth and health, ungraceful but fluid. And, to George, it emphasized the unmitigated, irreversible tragedy of the crescent scars above her temples.

She stooped and smoothed her sodden clothing to dry on the stones, then moved to the water.

"Wait," he called, jumping up. She turned as he laid a hand on her shoulder. "What about your contact lenses?"

"Oh golly, I forgot! Thank you, Mr. Sinclair."

"That's all right," he said gruffly. "You'd better call me George. We're friends. Wait. I've changed my mind. I'll come for a swim, too."

After lunch—a hunk of cold mutton with pickles and a loaf of homemade bread, washed down with heavily sweetened black tea brewed in a quart pot over a minute fire of bark and twigs—they fished. George, who had not condescended to use a hand line since school days, landed three sizable perch in the first half hour but thereafter was ignored by the Bunyip Pool's crocodile food. The girl fished from a small promontory of the ledge fifty feet away, squatting on her heels and intent.

When the perch stopped biting, George stretched out on the warm rock, face down, and dozed. He was aroused by a trickle of water on the small of his back and buttocks. Mary Dalziel was holding her string of fish over him.

"You're lazy," she said. "There isn't any bait on your hook."

"We've caught more than we'll ever eat," he protested. "Anyway, I like being lazy."

"Do you want to try for catfish? They start to bite as soon as it gets dark."

He looked at his wristwatch. "But that's not for hours yet. Hadn't we better get home by dark?"

"Why?"

"Won't Patty be worried?"

"She takes a lot of pills when she has a migraine."

"Do you want to try for catfish?"

"No. Not much."

"Then what will we do?"

"We could sunbake by the river. Then we could ride up to the top of Porcupine Bar and look out for miles. It's nice up there."

"All right, let's do that."

Apparently Mary Dalziel regarded fishing and riding as pleasures best indulged without the distractions of conversation. Sunbathing was different—or, perhaps, after three or four hours of nudity she shed deeper, more important inhibitions. Lying close beside George in the hot, coarse sand of a spit downstream from the entrance to the Bunyip Pool, she told him without prompting how Peter Mountfort had first brought her there when they were small, the first time she had come to visit Patty and Uncle Arch. A black-fellow had shown Peter where it was. The white stockmen wouldn't know about it because it wasn't a place cattle could get into. The Bunyip Pool was really a secret. Peter would be angry with her if he ever found out she had shown it to someone.

"I won't tell," George assured her. "Do you go there often by yourself?"

She shook her head. "It's not much fun on your own. Peter and I used to go a lot when he came up on holidays but he doesn't come home for the holidays anymore."

"Why doesn't he?"

"He hates David because David's queer."

Holy cow! *I hate that perverted animal . . . I wish to Christ I never had to set eyes on him again.* The ménage at Wandonning was not as convenient an arrangement for a middle-aged widow as the worldly-wise might suspect. George felt piqued with himself that the disclosure should come as a surprise.

"Did Peter tell you that David's queer, Mary?"

"No," she replied with complete indifference. "David's in love with Geoff Soames. Geoff's one of the jackeroos. They play with one another's dongs and kiss each other. I've seen them in David's bedroom."

As an item of intelligence it was something less than fascinating—and in any case irrelevant. Or was it?

"Tell me," he asked, "are you fond of Peter? Are you great friends?"

"Not now. He was different after he went to university. He doesn't come home any more. He goes to stay with Ben instead."

George drew a deep breath, quietly. "At . . . Ben's place?"

"Um. But Aunt Patty doesn't know. She thinks he has a job in Perth to earn money."

Gold—information—is where you find it, George told himself. Don't push your luck. Just calm down and follow the indicators. He closed his eyes—and opened them again when she said nothing more. She had turned over on her side and was looking at the base of his belly.

"You've got a big dong."

Well, it had to happen. Some bloody butcher had cut her brain, but her body was whole. He forced himself to remain perfectly still.

"Oh? It's just a dong."

"It's bigger than Peter's."

"Well, he's only a boy."

"He isn't. He's a man. He's almost as old as I am.

He doesn't get the horn when he looks at me any more."

"Oh well, it happens like that sometimes. Sometimes men feel like it and sometimes they don't. Boys always do."

"He used to try to fuck me, but I wouldn't let him. I just let him play with my tits and stick his fingers up me."

"Why wouldn't you let him?"

"I was scared. Peter's cruel. He likes hurting things. I was scared if he put it inside me he'd try to hurt."

"But if he was so cruel, didn't he try to force you to do it?"

"When he did I just grabbed his dong and rubbed it till it came. Then he'd stop. But after he made his fox traps I wouldn't go with him anymore."

"I suppose," George said, closing his eyes again, "all traps are pretty cruel things."

"These were. He made them out of big fishhooks and springer poles, and when the foxes got caught they just hung up by their mouths until they died."

Peter was clearly a poisonous young bastard, but what was his relationship with Ben Burnie? The conversation must be diverted from dongs and adolescent sadism to the friendship which apparently existed between Patty Mountfort's difficult son and the son of her recluse neighbor. The art of pumping Mary Dalziel was the art of simulating complete mental relaxation—the state of hazy, lethargic indifference and noninitiative assumed by competent agents presenting forged travel documents at alert frontier posts or airports of entry. George simulated a yawn and rolled over on his back.

"What about this friend of Peter's . . . what's his name? Ben? Is he cruel, too?"

"Ben's different. He's a real native. Peter only pretends."

"Pretends he's a native, do you mean?"

"Last year he got initiated into the tribe. He's got the scars on his chest. He showed me."

"What did you say?"

"I said I thought they looked silly because he had

white skin. He got wild. He said they showed he was a man and Ben's blood brother. Anyway, I don't want to talk about Peter. I don't like him anymore."

"All right. What do you want to talk about?"

Silence.

Then she said: "When are you going away?"

"I don't know. Tomorrow or the next day."

"Will you come back?"

"I should think so."

She took his hand and guided it to her breasts, wriggling closer.

"Don't you want to play with my tits?" she whispered. "You can put your dong inside me if you like. You wouldn't hurt me."

George sat up abruptly. "That's right, Mary. I wouldn't hurt you. You're much too nice. But I've got a better idea for now. Let's catch the horses and ride up to the top of Porcupine Bar—and then we'll go home and have fish for dinner."

On the long ride out of the sad, calm half-world of Mary Dalziel, George Galbraith wondered how pity could have survived in him after twelve years in the dirtiest business in the world.

CHAPTER 14

NIGHT was falling by the time George and Mary Dalziel had unsaddled, turned the horses loose, stowed the tackle, and walked back to the homestead from the stockmen's quarters. The Cessna was in its rusty iron shelter at the end of the landing strip and, although Patty Mountfort's bedroom was in darkness, there was a light in the gallery. The girl went off with her string of fish to the kitchen. Carlin was sprawled in a chair with a half-empty bottle of whisky on the table beside him. His face was flushed and set in sullen lines.

George said pleasantly enough: "Hullo, Carlin. Is Mrs. Mountfort still out of action? A miserable illness, migraine."

The Honorable David belched angrily. "You made an early takeoff this morning. I'd hoped to have a word with you. Give me ten minutes to clean up and I'll join you.

"Where the bloody hell have you been, Sinclair?" Carlin's voice was thick and slurred.

George stopped short and turned. "I'd take it quietly if I were you, old man," he said. "It wouldn't be considerate to upset Mrs. Mountfort any more than you have done already. It's no business of yours, but I've been out riding with Miss Dalziel."

"No business of mine! The damned hide of you! I run this property and I'm responsible for protecting the people I employ . . . and I say you had no right at all to go off anywhere with that girl, Sinclair. No right at all. She's mentally defective and incapable of protecting herself. Men'ally defective."

George walked back to the sprawled figure, drew up a chair with great deliberation, and sat down.

"My good chap," he said, "you're fuddled and I'm making allowances for that. But you're sober enough to get a few facts straight. In the first place, you do not employ anybody. You're employed yourself by Mrs. Mountfort on behalf of the Wandonning Downs Pastoral Company, which Hamilton Wrightson controls. I'm here on business for Mr. Wrightson and I'm Mrs. Mountfort's houseguest, not yours. If anybody's responsible for Miss Dalziel, it's Mrs. Mountfort."

Carlin started to struggle out of his chair, but George leaned forward, put the flat of one hand firmly against the man's chest, and pushed him down again.

"Easy does it, Carlin," he said. "Don't rush your fences. You may now care to explain why you think Miss Dalziel should need protection against me?"

The Honorable David was not an intelligent man, sober or drunk—and the truth was that he was fighting drunk. "Because," he bawled furiously, struggling to get up, "I can smell billy goat a mile off. You stink of it, Sinclair, stink of it! Take your hands off me, you filthy bounder!"

George rose, seized the Honorable David's patrician nose violently between thumb and two fingers of his left hand, and keeping his right hand low and his knees prudently together, jerked the man bodily upright. Then he gripped his right wrist, spun him, and applied a hammerlock with vicious force. Carlin's agonized yell was cut short as George clapped a hand over his mouth and pulled back hard.

"If you scream, darling," he murmured, "I'll smash your bloody arm. Stop trying to bite me with those absurd false teeth. Go away and take a cold bath. And when you're sober, I'll expect an apology and an explanation of why you're playing games with the Burnie tribe. Do you read me, lover boy? *Well, do you?*"

The arched, rigid body suddenly went slack. George loosened his grip and stepped smartly back. But retaliation was far beyond the Honorable David's competence at that moment. With blood streaming from his nose and his semiparalyzed arm clasped against his chest, Carlin ran staggering along the gallery toward the front door. He did not look back.

Who would have thought, George asked himself under the shower, that so large a man would have so few guts in him?

Nevertheless he wore his bush jacket to fish supper in the kitchen and one patch pocket sagged.

He was restless and irritable because a sunburned, saddle-chafed backside was plaguing him. Mary Dalziel did not seem to resent his taciturnity. She didn't want to talk anyway.

The following morning was even more than usually hot and still and a bank of bruised clouds lay along the northern horizon. George rose early, packed his bags, stowed them in the Land Rover, topped up the fuel tank from the pump in front of the machinery shed, and checked radiator, oil, and tires. Then he went back to the house and ate a breakfast of flapjacks, syrup, and bacon set in front of him silently by

Mary. She was not in a communicative vein. There was no sign of David Carlin and he judged it politic not to inquire. The Cessna was still in its crude hangar.

"Thank you for a very nice breakfast, Mary," he said. "Is Patty's migraine any better?" She shook her head vehemently. "Still, I'll have to see her just for a moment. I've got to go into Port Epsom on business."

"It won't do any good. She's taken her pills again. She won't be able to talk to you. She's asleep."

Unpleasant, George thought. Untidy, trivially tragic. You had to keep a sense of proportion, but Christ, what a country, what people!

"All right," he said. "I'll write her a letter explaining. Will you be sure to give it to her as soon as she's better?"

"Yes. When are you coming back again?"

"I don't know for sure. It depends how long my business takes. Tomorrow . . . the day after. I can't be sure."

"But you're sure to come back?"

"Yes. Honestly."

"David's gone away."

George became attentive. "Has he now? Where to? The plane's still there."

"He's gone away for good. He took all his things from his room and his car's gone."

So the Honorable David had bolted! That was interesting—very interesting because he would hardly bolt for a reason as slight as the humiliation of having his nose pulled and his arm twisted in retaliation for a drunken insult. George suspected that Carlin had been planning to break with Patty Mountfort for a long time. His violent outburst over the accident with the coffee cup was fair indication of it. The nose pulling had merely precipitated action. Perhaps Patty Mountfort knew why her manager should decide to run out on her at this particular time, but George felt intuitively that she did not—any more than she knew that her difficult son, Peter, spent his vacations on Silent Reach.

"When did David go, Mary? Do you know?"

"In the night sometime. I didn't hear his car start. He keeps it down near the men's quarters."

"The gray Triumph? Was that his car?"

"Yes."

"Do you know if he told Patty he was going?"

"I didn't hear them talking."

"Did you speak to Patty this morning?"

"Of course."

"Did you tell her David was gone?"

"Yes."

"What did she say?"

"She said 'Thank God' and asked me to give her her pills."

George stroked his chin thoughtfully. "Well, there doesn't seem to be anything I can do. But it's pretty awful for me to go off and leave you and Patty on your own."

"We're often left here on our own. Anyway some of the stockmen could be back tonight. It depends on the donkey drive."

"But it sounds as if Patty's very ill."

"Migraine doesn't kill you," the girl said indifferently. "If you're going into Port Epsom, I'd better hurry and fix you something to eat. You want to get over the Bondy crossing as fast as you can. There's going to be a storm."

The first pint-sized raindrops exploded against the windshield when George was still fifty miles from town. After ten minutes the downpour became so savage that he could no longer see the edges of the formation, let alone the way ahead. He braked, changed into four-wheel drive, edged as far to the left as he dared, then pulled the gearshift into neutral but left the engine running. The roof and hood of the Land Rover leaked like a sieve and he wondered how much drenching the ignition wiring would take before it short-circuited.

The wet season had started with a vengeance. George had seen the arrival of the southwest monsoon several times in Indian hill stations, but this cloudburst was more severe than any he had experienced.

After half an hour or so, the waterfall from the sky eased to heavy vertical rain and he decided that no good purpose could be served by further caution. He would drive as long as the Land Rover kept going, and take the chance of stalling in flooded creek crossings or skidding into a ditch. Every mile he could make on wheels would count if he was forced eventually to abandon the vehicle and footslog the rest of the way into Port Epsom.

The road surface by now offered as much tire traction as a river of tallow. The Land Rover progressed at ten miles an hour in small looping skids throwing up clouds of muddy spray. George's arms and neck ached from the continual battle with the steering wheel and his buttocks burned intolerably from friction on the thinly padded seat.

Nearing the Port Epsom junction, however, something happened to float him home on a tide of adrenalin, submerging the miseries of the flesh. Momentarily the intensity of the rain had increased. He was about to pull onto the shoulder of the road to stop when the flooded windshield was suddenly suffused by the blinding light of high beams from the headlights of a big car approaching at high speed in the middle of the road and sliding wildly from verge to verge.

There was nothing George could do. He simply put his left hand down hard and leaned on the horn, crouched in expectation of a head-on smash that seemed inevitable. But by some freakish chance of timing it did not happen. The car slid to the left. In the last split second its rear guard and fender tip scored a deep groove in the Land Rover's onside door. It spun in a complete circle, straightened up, and—accelerator on the floor—vanished behind the curtain of rain.

Half an hour later George pulled up outside the Betts and Salinger service bay. Arthur was padlocking his pumps for the night.

"G'day," he drawled. "I was just wonderin' about yer gettin' caught. Not a bad drop of rain for a kick-off. Which way did yer come in—from the Broome road or the Bondy?"

"The Bondy. Take a look at the near side door."

Arthur examined the damaged door panel without showing the faintest surprise or concern.

"Ar. The Bondy's tricky all right. What did yer hit —a tree or a marker post?"

"I didn't hit anything," George snapped. "Some suicidal twit in a station wagon sideswiped me near the turnoff. He took off like a bat out of hell when he came out of the skid. A big Ford, I think. Have you any idea who it might have been?"

"Did yer get his number?"

"Like hell! With all the shit flying I couldn't even be sure of his color."

Arthur spat disgustedly. "If he was headed for the Bondy at this time of day," he said, "I can tell yer his color in one, mate—black as the ace of spades! Jesus, I don't know why the wallopers don't blitz them Wongai bombs. Four out of five of 'em aren't even registered. Who do I charge the panel beating to?"

Stiff in every muscle, soaked to the skin, and already under attack by the advance guard of Port Epsom's evening mosquito invasion, George was in no mood for the civilities.

"Make the bill out to Hamilton Wrightson," he said, "and shove it up Oscar's funicular for collection."

At the desk of Bauhinia Lodge he caused some embarrassment by loudly demanding a room without a snake. His frame of mind was not improved by the news that the telephone lines to Broome and Port Hedland were down, but the Flying Doctor Base radio would relay urgent telegrams. He wrote:

DIAGULSKI CONWRIGHT PERTH
EARLY SUMMIT ESSENTIAL VISITATION FRUITFUL BUT INCONCLUSIVE NEED INFORMATION ACTION URGENTLY RING ME SOONEST

GEORGE ALGERNON

The expression of baffled curiosity on the receptionist's face as she checked the message cheered him somewhat. He dined with appetite and slept well after checking his bedroom appointments very carefully and reading seventeen chapters of Revelation in the Gideon Bible.

CHAPTER 15

OSCAR SALINGER sounded peevish at being bothered so early in the day, but recalled the names of the five Burnie children without difficulty. Benjamin, Charles, Edward, Max, Alison. Old Max's brood. Two were living at home, and the Gregorian mission at Barramundi Bay probably kept track of the others.

George sat pondering the list before ordering late breakfast in his room while he waited for a response to a call he had put through to Hamilton Wrightson in Perth. The exchange had notified that the trunk lines had been repaired overnight, but a cyclone warning was still out down the coast.

Halfway through George's bacon and eggs, the phone rang. Perth was on the line for Mr. Sinclair.

Diagulski's voice was faint and distorted beyond recognition by an appallingly noisy line.

"Colleague, this is Sinclair. Do you read me?" George yelled.

"Affirmative, colleague. Strength two. Speak up."

"This is a small town and the wire is open. Do you understand me?"

"Say again."

"I said this is a small town and the wire is open. Listen carefully."

"I get the message. I read you."

"Do you know what property I've been visiting?"

"Affirmative—if you didn't change your mind."

"I didn't change my mind. I need information."

"I got your signal. What information do you need?"

"I need information about the next-door neighbor's children."

"Say again."

"The . . . next . . . door neighbor's children. I need information about them."

"I read you. What sort of information?"

"Personality assessments. School records. Education."

"I understand. It may take time. The schools may not cooperate."

"That man who went to Melbourne on my behalf may be able to help. Conwright could be checking out the references of people applying for employment."

"I read you, colleague. Thank you for the suggestion. Is this urgent?"

"Affirmative. Urgent. And I have one more name. One additional name. The son of the lovely lady I've been staying with."

"What about him?"

"I want his school and university record, as well."

"Roger. I'll do my best."

"I'll bet on that, colleague. Tell the boss I must talk to him. Is he there?"

"Negative, but I will arrange."

"Good. Tell him the honorable gentleman with the false teeth has resigned. The honorable gentleman with the false teeth has resigned. He has bolted. Repeat, bolted. I may have frightened him."

He'd have given a lot to hear Diagulski's reaction to that intelligence but her reply was drowned in a burst of Morse and a furious squealing and crackling.

The exchange operator cut in with Olympian indifference. "I'm sorry. We've lost the connection. I'll have to call you."

George opened his mouth to observe, with appropriate expletives, that she didn't sound as sorry as she might, but then bethought himself. In this small town it was conceivable that at some future time he might need cooperation in the local telephone exchange. Besides he must break his bourgeois habit of being discourteous to inferiors. A peeress of ancient lineage had once warned him in bed that it was an unpleasant failing.

"Thank you, operator," he said in a tone of sweet

resignation. "I'd appreciate a call when the line's working again. You're very kind. Don't forget me."

No sooner had he returned to his breakfast tray than the phone beeped again. Reception sounded faintly scandalized. Two policemen were inquiring for Mr. Sinclair. Would he please come to the office?

George swallowed a mouthful of toast and said irritably: "I'm not dressed. If it's urgent business, ask them to come along to the room," and then he added "please." He slammed the receiver down.

Policemen. What the hell was breaking now? Had they found out something about the Excon dynamiting?

Evidently their business was urgent. George opened to an authoritative rap. His callers were tall, well-scrubbed men in sun-bleached drill and wide-brimmed felt hats—a gray-haired senior sergeant pushing the age of retirement and a young first constable.

"Come in," George invited. "But let me finish my coffee before you tell me the worst. There's more in the pot if you'd like some."

The senior sergeant smiled sparingly and shook his head. The constable did not register. George found the young man's type unsympathetic—a skinhead without a ducktail. Stormtrooper material.

"Are you Mr. George Sinclair?"

"I am, senior." George drained his cup and refilled it. "How can I help? Are you following up that statement I made to one of your chaps at Braund?"

"No, sir. I don't know anything about that. It concerns another matter altogether. I wonder if you'd mind coming over the road to the station."

"Not at all," George said cheerfully, "provided you tell me why."

The uniformed skinhead took an eager pace forward. "Look, if you want to do things the hard way . . ."

The older man rapped, "No need, Wilf. Mr. Sinclair's not having us on. We think you may be able to help us in our inquiries about an accident, sir. A serious accident."

George's eyes widened. "An accident—who to?"

"Mr. David Carlin, the manager of Wandonning Downs station."

"Carlin! What sort of accident?"

"It's all a bit complicated, Mr. Sinclair. I think it would be best if you came over to the station."

George shrugged. "As you like. Give me five minutes. You can wait at the desk, or I'll walk over myself."

"Look, you—"

George held up a hand. "Constable," he said somberly, "I give you my word you'll have to arrest me before I will consent to evacuating my bowels under police surveillance. I am a man of very regular habits. If you're not, I recommend bran. It's very effective."

It was a dismal office decorated many years previously in public-service green and brown. A pinboard covered with mildewed baize carried proclamations under the royal monogram. Another displayed reward posters—many with smudgy photographs of wanted malefactors so yellowed by time that one had to assume that the subjects had long since been called before a higher court.

The sergeant beckoned George into a smaller back room that smelled of drains, disinfectant, and linoleum polish. Skinhead glowered sulkily and retired when his senior suggested that he might like to get ahead with some of the paperwork out front.

"Take a seat, Mr. Sinclair. My name is Huskisson. What's happened to Carlin?"

The old policeman's eyes had a watchful expression. "I'm sorry to say Mr. Carlin is dead, Mr. Sinclair. His car collided with a semitrailer on the coastal highway between Broome and Port Hedland just after nine o'clock last night."

"Good God! What an appalling thing!"

It was an automatic, conventional response, but not wholly insincere. George was jolted by the news of the Honorable David's sudden death. He had entertained great hopes of Carlin—a live Carlin run to earth and under calculated pressure.

"Tragic business, this sort of accident. Happens far too often," Huskisson said expressionlessly.

"How on earth did it happen? In a rainstorm—a skid? I ask that because some damned fool belting along in zero visibility nearly collided with me coming in from Wandonning Downs yesterday afternoon."

"Mr. Carlin went off the road trying to pass a semi-trailer. He clipped it. His car rolled and he was killed instantly. You've been visiting Wandonning Downs homestead, Mr. Sinclair?"

"Yes. I stayed there a couple of days."

"When did you last see Mr. Carlin?"

"The night before last, between seven and eight o'clock."

"Did he mention his intention of driving south?"

"Not to me."

Huskisson took a pencil from a glass desk tray in front of him and began doodling ducks on his blotter.

"Were you and Mr. Carlin old friends?"

"No. I met him for the first time when I arrived at the homestead the previous day."

"Did you have business to transact with him?"

"No. Sergeant, if you'll tell me exactly what you want to know . . ."

"That'll be clear, sir, if you'll have the patience to listen to my questions."

Not quite the paternalistic, small-town cop he might appear! He had authority, he knew it, and would use the authority if need be.

George said: "Fire away. My time's yours."

"Did you visit Wandonning Downs socially? Or on business?"

"In a way on business."

"In a way? Could you explain that?"

"Certainly. I visited Mrs. Mountfort at the suggestion of Mr. Wrightson who thought she might be able to give me informally some information about a business matter in which he was interested."

"You're employed by Mr. Wrightson?"

"I'm retained by him as a consultant on certain aspects of group management."

"Would you have the power to negotiate a deal on Mr. Wrightson's behalf?"

George registered surprise. "A deal? Good Lord, no—not a deal of any substance. I simply advise. Really, sergeant, I don't see what this has to do with Carlin's accident."

"Possibly you don't. Do you know what time Carlin left Wandonning Downs in his car?"

"Not exactly. But it was some time during my second night there. He was gone when I got up about six o'clock next morning. The fact is, sergeant, Mrs. Mountfort and Carlin had a disagreement the night I arrived and Carlin walked out in a rage, saying he was fed up with his job. Mrs. Mountfort was very upset and the following day suffered an attack of migraine. I spent the day riding on the property with Miss Dalziel, Mrs. Mountfort's niece, and when we returned in the evening, I discovered that Carlin had been drinking. He was extremely offensive. I'm afraid to say we had words."

"I see. Did you come to blows?"

"Not blows. I merely pulled his nose to sober him up and sent him on his way. I didn't see him again."

Huskisson smiled faintly and began to frame the ducks on his blotter with elaborate curlicues. "What was the cause of the quarrel between Mrs. Mountfort and Mr. Carlin?"

"I don't honestly know. Carlin accidentally broke a coffee cup on the verandah after dinner. Mrs. Mountfort spoke sharply to him and that triggered his outburst. At the time I thought it was simply a case of nerves frayed by the oppressive weather. Short tempers on both sides. But it seems as if there must have been a much more serious disagreement in the background."

"Could your own business at Wandonning have caused the quarrel, Mr. Sinclair?"

"I very much doubt it. As it turned out, Mrs. Mountfort wasn't able to help me with my inquiries very much."

"What was the nature of those inquiries?"

George considered the question for a moment and then shook his head.

"Only boneheads and people with something to hide refuse to cooperate with the police, Sergeant Huskisson," he said, "but I don't feel I should answer that question without consulting Mr. Wrightson. His business interests are involved. My work for him is confidential—but quite legitimate. You've told me you're investigating a fatal road accident. Can I ask whether you're really investigating a suspected crime?"

The old policeman completely ignored the gambit. "Do you carry a letter of accreditation from Mr. Wrightson?"

"No. I carried letters of introduction to Mrs. Mountfort—and to Oscar Salinger, here in town. I've presented them."

"Have you any documents of identification—a driver's license or a passport?"

"Yes. In my baggage at the lodge. Do you want to see them?"

Huskisson smiled again. "No. We've already established your identity to our satisfaction, Mr. Galbraith-Sinclair. Or is it Sinclair-Galbraith?"

George drew breath slowly. Well, it had to come sooner or later and it didn't much matter.

"That," he said, "was commendably fast police work if Carlin's accident happened only last night at nine o'clock."

Huskisson's smile broadened. "Oh, we have our sources, Mr. Sinclair-Galbraith. Now perhaps we can advance one step further. What we're trying to establish is the ownership of a very large sum of money found among Carlin's effects in the wreck of his car. If you clinched a cash deal with him on behalf of Ham Wrightson, we would like to hear about it."

George was too taken aback to protest even genuine innocence. The pertinent question came out automatically. "How much money?"

Huskisson wagged the pencil disapprovingly. "Come, Mr. Galbraith, you're too old a campaigner to expect me to answer that. And you didn't answer my question. Did you do a cash deal with Carlin?"

"No. I didn't do any sort of deal—cash or otherwise—with Carlin or anybody else. And I haven't the faintest idea where the money could have come from. If I had I'd tell you."

"Fair enough," Huskisson said. "There's just one thing more. . . ."

"Yes?"

"It is not the practice of the police to release the names of fatal accident victims until the next of kin have been informed. As I understand it, Carlin's relatives are in England. Therefore his name may not be released for some days. I'm sure we can rely on your discretion on that point, Mr. Galbraith."

"Entirely, sergeant. I get your point. We consultants have to be very discreet chaps."

"In that case," Huskisson said, removing the top sheet from the blotter and tearing up his framed ducks, "I needn't trouble you anymore for the time being. For your ears alone, the sum we were speaking of runs well into five figures—in fact, halfway to six. That means the pressure is on to find the rightful owner of it. Good luck with your work for Mr. Wrightson. He's an influential and well-respected citizen in this state. I'll be sorry if he turns out to be involved and we have to question him, but, after all, Carlin was the employee of a pastoral company in which Mr. Wrightson has a very substantial interest."

CHAPTER 16

"HUSKISSON? Didn't even know his name, son. Only been here a week, relievin' the regular sergeant who was laid up and had to go south."

Oscar twiddled with his little blue mouth, removed a fragment of food with the nail of his forefinger, and went on: "Why the interest in the local cops, anyway?

Did they catch yer with yer pants down out the blacks' camp?"

Salinger humor. George laughed politely. "That's right. But I told them I didn't know she was underage so they let me off with a caution. No. I just wondered if Huskisson was a local. It was something else altogether that I wanted to talk to you about—privately."

In town a week . . . relieving. That added up. But a security man using a police uniform for cover didn't add up. Huskisson's vocabulary and speech tunes were not those of a policeman of his generation. In the upshot, Huskisson could be very good news—or very bad.

The fat man stirred in his chair uncomfortably and his voice was querulous.

"What's on your mind, Sinclair? The door's closed, isn't it?"

Flattery being a cheap lubricant of tongues, George felt he could afford to be generous.

"Look, Mr. Salinger," he said, "Ham Wrightson told me you're king of this town. You own it and know every damned thing that goes on here—and most of what goes on in the rest of the Kimberley. If I read him right, he looks on you as a sort of partner."

Salinger's piggy eyes were almost invisible. "Cut the soft soap, boy," he fluted. "I asked what's on your mind. You don't have to bullshit me."

Error of judgment. Salinger was nauseating, not stupid. So try it frontally. The target was wide enough.

"I need to know something. Suppose you were a top-class villain in Port Epsom, where would you look to make a few killings big enough to put a show like Betts and Salinger out of business?"

The blue lips pursed. "I don't like that sort of talk, Sinclair. Ham wouldn't like it neither. You better not push your luck. We operate legal."

George reached for a cigarette, lit it, and leaned forward confidentially. "You don't listen to me, Mr. Salinger," he said. "I didn't accuse you. I asked if you knew any ways and means of making big money illegally in this town. When they get that Stone Age telephone working again, call Ham Wrightson and tell him you don't like the sort of questions I ask and you won't answer them. See how you go. I can wait."

He started to get up. Oscar Salinger's hand shot out across the cluttered desk.

"Sit down, Sinclair, for Chrissake! Get off me back. Stop needling me. Tell me what you want to know."

"If you wanted to make a fast buck in this town," George said patiently, "what caper would you go in for?"

Oscar frowned, cleared wax from one ear, and finally gave vent to a hiccup which George interpreted as an expression of scornful amusement.

"You could get a blackjack game goin' out at the blacks' camp or sell 'em booze on credit between pension days. Twenty thousand a week of pension money goes into that camp. A couple of years back, I'd've said there was money in cattle duffin'."

"Cattle stealing?"

"That's what I said. But it's dead now. A while back you could've got two or three hundred for a prime bullock. Today you'd be lucky to get thirty or forty—if you could find a buyer."

"How was it worked?"

Salinger humped his shoulders. "Simple enough. Muster unbranded cattle on your neighbor's back paddocks, drove or truck 'em off somewhere, and slap your own brand on 'em. Look, son, I don't know what's on your mind, but if you're workin' up some fancy theory about Max Burnie makin' money outa duffin', you're up a gum tree. For one thing, he ain't got the plant for the racket. In any case, it ain't his form."

"So Port Epsom's a pretty clean town now?" George asked.

"More or less, I suppose." Salinger sounded grudging. "Not like in the old days when there was pickings in snide pearl buying off of divers up from Broome. Or even later when a man could make a few quid buying illegal gold off of desert prospectors. But when gold went on the free market, that was the end of that."

"Where did they shift the gold?"

"Where to? Singapore, Hong Kong, Macassar. Anywhere there's Chinese. They're great gold traders, the Chows."

"And *how* did it go?"

Oscar humped his shoulders again. George sensed the man's disquiet.

"I wouldn't know, son. I wasn't in it. But I can make a bloody good guess."

"Go ahead."

"There's an awful lot of fishin' boats workin' off the coast out there, hull down. Taiwanese, Nips, Koepangers—even bloody Russians. You work it out."

Inwardly George stiffened. Was it a light—or only a jack-o'-lantern? What was Carlin buying, or selling, worth fifty thousand dollars? To or from Taiwanese, Nips, Koepangers, bloody Russians?

"In the days when the IGBs were active, did any of them ever get caught?"

"Illegal gold buyers, do you mean? Don't be bloody silly. Who'd catch 'em. Customs? Two flat-footed demons from Customs come through about twice a year and a man can sniff 'em a mile away. Break it down!"

"They could feed the stool pigeons, couldn't they? Get tip-offs?"

"Yeah? Then it looks like they didn't because Customs never copped nobody around these parts in my time for gold smuggling."

"What about the navy? They arrest Taiwanese fishing boats every now and then for working inside the limit, don't they?"

Salinger opened his eyes wide. "Jesus, Sinclair," he breathed, "you're really a Brit, ain't yer? The *navy!* What navy?"

"You mean it's a wide-open coast for smuggling of any kind?"

Oscar Salinger did not deign to reply. He split a match and began probing. George leaned back in his chair.

"All right, Mr. Salinger," he said, "let's move to

another subject. Can you give me a rundown on David Carlin, the manager at Wandonning Downs?"

Oscar blinked. "The Honorable Dave? That wet cunt? What about him?"

"What's his form?"

"Form? None as far as I know. Except they say he's a pansy and goes for the private-school jackeroos at the picnic races."

"How did he come to get his job, do you know?"

"Not for sure. Somebody told me he was a mate of Arch Mountfort's in the air force. Arch had a bit of money when he took on the old place, but he was broke when he killed himself in his plane. The Honorable Dave just loafs on, I reckon. He never bothers me. We don't move in the same social circles, deah boy!"

"Does he gamble big—races, cards?"

"Dave?" Oscar giggled. "Oh, real big! Dollar bets and penny ante."

On his way back through the front office, George heard Eileen call: "Yer wife was on the phone, Mr. Salinger. Will yer call her back?"

George swallowed an unpleasant taste. It hadn't occurred to him that the man who owned Port Epsom might also own a wife, the poor wretch.

The rain continued, long after Cyclone Dora had shied away from the coast and hammered a tardy Indonesian fishing fleet off the Rowley Shoals—a steady, drenching, lukewarm downpour from a gunmetal sky.

George was acutely unhappy. He had exhausted every avenue of conjecture and was stalled until the weather moderated and communications with the outside world were restored. He was told by Codligoni that in bad wet seasons Port Epsom could remain isolated for days or even weeks.

However, on the third day the rain eased and shortly after three o'clock in the afternoon a light aircraft circled town, darting in and out of low clouds, and droned off toward the airstrip. At five o'clock, when George with immense self-discipline had returned to his maps and travel-time calculations, he was disturbed by a rowdy banging on his door and a rowdier voice demanding: "For Christ's sake, Sinclair, hide that bird in the bathroom and let me in!"

It was Chasser Fitzpatrick, soaking wet, mud-spattered, and bleary-eyed. He flung himself into a chair and gasped: "For the love of Allah, brother, get a couple of cold ones! I'm rooted!"

George went to the refrigerator. "All right, Chasser. Cool it and tell me the story. What the devil do you think you're doing flying around in this muck? Don't tell me you walked in from the strip!"

Fitzpatrick drained the can of beer before he replied. "That's right. You've picked it in one. I walked in from the strip and so did the boss man."

"Wrightson? You mean he's with you?"

"Yes. I brought him in from Halley's Circle. Holy cow, what a mess that is!"

George looked blank. "Look here, old boy, take a deep breath, count ten, and begin at the beginning. Halley's Circle is an Excon mine out from Hall's Creek, isn't it?"

The little pilot gaped. "Jesus, man, haven't you heard? The bloody kooris hit the tank farm with thermite. Two dead and four in the hospital. The radio news has been full of it. Where have you been?"

"All you can get from the radio in this sewerage farm is a ruptured eardrum," George said bitterly. "When did it happen?"

"Wednesday. Just before daylight—the same as the camp at Mullamurra. The hands didn't manage to get word out for twenty-four hours. Ham's close to flipping his top."

"I'm not surprised. Where is he?"

"In Mario's office on the phone, ripping strips off Oscar Salinger for not sending transport out to the field when we buzzed town. He wants to see you in half an hour after he's been to the police station."

"All right. Now let me get it straight, Chasser. The tank farm at the Halley's Circle mine was blown up at dawn on Wednesday morning?"

"Right."

"You say it was hit by bloody kooris. How do you know that?"

"Because the bastards wrapped a message round a lump of rock and heaved it through the window of the mine manager's office."

George stiffened. "A message saying what?"

"Something like 'Give us back our land you stole, Whitey' and it was signed 'The Midnight Riders.' "

"I see. Didn't you say something about thermite?"

"The manager, Don Tilley, said they used thermite. He ought to know. He's ex-Australian Air Force. Eight thousand gallons of diesel and twelve hundred gallons of high octane went."

"You said there were two dead."

"Yes. A fifty-ton Euclid they were trying to drive clear blew up. Fuel tank."

"Were any of the raiders sighted?"

"No. They didn't even leave tracks."

"Was all this on the radio?"

"Most of it—and a lot of bullshit about a Black Power gang, too."

"All right, Chasser. Hold your water while I find it on the map."

George shuffled through the survey sheets and studied one of them.

"There's no access track marked on this," he said.

"They only opened up the pit twelve months ago—put dozers and graders through from Millicent River like they did to Excon Four from Braund."

"Open-cast mining of copper carbonate for fertilizer? Right?"

"Yes."

George put the sheet down on the top of the pile.

"You look as if you could do with something stronger than beer, bird man," he said. "You won't be flying tonight so how about a whisky and a shower. You can tell me the rest later."

"Your mother was a virtuous and gentle woman, mate. . . . Hell, I almost forgot . . ." Chasser fumbled in his shirt and produced a limp envelope. "Diagulski sent you this. It's urgent. And she said to tell you that she got the info fast because Ham made a whacking donation to the school rebuilding fund last year—whatever that means."

"Diagulski's still in Perth?"

"Yes. She'll call you when they get a line back."

"All right. And wash your socks. You're on the nose, man."

George slit open the envelope and gingerly unfolded a single soggy sheet of typescript. He read.

Benjamin Sandamara Burnie. b. 12 Aug. 1948, Gregorian Mission, Barramundi Bay. Boarder, the Gregorian Preparatory and Collegiate Schools, Southam, 1959-65. Lederberg Agricultural College, 1966-67. Diploma with high distinction in farm management, animal husbandry. I.Q. 145. Brilliant but not academically minded. Unpopular, emotionally unstable, and aggressive. Suspended Lederberg 1967 for violent assault on dormitory mate but reinstated when provocation established (racist jibes). No known contact with schools or fellow students. Present address c/o Brother Martino, Barramundi Bay Mission, reserve of which has estimated population of 750, 40% full bloods.

Edward Naradjin Burnie. b. 18 Mar. 1951. Preparatory and Collegiate Schools, as above. Junior certificate, 1966. Average intelligence, placid temperament. At present believed working as mechanic on Jilgeric Downs native-cooperative sheep station, via Mundiwindi. Estimated population 300, mainly mixed bloods.

Charles Dagier Burnie. b. Oct. 1953, d. Mar. 1965, virus pneumonia, Princess Margaret Hospital for Children, Perth.

Maxwell Naninga Burnie. b. 27 Dec. 1955. Schools as above. Matriculated with four first-class honors, Commonwealth and state scholarships, B.A. (honors) politics and history, University of W.A. Postgraduate student, Australian National University, Canberra. Inquiries instituted.

Alison May Burnie. b. 28 Aug. 1961. Boarder, St. Columba Convent, Dandinup, 1970-74. Junior certificate. Intelligent, cooperative. Present address, Silent Reach station via Barramundi Bay. Department has no estimate of native population.

Peter Dorian Alexander Mountfort. b. 2 July 1955. Boarder, Wrestford College, Southam, 1967-72. Arts student, University of W.A., majoring anthropology. Radical, erratic, suspended 1974 for part in disorderly student demonstrations. Inquiries proceeding.

George read the text carefully twice—and admitted joyously that he was in love with Diagulski. He was, indeed, proud of the fact.

Hamilton Wrightson sat behind Mario Codligoni's desk. His appearance was alarming. He seemed shrunken by exhaustion. His weathered face had taken on a bluish tinge and a nerve was jumping and fluttering in one eyelid. He looked defeated—close to collapse. He motioned George to a chair wordlessly. When he finally spoke his voice was slurred with weariness. No greeting. A question.

"What do I do now, Galbraith?"

George looked hard at the man.

"You won't like my advice, Mr. Wrightson," he said gently. "Right now, go to bed and get twelve hours' sleep. There's not a single useful thing you can do before six o'clock tomorrow morning."

The prominent eyes were haunted—out of focus, peering almost furtively. "They've killed five of my men, Galbraith. A sixth could die in the hospital tonight. And you tell me to go to bed and sleep!"

"You don't fight wars without casualties. And you don't win them by chasing your own tail," George said.

"Wars? Christ, how can a man fight a war against people he can't see?"

"Try opening your eyes. I've pointed you in the right direction."

"Yes. I was a fool, Galbraith. I didn't buy that anomaly theory at first. Not the Black Power stuff."

"But you do now? This business about Max Burnie's sons . . . Diagulski told you what she found out?"

Wrightson nodded. "I suppose they could be mixed up in it," he said miserably.

George smiled. "I understand your distrust of theories," he said. "I wouldn't buy into Excon on the strength of Doc Margan's geophysical graphs either. I'd want to see assays of the ore body—when he'd found it. Every man to his trade. What about the money they found in Carlin's car?"

Wrightson started. "You know about that!"

"I know about it. Do you know where the money came from?"

"No. But I know it wasn't Carlin's—or Patty Mountfort's."

"Which means that Carlin was either an agent or go-between in somebody else's deal."

"But, for Christ's sake, man, what sort of deal?"

"I can't be sure. But I can make a guess."

"Then make it."

George studied the haggard face across the desk. The eyelid was still jumping.

"No," he said, "I won't go off half-cocked. By the morning I might do better than guess. I'm going to walk out on you now, but first tell me if you took the advice I gave you at Braund and approached someone at high level in Canberra?"

"Yes. As soon as I got back."

"And in Perth?"

"Yes. Perhaps this time we'll get police work. I raised hell, but I can't be sure."

"Did you give these people you approached a full summary of the conclusions I'd reached and how I'd reached them?"

"Yes. God knows how much got through."

"Enough—in Canberra anyway. Good. I've got

something to work on. We can go over details tomorrow. Go to bed now, man. You're in no condition to fight an angry rabbit."

Sergeant Huskisson was busy. He couldn't see anyone. What was the trouble?

George said "Too bad," took a blank card and a pencil from his wallet, scribbled "Halley's Circle—Urgent," and offered it to the skinhead constable with exaggerated diffidence.

"Honestly, constable," he said with equally exaggerated earnestness, "I think the sergeant would take a dim view of it if you didn't take that message to him right away."

The skinhead read it, shot a look of undiluted venom, hesitated, turned on his heel, and went into the inner office, shutting the door behind him. George learned from the notice board that he could earn £1000 reward for information leading to the conviction of the person or persons responsible for the murder of a Chinese miner at Hawker's Flat in 1961. Then the skinhead came back and jerked his head.

Huskisson was, in fact, busy. He was listening intently to the telephone, interjecting affirmative or negative grunts and occasionally asking the caller to say again. He gestured to a chair, and signed off: "Okay, Bruce. Keep me posted. Over and out." He put the phone on its cradle gingerly and mopped his face with a handkerchief already sweat soaked.

"Hard work at this time of the year," George said sympathetically. "I've tried to talk to Perth myself."

Huskisson picked up the card, fiddled with it, and laid it down again. In the outer office the skinhead began recording the devious formalities of law enforcement on a thunderously ancient typewriter. A dozen kamikaze beetles were dive-bombing the single unshaded electric-light globe above the sergeant's head.

"Halley's Circle, um?"

"Yes."

"You've got information for us?"

"Possibly—probably."

"Go ahead."

George chewed a thumbnail thoughtfully. There wasn't much point in continuing the fan dance. Huskisson knew who he was and what he was doing. He might approve or disapprove, or simply be indifferent. It was a point worth clearing up.

"I wonder, Mr. Huskisson, if you and I could discard protocol—be bold, bad flashers and open our raincoats as of now. Your case officer must be a long way away."

Huskisson's lined, rather cadaverous face was entirely blank for a moment, then split in a broad smile.

"I don't see why not, Mr. Galbraith. You go first."

George grinned back. "You're cheating," he said. "You've taken a peek already—probably at those dirty pictures they've got of me in Canberra. But I'll tell you something you probably won't believe. I'm genuinely ex-service. They bowler hatted me before steering me into this job. I'm excommunicated. That's official."

"I wonder why?"

"So do I."

"I also wonder why Wrightson approached the British high commissioner for help before he approached the Australian minister."

"Then we're in the same boat again. But I shouldn't be surprised. The Powers don't burden tiny little brains like ours with matters of high policy. We might get ideologically involved."

"Very true."

"Are you with the Australian Security Intelligence Organization?"

Huskisson looked pained.

"Hardly," he said. "I'm seconded from my state department for special duty with the Commonwealth police."

"For this operation specifically?"

"Yes. I've had experience of counterinsurgency work in Cyprus, Malaysia, and elsewhere. On secondment also."

"Well, well!" said George. "It seems as if my influential client has a bit more political clout than I thought. If I may say so without offense, you have a really ingenious cover—a temporary copper in one police force disguised as a temporary copper in another! But tell me, did your briefing include a digest of the reports I've made, verbal and otherwise, to Wrightson and his personal assistant?"

"Up to the Excon Four bombing—yes. Your line of thinking has been given a good deal more substance by events since you made your first analysis. That's not to say it didn't launch a rocket or two in the beginning. Wrightson was in a position to see that the facts were put before the right people."

"I haven't always had that luck in my distinguished career," George observed drily.

Huskisson snorted. "Who does in our game? But to get on with it. I'm less impressed with your zone-of-immunity theory. I think the odds are pretty long against it working out."

"Even in the light of what's happened over the last few days?"

"I don't see any connection between anything that's happened over the last few days and a batty old man who's running a few cattle on a property two hundred miles out in the bush from here."

Huskisson's tone was tart. George swallowed an equally tart response. After all, Huskisson hadn't reconnoitered Wandonning Downs.

So he merely cocked a superior eyebrow and said: "Let's take stock. Item one: David Carlin, manager of the property adjoining Silent Reach, is in possession of a large sum of money when he is killed in a road accident after quitting his job. Ownership of the money is not known—or how it came to be in Carlin's possession. It seems highly unlikely that it was his, but he could have been the go-between in a business deal. I was at Wandonning Downs when Carlin left. I had the impression without any evidence that his bolt was precipitated by my questions about Silent Reach."

Huskisson's lips barely moved. "Go on."

"Item two: at Wandonning I discovered that, unknown to Mrs. Mountfort, there's a close friendship between her son Peter and Burnie's eldest son, Benjamin. Young Mountfort spends his university vacations on Silent Reach instead of going home. He seems to be more than a little kinky about noble savages and dreamtime artifacts."

"How did you manage to—"

George held up a hand. "Wait. Don't interrupt my train of thought. Item three—*this*."

He took Diagulski's paper from his pocket and put it on the table.

"Go easy with it. The courier got wet walking in from the airstrip. The information was obtained at my request by Miss Diagulski, Wrightson's personal assistant."

Huskisson, as George had done, read the text carefully and twice, expressionlessly. "Is this the end of your train of thought?"

"No. Item Four: Max Burnie is said to have raised more than a quarter of a million dollars two or three years ago when he was in danger of having his lease canceled for failing to meet the improvement covenants. That's a tidy sum for a batty old man running a few cattle in the backblocks."

"You got that from Oscar Salinger, I suppose?"

"Yes. Item five: Halley's Circle. Fitzpatrick, Wrightson's pilot, tells me that thermite was used to destroy the fuel storage at the mine. Is that correct?"

"Go ahead. The line's all clear."

"Well, you don't buy thermite in every supermarket, or at a discount. So I come to item six. The explosion occurred at dawn on Wednesday morning. Halley's Circle is two hundred and seventy miles by road from Port Epsom. The distance is relevant. Remember that I was driving in from Wandonning through heavy rain about four o'clock on Wednesday afternoon—ten hours after the tank was blown. Two or three miles from the highway turnoff to town, I met a car traveling east at reckless speed in filthy weather. It skidded and clipped the door of my Land Rover, but the driver just straightened up and put his foot down again. The whole thing happened fast. All I can say is that the car was a dark blue station wagon of fairly recent vintage, probably a Ford. I can't be sure of the make and I had no hope of getting the number."

Huskisson's forehead wrinkled. "I'm afraid I still don't get the Halley's Circle connection."

"There's two hundred and seventy miles of connection—unsealed highway that's rough but will carry traffic at an average of thirty to forty miles an hour. A driver who knew the road, with a car in good condition, could easily cover the distance between Halley's Circle and Silent Reach in ten hours. But here's the rub. A monsoon storm broke during the morning and the Bondy must have been carrying heavy floodwater by mid-afternoon. I think the man driving that station wagon was driving like a lunatic in hope of getting over the river crossing before it became impassable. I don't think he had the chance of an ice cream in an atomic pile. If I'm right, that car's still on this side of the river. It would be interesting to know who owns it and who was driving it."

After a long, reflective minute, Huskisson rose, went to the door of the outer office, and called: "Wilf, come in for a tick, will you?"

The typewriter obbligato stopped abruptly. The skinhead came in and looked from Huskisson to George—hopefully until he saw that George was smiling at him.

"Wilf, you ought to know the score. Could we get a vehicle in to Wandonning station tomorrow?"

"Not a hope. The Bondy's broken its banks."

"What about as far as the crossing?"

A shrug. "Maybe a tow truck with chains would make it."

"Okay. Where's Constable Hogan?"

"He took the Willys out to the reserve. Some sort of blue was on between a couple of gins."

"Right. I have a job for you two, first thing in the morning. Take a tow truck on requisition from the garage and get out to the crossing as fast as you can. Locate and case a fairly new model station wagon, dark blue, probably a Ford, with some recent damage to the bodywork. It should be just off the road this side of the river."

Constable Wilf opened his mouth, but closed it again when he caught his sergeant's eye.

"If there's a driver or anyone else with the vehicle," Huskisson went on, "bring them in for questioning about an unreported road accident on Wednesday afternoon—a collision with a Betts and Salinger Land Rover. If it's abandoned, drive or tow it back into town."

The skinhead sounded deeply hurt. "But there's court on Monday morning, sergeant!"

"I know. Big deal. Three offensive behavior, eight d and d. Don't worry, Wilf. I'll see justice is done. We'll clean up the old town yet. But that station wagon's top priority."

When the policeman had gone, George remarked, "It must be nice to have Indians, chief. I've been wondering where I'd seen that chap before. I remember now. He was striving manfully to restore law and order on pension day. Pinching phantom piddlers against the publican's tin fence."

Huskisson did not respond. He reached for a pencil, began drawing ducks, and finally said: "You've done the decent thing, Galbraith. I'm grateful. You've put me in the picture weeks before I could have done it under my own steam."

"I doubt that," George said. "Besides, you've got resources to follow through and I haven't. We're not in competition, so there's no earthly reason why I wouldn't help all I can. But this is your scene, not mine. I'd understand if you didn't want a new chum getting in the way. Do you want me out from underfoot?"

The smile was very faint and the tone was very flat.

"I wonder if you know, Galbraith, that the internal security services of this country have never, until now, assigned competent personnel to investigate genuine aboriginal disaffection in the deep bush? Until now we've confined serious investigation and surveillance to the tent dwellers outside Parliament House. So my answer to your question is—there are unfortunately no feet for you to get under."

George nodded. "Understood and agreed. If I can do some useful pointing, then you may be able to whistle up the retrievers. I've an idea or two which would hardly be practical without the sort of action you can lay on. Can we discuss it now, or some other time?"

Huskisson stood up and mopped his face again. "Come on," he said. "There's a refrigerator in my quarters next door. When in Port Epsom, do what the Port Epsodomites do."

CHAPTER 17

LATE the following afternoon, Constables Wilfred Fischer and Bryan Hogan located a 1972 model Ford station wagon abandoned on the stony breakaway of a ridge overlooking the Bondy crossing, now under fifteen feet of turbulent floodwater. The car was concealed from the road by a dense stand of wattle and was spotted accidentally by Constable Hogan while he was searching for a private spot to air his hunkers.

The Ford's paintwork was dark blue under a thorough plastering of red mud. Its rear offside mudguard had been crumpled by a glancing collision.

It took more than half an hour to open the driver's door, check that no clue to the owner's or driver's identity had been left inside the car, and discover that it could not be driven because the rotor arm of the distributor was missing. It was a job for the tow truck.

Heavy rain began to fall again at sunset and the policemen decided to spend the night at Dongarra Lagoon homestead fifty miles short of the highway junction. They arrived in Port Epsom just before eleven o'clock the next morning, towed the Ford to the police-station yard, and signed in the truck with Arthur, who was later summoned by Huskisson to inspect the impounded vehicle.

Arthur's opinion was illuminating. He examined the damaged guard carefully, lifted the hood to peer at the motor, then straightened up and rolled a slim cigarette.

"Well, Arthur," prompted the skinhead constable, "what do you reckon? Was this the koori heap that clouted your Land Rover?"

Arthur licked the end of his cigarette copiously, spat out fragments of tobacco, and lit up.

"You're the Sherlock, Wilf," he drawled. "Take a gander at the paint marks on the Landy's door and you'll know. But I'll tell you something for free. This ain't no koori heap neither."

"Why? Have you seen it before?"

"Never set eyes on it."

"Then how can you tell it's no koori heap?"

Arthur affected surprise. "Are you kidding? Did you ever see a koori heap with four steel radials bloody near brand-new and a changeover motor that's not much more than run in? I'll tell you something else for free. This heap is hot—else why did they give it a one-coat spray job over the original white duco and fix it with expired license plates?"

Constable Wilf Fischer was stung. "Pig's bum they're expired!" he snapped. "They're standard-issue plates. I'm not blind."

"Then you're dumb. Them numbers was issued two years before this model Ford came off the line. Sure, people can have number plates transferred, but who puts beat-up plates on a brand-new car?"

"Okay, Arthur," Huskisson said briskly. "Thanks for the info. Notice anything else?"

"Bugger-all else to notice, sergeant," the balding mechanic pronounced. "They must've decided to dump her for keeps when they couldn't get across the Bondy. You'll have to be pretty tinny to pin down those blokes."

"No sweat. We'll trace them," Huskisson said. "In fact, Constable Fischer will begin the job at once at the Shire registration office. And I'm getting on the blower to the district inspector at Derby to start the wheels turning down the coast."

George Galbraith gazed at the beer can in his hand with an air of quintessential pessimism.

"All routine police work is so bloody slow, Huskisson," he complained. "It could take weeks to trace the owner through the engine number. Even finding the owner mightn't help, if Arthur's right and the car was stolen. We need to know who was driving it and what connection the driver had with Silent Reach."

Huskisson tugged at his chin. "Don't take your eye off the ball, man," he said. "The car may have been stolen but it wasn't dumped. It was parked. The driver intended to come back and continue his journey when the river went down."

George sat up.

Huskisson went on. "If you dumped a car, would you bother to remove the rotor arm to make sure it couldn't be driven away? If you dumped a stolen car near the flooded Bondy, would you bother to drive it onto high ground? Why not point it downhill, put it in low gear, and let it rip? You were right the first time, Galbraith. You're the anomaly expert, so try these items for size. If the car *wasn't* stolen, why was it fitted with expired license plates? Why was the original white paintwork sprayed over with a single coat of blue? Why does it look like a koori heap, whereas it's in first-rate mechanical condition?"

George relapsed into his gloom. The all-night session with Huskisson after a hectic three-hour session with Wrightson on security precautions had taken their toll. He was thinking in circles.

"All right, all right, all right! Back to square one. So you buy my original idea that it was the car they used to hit Halley's Circle. And they'd used it before to deploy the gang. Next time they'll spray it pink and fix another set of plates. Okay, prove any of it. You've got the bodies and the authority to raid Silent Reach. I haven't."

Huskisson's glance was sympathetic. George was even more tired than he looked. He was pink-eyed, pale, and his fingers were stained from chain-smoking.

"Don't get testy, Galbraith. You've done all you can for the present. Even if you had the bodies and the authority to raid Silent Reach, how would you go about it? Burst into the Burnie homestead waving a search warrant and yelling: 'Come clean! Where do you keep the thermite and the time fuses?' God Almighty, man, the KGB itself couldn't seal off a million acres of North Kimberley bush and mount a search that would turn up anything except by fluke."

George scowled unpleasantly. "Come off it, old boy, you're a pro," he said. "The KGB would crack this business in half a day and you know it. They'd pinch old Burnie and his boys and wire up their balls to a battery. But we don't conduct terrorist investigations in that way, do we?"

"Not in this part of the free world," Huskisson said equably. "I don't know about friendly powers like Chile and Indonesia and South Korea, but in permissive society we can definitely rule out the possibility of wiring up the Burnie balls to a battery. Why don't you go and get some sleep?"

George drained the beer can and heaved himself out of the chair. "I'll do that. How far do you think your people are prepared to cooperate with me, Huskisson?"

"What do you mean?"

"I'm not going to sit around on my sweaty ass in this slum while your chaps compile dossiers on the Burnie boys and their mates. I've been doing a bit of lateral thinking. Until now we've assumed that the operation against Wrightson has been financed by outsiders' money—by an unscrupulous competitor or more likely by political subversives bent on selling aborigines on Black Power ideology for its sheer nuisance value. But what if that assumption's wrong? What if the man who's running the Midnight Riders is footing the bill himself from the profits of some sort of criminal racket?"

Huskisson made no reply. He reached for a pencil and began adding to the gallery of ducks on his blotter. George experienced a surge of unreasonable irritation.

"For Christ's sake, comrade," he exploded, "get out of the groove, can't you? Try daisies or fat cats for a change. I asked a sensible question."

Huskisson threw down the pencil a little guiltily.

"What's a sensible answer? If you suggest some big money racket that could be run on Silent Reach, I'll make a profound comment."

George sat down abruptly. "The geography of this blasted heath is beginning to soak into my brains," he said. "This is a wide-open coast, practically uninhabited, and to all intents and purposes, unpatrolled. It's two hundred miles over the water to Indonesian territory—call it an hour's flying time in a modern light plane—or an overnight trip for a fast powerboat. Does that observation rate as a suggestion? Or do I have to spell out dope, currency, prohibited fauna, illegal immigrants, and stolen goods?"

The reflective expression of Huskisson's lined face did not change. "Turn me up one tittle of evidence along these lines and I'll show you how lateral thoughts bear fruit. But what can we do that we're not already doing?"

"We could follow the money Max Burnie spent on improvements to his property a few years ago. Do you think your Taxation Office people would play ball and trace that back to its source?"

Huskisson shrugged. "Probably—if they haven't already satisfied themselves that he raised it legitimately on loan or from the disposal of assets. The tax boys don't miss much. But I thought you were complaining about a sweaty behind. You won't get oil from that source overnight."

"I wouldn't expect it. I was wondering if, in all the circumstances, you'd bend the proprieties a bit and provide me with a new cover. All I'll need is a piece of paper."

"A piece of paper saying what?"

"That I'm a Commonwealth Taxation Branch investigator."

This time Huskisson reacted.

"Jesus!" he said softly. "That's Treasury business! That's dynamite!"

"I only want a sheet or two of letterhead. None of your crowd needs get his wrist slapped. I'll do my own forging and uttering."

"But that cover wouldn't fool old Burnie for a min-

ute," Huskisson protested. "Besides,
think a bogus tax man can get answ
policeman can't?"

George looked reproachful. "Really, c
said, "you don't do me justice. What I h.
was an excuse for dropping in for a chat
missionaries at Barramundi Bay. It would
esting to find out how they receive a bogus tax

Father Arnaldo Valdera, Superior of the Greg
Order's Mission to the North Kimberley—a c
munity of four priests, three monks, two lay brothe.
and five nuns—was a man of impressive presence. I
his late fifties or early sixties, he was over six feet
tall, barrel-chested, still flat bellied from long hours
spent in the saddle of a stock horse, and he wore a
majestic spade beard dramatically streaked wit!
white. His complexion was swarthy, his eyes deep s
and a piercing black, and his forehead high and
ceding. The soutane which he had donned for the e
ning meal in the refectory was immaculately w.
and his fingernails—as George observed when he
reached for a humidor on his desk and offered his
visitor a slim Cuban cigar—were carefully tended.

George accepted a match, lit his cigar, inhaled with
appreciation, and said: "It's very kind of you, Father Valdera, to receive us so hospitably. Brother
Martino was good enough to show us something of
the station while you were busy with . . . what was
it, the fortnightly issue of rations?"

The priest inclined his head. "To the pensioners,
yes. Two hundred are rather a handful. You're welcome, Mr. Sinclair. We get few visitors here. The
evening meal was quite an event. Your Captain Fitzpatrick is a lively fellow—tremendous sense of humor."

"Ah," said George with a faint frown by way of
insurance since Chasser had been definitely obstre-
perous. "Yes. As you say, a lively sense of humor."

"Um. Your first time in this part of the country,
Mr. Sinclair?"

"Yes, sir."

mpressed?"

Overwhelmed," George said.

The missionary laughed. "Yes, I remember my own oughts when I first came here."

He took a pair of pince-nez spectacles from a rawer, set them on his long, bony nose, and picked n a radio message report form.

"The Port Epsom police are rather cryptic. There's a request to cooperate. Government business. I take it you're not a policeman, Mr. Sinclair, or they would have given your rank."

"No, sir, I'm not a policeman." George reached into his pocket for an old plastic identity card holder that was as genuine as its contents were false.

"Then Aboriginal Affairs?"

"Australian Taxation Office," George said so un- emphatically that he might even have convinced the deputy commissioner. Father Valdera waved the card holder away after the briefest glance.

"Well now," he said, "that's extraordinary! Tax matters are not our concern here. The business af- fairs of the Order are under the control of the provin- cial office in Southam."

"Of course. The department is interested only to clarify details of this mission's business association with the owner of a pastoral property which adjoins the Barramundi Bay Native Reserve, a Mr. Max- well Burnie of Silent Reach station."

It is difficult for a luxuriant spade beard to register disbelieving amazement, but in this case it contrived to do so.

"Business association?"

"My information," George said in his most precise official voice, "is that Mr. Burnie has an agency ar- rangement with this mission under which the mission receives, holds, and dispatches to market beef cattle raised on Silent Reach."

"Good grief! An agency arrangement? In the legal sense, I suppose, yes. We do handle Max Burnie's cattle. But this has been going on for many years. We regard it as helping a good neighbor rather than a business transaction."

"I quite understand, Father Valdera," George said. "But I presume you keep a record of the services you provide Mr. Burnie?"

"A record?" The missionary still sounded disbelieving. "Yes, I imagine so. Since this is an official inquiry I would like the advice of Father Bridges who looks after our accounts. You met Father Bridges during the evening meal?"

Bridges? Yes, the square, redheaded man with bright blue eyes, a badly sunburned nose, and hands like freckled hams, who'd caught George's eye during Valdera's prolonged grace and winked, who'd assiduously circulated the pitcher of vinegary but potent wine, and laughed loudly at Chasser Fitzpatrick's off-color Irish jokes.

"Certainly, Father Valdera. By all means ask Father Bridges."

The priest rose and strode out of the room, soutane rustling, leaving George to gaze from the window into an overcast night sky where he could discern the looming bulk of an escarpment towering above a patchwork of cultivated land. After almost a century, Barramundi Bay Mission was still no more than an embattled bridgehead on the coast of an immutably savage land. Despite the clammy, blood-hot air, George Galbraith shivered as he stared at the inky hills.

The redheaded priest hurried into the room discourteously a pace ahead of his superior, impatiently knotting the girdle of the grubby white cassock he had worn in the refectory.

"Well now, Mr. Sinclair," he said with suspicious joviality, "so the cat's out of the bag at last! I've won a small wager on you—twenty cents that you weren't a detective. So you're a tax man. What's all this about Max Burnie fiddling his return?"

George frowned. "You're mistaken, Father Bridges. That wasn't my suggestion. I check sources of income on scores of pastoral and farming properties without detecting any understatement of earnings or any other form of evasion. It is simply a routine inquiry. I asked Father Valdera if the mission kept records of stock

and freight dealings with Silent Reach station. He said
the matter was in your province."

The spade beard wagged. "That is so. That is so."

The redhead hooked a chair forward with a thong-
clad foot and sat down. "Routine, eh? The tax man
cometh from afar—and by air, too. A memorable
visitation, Mr. Sinclair. What figures do you want?"

"The numbers of cattle turned off the Burnie property through the mission, and inward ship freights
held for collection. Service fees or commissions
charged."

"We don't charge commissions. Mr. Burnie reim-
burses us for out-of-pocket expenses like stockmen's
wages. The mission has staged cattle and freight for
Silent Reach for the best part of thirty years. What
period of time are you interested in?"

George plunged manfully on. "The last five years
will be sufficient, Father," he said in a prim, no-
nonsense voice.

Father Bridges shot an inquiring glance at his superior, who nodded. "An hour in the morning should
clear it up. Directly after breakfast, Mr. Sinclair?"

"At your convenience, Father Bridges."

The bright blue eyes twinkled. "I take it you
haven't interviewed old Max himself yet. Um?"

"Not yet."

The younger priest laughed. He sounded genuinely
amused. "You'll find it quite an experience. He's a
memorable character. Have you made an appointment
to call at the homestead?"

George decided there was no harm in playing it by
ear.

"I believe the Native Welfare people are due to
make a routine visit," he said indifferently. "It'll
probably be possible to travel with them. Surely it's
unusual for so large a property not to operate a radio
transceiver or maintain an airstrip?"

The missionaries exchanged glances.

"Well," Father Bridges said, rubbing at his peeling
nose, "I'd say someone in high places must have decided to lean on Max again, wouldn't you, Reverend
Father?"

The superior cleared his throat warningly. "That hardly concerns us, Father. Such policy matters are probably of no interest to Mr. Sinclair either."

"Don't you believe it! Everything's grist to the tax man's mill, eh, Mr. Sinclair?"

"I'm sorry, I don't quite follow," George said woodenly. "As you know, costs incurred in maintaining an airstrip and radio communications are legitimate operating expenses and tax deductible."

"Which is an advantage only if you make use of the installations," Father Bridges observed drily. "And Max won't, of course, even if he's forced to put them in. He's opposed to establishing any links with the outside world. He's even opposed to making money, which is why I'm surprised the Taxation Department has any interest in him. Silent Reach is run to provide subsistence for the Burnie family."

"That includes Mrs. Burnie's tribal relatives, I believe," George said.

"Ah, I see you've been briefed. Native Welfare, no doubt."

George was not to be drawn onto ground as shaky as that. It was time to display a little inquisitorial muscle. The redheaded priest was too firmly steering the conversation.

George said: "A leasehold property of that size cannot be run solely as a subsistence proposition. A considerable cash flow must be generated to pay even nominal rents and meet the cost of statutory improvements."

Father Valdera nodded and fingered his beard. "Most cattle stations in the Kimberley these days are being run at a loss, Mr. Sinclair."

"That's very true, sir," George conceded. "The industry is going through a difficult time. The only people in a satisfactory position are those with considerable reserves or a secondary source of income."

"Neither of which, by my reckoning, Max Burnie has," Father Bridges said in an uncompromising tone. "Well, Mr. Sinclair, if you'll see me in my office in the morning, I'll do what I can to help."

"Of course. Thank you."

No dice. The reverend gentlemen were not to be seduced into gossip. George wondered why. He could have goofed his approach, but how? They had not challenged his authority to request details of business with Silent Reach. An hour or two in the morning with the redhead might yield results, but it was doubtful. The redhead was also a hard head.

Father Valdera said: "Brother Martino will have shown you to the room prepared for you, Mr. Sinclair." The beard tilted benignly. "I must bid you goodnight. Father Bridges will see that you have everything you require before you retire. You'll excuse me, I know. I have some urgent correspondence. Sleep well."

Nunc dimittis.... And definitely no dice.

The Barramundi Bay Mission's guest room was a stone-walled chamber of considerable size with a shuttered window leading out to the verandah some fifty or sixty feet from the superior's study. It was furnished only with two hospital beds under voluminous mosquito nets hung on ceiling hoops, a painted chest of drawers, a Victorian washstand with water bottle, ewer, basin, and chamber pot, two cane-bottomed chairs, and a framed oleograph of the martyrdom of St. Sebastian.

The redheaded missionary followed George through the door, glanced around, and jerked his head toward the washstand. "Don't be inhibited about using the period piece," he said. "It's a long trek to the lavatory block. I see your bag's here. Is there anything you'd like?"

"No thanks, padre. I'll be quite comfortable."

"You wouldn't be requiring a sedative, by any chance—in the form of a tot of rum?"

Surprise, surprise! The breezy Father Bridges had decided to launch his own fishing expedition. George grinned. "Insomnia's an awful thing, padre. If you advise, I consent."

"Then come on. I'm just across the way. We'll hear Fitzpatrick when he comes back and he can join us if he wants."

The priest's small bedroom was in cheerful disorder. Its furniture included a plywood closet with a warped door. From its depths the priest abstracted two shot glasses and a quart bottle.

"Sit yourself down," he said. He poured two minute measures of liquor with great care. "One thirty-five degrees proof but a good thirty-five years old. There's water if you prefer, but I don't hold with desecration."

George sat, sniffed the glass cautiously.

"Powerful," he pronounced.

"Jetsam from a British navy oiler that ran aground in these parts during the war. We bottled the last of it from the hogshead five years ago. Your very good health."

George sipped and suppressed a gasp.

"Memorable," he said. "Memorable. Generous of you."

"You're from the old country, Mr. Sinclair?"

"How could you tell?"

The priest laughed pleasantly. "Been with the department long?"

"Not long. This is my first tour in the bush."

"You'll find your visit to Silent Reach . . . illuminating, I think."

"So you implied. Mr. Burnie is really eccentric, I'm given to understand."

A faint shrug. "As an accountant, you'll probably find him so. He has a quaint way of saying that a ton of barbed wire or a drum of kerosene or whatever costs so many bullocks, not so many dollars and cents."

"Bullocks as currency, eh? Unstable perhaps." George made it sound priggish, befitting an accountant. But he was intrigued. "Does Mr. Burnie estimate the cost of educating his children in terms of bullocks?"

Father Bridge's smile was wry. "By jove," he said, "you tax chaps know your stuff, don't you? As a matter of fact, believe it or not, he did. Term and other fees for the children were paid by this mission from credits established from the purchase of Silent Reach cattle. On the subject of eccentricity, I don't think that Max Burnie is much more eccentric than our community here. In some areas we have common aims. We share a conviction that the welfare of natives is best served by insulating them from the conditions that exist in Port Epsom and other towns in the North West."

"Apartheid of a sort," George said, tilting his glass.

The priest was not amused. An angry spark lit his eyes. "The choice, Mr. Sinclair, is between apartheid —of a sort, as you so politely add—and the type of integration afforded by apostles of progress like Oscar Salinger. I take it you met Port Epsom's leading citizen?"

George held up his hands. "Barley, Father! I wasn't criticizing. Until a few weeks ago, I don't think I'd ever set eyes on a full-blooded aboriginal and yet here the natives are a substantial majority in the community. That's why I used the term apartheid, of a sort."

The priest's expression acknowledged the concession.

"A dry argument, Mr. Sinclair. The other half, perhaps?"

This time the measure in the shot glass was more ample.

"Tell me more about the Burnie establishment, padre. In Port Epsom they said the old gentleman would probably run me off the place with a shotgun."

The responding chuckle was sardonic. "Not unless you make an offer to buy the place or sell him machinery. Max is a gentle, peaceable man—a philosopher in the old-fashioned sense of the word. I should have thought the Native Welfare people would have told you that."

"Do you see much of the family down here?"

"Not so much now that the children have finished their schooling. They stay with us, coming or going. Otherwise . . . well, Max or the eldest, Ben, comes through with the cattle or to pick up shipments of stores. Ellie—Mrs. Burnie—is a devout woman and until her health began to fail two or three years ago she always attended Easter and Christmas services here. A remarkable person. She was the first full-blood aboriginal girl in this state to become a triple-certificated nursing sister. I believe she and Max met when he was a patient in Broome hospital after he returned from the war. That was long before my time, of course, but Father Valdera remembers. He married them in the church here."

"But you yourself have had a long and cordial association with the Burnies, Father?"

"Yes. Unhappily, Max Burnie doesn't subscribe to the Catholic faith, Mr. Sinclair. He is firmly agnostic. But for all that, we've found him a good man and a loyal friend of the natives who live on his land. Or, as he puts it, on whose land he lives. That is why we would be . . . distressed if he were in any trouble with the government."

In George's experience, the best way to gauge the quality of a smooth operator was to try him out on rough going.

"I shouldn't worry, Father," he smiled guilelessly. "If the old chap's accountancy were more conventional, the explanation would probably be quite obvious."

"The explanation of what?"

"Of why Mr. Burnie has for some time been able to spend amounts of money very substantially in excess of the income he derives from the sale of his beef cattle. He has mining interests—mineral leases on the Bondy River. I've been wondering if it's not just possible he's working alluvial gold which, as you know, is not taxable in the hands of the producer. If that's the case, he may or may not be contravening state mining regulations by not notifying a strike, but the matter would be of no interest to my department."

The redheaded priest fumbled under his gown and produced a rumpled packet of cigarettes.

"Smoke, Mr. Sinclair?"

"Thanks, but one of my own if you don't mind."

When both cigarettes were glowing, Father Bridges blew a smoke ring expertly and said: "No. Max has alluvial tin leases on the Bondy. They were worked

out years ago commercially but he keeps the tenements up so that his natives can earn a little money
for tobacco when they're so inclined. The country's
not auriferous. Four or five years ago, the hills out
there were crawling with young geologists in big
boots proving it—drilling holes and cracking rocks
and waving geiger counters about. No gold, no uranium, no bauxite, no oil, nothing, thanks be to God."

"Blessed are the poor," George said. "I get your
point. You can do without multinational mining companies for neighbors. Well, good luck to you, padre.
Keep up the good work." He swallowed the last of his
rum.

"And one for the road, perhaps?"

George laughed and shook his head. "No thanks.
I've been indiscreet enough as it is."

"But not unintentionally, Mr. Sinclair," the priest
said with a faint smile. "Yours is a job that demands
finesse. We'll say nine o'clock in my office, shall we?"

One by one, the lights in the rows of square, fibro-
cement cottages built to house the mission's married
couples and their children dimmed and went out. But
in front of the native *wurlis,* where the pensioners
slept huddled under thin rags of blankets, the small,
fitful watch fires set the limits of darkness.

George turned down the hissing gas lantern in his
room and sat on the foot of his bed, looking through
the window and wondering whether to stroll down to
the hangar where Chasser Fitzpatrick was determined
to sleep. In his words, there were too many white
teeth and eyeballs about for him to be happy about
leaving the Cherokee unattended. Chasser's nerves
were frayed by the Halley's Circle bombing. But a light
rain was beginning to fall when George stepped out
onto the verandah and he decided that there was little
point in getting wet and mosquito bitten merely to
boost the little man's morale for an hour or so.

A shaft of light was still shining from the superior's
study window. George reflected for a moment, then
walked quietly toward it, keeping close to the wall.
His intuition had been right. Father Valdera was

talking with his second in command, but the ecstatic croaking of the cane toads made their conversation unintelligible until George moved closer and stopped a bare yard from the open venetian shutter.

"I don't believe Max would have made a decision like that without telling us, Michael. He said nothing about having to meet unexpected demands again. It worries me. It's not like him."

"No. But the taxation people got their information from somewhere. This Sinclair fellow is too sure of himself for there to be any mistake. Max has done something infernally silly, that's plain. But *why*, Arnaldo, and how? That's what I can't understand."

There was a long silence. When the redheaded priest spoke again, he was standing within arm's length of George, looking out into the night.

"I know it's a bad time of the year, but have you considered making a trip over the hill? The man should be warned."

"To what purpose? If he has had a change of heart, there's nothing I can do about it. I have no influence on him."

"You have influence with Ellie."

"No, I'll not involve her in this—and you know why. When God's will is done and she goes I don't think Max will be so far behind. I've given it thought, Michael. This business can't be kept secret forever. We have to face that."

"When his father dies, what will Ben do?"

"Does it matter?"

"He'll inherit. When he does, he won't stay long with the tribe."

"I shouldn't be too sure of that. After all, he chose to come home to his own people. The other boys didn't. And when Alison went through a few weeks ago, she told Sister Mary Antony that she wants counsel about entering the convent after her mother dies."

"Does Ben know how his father got the money for the fencing?"

"I don't know. I doubt it. It's strange they're not closer."

Father Bridges turned away from the window and

moved back into the room. "What father is close to
his son these days, Arnaldo? Even in the tribes the
old men have no authority. I'll be off now. But think
again about warning Max."

"When is that man going, do you know?"

"The tax sleuth? Tomorrow, I suppose. It won't
take me long to give him what he's asked for."

"I don't like him, Michael. He's two-faced, glib—a
deceitful man. We'll talk again after he's gone. I'll decide what to do. Good night."

"Good night."

"And up you, too, for the rent, you Tridentine old
bastard!" George muttered under his breath as he
padded hastily back to his room.

Lying naked under the musty mosquito net, he
cursed his luck. Twice had crude eavesdropping
brought him tantalizingly closer to a solution of the
puzzle of Silent Reach. And twice crude eavesdropping had in the upshot left him baffled because he had
been unable to eavesdrop long enough.

CHAPTER 18

GEORGE Galbraith looked up from the stock
and stores tallies on Father Bridges's desk and sucked
at his pen thoughtfully. Something unexpected must
have broken, otherwise Roger Huskisson would not
have sent such a signal. But it was all to the good.
For the time being, there was no further mileage to be
made at Barramundi Bay, and any excuse to hurry his
departure was welcome.

"Are you sure there was nothing in the message
about the matter being urgent, Brother Martino?" he
asked.

The nuggety little Catalan monk who doubled as
the mission's studmaster and motor mechanic looked
affronted. He was not the sort of man to ignore urgency.

"I have given you all the message received, Mr. Sinclair," he replied huffily. "Port Epsom police to this mission. Please request Mr. George Sinclair land Wandonning Downs before he returns Port Epsom. Ends. That is all."

"Thank you, Brother Martino."

"You're welcome," he said coldly.

Father Bridges did not trouble to conceal his curiosity. He marked a place in the daybook he was searching and asked: "Nothing wrong, I hope?"

George frowned.

"Police requests always mean something's wrong. But why Wandonning? As far as I know, the department has no business at Wandonning. Do you happen to know the station people, Father?"

The redheaded priest shook his head.

"Not really. I've never visited the homestead. It's well beyond this parish. But as a matter of fact, the manager put down on the strip here a few weeks ago when he ran short of fuel returning home from Darwin. A Mr. David Carlin. He stayed with us overnight."

George raised his eyebrows. Darwin was only one hundred and twenty air miles away. Yet Carlin had run out of fuel. Odd.

"Sounds rather careless of Mr. Carlin," he said offhandedly. "Or was the weather bad?"

Father Bridges grinned slyly. "No, but it had been bad the night before. Mr. Carlin was a very tired man when he landed. A good night's sleep set him up."

"Ah," said George. "Quite! And speaking of weather, was there an aviation forecast on the radio this morning, Brother Martino?"

"*Si.* Thunderstorms among the mountains in the afternoon. Another cyclone is coming. The cloud will build up."

"Awkward," George said. "I'd better alert Fitzpatrick. He's a fussy fellow about thunderstorms and cyclones, for which I'm duly grateful. I'm sorry, Father Bridges, but I think we should get away as soon as possible if the weather's breaking again. These figures aren't complete, but I'm already satisfied that there's no point in bothering you further."

The priest grinned again.

"In your line of business . . . yes, I understand. Brother Martino can take the runabout down to the strip and give Captain Fitzpatrick the bad news. And, Brother, stop off at the kitchen and tell Sister Consuela to prepare an early lunch for them. Also tell Sister a large loaf of bread, beef, and bottles of wine for our guests to take. Captain Fitzpatrick might have to put down on one of the old fighter strips up the coast if the weather closes in."

"Understood, Father. I go."

The remnants of George's conscience pricked him. When the Catalan had stumped off, he cleared his throat. "I hardly know the form of acknowledging your hospitality, Father. Does the mission have a contribution box or something of the sort?"

"The provincial's office at Southam is always pleased to receive voluntary contributions, but there is nothing obligatory about it." The reply was a formality. "By the way, I'm told your pilot spent the night in his aircraft. The poor chap must have been terribly uncomfortable. Why on earth did he choose to do that?"

"He's sensitive about security, Father, particularly since the Halley's Circle bombing. He flies for Conair, you know. Hamilton Wrightson's concerns have had more than their share of accidents lately, and airplanes are rather accident-prone machines."

The bright blue eyes were frosty. "Sabotage prone, you mean?"

George made a deprecatory gesture. The priest closed the day book with an air of finality.

"I'm afraid you've been wasting your time with us, Mr. Sinclair, but we've enjoyed your company. We know all too little of things that go on in the outside world. Shall we explain to Father Valdera now that your visit has been cut short?"

"I was about to suggest it," said George with a faint smile. "And I assure you that I haven't been wasting my time. On the contrary, this visit has been thoroughly worthwhile for a department that must work with processes of elimination."

Half an hour after takeoff, at an altitude of eight thousand feet, Chasser Fitzpatrick eased the throttle forward, dipped the starboard wing, and banked smoothly away from the boiling column of cunim over Mount Hatter.

"Negative, colonel," he said against George's ear. "We'll have to make the recon next time round. Silent Reach is not just silent, it's invisible. Besides, I promised my mum, scout's honor, I'd never fly into an Aunty Jack."

"An Aunty Jack?"

Chasser's teeth flashed in his three-day stubble. "In-joke," he said cryptically. "Aunty Jacks rip yer bloody wings off!"

George did not reply. Chasser's humor could be tiresome. He cocked his eye at the gyrocompass, then peered down at tree-spotted hills already hazed with driving vapor.

"What now, captain? Do we turn back—or look for an old fighter strip?"

Fitzpatrick snorted. "Be your age! With two hours' fuel in the billycan, we could go upstairs and divert to Broome if we needed to. We'll stooge around and see how it looks over the Ferdinands. But where was I? About this old character in the pensioner line. . . ."

The hole through the clouds, fifteen hundred feet deep and fuming, could hardly have opened more conveniently. At its bottom, yellow floodwater shone where the Bondy rushed out of its gorge and spewed over the samphire flat on the approaches to Wandonning. Chasser put the little aircraft's nose hard down, rolled out of the dive below the cloud base, and leveled off at two hundred feet. He circled the homestead and made one low pass over the strip. It was a foot deep in young grass and blotched with pools of groundwater.

"Greasy as a nympho's G-string," Chasser pronounced. "How keen are you to land, governor?"

"It's your department, driver," George replied stoically.

Chasser climbed away, flipped his throat-mike switch, and exchanged gabble with the Port Epsom tower. Then he eased the yoke forward again.

"Hold on to your neck," he said. "Epsom's closed and Sunday's too far away."

It was neat—a paste-on landing that left a long wake of muddy spray. The station Cessna was still standing forlornly in its shelter. Chasser ran up to the little gravel apron and switched off.

"What—no brass band? I thought we were invited, George."

George stepped down and looked around. Nobody had come down to the strip to meet them. It was puzzling.

"I didn't see anybody when you buzzed the house," he said. "I wonder what the devil—"

"Wait!" Chasser lifted a hand. On a fitful wind ahead of the rain, there blew in the growl and whine of an old motor, overrevved to get tire traction in the mud. George spotted the cab of the homestead utility truck lurching toward them through fender-high kangaroo grass.

"Better get your dilly bag out of the back," Chasser told him. "Patty's stuck with us, whether she likes it or not. We won't be cracking a cold can at the lodge tonight. There's ten-tenths cloud over those hills."

George acquiesced gloomily. He wasn't looking forward to a session with Patty Mountfort without first getting a briefing on progress of the police inquiry into the death of the Honorable David. Patty knew more than she'd told, but she would need delicate handling.

Chasser Fitzpatrick was staring at the approaching truck. "Well, blow me over!" he called. "Look who's here! Surprise, surprise!"

George peered, blinked—and felt his heart turn over.

"Diagulski! What in the name of—"

She braked hard, flung the door open, and stepped down from the cab without a word of greeting. George dropped his impulsively outstretched hands.

Her lips were pale and chapped. She passed the tip of her tongue across them before she spoke.

"You're too late. You've missed them. They took off just before ten o'clock."

Chasser glared at her indignantly. "Who's too late for what? What's the bind, Diagulski? Who took off?"

"The helicopter ambulance from Derby. Didn't you get a police message at the mission, Sinclair?"

"Yes—to land here before returning to Epsom. Nothing else. What's wrong? Has there been an accident?"

"No. Put your gear in the truck, Chasser. Get in, don't just stand there! No, it wasn't an accident. Patty Mountfort took an overdose—and Mary Dalziel's gone missing."

The little pilot's eyes popped and his jaw sagged. "Sweet Jesus!"

George expelled his breath slowly. "Okay, Chasser. We'd better move. Leave the rest of it till we get up to the house, Diagulski. Do you want me to drive?"

"No. I'm perfectly capable of driving myself," she snapped.

"Then unwind—and keep your foot off the accelerator," he said coldly. "I don't feel like walking. And less like digging trucks out of bogs."

They rode the half mile of tooth-loosening jolts and dizzy skids in silence.

The house was empty. They filed indoors, still without speaking. George found an opened bottle of brandy on the dining-room sideboard and carried it out with three glasses to the gallery.

"Where are the stockmen, Diagulski?"

"Out looking for the Dalziel girl."

"You're here on your own?"

"Yes."

"I see. Better begin at the beginning. Here, you can use a drink by the look of you."

She swallowed the spirit in a single gulp. Chasser held out his hand for her glass. "Have the other half, mate," he said.

"No. When did you leave Port Epsom, Sinclair?"

"Tuesday. Chasser flew me down to that mess at Halley's Circle. We called at Barramundi Bay on the way back and stayed overnight. A message from Sergeant Huskisson told us to land here. It didn't say why."

"All right. Now I know where to begin. Ham and I came up to Epsom in the Beechcraft the day before yesterday. There were two policemen with us—a superintendent from the Criminal Investigation Department, and an explosives expert. Ham planned to take them down to Halley's Circle and return by way of Mullamurra and Braund. He told me to drop off at Epsom and try to get into Wandonning by tow truck. He was worried about Patty Mountfort because the station radio hadn't been answering scheduled calls, and there's some sort of fuss about David Carlin's personal effects."

"Yes," George said under his breath. "There would be by now."

"The tow truck couldn't get across the river. In that case, I was to wait at Epsom until you and Chasser got back and then fly in with you if the strip here was serviceable. Yesterday evening the base operator tried to reach Patty again, but again there was no reply. Just after the regular schedule finished, one of the stockmen, Willy Schrieber, came in on the emergency frequency. The channel was noisy and his English isn't good. All the operator could understand was that it was a Mayday and the missus had 'taken something.' He kept repeating that it was a Mayday. Base called the police and they arranged for the ambulance helicopter to fly in from Derby at first light this morning. Sergeant Huskisson thought I should travel with them because a nursing sister wasn't available."

"Did Huskisson come in with you?" George asked sharply.

"Yes. He said to tell you to wait. He'll be back as soon as he can."

"Right. Was Patty dead when you got here?"

"No. Her heart was still beating but she was in a coma. The doctor said she might live if they could get her to a respirator in time, but he didn't hold out much hope. She'd taken a whole bottle of barbiturate tablets. It was beside her bed, empty."

"Who found her? You said Mary Dalziel is missing."

Tamara Diagulski knuckled her eyes angrily.

"For God's sake, Sinclair, I can't tell you everything in one breath! I'm trying to tell you what I know, step by step. I'm trying to be clear." She paused. "Give me the other brandy, Chasser, I've changed my mind."

Chasser put the drink into her hand.

"When the helicopter landed, three of the stockmen met us—Schrieber, the man who made the Mayday call, and two half-caste Spaniards—Chileans I think they are. It was lucky I speak German. Schrieber's English is awful. He told me that he and the others had been out moving cattle from a flooded area downriver. The foreman, Barratt, stayed to repair broken fences but the rest got back late in the afternoon. Mary Dalziel usually prepared meals for them and when she hadn't appeared at the quarters by nightfall, they came up to the house. They found Mary in a state of collapse. She said the missus was dead—she'd poisoned herself with pills. Willy went to the bedroom and saw Patty lying on the floor by the bed. He was scared to touch her. Then he went to the radio in the office. He'd never operated it, but he worked out the typed instructions on the panel and sent the Mayday call. The Flying Doctor Base gave him first-aid instructions. He understood them, but he was still too scared to touch her."

"The stupid bloody clot!" Chasser Fitzpatrick burst out. "If she was still alive this morning—"

"Shut up, Chasser," George rapped. "Go on, Diagulski. Did Schrieber explain why he was frightened to touch her?"

"He wasn't sure she had poisoned herself. He thought she could have been killed by the person who attacked Mary Dalziel."

"What! *Attacked,* did you say?"

"Yes. Yesterday, or the day before, somebody

beat her up. When we found her in her room, her face and throat were a mass of bruises. But she wouldn't—or couldn't—tell us who did it. Or why. We couldn't get a word out of her. She just stared at us blankly."

"Was she seriously hurt?"

"The doctor examined her. He said the physical damage was trivial though she'd been punched and half strangled. The worry was Patty. She was barely alive, but unmarked by violence of any sort. The doctor put a tube in her throat and we got her into the ambulance. I went back to fetch Mary from her room, but she wasn't there. She'd disappeared—run away. If Patty was to have any chance the helicopter couldn't wait. Huskisson decided it would be best if I were here when the stockmen found the girl and brought her in. That's why I stayed. But . . . but the stockmen haven't found her. They've been away for hours."

"Are you quite sure," George asked gently, "that the girl ran away? Are you sure she wasn't *taken* away?"

Diagulski shook her head. "After the ambulance took off, Schrieber discovered that her saddle and bridle weren't in the tack room behind the store and her stock pony was missing from the yard. Huskisson said to tell you he'd be back before dark."

"Monkey's bum he'll be back before dark!" growled Chasser. "The ceiling's down to three hundred already. I'll get Epsom tower on the blower again and give them the lowdown on the weather here. That cyclone's moving inland. Do you want to talk, George?"

"No. Just ask them to report to the police that we've landed and we'll wait out the weather."

When Fitzpatrick had gone, he asked: "Diagulski, how well did you know Patty Mountfort and her niece?"

"Not very well. Whenever I came here it was always on business—following up some 'please explain' or 'please expedite' from the pastoral manager. The property isn't well run. I don't think it ever was, even in the good times. I didn't enjoy coming and Patty didn't enjoy having me."

"How bad was her financial situation?"

"Not bad enough to drive her to suicide, unless she had debts or commitments I don't know about. The property isn't paying, but Ham saw to it that she had enough to live on."

"Then you don't know or suspect anything about the Wandonning setup that might account for her attempting suicide?"

"Patty was a neurotic woman. You must have seen that. She hadn't the resources to stand the loneliness of her life here, Sinclair. And there was bitter ill feeling between her and David Carlin."

George nodded. "Yes, bitter sexual ill feeling. She was worried about Carlin's influence on her son Peter. She needn't have been. Young Peter's peculiarities aren't homosexual—they take a different direction. Carlin's death couldn't contribute to her suicide attempt. We have to look elsewhere for a reason—and for an explanation of how that poor little devil, Mary Dalziel, has become involved in the dirty doings at Wandonning."

George was acutely aware that Hamilton Wrightson's girl Friday was looking directly into his eyes for the first time since he had run to meet her at the landing strip. Bewilderment? Fear? Appeal? He couldn't be sure.

"Dirty doings?"

"What else, for God's sake? If the doings weren't dirty, why did someone beat her up and why did she run away?"

"Maybe someone threatened her with a worse beating if she told outsiders what she knew. Maybe she was afraid of police questioning. Is that what you're suggesting, Sinclair?"

"No. Mary Dalziel isn't the sort to scare. Some infernal witch doctor in a surgical gown cut her forebrain to suppress the symptoms of mental illness, but he didn't cut her physical courage. I don't believe that girl could be intimidated by physical violence or the threat of it. She was beaten up and she ran for other reasons."

"Then why wouldn't she speak—tell us what happened, who attacked her?"

"I can't answer that, but I'll swear it wasn't because of intimidation, or guilt for anything she'd done."

The violet eyes seemed very large in the small, brown face. Again she moistened her lips.

"You sound quite sure of it, Sinclair—as if you understood Mary Dalziel much better than most people who knew her would care to claim."

"I think I do. Yes."

"But it's understanding on the strength of a brief acquaintance, isn't it, colleague?"

He caught the muted irony, the little quirk of skepticism in her voice. His reply was deliberate.

"Brief, yes—but not without intimacy. You see, we spent the best part of a whole day together, stark naked and unashamed, sunning ourselves on the riverbank."

The violet eyes held his for another moment. Then she looked away and set down the brandy glass. When she spoke her tone was cool, but without the faintest inflection of either surprise or animus.

"I suppose there's a point in telling me this, other than to explain your . . . instant understanding of a mentally disadvantaged girl."

"Yes. I'm telling you to explain that she liked and trusted me in much the same way as a child might. She was lonely, like everybody else in this wretched household. She badly needed someone to talk to. She needed someone who would listen and not make comments or judgments. And what she told me triggered the breakthrough to a solution of this entire, twisted, cat-and-mouse business."

Breakthrough. The word came to her as a blow. She flinched. If George had been less completely absorbed in her presence, less physically responsive to the nearness of the slim, graceful body with its small, jutting breasts and lean, smooth flanks, he would not have perceived the flash of fear, for her suppression of it was instant. She turned away from him.

"You've got an uncanny instinct, Sinclair."

"For what?"

"Breaking down people's defenses with your charming, wacky arrogance."

You've got to face it sooner or later, George told himself. There can't be any future with Diagulski while she's holding out on you.

"The charming, wacky arrogance of the Galbraiths doesn't work so well with you, does it, Diagulski?" he said. "After all, Mary Dalziel has very little to defend or conceal. On the other hand, you have. You're going to have to make up your mind about whose side you're on."

She whirled, taut with resentment.

"Will you explain that, Sinclair?"

"Not now." He spoke with gentle flatness. "It'll take time and privacy. The explanation's personal—and complicated. All I can say is this—no matter what side you opt for I don't want you hurt. I think you know why."

Willy Schrieber and the two Chilean stockmen rode up to the homestead as night was falling—alone. They had picked up the tracks of Mary Dalziel's pony at the eastern gate to the home paddock and followed them for a mile or so until they lost them on stony ground. They had spent the afternoon in the rain quartering the sparse scrub on the hillsides under the rock spine of Porcupine Bar without finding any further trace of the girl. There was, Willy explained, no use in continuing the search after dark. They would go out again at first light if the Fräulein wished, but the police would do better in a helicopter.

Diagulski said she would radio the police for instructions. If the men came up to the kitchen in an hour she would have a meal prepared, unless they preferred to cook their own food in their quarters. Willy, a slow-moving, bullet-headed man in his midtwenties, looked more cheerful. The Fräulein was very kind. It had been hard riding and they had had noth-

ing to eat in the middle of the day. He hoped there
would be good news about Frau Mountfort. It was
very sad. She was a good employer. He did not think
that Fräulein Mary would come to harm from one
night in the bush. Perhaps she would return home of
her own accord when she got hungry.

When the men went off to unsaddle, George said:
"Your German's very good, Diagulski. Where did you
learn it?"

"My foster parents spoke German in the home—German and Yiddish," she said indifferently. "They came
from Breslau."

"Here, to Australia?"

"Yes, by way of a DP camp in Trieste. They arrived in 1947."

She did not elaborate and George dared not probe.
A foster child. Breslau. German and Yiddish. Polish
Jews. His mind reeled with questions. With an effort,
he put them aside.

"If you want help in your new job, colleague," he
said lightly, "you can count on me. I peel potatoes and
boil water very efficiently. Once upon a time, many
years ago, I was a boy scout, in the days before they
abolished the daily good deed as too heavy a responsibility for young mods."

After the evening meal they played three-handed
gin rummy until Chasser Fitzpatrick's emergency carton of beer, retrieved personally by the eternally
thirsty little man from the Cherokee's luggage compartment, had been consumed. Shortly after ten
o'clock the light globe dimmed because the fuel tank
in the engine shed had not been refilled. George found
hurricane lanterns in the kitchen and brought them
back to the gallery, but Chasser yawned noisily and
hoisted himself out of his chair.

"Sorry, folks," he said, "but I've had it. I slept in
the kite last night and I don't mind telling you those
Barramundi Bay mosquitoes are a special breed. They
make a noise like bloody electric lawn mowers. I
didn't mind that, but it was their bragging that kept
me awake—arguing about whether to eat me where I
was or drag me down to the river."

"I know," said Diagulski wearily. "They decided to eat you where you were because they were scared their big sisters would hijack you if they pulled you outside. You'd better sleep in David Carlin's room."

Fitzpatrick pulled a wry face. "And a gaggle of sweet dreams to you, too, old thing. Be careful. Random samplings by Gallup show that thirty percent of all British private eyes are sex maniacs. Take a spanner to bed with you."

"Oh, get knotted, Fitzpatrick," George exclaimed irritably. "The lady and I don't feel strong enough right now to laugh. Another time, eh?"

The pilot looked startled, then pursed his lips absurdly and produced an enormous shrug.

When he had gone they sat for a while, watching and listening to the rain falling on the avocado and hibiscus bushes in the courtyard garden. Somewhere in the timbered belt to the north of the house a boobook owl began its soft, doleful calling. Myriad frogs beat out their ecstatic rhythms on the drumskin of the night.

She spoke at last. "Why did you say I'd have to make up my mind whose side I was on, Sinclair? Why did you say I had things to conceal?"

"Later, Diagulski," he said softly. "Our mutual friend is jumpy—and inquisitive. I don't blame him."

"No. I understand. Very well. Half an hour?"

"An hour to be on the safe side. I'll be in my room."

She smiled faintly, rose, and called over her shoulder as she walked away: "Good night, Sinclair. You need a night's sleep yourself."

It was longer than an hour. He sprawled on the guest-room bed, chain-smoking, staring at the resident gecko's skittering forays across the ceiling, and separating in his mind yet again the linked factors from the loose ends, the explained facts from the unexplained. Most pieces of the jigsaw were still chaotically disordered, but a picture was beginning to form which excited the compulsive curiosity that had for years sustained him in an otherwise increasingly distasteful trade. Where did Diagulski fit in? Diagulski, the bitter-sweet complication.

At last he heard the soft shuffle of her slippered feet in the corridor, sat up, and turned the wick of the hurricane lantern higher. The door opened. She had changed jeans and cotton shirt for a loose robe of green terrycloth and brushed out her braids into the ash-blonde cascade that he remembered from the afternoon of surprises at the Golden Galleon. He felt his pulse quicken. He pointed to the end of the bed. She nodded and sat down.

"I'm sorry it was so long. As soon as the little man lay down he started to die of thirst. He got up again and raided the bottled beer in the kitchen fridge. He's asleep now."

"Good."

"Can I have a cigarette, please?"

He opened a new pack, lit two. She drew at the smoke nervily.

"What's wrong, Sinclair? What's happened?"

He forced himself to ask it, the crucial question.

"Why did you and Ham Wrightson both omit to list the Frenchman's Bay mining leases among the concerns that Conwright controls? Why didn't you tell me the real reason why he's been trying for years to force Max Burnie to sell Silent Reach?"

Silence. Then she took the cigarette from between her lips and said unsteadily: "My God, Sinclair. You *are* good, aren't you?"

"So? I asked you why, colleague. A straight question."

"Because . . . because there's no connection between Frenchman's Bay and the sabotage. There can't be. Why should you be told something you didn't need to know to do your job? You've worked in intelligence for years, and you've accepted need-to-know restrictions as part of the security of any operation. When people had to limit your knowledge, you didn't accuse them of being on the other side."

He looked down and saw that she had already stubbed the cigarette. Her fingers were plucking distractedly at a seam in the sash of the terry robe. He leaned forward and put a hand over hers.

"Don't do that, Diagulski. It's unprofessional."

She drew back from him furiously, bunched her fists.

"The analogy's wrong," he went on. "I'm no longer a part of the intelligence community, so I'm not subject to its disciplines. I don't accept need-to-know restrictions from Hamilton Wrightson. I agreed to help him on the condition that he held nothing back from me. He's cheated on that score. There *is* a connection between Frenchman's Bay, Max Burnie, and the Silent Reach saboteurs. The missionaries at Barramundi Bay know how Burnie gets money when he needs it. As soon as Roger Huskisson and his shower of special-branch bodies crack down on this Midnight Rider junketing, they'll know too. The whole bloody world will know! What sort of secret do you think you're helping Wrightson to protect, Diagulski?"

A dew of perspiration was on her forehead and her voice shook, but her hands were quiet.

"What do you think there's in it for you, Sinclair—hush money?"

That hurt. Inwardly he flinched—as she had flinched when he claimed the breakthrough. And his recovery, like hers, was instant.

"For an intelligent woman, Diagulski, you're an awful little fool when the heat's on. You need wider experience in double-dealing. If I wanted hush money, I'd go direct to Wrightson. If I wanted money of any other sort, I'd go elsewhere—to other parties who might be interested. Why should I badger you? I've earned Wrightson's fee and I could take it now with a clear conscience—then sell the other information to the highest bidder. Or I could get out from under and save myself a hell of a lot of trouble."

"Then why don't you?" she demanded passionately. "You've done your job as a puzzle-solving machine, you cold-blooded, two-legged computer! You don't give a damn about anybody or anything except processing information."

George drew a slow, deep breath and plunged.

"Wrong again, Diagulski-as-a-term-of-endearment. I care about you, Diagulski-as-a-person, more than I've ever cared for anyone else in my life. I'd willingly . . . become a one-legged computer without any blood at all to save you from being used up by Hamilton Wrightson any more than he's already used you up."

The anger, the hostility, in her eyes faded. They filled with tears. Her taut body went suddenly slack.

He said gruffly, without moving: "For God's sake, Diagulski, don't cry. I'm not asking you for anything—except to believe me. Whose side you're on doesn't matter to me as long as you don't get hurt."

"Why should I get hurt, Sinclair?"

"You're riding behind Wrightson, and Wrightson's riding for a fall."

She had turned her face from him to hide the tears. "I can't run, Sinclair," she said hoarsely. "I can't!"

He rose and stood over her, took her shoulders between his hands, and turned her almost roughly toward him.

"Look at me, Diagulski! You say you can't run—so look at me!"

Her eyes were tightly, stubbornly closed, her mouth slack and trembling. She looked even more worn and exhausted than she had in the Coolgardie room at Braund—younger, more vulnerable, more direly in need of help.

"I'm not asking you to run, my dear. I'm asking you to stop running, because you're heading into a kind of self-destruction. I love you and I can't stand the thought of what could happen to the rest of your life if you burn yourself out helping Wrightson."

"Don't, Sinclair. Please. I know."

He straightened, took a fresh cigarette and held it, looked again at the small, crouched figure—the veil of hair gleaming in the lamplight.

"You've had enough for one day. So have I. You'd better go and have some sleep. I'll get you a drink. Come on."

Then, as he stooped over her, her arms went around him, clinging fiercely and convulsively. Her face was wet against his belly. The surge of her surrender and her need scorched him.

"Please . . . please, Sinclair. If it's true you love me, don't send me away now."

The terry robe fell from her shoulders. She was naked and he bared his own body. Small, hard breasts pressed against his intolerably tumid sex. Panic clawed him as, in a moment of uncontrollable ecstasy, his loins gushed. Yet, even as the tide of release ebbed, he felt new potency gathering in him again. He unlocked the clinging arms and drew her upward. Then her mouth opened to his kiss and her body arched as he mounted her.

"Wait, my darling," she whispered, "wait for me. I can't bear to be alone anymore."

CHAPTER 19

MARY DALZIEL'S stock pony was tethered under the casuarina trees that gave shelter near the Bunyip Pool. George had felt sure that she would come to this place, but he had not realized how high the floodwaters had risen in the gorge. The Bondy was half a mile wide, booming and snarling as it bore its burden of silt and debris and shattered, gyrating logs through the stone narrows.

The pony was tethered, not hobbled. Mary Dalziel was not far away. He would wait. It was futile to search for her in the steady downpour that had cut visibility to less than a hundred yards. He would wait within sight of the pony, at least until the light began to fail. Then if he had guessed wrong, he would ride back to the boundary riders' hut and camp overnight. A great deal depended on the girl's state of mind, on how severely she had been shaken by the violence of events at the homestead and Patty Mountfort's suicide attempt, but the fact that she had troubled to tether her horse suggested that she was not wandering blindly in shock. Probably she was sheltering in some hideout in the rocks that she had discovered long ago.

Fifty yards from the she-oak grove and within sight of it, he found his own shelter in the lee of an undercut granite boulder. He dismounted, unsaddled, and tied his horse's reins to a sapling. He settled down to wait until Mary Dalziel came for the pony.

The inactivity was no trial of patience. He needed time to think, and plan what to do now that his obligation to Hamilton Wrightson was ended.

Huskisson could take over the sleuth's job, find the missing pieces, and fit them into the picture. He had government authority, men, and equipment at his command to solve what was in essence a grubby Australian problem in race relations created by the greed of four generations of exploiters, and perpetuated in the fifth generation by men like Wrightson in whom the lust for land-taking was still untempered by conscience. God knew there was nothing novel about it. It was paralleled all over the world.

He, George Galbraith, had no debts of loyalty to discharge. Callaghan, and the sick, parsimonious, and increasingly impotent service in which he held rank, could make no claim. And Wrightson had reneged by holding back on his bargain to put his cards on the table.

Curiosity, the old fascination with untangling the web of an intrigue, still endured in George—but it had become submerged by his determination to extricate Tamara Diagulski from her involvement with Wrightson before the oncoming crisis of violence broke the man. Diagulski's work load had brought her already to the brink of collapse. When the real crunch came, holding back on his bargain to put his cards on the table.

With the intense supplication of which only an agnostic is capable, George prayed that her sexual surrender had been more than an explosive release of tension, that she loved him as totally as he loved her. And that the truth of it was their future.

Mary Dalziel walked out of the stringybark scrub at four o'clock in the afternoon, barefoot, soaked to the skin, carrying her riding boots in one hand and dragging a dead perenty lizard with the other.

George waved as she approached but remained sitting on his saddle blanket under the overhang. She wore mud-spattered jodhpurs and a torn army shirt. The bruises on her face and throat were still livid against the streaked pallor of her skin. She looked down at him.

"So you did come back."

"Hullo, Mary. Of course I came back. I said I would. Didn't you think I'd keep my word?"

"Yes, but I didn't know when. Have they gone yet?"

"Who?"

"That horrible old policeman and the people who came to take Aunt Patty's body away."

"She wasn't dead. They took her to the hospital in Derby."

The girl's eyes widened, then narrowed.

"She wasn't breathing," she said.

"The doctor said she was. She was only unconscious. Anyway, what's this about the policeman? He's a very decent old boy. There's no reason why you should be scared of policemen. You haven't broken any law."

"They'd have taken me to the hospital with Aunt Patty, wouldn't they?"

"Oh, I don't know. Maybe. You were pretty scared and upset, weren't you?"

"I won't go, Mr. Sinclair. I won't. They can't make me. I won't go to the hospital again—ever."

So . . . she'd bolted out of fear that she would be sent to an institution if Patty Mountfort wasn't around to give her a home.

"Well," he said with feigned indifference, "if that's how you feel, it's all right with me. Come under out of the rain for a bit. Do you want a cigarette?"

She threw down the riding boots and dropped the lizard, and sat beside him. He lit a cigarette and handed it to her.

"What did you kill the young crocodile for, Mary?"

It worked. She laughed, choked on smoke, and laughed again.

"Gee, you *are* a newchum! It's not a crocodile. It's a perenty—a lizard. The blackfellows say it's good bush tucker. I was going to have it for my tea, roasted in the ashes."

"Back at your camp?"

Again suspicion—caution. If he was too damned clever, he'd lose her. She'd stop talking.

Against her silence he ran on: "Well, you needn't eat lizard tonight. I've got tins of meat and that unleavened bread you Australians call damper. I've even got some whisky in a flask. If you hadn't turned up today, I was going to camp in the old boundary hut and go on looking for you tomorrow."

"How did you know where to look?"

"Well-l, I didn't really know. But I remembered you'd told me when we were going to the Bunyip Pool that stockmen didn't come this way because it's too rough for cattle. Then I spotted your horse and just waited. He was tethered, so I knew you'd be back for him."

She nodded slowly, brows knit. "You couldn't find my camp, Mr. Sinclair. I could hide there for always if I wanted to. There's plenty of tucker in the bush—fish and nardoo and water-lily roots. You didn't really think it was a crocodile, did you? You were kidding, weren't you?"

He laughed uneasily. "Yes, it was only a joke. But it's true I'm a newchum. I don't know anything about bush tucker. I'd starve out here."

"You said you'd got some whisky. Can I have a nip now, please?"

"If you like. Don't you want something to eat first?"

"Whisky goes further on an empty stomach."

He unbuckled the saddle bag, rummaged, and drew out a stale damper, a can of beef, and finally his pocket flask. She tilted it against her mouth, swallowed, and shivered.

"You must be hungry. Have you eaten anything since you went bush?"

She shook her head. He opened the can with the

key soldered to its base and handed it to her with some bread.

"Don't you want some yourself?"

"Not yet. I had beans for lunch. There's another tin of meat for supper—or you could bake your crocodile!"

She giggled and began eating—at first slowly, chewing each mouthful painfully, then more voraciously as her stomach juices flowed. He watched in silence until the last crumb of food had disappeared. Then, looking away, he said: "By jove, you were hungry! Is your face still sore?"

"Not very, if I don't touch it."

"How did it happen?" A throwaway question, pitched as if he wasn't interested.

"Peter punched me."

"Peter? Peter Mountfort, you mean?"

"Yes. He's mad—much madder than me. I hate him."

George was careful to leave a reflective pause.

"Um. Can't say I blame you. Have another smoke?"

"Yes, please."

"Here . . . I didn't know Peter was home. He wasn't at the house when I left. Why on earth did he punch you, Mary?"

"Because he thought I was lying. I told him David Carlin had run away for good—took all his things and drove off. Peter went crazy. He grabbed me and shook me and kept asking where David had gone to, where was he hiding."

"But *why?* Surely Patty told him about David Carlin? Why should he punch *you?*"

"He hadn't been to Aunt Patty. He didn't want her to know he'd come looking for David. He didn't want her to know he'd been staying all the holidays on Silent Reach with Ben Burnie. He waited around at the windmill in the horse paddock until I went down to check the pump. Then he came out of the bush."

"Was Ben with him?"

"I didn't see him, but there were blackfellows with guns back in the bush. On horses."

"Then what happened?"

"He tore up to the house and went to see Aunt Patty in her room. After a while they had a frightful row, and shouted and screamed at each other. I heard them smashing things. Then Peter rushed out and jumped on his horse and rode off. I suppose he's gone to live at Silent Reach. I don't think he'll ever come home again."

"I see," George said. "Oh, well. He's gone. Poor Patty. It would have been a terrible shock. She must have swallowed all those pills to try to get some sleep."

Her look of contempt seared him. "She swallowed them to kill herself," Mary Dalziel said acidly. "You needn't soft-soap me. Aunt Patty's dead, isn't she? You're only telling me she's alive so I'll go back with you. But I won't. If Aunt Patty killed herself, it was her business. And it's my business if I want to stay here. I'm not doing any harm. Nobody's sending me to an asylum, that's all."

"Nobody's trying to send you to an asylum, Mary," he said, "and what I told you is true. Your Aunt Patty's in the hospital at Derby. She was alive when they took her away and I suppose she'll come back when she's better. But all right, it's your business if you want to stay in the bush. I can't make you go back with me. You're grown up."

She was watching him intently, searching his face as if for some sign of the shabby deceit that he knew he must contrive in the end in his attempt to persuade her.

"What are you going to do?"

"There's not much I can do, is there? I'll have to . . . tell the others I found you and you don't want to come back. I can't let them go on searching when I know you're safe, can I?"

"No, I suppose not. But if the police chase out here to bring me back, they won't find me."

"No. I realize that." He hesitated, weighing the words. "Look. If I could promise, really promise, that you could stay on at Wandonning, just be a caretaker and keep house for the new manager they'll have to hire instead of Carlin, if I could *promise* no one would try to send you away to a hospital, would you come back?"

She frowned. "You couldn't promise. You're not my guardian. Aunt Patty is."

"That's right. I can't promise now. But if I fixed it, absolutely for sure, that I could promise—then would you come back?"

The frown deepened.

"Maybe. I don't know. If you fixed it, I'd have to think."

He stood up. "Okay. I'll have to go, or I won't get to the house before dark."

"Aren't you going to camp at the boundary riders' hut?"

"Not now that I've found you. I have to tell Willy and the rest to call off the search—and start fixing it for you to come home. I'll leave the saddle bag. There's more food and cigarettes, and some aspirin if your face hurts. And here, the whisky. There's not much, so don't drink it all at once and don't lose my flask. It's my good-luck piece, but I'll lend it to you. I'll be back tomorrow. Keep a lookout for me."

She watched in silence while he saddled up. When he had mounted, she called: "I've made up my mind, Mr. Sinclair. If you can promise, I'll come home."

He lifted an arm in acknowledgment and rode away without looking back.

He let the horse set its own pace through the hock-deep mud of the old cattle path. Incredibly, the downpour had become even heavier as the afternoon advanced. Every hollow on the hillsides gushed storm-water. The dun-colored savannah shivered and wavered behind veils of rain. Within minutes of leaving the casuarina stand he had lost all sense of direction, but the horse seemed to know where it was going. When the ground flattened out below the bar, it broke into a shambling, uneven trot. The sodden saddle chafed his sweating thighs and buttocks. He itched with heat rash and every muscle ached. A profound de-

pression engulfed him. Disconnected fragments of recollection crackled in the circuits of his brain like static.

I can't run, Sinclair. . . .

He was clinging to the straw of a fool's hope. Diagulski wasn't in love with him, whatever the needs of
her frustrated body. She was in love with Wrightson's
ambition to wring something out of this damnable,
savage country. When it came to the moment of decision, she'd stick with Wrightson. She was liberated—
any man's equal in a battle to acquire possession and
power—and willing to destroy herself to prove it.

Possession! Christ, what did George Galbraith pos-
sess except skill in the noxious trade of sniffing out
dirty secrets in the back alleys of international traffick-
ing? Where did *his* future lie? What did *he* have to
offer a Tamara Diagulski except stud service?

Get out. Throw the bones of what he had learned
from the missionaries and Mary Dalziel to Huskisson.
That wrapped up the case against Silent Reach. Let
Huskisson fight the good fight to save the moneybags.
Let him play guard dog for the white man's loot and
fend off the dingoes—George Galbraith was out. And
tonight he must know, once and for all, if he was out
alone.

Random flashes of memory. . . .

Give us back our land you stole, Whitey.

*He's a man of broad vision. . . . He believes in his
country and its future.*

*I had the leases sewn up. . . . For ten years I had
the sense to keep my trap shut . . . sweat it out.*

*Frenchman's Bay's been a dead duck for more than
five years. . . . Find me a reef and the ground, and I'll
believe you know how the drift runs.*

*No gold, no uranium, no bauxite, no oil, nothing,
thanks be to God.*

The answer suddenly surfaced in his mind. It didn't
come as a revelation. The answer had been there all
the time, obscured by a fog of side issues. He was not
elated—merely relieved that he wouldn't have to con-
fess to Diagulski that behind his bluff he had not been
able to put a name to the treasure of Frenchman's
Bay and Silent Reach.

A department that works with the processes of elimination.

The stockmen's quarters and the house were in complete darkness. The front door stood open. He shouted above the pervading mutter of the rain: "Diagulski! Fitzpatrick! Hi, there, where are you?"

Rain. . . . Then one of the cattle dogs chained on the verandah of the quarters started to howl—a thin, soaring thread of melancholy woven into the night. The cold finger of premonition touched him. He groped for the light switch in the passageway and snapped it down. The globe glowed red for a second, then went out. No one had recharged the accumulators.

There had been a hurricane lamp on a table in the gallery the night before. He scraped a match, moved forward and touched the flame to the wick, stood listening intently. Nothing. No one was in the dining room—or the bedrooms. He checked, rapidly, methodically. So . . . try the kitchen block at the end of the covered walkway.

Chasser Fitzpatrick's body lay just inside the fly-screened door, arms flung wide and eyes staring. A shotgun blast had ripped away the side of his chest, but his heart had pumped on long enough to spray the ceiling with arterial blood.

CHAPTER 20

TWELVE hours after George Galbraith made contact with the Port Epsom Base on the Mayday frequency, Constables Fischer and Hogan with two young men from the Native Welfare Department crossed the Bondy in a flat-bottomed aluminum flood boat powered by an outboard motor. It was a tricky, hazardous operation—first towing the boat behind the Betts and Salinger truck on the badly washed-out beef

road, and then ferrying the river which was running at
twelve knots and eighteen feet above its flood banks.
On the homestead side it took an hour to dry out the
wiring of their trail bikes which had been submerged
when the boat shipped water after being rammed by
a tree trunk. It took another hour for the bikes to negotiate the samphire bog.

The land party reached its destination at ten thirty
in the morning and found a Bell helicopter with Conair markings parked in the horse paddock. It had
touched down half an hour earlier with Roger Huskisson and two Commonwealth plainclothes policemen.
The rain clouds over the Ferdinands had lifted enough
to let the chopper pilot sneak over the ridges at tree-
top altitude.

Huskisson hurried out of the house to greet the ar-
rivals.

"Good show, Wilf," he said laconically. "You made
time under these conditions. I'm sorry you had to do it
the hard way, but the weather gave us a break. Look
in at the kitchen. Unpleasant. I'm with Sinclair in the
dining room, taking him quietly. He's had a rough
night. Give us another few minutes and we'll call a
meeting to get things organized and moving. Meantime you men could do with a smoke-oh."

The skinhead glowered, sucked at the back of his
hand which he had scorched on the exhaust when
bulldogging his cycle out of a drainage table. He
jerked his head toward the kitchen.

"Shotgun? Was the Bertie Wooster right?"

Huskisson nodded. "Yes. Bush artillery. Messy."

"What about the girl—Dumski or whatever her
name is? Abducted or blown through? Could she have
used the gun?"

The old policeman's face was bleak.

"We haven't got the story yet, Fischer. We will."

"You bet we'll get it!" sneered Constable Wilfred
Fischer. He turned to join Hogan and the Native Welfare men who were stripping off their protective clothing on the porch.

Without raising his voice, Huskisson said: "Just a
minute, Constable Fischer."

"Yes, senior?"

"For your information and in the strictest confidence. It'll save your face. The Bertie Wooster is one of our mob—and very high powered at that. If you want to make friends in the right quarters, forget the wisecracks and just listen, eh?"

The expression on Fischer's face was the only spectacle that day from which Huskisson derived the slightest amusement.

George, slumped in a chair at the dining table, straightened his back painfully, as Huskisson reentered the room.

"The ground party," Huskisson said.

"Yes, I heard."

Huskisson sat down.

"Well, you've roughed it out. You got back here about eight twenty and found Fitzpatrick's body. The house and quarters were in darkness. There was no sign of Miss Diagulski—or the stockmen. When did you last see them?"

"They came for breakfast at six and left about half past to continue the search for Mary Dalziel. I followed an hour later. Diagulski and Fitzpatrick came down to the horse paddock to help me catch a mount. They were still there when I rode off."

"If you had a pretty good idea where you'd find the girl, why didn't you tell the stockmen?"

"Because I didn't want her disturbed any more than she already was. You know what her mental condition is like. I needed the information she had to give me."

"She gave you information?"

"Yes."

"What?"

George told him—in precise, measured, dead tones. As he talked, Huskisson studied him, trying to fathom what was going on behind those bloodshot, narrowed, and unwinking eyes. The man's whole face had changed. He seemed to have aged twenty years since their first meeting at Port Epsom. His skin, once ruddy with desert sunburn, was the color of yellow wax. But, good God, he'd shaved this morning! *Shaved!* Holy cow! Mad dogs and Englishmen!

Huskisson started, snapped his attention back to what George was saying.

"Repeat that. I was trying to work out something. Sorry."

"I said the girl didn't give any estimate of the size of the party with Peter Mountfort. She merely said there were armed blackfellows back in the scrub."

Huskisson grunted and sat for a moment, thinking it over. Then he asked: "Why did they have to kill Fitzpatrick? What point was there in raiding the homestead? Carlin was gone. You think the place hasn't been ransacked and valuables stolen."

"I believe," George said, "that Chasser Fitzpatrick was shot either because he resisted, or because he recognized one or more of the gang who had come to abduct Diagulski."

"Abduct? What makes you so certain the gang came to abduct her?"

George did not reply immediately. He rubbed his eyes and shook his head violently, as if fighting back drowsiness.

"Huskisson . . ."

"Yes?"

"I know Diagulski was abducted. I've got proof of it. Do you want to trade?"

The old policeman's face hardened.

"Trade what for what?"

"Information—for the promise that you will not, under any circumstances, take action on that information for at least seventy-two hours."

"What! If you've got information we can act on, it's vital we act on it immediately."

"No. It's vital you don't. Don't haggle. No embargo on action, no information. I mean that."

Huskisson made an angry gesture.

"Promises made under duress aren't binding, Galbraith. For God's sake, man, don't you think I'm in a better condition of mind to exercise discretion than you are!"

"Very well. Agree not to disclose the information

to any other person until the time's up. I can trust you to come to the same conclusion as me, but I can't trust someone with more rank not to overrule you."

Huskisson's smile was very slight indeed.

"All right, Galbraith. This conversation is post-dated seventy-two hours. If anybody gets clobbered for withholding information, it's you. Agreed?"

George said nothing. He took a single sheet of Wandonning Downs Pastoral Co. letterhead from the patch pocket of his safari jacket and laid it on the table. It had been folded once. On one side was typed: TO HAMILTON WRIGHTSON—URGENT. On the other side the message read:

It will cost you $500,000 to get her back alive. You'll get your orders care Derby P.O. next week. Follow them out exact. If you bring in the fuzz or try any tricks we'll send you her ears. You'll never find the rest of her.

MIDNIGHT RIDERS

Huskisson absorbed it, word by word.

"Where did you get this?"

"I found it on the table in the gallery. I didn't see it until this morning because the power had failed."

"Typewritten."

"Yes, here on the old Remington in Carlin's office at the store. I checked the typeface."

Huskisson nodded slowly and stood up.

"I go along with your reasoning. Ground parties couldn't operate in this weather. There's nothing we could do except put up spotter aircraft when the cloud clears. If by the millionth chance they did pick up a group of natives on the move—"

"There wouldn't be any evidence left by the time the police intercepted them," George broke in harshly. "Yes, you get me. There must be no move to alarm or press them until the ransom money has been paid and Tamara Diagulski has been released."

The old policeman was clearly troubled. As he started to reply, Constable Hogan came in without waiting for an answer to his rap on the door.

"Senior, about the photographs—"

Huskisson whirled on him. "Get to hell out of here and stay out until I call you, Hogan!" he roared. The man gaped and backed out. "And close the bloody door after you!" Then to George, quietly: "Two points. Can and will Wrightson pay half a million dollars in ransom? If he does, can we be sure that the girl will be released unharmed? You know a snatch doesn't always work that way."

George's voice was devoid of emphasis. "Wrightson can raise half a million easily and he'll pay it. I can assure you of that. And provided they haven't killed the girl already, I believe I'll have the means to assure that they'll release her unharmed."

"*You* have the means—*you* can assure? I don't understand you."

George put his hands on the table and rose painfully to his feet.

"You'll understand me in time, Huskisson," he said. "Do you know where Wrightson is now?"

"He was in Perth last night. We phoned him the news. If planes could get through this morning, he's probably in Derby or Port Epsom now, waiting for another break over the hills. Look, Galbraith, don't you think you'd better explain yourself? What sort of means have you got to assure anything?"

George turned away. "No. If I explained myself, you'd only have another problem on your mind—and one you can very well do without. Right now, I'm not up to an argument. I'm buggered. I've had no sleep in the last thirty-six hours, and damned little in the twenty-four before that. I propose to snatch enough to keep me going. Be a good chap and have someone wake me at three. I want to leave not later than half past."

"Leave! For where?"

"I want Mary Dalziel back tonight if possible. I hope Wrightson's here before I leave because I'd prefer . . . never mind. The point is . . . no, never mind the point either. I'll talk to you before I go. I'll make more sense then. Ease me through your pack of sleuths, will you? I'm feeling pretty brittle."

"All right. Do you want me to detail a couple of men to go after the Dalziel girl with you?"

"It's the last thing I want. If I'm alone, she'll show. If I'm not, she probably won't."

"You're pushing your luck, man, riding alone."

George sighed. For the first time, his voice revealed his desperate weariness. "Belt up, Huskisson. You've studied the pattern of their operations. At this minute there isn't an original Australian, friendly or hostile, within fifty miles of this house."

CHAPTER 21

ROGER HUSKISSON watched the ambulance helicopter rise from the horse paddock in a maelstrom of groundwater and grass blades, and tilt tipsily toward the rain clouds still boiling over the Ferdinands. The removal of Chasser Fitzpatrick's body, strapped in black plastic sheeting and blankets, and the embarkation of a stony-faced Mary Dalziel to be accommodated at Bauhinia Lodge until other arrangements could be made, had relieved the immediate pressures, but Huskisson knew only too well that the respite was temporary. The pile of telegrams, phone messages, and departmental memoranda brought in by the ambulance pilot presaged an invasion of officious top brass and, worst of all, reporters.

The police routine was fully launched. Photographs of the corpse had been taken and sent for processing, measurements made and noted, a pro-forma search conducted for discharged cartridge cases and the murder weapon. One of the Darwin men had dusted the house for fingerprints. Constable Hogan, with the aid of a Native Welfare man who spoke a little schoolboy German, was conducting a painfully slow interrogation of Willy Schrieber who had ridden in early that morning with the news that the two Chileans had linked up with the foreman, Barratt, but all three of them had been cut off by floodwater at the Landy Creek mustering yards, fifteen miles west.

Willy Schrieber was emphatic that he had not seen Miss Diagulski or a party of aborigines, and he did not think the others had. The Landy mustering yards were now an island. The men would soon need food. Huskisson decided that Hogan could organize a relief party after he had extracted what scant information the young German could give him.

George Galbraith returned to the house ten minutes after the big helicopter's departure. Huskisson met him on the porch.

"No trouble?"

"No. Her mind was made up and she rode fast."

"I wondered."

"So did I," George said. "I felt an utter bastard telling her that she could talk things over with her Aunt Patty when I knew her Aunt Patty died last night. Wrightson will have to make proper arrangements about that girl. Do you know why he didn't come in on the chopper?"

Huskisson hesitated as if choosing his words.

"Yes. We've got problems, Galbraith. It's a longish story. Better sit down."

"Why?"

"I said it was a longish story. Taking last things first, Hamilton Wrightson is still in Perth. I have the message here. I've just finished reading it. He collapsed at Perth airport this morning and was taken to the hospital where he was admitted to the intensive-care unit. Stroke, heart attack, or general collapse from strain. They don't know yet."

George's visible reaction—or lack of it—was so unexpected that Huskisson felt a stab of alarm. George simply sat down—in exaggerated slow motion. Not a muscle in his face twitched. He didn't even blink. Again in exaggerated slow motion, he lit a cigarette with a rock-steady hand.

"Can I see the message?"

"Here." Huskisson passed it to George who read it, nodded, and passed it back.

"From Doc Margan, eh? Deputy Managing Director, Technical. I hadn't realized he was so high up in the Conwright hierarchy. Silly of me. A down-the-liner would hardly be in on Frenchman's Bay, would he?"

Huskisson stared. "In on what? What are you talking about?"

"Sorry. Just thinking aloud. That's *my* longish story. After you, old man. But first, do you know Margan's ETA?"

"No. I presume he'll have a seat on the Bell with the pilot who's coming in to fly Fitzpatrick's aircraft out."

"I see. Now let's have the first things first."

"Are you feeling ill, Galbraith? You look a bit below par."

"I can't imagine why." It was sarcasm without intonation, doubly bitter.

"Sorry, I didn't mean it that way," Huskisson said placatingly. "I thought you might like more sleep. For the moment there's not much we can do."

"No. Apart from being rather old and tired and triste, I'm perfectly all right, thank you. No stroke, heart attack, or collapse is imminent. Go ahead with the rest of the news."

Huskisson fidgeted. This preternatural calm bothered him. The man had so far voiced no word of regret or outrage at Chasser Fitzpatrick's murder nor, oddly, had he shown concern for Tamara Diagulski. His only expressed anxiety was for Mary Dalziel. And now he had not batted an eyelid at the bomb-shell news of Wrightson's illness. George Algernon Sinclair Galbraith's strange personality had been transformed into an even stranger shape by the events of the last few days. He was not the same supercilious, self-assured, absurdly youthful-looking man who had written acute and convincing intelligence reports for Wrightson. Nor was he the cynically amiable agent who had volunteered information, promised co-operation, and offered to withdraw gracefully from the field if the authorities wanted him out of the way in a politically tricky situation. That man had been formidable enough but the man sitting across the table was a dangerous man. Roger Huskisson's career in undercover police work on three continents spanned more than thirty years. He recognized dangerous men, whatever their affectations and whatever side they were on, when he encountered them.

"Apart from what's happened here, Galbraith," he said, "things have been moving at a hell of a pace elsewhere. What started as a campaign of sabotage against Wrightson—a private grudge fight—has now triggered off acts of sabotage against white property owners all over the country. Groups of armed aborigines have started terrorizing isolated homesteads in the Northern Territory and western Queensland, and there have been riots and demonstrations in some mining settlements. You foresaw almost from the outset that the trouble wouldn't be confined to Wrightson's enterprises—because nothing succeeds like success. The vendetta against Conwright has become a model for Black Power action elsewhere."

"Clever me," George murmured. "What have the alert forces of law and order done about it?"

Huskisson bit his lip—hard.

"The forces of law and order," he continued in a somewhat strangled voice, "acting on your reports to Wrightson, have obtained documentary and other evidence that proves that a Black Power organization does exist in this country and is stepping up its activities. The latest development in Canberra"— Huskisson tapped his sheaf of messages—"is that Max Burnie, junior, and two Singaporeans at the National University have been arrested and charged with the illegal possession of explosives and firearms which were discovered in a Commonwealth police raid on a Belconnen house rented by a group of Asian and African students. It would seem that they were caught with their pants down, because as well as explosives the haul of paper was sensational. Further arrests and more serious charges are pending. Other raids have been made by police and security men in Perth and Darwin, but I've not yet heard results."

George Galbraith butted his cigarette, selected another from the packet, examined it, lit it, and blew smoke.

"No comment, Galbraith?"

"Of course. Damned good show—particularly if they can persuade one of the young bastards to sing before a civil-liberties lawyer gets to him. But it doesn't do much to solve our immediate local problem, does it?"

"In the long haul, I think it could provide a complete solution to all our problems."

"For yours, maybe. But for mine there's no long-haul solution. It's got to be short haul—very short haul indeed."

Huskisson pondered a moment and said: "Yes. But before we come to that, there are other developments you should know about. The Ford station wagon that clipped you has been traced. It is owned by Ted Burnie, the mechanic at Jilgeric Downs native cooperative, who claims that it was stolen, or borrowed without his permission, last month. The West Australian police are going through Jilgeric with a fine-tooth comb right now. They've turned up the fact that Ted Burnie has purchased three other good secondhand vehicles from Geraldton dealers in the past two years and paid cash for them. He claims to have sold them to other natives without the formality of transferring the registrations."

George eased himself in his chair, leaned back, and studied the ceiling. "Ah, yes," he said. "Edward Burnie. The Burnie boy of average intelligence and placid temperament. Tell me, Huskisson, has the great Canberra crackdown implicated Max Burnie, senior, or number one son, Ben?"

"No. Not so far."

"Peter Mountfort?"

"Canberra hasn't yet found anything that puts the finger on him. Perth detectives have been checking him out. The university people describe him as a brilliant anthropology student with a one-track mind who crashes every subject except his speciality. He hasn't attended lectures or tutorials for two terms and his associates deny any knowledge of his whereabouts.

Mary Dalziel's story to you is the only evidence that
he has contact with the Burnies."

"Have you made any progress in tracing the money
in Carlin's car?"

Huskisson scowled. George had touched a sore
point.

"None at all," he replied. "Carlin flew the station
Cessna with Mrs. Mountfort to Kununurra to buy
booze. Otherwise he doesn't seem to have been off
this property since the Fitzroy Crossing picnic race
meeting in September. Either the head stockman or
one of the station hands or jackeroos has been making the weekly run into Port Epsom by road for mail
and stores."

"Nothing has been turned up at the airstrips?"

"What do you mean?"

"Did Carlin lodge a flight plan at Port Epsom for
the trip to Kununurra?"

"Yes, he did. The air regulations require a flight
plan to be lodged for trips of more than fifty miles.
Station people bend the rules a bit, but not too far or
too often."

"Naughty," murmured George.

"Eh?"

"One of the priests at the Barramundi Bay Mission
told me Carlin made an emergency landing on their
strip only a few weeks ago because he'd run out of
fuel on a return trip to Darwin. His explanation was
that he'd had a heavy session the night before and
forgot to check his tanks. He looked pretty frayed so
they persuaded him to stay at the monastery overnight."

For a fraction of a second Huskisson's face registered surprise and disbelief, then he leaned across the
table and said softly: "Carlin didn't put down at Darwin or any other government airport within Cessna
range of here. That's been established. So he must
have been visiting other station properties and, shit,
that really complicates it!"

"Are you open to suggestions?" George asked.

The old policeman glared at him, then stifled his

surge of irritation. "Proper or improper?" he demanded.

Remotely, George smiled. Some of the masked tension in him seemed to ease.

"It would be interesting," he said, "if your troops could ferret out how much aviation fuel Carlin bought in the last three or four months—both from his ordinary source of supply, which I'd take to be Betts and Salinger, and elsewhere in these parts. It's my hunch that you'll find the Wandonning Cessna has put up many more flying hours than are recorded in its logbook. Also, if you examine that plane you'll find that it has been modified to accommodate an extra fuel tank in the back-seat passenger space, which would increase its flying range by fifty or sixty percent. And, on another tack—"

"Hang on, man." Huskisson held up a hand. "Not so fast. One tack at a time. Suppose your hunch works out, where does it get us?"

"If Carlin was flying long distances secretly, he was flying for an illegal purpose. So then I arrive here and start asking questions about Silent Reach and the Burnies. He loses his nerve and bolts—with fifty thousand dollars. It's conceivable that the money was his share of the take on several deals, but it's unlikely because, first, the sum's too large to be a go-between's slice and, second, Peter Mountfort is so steamed up that he comes looking for Carlin with a gang of bully boys. When he hears Carlin has bolted he blows his stack and beats up Mary Dalziel because she can't tell him where he's gone. That's a credible reaction in a psychopath. He storms up and confronts his mother, probably thinking she may have an idea of Carlin's whereabouts. We'll never know exactly what happened between the pair of them, but by now he's totally committed to his lunatic ideal and possibly blurts out the truth. It's a side issue. The crucial point is this: Carlin absconded with money that had been entrusted to him to make, or more likely to complete, a purchase for the Silent Reach gang. He probably acted as a go-between on previous occasions. You don't get two guesses at what sort of shopping he was doing."

Huskisson's leathery face creased in concentration. "One objection, Galbraith," he interrupted. "You can't carry much shopping of that size in a Cessna 170 with an extra fuel tank in the back seat."

"He wouldn't do any actual carrying. He was far too nervous a nellie. I think he made contacts, paid over money, arranged places and dates of delivery, passed messages. It's a pure guess, but I suspect the goods are bought and supplied illicitly from Indonesian sources, and are landed from a fishing boat at a pickup point somewhere along the coast. Whether you've got the resources to test that theory, I don't know."

Huskisson laughed—obviously without feeling at all amused.

"You know about our resources all right," he growled. "Well, did your Barramundi Bay caper turn up anything else?"

"Yes," said George flatly. "I know how Max Burnie gets money when he needs it. The good missionaries seem to know too, but they don't feel disposed to take a hand in the game."

Huskisson stiffened with shock. He stood up abruptly. George watched him, eyes narrowed, until he spoke. "I'm sorry, Galbraith, but I can't open my raincoat this time. I'm under orders not to discuss that aspect of the case. I don't agree with the orders but I have to obey. I'm truly sorry because I realize that we wouldn't have got any distance in this business without your spadework and cooperation."

George rose, too.

"Don't feel badly about it, Huskisson," he said. "I understand your position. I've also served my time in resources diplomacy. But now I'm out. My interest in this business is confined to one single objective. If Tamara Diagulski is still alive—and I believe she is —I want to assure that she stays alive and is released unhurt."

"Good God, Galbraith, don't you think that's our objective, too!"

"I don't doubt it for a moment. But I don't think Diagulski's safety has top priority with the people who give you your orders. It ranks behind what you'd call the national interest, doesn't it?"

Huskisson flushed, opened his mouth to reply, then changed his mind.

"Wrightson's collapse," George went on, "is an utter bloody disaster. If he's seriously ill he won't even be told of the ransom demands, let alone be able to make arrangements to meet them. So my plan won't work—unless you know someone else willing to put up half a million at short notice to bail the girl out. A humane federal treasurer, perhaps?"

Huskisson ignored the jibe.

"What was your plan anyway?"

"Simple enough. The sort of deal they're probably used to swinging with little gentlemen over the water who are prepared to supply consumer commodities such as thermite charges, machine pistols, and maybe a few surplus FN rifles mislaid in Vietnam by our great and powerful friends. Half the cash on confirmation of order, half on delivery of the goods under security conditions satisfactory to both sides. It's an arrangement that usually works when the parties are satisfied with what they each stand to gain. I know that from past experience."

Huskisson moved uncomfortably.

"We shouldn't hold back the ransom note any longer, Galbraith. With Wrightson out, the top brass will need all the time they can get to work out alternatives."

George said, after a moment's consideration: "Tell you what, Huskisson. I'll release you from our gentleman's agreement if you'll do me a favor."

"What?"

"Use your police radio to contact Doc Margan urgently. Ask him to give me authority to use the Excon helicopter and its pilot for half a day. If Margan's already on the way, I'll ask him myself when he arrives."

"The pilot would have to lodge a flight plan."

"Yes. Cross-country from here to Barramundi Bay. A terrain study, shall we say?"

Alarm flared in Huskisson's eyes. "Jesus, man, you can't come at that! You said yourself they'd do away with the girl if they thought we were on their tails! I agreed to hold the ransom note—"

George's restraint cracked.

"Don't be a fucking fool!" he spat. "I won't be flying within twenty miles of them. What do you think I am?!"

"Do you mean you know where they are?"

"No. But I'm bloody certain I know where they're not!"

CHAPTER 22

It was important to strike the right balance of ambiguity. George read the final draft again.

Dear Father Bridges,

I am addressing this to you personally rather than to Father Valdera because it is in no sense an official communication and I hope you will be kind enough to destroy it after reading it. During my brief stay at Barramundi Bay I obtained the impression that your community has for many years had more than a casual concern for the welfare of your neighbors, the Burnie family. I am venturing to write this on the assumption that my impression was correct.

Since coming to Wandonning Downs I have learned that certain younger members of the family are in serious trouble with the authorities and that as soon as the station roads are trafficable again, police and Native Welfare officers will be visiting Silent Reach homestead to make inquiries. I am sure you will agree that the Burnies would appreciate support in their difficult situation, and the presence of reputable witnesses when the official visitation takes place.

I hope that you are not embarrassed by my indiscretion in imparting this information to you without official authority to do so.

Please convey my respects to Father Valdera.

With thanks for your recent hospitality and help,
Yours very sincerely,

They couldn't very well ignore it. They were involved, whether they liked it or not.

George signed and folded the letter, enclosed it in an airmail envelope endorsed *Urgent and Personal.* and tucked it into his shirt pocket. Then he made a final check of the contents of his airline bag, slung the strap over his shoulder, and walked slowly down to the horse paddock where the little Conair Bell had landed an hour previously. Huskisson, who had been waiting at the stockmen's quarters, fell into step beside him.

"No complications?" George asked.

"No. Margan gave you the authority to use the machine without questions. The pilot's cleared for Barramundi Bay and return. That's what you wanted, isn't it?"

"Yes. That's where he's going."

Huskisson coughed self-consciously.

"I don't know exactly what you've got in mind, Galbraith, but I've a damned shrewd suspicion. You're taking one hell of a risk again."

"Visiting my missionary friends? Come off it, old man."

Huskisson shot him a sour glance. "Am I expected to believe that?"

"Yes—officially. That's what I've told you—and the chopper's cleared for Barramundi Bay."

"And return."

"Quite."

"I can't guarantee to give you a quick backup if you get into trouble, Galbraith. With Wrightson out of it, I don't know what sort of decisions are being taken up the line."

"None," said George, deadpan. "They're appointing a subcommittee to draw up the terms of reference for a board of inquiry to be convened to make recommendations to the minister. No provision was made in the estimates for a slush fund to meet terrorists' ransom demands. Or didn't you know?"

"That's not fair, Galbraith."

"I didn't realize this was the sort of game you had to play fairly, old boy. I've no intention of waiting around for the experts to arrive and fuck things up."

"And that's pure bloody arrogance!"

"It's pure bloody experience," George said equably. "I call to mind a story that Chasser Fitzgerald told me on the flight from Halley's Circle to the mission—the one about the army and the emus."

"The what?"

"According to Chasser, some years ago there was a bad drought in the sheep country, driving a plague of emus down south to invade the wheat areas. They played merry hell with the crops. The experts decided to mount the biggest emu shoot in history. They called out the army with Lewis guns and Lee Enfields. End result—five dead emus and five hundred thousand empty cartridge cases. Not to be beaten by a bunch of featherbrained birds, the experts planned to build an emu-proof fence. It cost God knows what and took two years to complete, by which time the drought had broken and nature had restored the balance. Was that a true story, or was poor old Chasser romancing?"

Huskisson did not reply. He knew that, give or take a few emus or a few thousand cartridge cases, it was true. He also knew that however much one admired George Galbraith's talents, there were times when it was damnably difficult to like him.

The helicopter pilot, a raw-boned veteran of twenty-six who had learned his trade in gunships over the Mekong Delta, was standing by his machine voicing to Constable Fischer views on wogs, gooks, kikes, and nigras—views with which the energetic young arm of the law emphatically agreed.

"Bradley's the name, isn't it?" Huskisson asked.

"Joe," said the pilot, redeploying his wad of gum. "Sho't fo' Joab."

"This is Mr. Sinclair."

"Uh-huh. The Doc said it was a Mistuh Sinclair. Happy to drive you, suh."

"Happy to have you drive me, Joe. Barramundi Bay. Got the map sheets?"

"Sho' have. Wanna look?"

"Later on will do. All systems go?"

"Yes, *suh!*"

George turned to the old policeman and held out his hand.

"Even if the emu shooters arrive, be a good chap and persuade them to hasten slowly. I need a couple of days. By the way, I've left a note for you on the lowboy in my bedroom. Covers a contingency. Eyes only."

Huskisson compressed his lips. "I hope to God you're doing the right thing," he said in an undertone.

"I'm doing the only thing." George turned to the pilot. "Okay, Joe, let's get cracking."

"Have a good trip, sir," said Constable Fischer diffidently.

George's mouth twitched slightly.

"Thank you, constable—kind of you."

Joe looked at the small circle George had drawn with pencil on the plastic map guard, nodded, and reached to reset his compass.

"No problem to that, suh. Mill, and bull corral. Right?"

"Right," said George. "Have you flown over this country before?"

"Nope. Never so far north. I worked a season on seismics outa Excon Four. Contract's up. Woulda been stateside now if the big chief hadn't gotten this coon trouble and needed choppers on standby. One season's enough in these parts. No tail worth chasin'—and they ration the booze."

"Check. Were you in on the search for those two fellows who went missing from Excon Four?"

"Uh-huh. Lousy way to die, a spear in your back, but I guess it was better'n what we'd thought—thirst."

It took a moment to penetrate. George leaned sideways.

"Sorry," he said, raising his voice and gesticulating. "Ears. What did you say?"

"I said a spear through your back is a lousy way of dyin'. They never found the body of the second guy, Jack Lightning, but I reckon he musta got his the same way."

"Yes," said George through his teeth. "Yes. I reckon he did. Were you around when they found the young chap?"

"Sho' was. Threw snakes eyes and got the job of carryin' the bag to Meekatharra. When they have been two, three weeks in the water they ain't no bunch of roses. No, suh!"

George closed his eyes.

They'd found Nathan Ebbet's body before he had arrived in Port Epsom, and yet the discovery was classed as something he didn't need to know.

Well, what odds? It didn't matter what they hadn't told him. Not any more.

Thirty minutes after takeoff, Joe Bradley said: "I calculate that the mill an' corral oughta be comin' up on two seventy, suh. Want I go down and yo' take a look?"

"Yes."

"Homestead's jest next valley over—say five miles. Wanna look there, too?"

"Negative, Joe. We can't see them, they can't see us. Right?"

Joe Bradley shot a sidelong glance at his passenger and cocked an eyebrow.

"Okay. You're callin' 'em, boss. This wind they won't hear us, neither."

He put the little helicopter down to fifty feet and hovered. His map navigation had been commendably precise. Dead ahead, a small branding pen and windmill crouched on the narrow-gutted valley floor, lapped by a rising tide of kangaroo grass. There were no signs of life, animal or human. George took the letter to Father Bridges from his pocket and clipped it onto the pilot's map holder.

"Thanks, Joe," he said. "Nice going. If you'll deliver that to the Barramundi Bay Mission, you've wrapped up your part of the job. This is where I get off."

Bradley almost choked on his wad of gum. His eyeballs bulged.

"Get off! Godamighty what's eatin' you, mac? Not *here!*"

"That's what the man said, Joe. Can you set the chopper down, or do you want me to use a stirrup?"

"What man said yo' was to get off?"

"My boss man. General Callaghan. You were briefed, weren't you?"

"Doc Margan briefed me to fly a passenger to Barramundi Bay, an' maybe look at some country on the way if he wanted. He never said you was no G man."

"Then," said George in his most penetrating voice, mouth against Bradley's ear, "some cocksucking sonofabitch has fucked things up. Check it out when you get back from the mission with the old state cop who saw me off. But for Christ's sake, don't go shooting your mouth off to anybody else. Can you set me down without the winch?"

Joe Bradley frowned in perplexity for about five seconds. Then his jaws began to move again in the rhythm of rumination. Half a minute later he put the Bell down, in the center of the branding pen.

I'm bloody certain I know where they're not. . . . The boast was now a wager he couldn't afford to lose.

Max Burnie's house could be observed clearly only from the crest of the crumbling basalt ridge that towered over it to north and east. It was screened on all sides by overgrown hedges of bauhinia, oleander, and bamboo, set like levees to protect the home pound against the flood of somber cypress and cabbage gums flowing out of the hills.

George Galbraith lay on his belly for a while, studying the layout through a pair of race glasses he had found in Patty Mountfort's bedroom and appropriated against emergency, together with a five-inch flick knife from one of the stockmen's bunkside cabinets.

The Silent Reach homestead was small, uncompromisingly square, weathered, and primitive. Its exterior walls were of wedge-split or pit-sawn planks, unpainted and bleached to silvery gray. It was roofed in iron and shaded by old mango and tamarind trees. Behind it were five outbuildings, walled like the house but roofed with sheets of bark.

Sector by sector, George scanned the tiny complex. The only sign of habitation was a filmy smudge of wood smoke rising at the rear. He had been watching for an hour. His journey from the stockyard, following a switchback cattle track, had taken five hours—two of them spent wading knee-deep in the henna-colored mud of a paperbark swamp. The experience had shaken him. For the first time in his life, he was traveling alone and on foot in unfamiliar, confusing, and difficult terrain, with no way of retreat and no means of summoning help. His relief at regaining firm ground had been tempered by several nauseous minutes occupied in removing with a lighted cigarette end a dozen black, looping leeches that had attached themselves to his crotch.

A final sweep with the glasses. No movement. The westering sun burned through his shirt. He wriggled into shadow and stood up slowly. From the airline bag he took a clean jockstrap, canvas shoes, and a pair of slacks.

The comfort of clean clothes and dry shoes heartened him. He slipped the flick knife into his pocket and crammed the little pistol into one of his discarded boots, which he wrapped in the muddy shorts and stowed in the airline bag.

Blue slacks with knife-edge creases. Would sartorial elegance add to the surprise of his arrival at Silent Reach? A good deal might depend on surprise.

George slung the bag over his shoulder and began his descent to the homestead.

A picket gate opened to a narrow path of brown pebbles, curving between rain-battered borders of salvia, petunias, flame nettles, and crotons. Somebody loved this flower garden and spent time cultivating it. Was it Max Burnie, the batty old man who hunted wild cattle? Or Ellie, his ailing black wife who was a devout Catholic, a triple-certificated nurse, and the mother of three sons who were at least accessories to murder, arson, and kidnapping? Or Alison, the intelligent and cooperative girl who contemplated entering the convent when her mother died?

The verandah deck was scrubbed and spotless. Ferns and orchids in wire baskets hung in profusion from the peeled sapling posts that supported the roof. George's rubber-soled shoes made no noise as he approached the entrance to the breezeway.

He rapped loudly on the wall and called: "Hullo, there! Hullo! Anybody at home?"

There was no answer. He knocked and called again, even more loudly. Then a bell like a small school bell sounded in the house—a single stroke that bled away into silence.

With a prodigious effort of will, George turned his back on the breezeway entrance and stood at the edge of the verandah, looking without really seeing toward a patch of cropped buffalo grass under one of the tamarind trees. A little wicker table and a single sea-grass chair had been set out on it.

A minute passed . . . two. He sensed someone watching and turned his head to find himself staring down the barrels of a 12 gauge shotgun. Behind them was a dusky, heavy-featured face and two terrified brown eyes.

"Come off it, young lady," he said in a tone of mild protest. "That thing could go off and you wouldn't want to kill me. I'm not a bushranger."

"What do you want?"—almost a whisper.

"If you're Alison Burnie, I want to see your dad on business."

"Where are the others?"

"What others? Oh, I see. . . . There aren't any others. I'm on my own. *Are* you Alison Burnie?"

"Yes."

"Father Bridges was telling me about you only the other day."

The barrels wavered and sagged.

"You're from the mission?"

"No. Not exactly."

"Then who are you?"

"My name's Sinclair—George Sinclair, and I want to see your dad on important business."

"Dad's not here"—then, hastily—"but he'll be back any time now. He's only down at the harness shed."

"Good. I'll wait. Is it okay if I sit out there under the tree till he comes?"

"Where's your horse?"

"Haven't got a horse. I walked."

The gun barrels flicked upward, so fast that he flinched.

"For heaven's sake, Alison Burnie," he said in schoolmasterish accents, "put that gun away before you have an accident with it. Shooting people, even by accident, won't do you much good if you want to enter a convent, will it?"

The effect of his words was startling. The girl's face crumpled with consternation. One hand flew to her lips.

"Oh, no!" Her voice dropped to a half whisper. "Sister Antony promised me! She promised she wouldn't say anything. . . . Is that why you've come to see Dad? Oh, please, please don't. He isn't a Catholic. He'll only go mad. He'll blame Mum—and Mum's so sick. Please!"

Tears welled in her eyes. The wide mouth drooped and quivered. She dropped to her knees on the sanded planks, covering her head with her hands. The preposterous notion that he was some sort of ecclesiastical official come to discuss with her father the possibility of her entering a convent had thrown her into blubbering panic. Then, as he stared amazedly, a memory shutter clicked.

Alison Burnie was the girl with the crocodile-hide satchel who had sat beside him on the flight from Melbourne to Perth.

"Forget it, Alison," he said. "I haven't come about that. Our business is altogether different. I absolutely promise I won't tell him what I overheard Father Valdera say."

George had a very persuasive manner with young females when he tried. She dropped her hands.

"Who are you, mister? How did you get here?"

"It's a long story, Alison—and it was a long walk. Will it be all right if I sit under the tree until—"

The bell rang again. This time it was muted almost instantly. Alison Burnie bounded to her feet, rubbing a forearm across her eyes.

"Gee, that's Mum. She wants to know who it is. She'll be scared. I've got to go. What shall I tell her?"

George smiled reassuringly. "It's perfectly all right, Alison. My name really is Sinclair and I really have come to see your father on business. I'll explain to your mother myself if you—"

"No. No, please. Mum . . . Mum can't talk to anyone. It's . . . she's . . . she's got a cancer in her throat."

The girl vanished into the dark of the corridor. George stood for a moment thinking, trying to adjust his mind to anticlimax. Then he walked heavily along the verandah toward the sea-grass chair under the tamarind tree. On the way he paused to pick up the shotgun. When he broke it, he found it was unloaded.

He felt a little sick—queasy with the growing suspicion that his calculations of the probabilities had all been disastrously astray.

Even at first sight Maxwell Burnie was, as Father Bridges had said, a memorable character. He was a man of extraordinary physique—abnormally tall and abnormally thin and long legged. He walked with a peculiarly stiff and jerking gait like a crane. George judged him to be about seventy years old. His narrow face was dominated by a great, bony, jutting nose and underpinned by a small, jutting chin over leathery dewlaps. He wore the uniform of a bygone generation of Australian bushmen—white moleskin trousers tucked into rawhide boots, a faded tartan shirt, and a stockman's hat of great antiquity.

George rose from the sea-grass chair and found

himself scrutinized from above by a pair of large, golden eyes—mild, wary, and all seeing like those of a very experienced billy goat. George was six feet tall, but Max Burnie topped him by a good five inches.

"Mr. Max Burnie? My name is Sinclair." The old man made no acknowledgment. "I apologize if my arrival alarmed your wife and daughter. I expected to find you at home."

A slow, completely indifferent appraisal. "I am at home—and I'll come to the point. We don't welcome uninvited visitors on this property. How did you get here?"

The voice was deep, controlled, and accentless—the voice of an educated man, not a bush hatter. Max Burnie's concern for the education of his children was understandable. George pulled himself together.

"Actually," he said, "I came by helicopter. And, as I told your daughter, on foot."

A slight frown. "You mean you made a forced landing on my property."

"No, sir. I had my pilot set me down at the stockyard on the other side of the ridge, and I followed a cattle track here to the homestead."

The goat eyes looked even milder—and even more wary.

"What did you say your name was?"

"Sinclair."

"Well then, Mr. Sinclair, I'll give you a bit of friendly advice. Follow the track back again and have your pilot pick you up. We've got no business together —whoever you are and whatever your proposition. You're a trespasser and I'd prefer you to get off my place of your own accord peaceably. I don't want to have my men run you off."

The extraordinary thing about the old man, George thought, was his self-possession. His indifference, to whatever the apparition of an uninvited visitor in pale blue slacks might portend, was total. He was concerned only to evict the intruder as quickly as possible. He was not even curious—and that lack of curiosity was disturbing. If genuine, it implied that Max Burnie knew nothing of the murder of Chasser Fitz-

patrick or the abduction of Tamara Diagulski; con-
ceivably he knew nothing of the activities of the
Midnight Riders, either. But surely that was absurd.
It had to be absurd!

"I'm afraid, Mr. Burnie," George said, "I've got
bad news for you. About your sons."

A flash of alarm—or had he imagined it? Certainly
no more than a flash.

"What about my sons?"

"May I suggest you sit down? This may be a
shock."

Max Burnie straightened himself stubbornly. "Get
on with it."

"Very well. What I'm going to tell you will be confirmed by the police when they arrive here in a day or
two. And by the missionaries at Barramundi Bay.
You—"

"I said get on with it. What's happened? Say your
piece."

George shrugged. "Max has been arrested in
Canberra and charged with sedition and the illegal
possession of arms. Ted is being questioned by the
police about sabotage. Ben and Peter Mountfort are
wanted for the murder of a man named Fitzpatrick
and the abduction of a woman named Tamara
Diagulski from Wandonning Downs homestead."

For a moment the goat eyes blazed with outraged
disbelief. Then the flame went out and the old man
staggered as if someone had dealt him a rabbit punch
from behind. He groped for the support of the garden
table and folded his body into the chair with a shuddering expulsion of breath. George noticed his hands
for the first time. They were pale and papery and hid-
eously deformed by rheumatoid arthritis.

George said quietly: "Can I get you something, Mr.
Burnie—water, whisky? I have a flask."

"No."

"I'm sorry I had to break it that way, but you
didn't leave me much option."

"No. Who are you? If you're not police, why have
you come here?"

"I'm not police. You could call me . . . a private detective, I suppose. I've come to try to do a deal."

"What sort of deal? Who with?"

"With Ben. If he agrees to let the girl go unhurt, he'll get the ransom money under conditions that'll give him a chance of leaving the country by the same means and route he uses to bring in guns and explosives."

Max Burnie stared into space, then slowly wagged his head from side to side. George could read nothing in the deeply lined face. The shock had passed. The old man's resilience was uncanny.

"Guns and explosives, eh?"

"How did you think the boys were spending your money, Mr. Burnie? On demonstrations and pussy propaganda?"

"What money?"

"Your money—the money you've been giving them."

Max Burnie frowned for a moment, then chuckled —a chuckle of amused contempt.

"You're a piss-poor detective, Sinclair, to fly that kind of kite. I've never given my sons money since they finished their schooling. I don't make money on this place, so I couldn't give them any even if I wanted to. The bullocks I turn off pay for the lease and a few station stores. I don't hire hands, so I don't pay wages. My wife's people work the cattle how I tell them to. Otherwise they have the run of their tribal country as they always have. I've got no use for money."

Don't challenge him on that pack of lies! Softly, softly!

"Ben has a use for money. Why else do you think he kidnapped the girl?"

The old man's lips tightened.

"I don't believe he kidnapped any girl. Ben's a bad bastard. That's no news to me. I've never had any time for him since his balls dropped. But he's not a bloody fool."

George said harshly: "If he didn't kidnap her, his gang did. They left a ransom note. That's why I'm here. Hamilton Wrightson's willing to play ball. He hasn't shown the note to the police. He'll pay half a million in cash to get the girl out safely before the police move in. Ben would have time to give them the slip."

Some part of it got through. Max Burnie's mouth sagged with astonishment. He put his crippled hands on the table and leaned forward.

"Hamilton Wrightson will pay half a million! Suffering mother of Jesus! Did you say *Hamilton Wrightson?"*

"Yes. The girl is Wrightson's—"

The old man made a strange, choking noise in his throat. Then he threw back his head and bellowed with laughter—bellowed until he gasped helplessly for breath. George felt an ice-cold lump congeal in his belly. Salinger had said it all. Burnie was a raving madman.

"Mr. Burnie," he pleaded when the paroxysm passed, "I must get in touch with Ben. Don't you understand? You've got to help me!"

The long body reared up from the chair with agonized effort. "I can't help you. I haven't seen Ben in four months. If you hadn't told me otherwise, I'd have said he'd gone walkabout down to the dry country with the rest of the Nijama people, as they do every wet season."

"Ben and his gang are here on Silent Reach and you know it!"

"I don't know it. But if they are, then go find them, son. I can't. I haven't been able to fork a horse in more than three years. They could be a mile from here and I wouldn't know unless somebody told me."

Stricken speechless by the realization of abysmal failure, George watched the old man walk away, too proud to hobble, balancing on his stiff, stick-thin, white-trousered legs.

Go find them, son. . . .

Go find them in fifteen thousand six hundred and twenty-five square miles of trackless mountains and scrublands and sandhills. Go find them in a million acres—or ten million. What was the difference?

George Galbraith sat under the tamarind tree until darkness fell. No one came out of the house. No light showed within it but the scent of green sandalwood, burned to keep mosquitoes at bay, drifted from the breezeway.

The mosquitoes were savage. He rose and walked to the verandah, squatted cross-legged on the deck. He could wait. He'd learned the tricks of waiting, of physical and mental discipline—discipline strict enough to let the mosquitoes bite long and suck back their own poison, and to put away the memory of Tamara Diagulski's body. The fireflies helped. Watch the fireflies and acquire the wisdom to enjoy antirhythm, the tranquility of waiting without expectation.

Her voice was very soft, but it rasped on his half trance. He winced.

"Mr. Sinclair . . ."

"Yes—what is it, Alison?"

"Dad says to tell you you can camp here or in the cookhouse, whichever you like."

"Kind of him. Tell him thanks."

"You can't come inside on account of Mum. She's pretty bad tonight. Strangers in the house upset her."

Apology? The youngster was embarrassed. He felt vaguely sorry for her. It must be a hell of a life for a teenage girl, even a convent-tamed one.

"It's all right, Alison. I understand. I'll be okay," he said.

"I'll sneak out a bit of meat for your tea later."

"Not if it'll get you into trouble. I can wait. But I'd like some water, please."

"There's a bag by the cookhouse door. How long are you going to wait, Mr. Sinclair?"

"I don't know," he replied. "Until the police come —tomorrow or the next day."

She gasped. He could sense the stiffening of her body.

"The police!"

"Yes."

"But why? Why are the police coming?"

"Didn't your father tell you?"

"No. Has Dad done something? Is it the Pasture Board again?"

"No. It's your brothers, Alison. They're in bad trouble. Max has been arrested and the police have been questioning Ted. Now they are coming for Ben."

"Oh . . . oh, my God!" It was an exclamation of anguished dismay, not surprise. "But . . . but Ben isn't here!"

The worm of cunning that always lived in George's brain moved. . . . It was just possible. *Christ, of course it was!*

He dropped his voice to a whisper. "Ben mightn't be here at home but he's on the property."

"He isn't. He isn't! He's gone with the Nijama to the sacred grounds by the river. He goes every year. If the police come looking for him it . . . it'll kill Mum. What can I do, what can I do?"

"Hush, Alison! Do you want your dad to hear and call you inside? Ben's here all right. Your father doesn't know where he is, but you do."

"No, I don't."

He waited. She added nothing to the flat, stubborn denial.

"Alison . . ."

No response. There wasn't time to wheedle—so try scaring the daylights out of her. Gamble on the one trump card.

"The money you brought on the plane from Melbourne wasn't for your father, was it? Your father didn't know anything about it. The money was for Ben. Don't you remember me? You came and sat beside me when the woman was taken ill."

She was very young, however deeply involved with her brothers' crimes. She was too stunned by what he had said to dissemble. This time her gasp was almost a sob.

Don't chicken out of the bluffing game now, Galbraith. Press your luck.

"You took the rough stones to Max and he sold them and sent the money back to Ben. Your father didn't know Ben had stolen them, did he?"

"He didn't steal them. He didn't! He bought them from the gins for tobacco, just as Dad used to. They find the carbonados in sluice boxes and coolamons when they're washing for tin. It takes ages to collect just a few."

Carbonados?

The penny was slow to drop. In Africa, the term for industrial diamonds was *boart*. Or was there some technical difference? No matter. When you'd washed away all the possibilities, diamonds remained in the bottom of the pan. Diamonds were the only mineral that Max Burnie in his situation could have mined, transported, and sold secretly to raise the large sum of money he needed to avoid cancellation of his lease. The girl evidently didn't realize that carbonados were discolored, flawed diamonds, nor did the gins who picked them out of the tailings of small alluvial tin workings all along the river and its tributary creeks. But Hamilton Wrightson knew what the sands of the Beechover carried—and so did Ambrose Fergusson. That cunning old fox would never have risked involving himself and his masters in Wrightson's operations if they didn't embrace something much more important than penny-packet gemstone mining.

"Doesn't your father know Ben's buying carbonados from the gins?"

"Of course he doesn't. He doesn't think Ben knows about them."

"How did Ben find out?"

"Mum told the boys when she . . . she got sick. She thought they ought to know."

And old Max didn't? Interesting—but irrelevant.

"Alison, come closer so you can hear me. I know you know where Ben is, and you've got to warn him. Tell him the police are after him and they know he's somewhere on Silent Reach. If he's not warned, he won't have a chance. They could even shoot him if he tried to escape."

"But he hasn't done anything!" she whispered furiously. "He didn't steal the carbonados. They came off the native tin claims. I told you."

Oh, God! Not another knot in the tangle! This

bloody little simpleton *must* know what her brothers had been up to. She'd run parcels of Silent Reach diamonds across the continent to Max in Canberra who sold them and sent her back with the cash to Ben. They'd trusted her as a courier.

"You must take the message, Alison. Listen carefully. Tell Ben I've come from the friends who helped Max in Canberra. He'll understand. Tell him the . . . his friends say that if he lets the girl go they can make sure he gets the ransom money. Tell him I came here alone and unarmed to give him the details, and I'll meet him anywhere he likes. But it must be soon because the police are going to use helicopters to direct their ground parties. When that starts—"

The bell seemed to rip every nerve in his body.

"Alison, please—"

But she was gone.

George sat for a long while watching the fireflies before he went in search of the water bag. He detested the thought of what he would probably have to do in the morning. There was something gentle and appealing about the poor little bugger.

CHAPTER 23

THE feather-light touch of fingertips on his eyelids dragged him into raw wakefulness. The old reflex was there, but sluggish. He drew up his knees and began to roll, but before he could lash out a palm was pressed on his mouth gently.

"Hush! It's me—Alison. Don't talk. Mum's awake and she might hear. Come on. Don't make a noise."

She seized his wrist and tugged. He scrambled groggily to his feet and followed her, bent almost double. The moon had set and the night was very dark. She led along the side verandah to the rear of the homestead, through the cookhouse—a bark-roofed open shed in the center of which a great mound of wood

ash and charcoal was piled. The glow of embers silhouetted an array of battered, blackened billycans
and cast-iron colonial ovens hung by wire hooks from
crossbars. Silent Reach was equipped at least to feed
its tribal retainers.

Once clear of the house, George freed his wrist
and halted. "You'd better tell me what it's all about,
Alison. Where am I supposed to be going?" He spoke
quietly but clearly.

"Hush! Not here. Too close. Only to the corn shed.
Give me your hand and I'll show you. Hurry. It'll be
light soon."

George shot a glance at his watch. Four o'clock. His
head was clearing. The pressure of her hand was
insistent, but somehow reassuring.

"Watch out!" A split-rail fence. "Here . . . climb
over. It's quicker."

He sensed rather than saw the bulk of the corn
shed, and ran the fingers of his free hand along the
wall to orient himself. The girl stopped. "Wait!"

He was alone. He flattened his back against the
wall and eased the flick knife out of his pocket.

"Elewee . . . ngaya ngairi!"

"Owei . . ."

Rustling. A scrape and a pale glow. . . . Alison
Burnie, holding a misshapen tallow dip in her hand,
beckoned him into the shed.

"Close the door."

He turned, saw movement out of the corner of his
eye, and whirled. An ancient aboriginal woman, clad
in a ragged, gray mother hubbard, was squatted between two empty corn bins, looking up at him. The
whites of her eyes gleamed like polished bone.

"This is Elewee, Mr. Sinclair. She's my auntie. I've
told her and she'll take you."

"What!"

"She'll take you to Ben."

He closed his eyes.

"But Alison . . . you . . ."

"I can't, Mr. Sinclair. Please understand. Mum's
very bad and I can't leave her. She's going to die and
Dad can't do anything to help. He can't even lift her

up because of his rheumatism. She keeps wanting me all the time."

He nodded dumbly, not trusting himself to speak.

"It isn't far, Mr. Sinclair. Elewee knows the way. It's her country."

"Where is it, Alison—how far?"

"Up the river, past the reach and Elumkuranji. In the hills. Elewee knows the way."

"How far?"

"Tomorrow sometime. Elewee is very old. Maybe tonight she'll have to stop and rest. If I could go, it would be tomorrow morning."

"I meant how far away in miles."

"I don't know."

"Could you show me on a map?"

She shook her head impatiently. "Elewee knows the way. I don't understand maps. The nuns never taught us geography at school. I've caught my horse for you. She's saddled up and I've rolled a swag for tonight."

"Where?"

"Just outside. You'll have to hurry. It's getting light."

"Alison, I . . . I've got to get my bag—the red one I had on the verandah."

"There isn't time."

"There'll have to be. It . . . it's got things in it, papers to show to Ben. Otherwise . . . maybe he won't believe I've come to help him get away. Wait for me. I'll fetch it."

"No! I'll tell Elewee . . ." She turned and spoke in a low, guttural mutter, seeming to give directions. The old black woman vanished in the shadows.

"When is Father Bridges coming, Mr. Sinclair? Do you think Sister Mary Antony will come with him?"

He passed a hand across his forehead. Predawn chill was in the air but he was beginning to sweat profusely. "I only know that someone is coming from the mission to warn your father that the police know about the carbonados."

"But Dad hasn't done anything wrong! It wasn't

wrong to buy them from the gins. It wasn't wrong of Ben, either."

"I don't care about the carbonados or the rights and wrongs. The important thing is for Ben to collect the money for that woman his friends took as a hostage, and escape before the police trap him. We can arrange for a boat to pick him up on a beach somewhere—or perhaps an airplane—and get him out of the country until the fuss is over."

Alison held the now flaring and guttering dip higher.

"Why do you want to help Ben, Mr. Sinclair? You don't know him. You're *balanda,* a white man."

Be careful. She's starting to think.

"No, I don't know him—only about him. He's a freedom fighter. Millions of white men all over the world want to help freedom fighters, Alison. *My* people do. They helped Max and Ted until someone blabbed and the police caught them."

"Someone blabbed?"

"Yes. Someone talked. It must have been that. How else could the police find out?"

"Who are your people, Mr. Sinclair?"

He rubbed his forehead with his forearm. Jesus! George Galbraith, star of the field agents' class of '67, sweating like a pig under interrogation by a fifteen-year-old girl!

"I can't tell you that, Alison. It's . . . political."

"But Ben and Max know."

"They have to. But the fewer people who are in on the secret, the less chance there is of its leaking and causing trouble."

"You mean you think I'd blab. I wouldn't."

"No, of course not willingly. But the police have ways of making people talk. They *can't* make you tell what you don't know, Alison. If Elewee is taking me to Ben, do you want to send him anything?"

"No. Elewee will tell him about Mum. Do you think Max and Ted will go to jail, Mr. Sinclair?"

Think, you clot, think! Believe what you say!

"They'll have good lawyers. Maybe they'll get off . . . with a suspended sentence or something like that. But I'm afraid Ben will go to jail if they catch him.

Ben's friends kidnapped a woman at Wandonning Downs homestead and a man was shot dead."

"Ben wouldn't shoot anybody!" She was aghast, not angry.

"Maybe not, but one of his friends did. Freedom fighters have to shoot people sometimes, and sometimes freedom fighters get shot."

Christ, Mary Dalziel would be sickened by him! But then Mary Dalziel had been "in advertising"—which provides a more catholic education in the techniques of duplicity than the nuns of St. Columba junior school at Dandinup.

Elewee walked ahead on frail, pipe-stem legs spotted with ulcer scars, leading the horse by a frayed, hemp halter. At daylight she dropped the lead and he gathered it in coils across the pommel on top of the swag —a roll of a rancid-smelling gray blanket and mosquito netting containing solid bumps of God knew what.

My auntie . . . blood sister of the "remarkable person," the first aboriginal girl to become a triple-certificated nurse? Or did "auntie" merely signify clan relationship? He wondered how old she was. Fifty? Sixty? Seventy? No telling. She moved effortlessly, surefooted, never faltering on broken ground. Alison Burnie's bay mare ambled docilely, like Don Quixote's Rosinante, head and lip drooping, but at a steady pace. Yet Elewee was always ahead.

Upriver. That meant roughly northeast. He could hear the stream grumbling in the distance but he could see no landmarks to commit to memory. That was not worrying as long as the river was within earshot, but when the sound of water faded away he felt uneasy. He was not at all sure that he could retrace the route if the need arose. When Elewee struck up from the swampy flats toward high ground, she seemed to be picking her way through a maze of tracks littered with donkey, cattle, and kangaroo droppings.

The flies were appalling. The mare snorted, tossed her head, and switched her tail frantically. Only El-

ewee was indifferent. She moved in a palpitating cloud
of insects, not even bothering to brush them away
from her eyes.

Yet physical discomfort was unimportant by comparison with the consciousness of failure that be-
deviled George. He had based his tactics on the
disastrous misapprehension that old Max Burnie
would have a pipeline to the sabotage gang and
a specific knowledge of its operations. He had been
completely wrong. But for the pure chance of meeting Alison he could have played no further part in
the desperate dicker for Tamara Diagulski's life.

There was only one hope left. He might still con the
gang into believing that Hamilton Wrightson had
agreed to meet the ransom demand. But the man
who had masterminded the strikes against Conwright properties must know that Silent Reach was no
longer secure. Maybe he was already on the run.

Early in the afternoon George and his decrepit guide
passed out of the Silent Reach pound by way of a defile in bare, red rock that radiated blistering heat.
Beyond it the downs flattened into a wide, scrub-
covered plain through which the Beechover snaked
toward its rendezvous with the Bondy. On the far
horizon, fifty or sixty miles away, the tabletops and
towers of the Riddoch Range marked the frontiers of
the sand desert. Southward in middle distance a single
trachyte spire, core of a volcano that died in Meso-
zoic times, thrust its bulbous tip a thousand feet above
the treetops.

Staring at it, he remembered. On the flight from
Braund to Port Epsom, Chasser Fitzpatrick had
pointed out a vast needle of rock east of them and
said that Conair pilots called it Pike's Prick. Chasser
made a caustic comment on the fact that the Division
of National Mapping had given it some unpronounce-
able aboriginal name and marked it PD—position
doubtful—on the latest sheets.

Elumkuranji? Maybe—almost certainly. Past Elumkuranji . . .

George was becoming light-headed from lack of

food. He gazed at Elewee in misty wonderment. The old woman couldn't keep going forever. Or could she? She'd been walking ahead of the horse without once pausing to rest. But she must be very old. Maybe tonight she'd have to stop and sleep. A sentence floated into his mind from a book idly read centuries ago in that ticky-tacky little city of paper pushers, two thousand miles east beyond the empty horizon: *To the native, the average white man appears limp-bodied, lacking in stamina, muscle-bound, near-sighted, and pretty much of a fool in the bush.*

Pretty much of a fool . . .

For the last two hours of daylight, they skirted a long pool contained by banks of bald, weathered granite. It was a great expanse of clear, unruffled water, beautiful and inviting. But within minutes of sighting it, George became aware of eerie abnormality. The rock crevices and occasional shingle bars were bare of vegetation. There were no white-limbed river gums with their feet in the wet sand; no birds or aquatic beetles or clouds of midges; no animal tracks or dung. He steered the mare toward the rock rim. She fidgeted and pulled on the bit, snorting protest. He dismounted and scooped up a handful of water, wet his lips—and spat explosively. It was alkali in almost corrosive concentration.

Mary Dalziel's vague story of how Max Burnie's station got its name had been true. Silent Reach was silent because it was dead!

At last light, Elewee yielded to her years. She stopped, waited until the horse had come abreast of her, and took its bridle. George slid to the ground gratefully, stiff in every muscle, chafed, and a little dizzy.

"Close up camp, boss. Orright?" They were the first words he had heard her speak.

"Ben's camp, Elewee?"

She shook her head.

"Camp bilong Ben, little feller longway. Camp bilong you-me. Morning time we go, bringen Ben close up arpinoon."

The sand under the rock slab by which she halted was smooth and clean. He dumped the saddle and swag on the ground. Elewee removed bridle and bit, unrolled the halter, and led the mare away through undergrowth. There must be a soak nearby. He hoped to God that the water in it was fit to drink.

It was already very dark. He rummaged out a pencil flashlight from the airline bag and untied the cord around the swag. As well as two bundles wrapped in pandanus leaves, it contained a smoke-blackened quart pot, a rusty army mess tin, and an oval water bottle covered with khaki felt nibbled to filigree. The bottle was heavy. He unscrewed its metal stopper, sniffed, raised the neck to his mouth, sipped cautiously, and then gulped at the sweet and pungently bitter tea.

By the time Elewee returned he had gathered a few twigs, set them alight, and was fossicking for more fuel. Somewhere out in the darkness he could hear the mare moving restlessly.

"Find water, Elewee?" he asked hopefully, holding up the quart pot. She took it and went off again. He explored the leaf-wrapped bundles—two small dampers, gray with ash and flint hard, and what looked like the shank end of a leg of yearling beef, charred to a cinder on the outside, bloody at the bone. It smelled faintly putrid, but his mouth flooded with saliva when he stripped off a few slivers with the flick knife and chewed tentatively. Later, he thought, he would recook the bone meat over the coals. He suspected it was flyblown but decided not to make sure.

When Elewee brought the filled quart pot, he put it by the fire and opened the mess tin. It held a knife-fork-spoon combination, two paper spills of sugar and tea, and two pathetic chocolate bars, liquid in their colored foil wrappers. Poor Alison, candidate bride of Christ!

He spread the blanket, squatted, hacked a flinty damper in half, impaled one portion with the knife, and held it out toward the old woman. She hesitated, then took the food, and stepped back into the shad-

ows beyond the firelight. He sensed her watching him
—watching and assessing every move.

He ate slowly, chewing each mouthful to liquid,
and forced himself to swallow. The bitter tea from the
flask, diluted with hot water out of the pannikin top of
the quart pot, helped. When he was sure he would
not vomit, he lit a cigarette, smoked it lying on his
back, flicked the butt into the dying fire, pulled a fold
of net over his face—and slept.

CHAPTER 24

ELUMKURANJI rose out of the pile of slabs
and boulders that had been stripped from its volcanic
cone by the heat, cold, rain, drought, and wind of a
million years—a gigantic, fissured finger raised in
warning to any reckless alien who might be tempted
to invade the sullen, trackless plain beyond it. Alison
Burnie had said her brother's camp was up the river,
past Elumkuranji, in the hills. George and his guide
came abreast of the spire at noon and were past it
by one o'clock in the afternoon, but he could see no
hills. A few flattened, treeless ridges extending east-
ward from the base of the pinnacle seemed more like
the top of a sunken tableland that had been split in
several directions by small canyons.

Elewee had boiled the quart pot at dawn, crouched
over a minute twig fire. George, although he was now
savagely hungry and feeling weak, could not stomach
the remains of the meat. He gave the bone to the old
woman who mumbled at it avidly with toothless
jaws, saliva running down her chin, enveloped in her
personal miasma of flies. He decided to keep the second damper in case Ben Burnie proved no more
hospitably disposed than his father.

Again Elewee traveled twenty yards ahead of the
mare, still tireless, veering toward the easterly ridges.
The going was rougher, but she followed a defined

track along a stony gully which narrowed to a ravine between rock walls that gradually gained height.
They were gouged by cave mouths and striated by
deep ledges.

Soon after the sun dipped below the rim of the ravine, he rounded a bend and found Elewee squatted,
waiting for him. He swung out of the saddle.

"Smoke-oh, Elewee? Ben's camp is close up, eh?"

"Elewee no can bringen camp bilong Ben little feller close up. Boss, you go." She pointed. "You no can
lose-im Ben. E can finem you. Orright?"

"Well-l," George said. "So you're opting out, old
dear, are you? Or is it that you're not allowed into the
gentlemen's club—except on ladies' night?"

She stared at him with bleary incomprehension.

"You givem nikki, boss?"

"What?"

"You givem nikki?" She mimed smoking a cigarette.

"Oh . . . yes, for sure." He unzipped the airline
bag, took out an unbroken pack of cigarettes, and
handed it to her. Her mouth split in a delighted grin.
The pack vanished down the neck of her mother hubbard as if by sleight of hand.

"You know," George said, grinning back at her,
"for one dreadful moment I thought you were solicit-
ing a gratuity of a different sort. What's the score
now? We wait?"

She shook her head. "You go, boss." She pointed
again. "Ben e finem you."

He looked long and thoughtfully at the sides of the
gorge ahead. When he turned back, Elewee was no
longer there.

The thin whine of a bullet whiffling past his head and
the crack of the shot did not surprise him. The mare
pig rooted halfheartedly. He reined her in, patting her
neck, and when she had quietened he simply sat waiting.

At first he could see nothing among the stunted
white gums that were scattered over the shallow depression to which the track along the ravine had led.

Then as his eyes accommodated themselves to the sharp contrast of light and shade, he thought he could discern in the deep purple shadow cast by the north-western rockface the line of a fence and the shape of a building.

Movement . . . perceived from the corner of one eye. He turned. Thirty feet away a tall, very black man carrying a rifle loosely at the ready stepped out of the bush and slouched forward. He wore stockman's rig—tight denim trousers held up by a broad, brass-studded belt, a khaki shirt, high-heeled boots. He motioned with the rifle barrel—an unvoiced but unmistakable order. Get off the horse!

George dropped the reins, languidly raised his empty hands shoulder high, and let them fall again.

"Not me, Jack. I've come to see Ben Burnie. Where do I find him?"

The rifle muzzle dropped to cover him, steadied.

"Giddown, whitey!"

"And you get fucked, you ape," George drawled. "Where's Ben Burnie? Don't you understand English? Where's Ben Burnie?"

A long—a very long—pause of confrontation. The black man stepped back. A second black man, then a third, appeared out of the scrub. The newcomers were not armed. The man with the rifle muttered something to them when they came up behind him. One turned and loped away. The other walked forward warily and took the mare's bridle. She pulled back.

George patted the mare's neck again. "Giddap, Rosinante," he said. "We're off to see the wizard." The rifleman paced behind, holding his weapon across his chest.

Yes. It was a fence all right, post and rails enclosing three sides of a stockyard. The fourth side was the cliff. And there were two buildings, not one—bark-walled shacks, ten feet by twelve or a little larger. Three men emerged from the nearer hut, one walking ahead of the others.

Ben Burnie? Yes—almost certainly, although his skin was much darker than Alison's. He was powerfully built, not more than five feet nine or ten, with the broad, flared nostrils and heavy, wide lips of the Australian aboriginal. Caucasian genes showed out only in the shape of his skull and a tint of copper in the thick, close-cropped hair. He wore jungle-green shorts and nothing else if you discounted copper-wire armbands above his elbows.

"Are you Ben Burnie?"

Strange eyes—prominent, light brown with a glint of red. They told nothing. His face was expressionless, stony.

"I could be."

"Well, if you are, I've got a message for you."

"How did you get here?"

He hadn't asked about the message or its sender. Only one question, "How did you get here?"

George looked the man up and down. "On this spirited animal, Alison's mare. Fifteen years old if she's a day. You ought to recognize her."

"Alison sent you?" The flat inquiry held no surprise.

"Yes, with a message."

"How did you find me?"

George wrinkled his forehead and scratched behind his ear elaborately.

"Actually," he said, "I followed an old lady."

"You insolent, spying bastard!" The explosion came from the man behind Burnie. Burnie spun.

"Keep out of this, Mounty! Shut your stupid trap!" It was a drill sergeant's roar and it commanded a moment of complete silence.

George looked past the stony-faced leader of the reception party for the first time. Peter Mountfort . . . good God! He was naked except for a *naga* cloth on a waist string and a headband that confined greasy, black hair falling below his shoulders—a bizarre, bottle-shaped figure with a soft belly, broad hips, and long, slender legs. A grid of white, raised scars lay across his narrow, freckled chest, more like collodian fakes than keloids. Every physical feature of the youth was ludicrous except his eyes. They were narrowed, blue gray, diffusely glazed like the eyes of a drug addict—or a psychopath. By comparison, Ben Burnie's eyes were benign.

"You answer me, mate." Cold, and still controlled. Formidable. Watch it.

"I have answered. Alison said the old lady was your aunt—name of Elewee. Does that make sense?"

Silence again. Then at last—"What message?"

"Can we talk in private?"

"What message?"

George raised his hands again, still languidly—and ironically. "Okay, Ben. Have it your own way. It's a message from Ham Wrightson. He agrees to your terms. No haggle. Half a million in any currency you name—or gold, though gold would take a few days longer to raise. He'll complete the deal under any conditions and in any place you say. The only thing he wants is proof that the girl's alive and you'll really turn her loose."

No response. The eyes and the dark, stolid face revealed nothing.

George shrugged and went on. "Half a million could buy a lot, Ben, if you get out ahead of the pigs fast enough. Max and Ted didn't. They were caught. You ought to get set to blow. We could fix it to make the swap over the water, if you like. The characters Dave Carlin dealt with would probably oblige and arrange it. There'd be no pigs to worry about over the water, would there?"

Ben Burnie smiled then—a flash of square, white teeth.

"You're peddlin' a load of bullshit, mate," he said softly, parodying the bush vernacular. "Who's this sheila you're talkin' about?"

George felt his breath leave him. So. Finish. End of line. A small motor began to whirr in his brain. Ben Burnie glanced away. "Do you know anything about a sheila, Mounty?"

The long-haired, freckled foster brother of the Nijama licked his lips.

"Ben, don't you reckon maybe we ought to . . ."

"Do you? Well, do you?"

"No, Ben."

"No, you don't know what?"

"No, I don't know anything about a sheila."

George reached into the breast pocket of his shirt, took out a cigarette pack, shook it open, drew out a cigarette with his lips, and patted his other pockets as if in search of matches.

"Must have come to the wrong address," he said. "Still .. . *if* you're Ben Burnie, I've got a letter from your sister. She's worried about your mother . . . wants you to know the score."

He twitched the holdall from his hip onto the swag roll, opened it, fumbled vaguely.

Point of no return. *Commit!*

The mare under him sidled to the surreptitious pressure of his heel. He took the pistol from the bag. Almost nonchalantly, he shot the man with the rifle through the solar plexus from a range of twenty feet —and the man holding the bridle through the throat from a distance of six inches.

There was no chance of a third shot. The mare squealed, reared wildly, spun—and bolted. George did not try to look back. He had lost a stirrup and nearly lost the Browning.

A quarter-mile beyond the point where the ravine opened out, he had his mount under control and eased her back to a trot, then a walk. He soon saw what he was looking for, pulled up, and climbed down. The mare was in a lather of sweat, trembling with fright.

Committed, George felt nothing. The computer was programmed. Without hurry, he unlashed and unrolled the swag. Taking his boots and soiled clothing from the airline bag, he rolled them in the swag and put it back on the saddle. He packed the airline bag with the remains of the damper, the refilled water bottle, and the quart pot.

The halter? Yes—conceivably useful. He coiled it tightly and laid the coil beside the airline bag. Then he looped the reins and knotted them so that they could not trail. The mare's flanks were still heaving.

He positioned himself carefully, opened the flick knife, murmured "Sorry, old girl," and plunged a half inch of steel into her rump. Her scream echoed and reechoed between the cliffs, and he could still hear in diminuendo the drumming of hooves and the clatter of flying shingle as he hoisted himself over the rim of a high ledge in the rock face. He had selected it because it gave a clear view of a short section of the track below and also afforded concealment from pursuers following the track.

It was by no means an ideal hiding place. In full light, alert hunters on horseback would certainly be able to see part of his body if they were looking for their quarry on the cliff fifteen or twenty feet above eye level, but George dismissed that risk as negligible. His adversaries might be able to appear and disappear like genies in the shadow-dappled scrub, but he was sure they lacked the imagination to anticipate that he would double back, at least so soon. The imponderables were how far and fast Alison Burnie's mare would travel before she foundered or broke a leg, how soon the hunters would discover they were chasing a riderless horse—and how much time they would waste trying to track down its missing rider. He was certain he would be pursued. Burnie simply could not risk letting him escape to lead police parties to the hideout.

So George waited, flat on his belly, behind the partial cover of a loose slab of rock that had fallen and come to rest near the ledge's rim. He waited without making the slightest movement. The shadows were deepening and the blistering heat of the afternoon was already tempered by the sunset breeze. Good.

Fifteen minutes . . . twenty . . . twenty-five. Then he heard the first rider approaching at a brisk trot. There was a holster on his saddle with a carbine butt protruding. The man did not lift his head. He rode leaning forward, scanning the ground ahead.

Two more rode close together, almost abreast. A hundred-yard gap. Then three in file. None of them looked up. The clip-clop died away.

George moved slightly, then froze again. No, give it ten minutes.

Wise. Ben Burnie, riding faster to catch up with the front runners, passed without an upward glance.

That made seven men—plus the two who wouldn't ride again. Nine—and Peter Mountfort, who had not appeared. How many others had been left to garrison the hideout?

Well, go find them, son. Delay would only whittle away any advantage he might have won by backtracking.

George Galbraith had been excellently trained in his job, and the very essence of instructions on field operations was to identify and concentrate on an objective, and to act swiftly once a plan of attaining the objective had been formulated.

He climbed down from the ledge and walked along the ravine into the shallow valley, openly, briskly, but without haste. Fifty yards beyond the rocks, he left the track for the cover of the sparse scrub, slowing his pace to a saunter and moving where possible in the shadows that were deepening and lengthening as the sun sank.

There was stillness in the darkening valley—and no sound but normal bush sounds. George halted beside a thicket of thorny acacia within clear view of the bark huts and the little stockyard. He scanned them and the intervening ground methodically with the race glasses.

Still no movement. The small clearing around the huts was littered with refuse of rusty cans and unidentifiable garbage. It might be difficult to cross silently. Next to scan the limestone wall under which the squalid encampment was sited. Like the sides of the access defile, it was pitted with ledges and holes, but the optical quality of the small binoculars was too poor for him to learn anything useful.

Where was Peter Mountfort? Was he alone? Where was Tamara Diagulski—or her body?

Twilight came and went quickly.

George moved again when he could no longer discern the mass of the buildings, and he froze as a flickering light appeared suddenly in the nearer hut. It shone through the chinks between the wall slabs and

from under the eaves—yellow, faint, and diffused by
smoke. Someone must be building a small fire. The
light strengthened and steadied. A lamp had been lit.
So much to the good. It is always difficult to see at
night from a lighted room. Now was the safest time
to make the final approach.

George bent double and made for the base of the
cliff to the right, feeling his way among the litter with
hypersensitive feet, every nerve tuned to concert pitch.
He was aiming first at the hut that was in darkness.
His fingers touched the wall, found a crevice, and he
put an eye and then an ear to it.

Blackness and silence. So take a gamble. The
chances against anyone waiting inside were hundreds
to one.

He pulled the pistol from his waistband, thumbed
off the safety catch, and eased the pencil flashlight
out of the bag, sliding along the walls until an explor-
ing toe found the sapling doorframe. The entrance
was screened with sacking. He pushed it gently aside
and stepped in. The pistol back in his belt, he cupped
one hand around the flashlight and began to quarter
the floor of the hut. At the second sweep the tiny
spot fell on a dark body sprawled facedown on the
earth floor. George uncupped the light long enough to
make sure it was a dead body—the body of the man
with the rifle—and that it was not alone. Farther back
lay the corpse of the man whom he had shot through
the throat. The head lay in a pool of blood. The casualties had been dragged under cover and abandoned.
That, too, was encouraging. If Ben Burnie had left
part of his force in camp, surely the dead would have
been treated with a little more ceremony.

George switched off the light and stepped into the
open again. The fire in the second shack was now
burning brightly. There was a smell of meat cooking
which reminded him of his hunger. He contemplated
taking a couple of the Ritalin tablets contained with a
small store of emergency drugs in the plastic sponge
bag issued to field agents before a mission and sar-
donically called "the panic pouch." But they would

take too long to work and, in any case, hunger had not yet seriously impaired his physical capabilities.

Commit again.

Gun in hand, without any further attempt at concealment, he strolled ten yards to the occupied shack, pulled back the sacking curtain, and walked in.

Peter Mountfort was crouched in front of a stone hearth holding an iron frying pan over the fire. He was alone and he did not hear George enter. With precisely calculated force, George clubbed him on the base of the skull with the pistol butt, seized his hair from behind, and jerked him back sharply before he could slump into the fire. Then he turned the flaccid body over with his foot.

Too hard—or was he thin skulled? That was always the risk. No, his pulse was strong. In five minutes, or ten at the outside, the adopted brother of the Nijama tribe would be aware of his headache. George hoped that their business together would not be interrupted by any returning members of Burnie's gang.

Meanwhile he checked the contents of the hut. A canvas camp stretcher with mosquito net, blankets and a beanbag pillow, a small casewood table and stool under the kerosene lamp swinging from a rafter. A saddle, saddle blanket, girths, and a bridle hooked up on four-inch nails driven into sapling wall studs. A stripped, short-barreled .303 rifle and an ammunition belt hanging on another wall. Cans of food ranged in a makeshift cupboard, a little flywire meat safe, and a four-gallon drum of water.

George smiled grimly. Peter Mountfort's abjuration of civilization, his defiant dropping out to the primitive life-style, had been something less than total. He had even changed for dinner—from *naga* cloth and headband into dirty shorts and a sleeveless shirt.

Rope or cord? Yes, there was a coil of heavy cuttyhunk fishing line below the ammunition belt. George worked fast and dextrously, lashing the unconscious man's thumbs and big toes together. But it was insufficient precaution. As George planned it, some movements by the bottle-shaped man would soon be entirely involuntary. He retrieved the halter from where he had dropped it outside with the airline bag, and bound Mountfort's ankles, knees, and elbows firmly.

Next get a gag ready, but don't fix it until he opens his mouth to scream. If he vomits into a gag he might suffocate himself. A wad of cloth torn from the shirt will do the job when the time for silence comes.

The trussing took three or four minutes. George straightened his back, took the rifle from the wall, checked that the magazine was full, tested the bolt action, and buckled the cartridge belt around his waist. He laid the rifle on the camp stretcher, near at hand. Then he turned his attention to the cupboard. The strips of meat that Mountfort had been frying were charred beyond edibility.

Can opener? Yes, on a shelf. Beef and vegetable stew. George, seated on the stretcher, was halfway through his meal when the bound man groaned and sitrred. George continued eating—and listening. A second groan did not come until he had finished the beef stew and was fighting back the almost over-whelming temptation to open another can. He stood up, unhooked the lamp, and held it close to the narrow face. The man's eyelids were twitching.

Foxing? No—not quite, but probably preparing to fox. George scooped water from the drum with the can and emptied it in a steady stream between the slack lips. Peter Mountfort swallowed, choked, and opened his mouth to yell. George slapped the gag between his teeth neatly and fastened it behind his head.

"Welcome back from the dreamtime, warrior," he said. "A little more water will help clear the head, eh? Then I'll give you a minute or two to gather your wits and reflect on the wisdom of cooperation. They tell me you're a university man, so I don't have to talk down to you."

He turned to the fire, selected the longest, straightest stick from a pile beside the hearth, and thrust its end into the coals. He said nothing more until the tip was well alight. "When we met before, Comrade Mountfort, you agreed with your intrepid leader, Ben Burnie, that neither of you knew a woman called Ta-

mara Diagulski. It was a silly sort of lie. It cost two of
your gang their lives. Are you hearing me clearly—
understanding me?"

Glittering, hate-filled eyes answered the question.

George went on: "Good. We can get down to
business. I'll be frank with you. You're simply not going to believe that a nice, fresh-faced English spy like
me is capable of doing the most appalling things if he
doesn't get answers to his questions. I don't look the
type to drive my mother to suicide, or beat up mentally crippled girls, or catch foxes with fishhook traps,
do I? But I assure you I'm quite capable of inflicting
much worse pain on types who are capable of such
unchristian acts. I'm trained for it. I don't particularly
enjoy the work, but I'm good at it."

Was fear showing in the mad eyes now, as well as
hatred? Perhaps—but any fear there might be was
far from blind, unseeing terror. George took his firestick out of the coals.

"I'm going to light a fire under your bare backside,
Mountfort, before I ask you any questions. A warm-
up, eh? It may convince you that I'll do exactly what
I promise if you refuse to answer questions when I
put them to you."

Within seconds of the glowing end of the stick burning a hole through the skin of his buttocks, Peter
Mountfort fainted. George checked his pulse and his
pupils, and again reached for the water can.

"Take your time, laddie," he said when the bound
man's muscles stiffened and he began to shake uncon-
trollably. "Meditate on your good fortune. You're
suffering much less pain than the men who were
burned when you bold freedom fighters sneaked up
in the night and blew up Excon Four and Halley's
Circle. If you hand it out, then you must expect to
take it, sooner or later. Now we can come to the
point. I will ask you a number of questions. If you refuse to answer any one of them, I will castrate you.
You may die of pain or shock, or subsequent infec-
tion, but I'll do my best to prevent that by injecting
morphine and cauterizing the wound. I'd prefer you

to survive and spread the word that the good old days are gone forever for the Midnight Riders."

George opened the flick knife and tested its point with his thumb. "Nod for yes. Shake your head for no. Question one. Is the woman you abducted, Tamara Diagulski, alive?"

Terror now. . . . The freckled, contorted face was streaming with sweat. The freckled, twitching body stank of terror. But instead of nodding or shaking his head, Peter Mountfort closed his eyes stubbornly.

"Heigh-ho," George said very softly. "So be it." He bent down, ripped open the fly of the man's shorts, and pressed the knife tip delicately into the side of the blue, shriveled scrotum. Mountfort's body arched as if in the final convulsions of tetanus. Then he began to nod his head backwards and forwards, backwards and forwards.

George grunted, stood upright. He felt incredibly hollow, lightheaded, relaxed.

"A timely change of heart, old boy. I take it you realize that if you turn out to be lying, you'll lose your balls anyway. Now I'm going to undo that gag. Puke if you want to, but don't squeak."

Mountfort drew in wet, choking gulps and started to blubber.

"For Christ's sake, little man," George said, "don't go on about trifles! All you've got is a lump on your skull, a burn on your bum, and a little slit in your ball bag that hardly needs a stitch. But it would be very, very easy to make your private sector a disaster area if you duck shove. *Where is she? Where's the woman?*"

Through chattering teeth, in a whisper—"Here."

"Here where?"

"In the caves—half a mile."

"Who's with her?"

"No one . . . no, please, *please!* There can't be anybody with her."

"How many of you are camped here?"

"Eleven."

Eleven? One unaccounted for, if Mountfort had included the casualties.

"Only seven went with Ben," George said. "Two are dead in the shack next door. Where's the other one?"

"Bosek went over the hill on the horse trail to warn the others. Ben sent him."

"How many others?"

"Five or six. I can't be sure."

"How far away are they? Be careful!"

"Three hours."

"And three back?"

"Yes, I suppose so."

"And Ben left the girl unguarded. Why?"

Terror glittered again in the bloodshot, streaming eyes.

"Quick!"

"Because . . . because she can't get away. She hurt her leg."

Part of the truth—not all. Far, far from that. . . . But leave it.

"Why didn't you go with Ben and the others? Why were you left behind?"

No answer.

"Shall I tell you, Mountfort?" George stooped and advanced the knife point. "Because Ben said: 'You got me into this, Mounty, with your kidnapping lunacy, so you can bloody well get me out of it. See you make a tidy job of it before we get back—*or else!*' That's pretty much the story, isn't it?"

No answer. The knife point rested lightly on blood-streaked, quivering skin.

"No, no! Oh, God, no! I wasn't going to do it! I wasn't. . . . I couldn't. . . . I swear I couldn't have done it! I swear!"

George withdrew the knife. "Don't be modest, little man," he said. "If she was quite helpless, you'd have worked up the nerve all right. Well, we're now going to see just how much truth you've told. I'll untie you in a minute, after I've done a job or two like commandeering your iron rations. You will then lead me with the lamp—and carry the food. I shall be walking just behind you within arm's length. If anything goes wrong, if anyone challenges us or you have even the slightest accident, you'll get six inches of steel up your asshole for starters. And a bullet in your kidneys if I have to put you down in a hurry."

CHAPTER 25

IT was very dark at the foot of the cliff. Mountfort's bare feet made no sound on the stone rubble. He walked bent almost double, carrying the blanket bundle over one shoulder and holding the light at waist height. George followed a yard behind, disconcerted because he could see nothing beyond the small circle of light. His ears strained for any noise that might signal danger. Once a shadow passed across the field of his vision and he felt a soft, glancing blow on his forehead. He stifled a gasp.

A bat. . . . There were colonies of them in the caves, coming out now for the night's hunting.

Steady yourself. . . . Watch where you put your clumsy hooves. And watch Mountfort at the same time, even if his state of abject terror seemed to grow rather than lessen. He was whimpering spasmodically. Then he suddenly stopped.

George reached forward and laid the flat of the knife against the man's bare rump.

"Keep going, comrade. Just keep going, slow and steady."

"I can't. . . . We've got to climb."

"Climb where to?"

"The ledge."

"Here?"

"It . . . it's the only way. Up."

"It had better be," George said coldly. "Give me the light. Careful!"

He took the light and held it high. It illuminated twenty feet of vertical limestone against which a small tree trunk was propped. Shallow toeholds had been hacked through the bark to provide a primitive ladder that presumably gave access to a rock platform, invisible from below.

If Mountfort had enough guts, or desperation, in his soft belly to attempt a break, here was the place. If he climbed first, he would be concealed by the ledge and could possibly bolt, using the advantage of familiar ground. If he waited below to follow, George could not hope to keep an eye on him, with or without the light, while he himself was scrambling up that infernal pole.

Think, but don't let him suspect uncertainty. While you think, keep the revolting little bastard cowed.

"Sit down, Mountfort. Before we go on, I want to know more. Who used the shotgun in your mother's kitchen? You? Ben?"

"No."

"Then who?"

Mountfort's eyes were fixed on the knife.

"Bosek. He . . . he had to."

George bared his teeth in a wolfish grin. "Of course he had to. Self-defense. But we must hear what the lady's got to say on the point. And by the way, you've seen my face before, haven't you?"

"No."

"Come now—not even in a telescopic sight? The spy at the Golden Galleon. You were in Perth at the end of October, weren't you?"

"No."

"Then the police must be wrong. I'm a fair man. Sometimes the police are wrong. I'll give you the benefit of the doubt. Who tipped you off that Ham Wrightson was hiring a shit-hot hatchet man to cure his sabotage troubles—young Max in Canberra?"

No reply. George sighed gustily.

"Okay. Your choice. Aren't you convinced I keep my promises?"

Mountfort's voice rose in a thin wail. "Oh, Christ! You're mad! No, don't . . . don't! Yes, it was Max."

George took the hank of heavy fishing line from beneath the rifle sling over his shoulder, unknotted it, and paid it out in coils. "You know, little white brother of the Nijama," he said, "those generous sponsors of yours with diplomatic immunity ought to have staked you to a year's study abroad. The PLO and the Black September lads don't fuck about with warning shots, illiterate paste-up notes, and snakes between the sheets. That's kids' comic stuff. As an apprentice terrorist, you don't know your ass from your elbow—and that goes for the mighty Ben, too. Now, let's see. . . . A running noose nice and tight around your neck, so. The line hangs down your back. I give you fifteen feet of slack—then fasten the line to my belt, so, with the gear tied onto the other end. You climb, I follow. Try anything silly and I pull the slack—you strangle. If I fall or you fall, the same thing happens, only quicker. You can haul the gear up later. Is that clear?"

It became patently clear. Mountfort was almost black in the face and on the point of collapse when George, who had taken no chances at all, finally loosened the cord as he clambered off the notched pole.

The ledge was at first narrow, but it widened rapidly and its overhang deepened. The rock was riddled with holes of indeterminable depth—pitch-black cavities which the unfocused light of the kerosene lamp could not penetrate.

The tethered man stopped again, turned, and fell forward on his knees.

"Get up, you groveling little prick! Is this it?"

A whisper, rising to a desperate whine. "I've got to explain something—talk to you. You've got to listen, Mr. Galbraith. You've got to . . . Jesus, but you've got to!"

George felt his belly knot with apprehension. Mountfort's face was a contorted mask of terror. He was shuddering so violently that his legs could hardly support his body.

Had he been lying, after all? Was Diagulski really alive?

"If she's not here, get going, Mountfort. Save your breath—"

"It wasn't my idea, Mr. Galbraith. I swear before
God it wasn't!"

"What wasn't your idea?"

"Bringing her here. . . . It was Ben. He made me.
He knows the others won't take any notice of me. . . .
He ought to have kept her down at roadhead."

"Kept her *where?*"

"Roadhead. Where we've got all the stuff . . . the
transport . . . off the old beef road. . . . I swear
before God, Mr. Galbraith, I wouldn't have done
what Ben told me to. I wouldn't! I couldn't . . . oh,
Christ, I tell you I couldn't . . ."

George seized a handful of greasy hair and yanked
the gibbering man to his feet. "You've got a good
memory for the names of people you have never seen,
Mountfort. And I've got a good memory for lies—and
promises. Get going—and stop shitting yourself, you
cowardly bastard. Give me the light now."

The cave had been used by nomadic Nijama tribesmen for centuries. Its floor was roughly oval, perhaps
fifty feet long and twenty feet wide, covered with
layer after layer of hearth garbage, ash, and charcoal.
Smoke-blackened stalactites festooned the deformed
dome of its roof, so lofty that the light of the lantern
scarcely reached it.

Tamara Diagulski was sitting with her back propped
against the base of a broken stalagmite, bare legs
extended in front of her. One foot was turned outward at an unnatural angle. She had been stripped
violently. Blood-streaked jeans were wound around
her hips like a loincloth and the rags of her shirt
around her breasts. Her unbound, matted hair had
fallen forward over her face. If she had not raised one
forearm listlessly as the light came close he would
have believed her dead. He understood the brutish
perversions of guerilla warfare too well to have the
faintest doubt about what had happened to her.

For one breathless moment of paralysis after the
bullet of comprehension ripped into his brain he felt
nothing. Then a red, searing tide of fury drowned
him. He spun on the balls of his feet with lightning

speed, grabbed the collapsing Mountfort by the throat, and smashed the pistol butt down again and again on the top of his skull with every ounce of force that hatred could release.

Patty Mountfort's psychopath son was dead before George Galbraith dragged his body out onto the ledge and rolled it over the cliff.

"Diagulski . . . colleague . . . it's me, Sinclair. Open your eyes. It's Sinclair. You're all right."

He knelt and parted her hair gently and thrust it back. Her eyes were open, not closed—dilated, unblinking, almost luminous. God knew what they were looking at—neither him nor the light.

"Look at me, Diagulski. It's me, darling. Truly. Sinclair."

Her lips parted but she did not speak. Then she began to roll her head from side to side, slowly at first, then faster and faster. He took it between his hands and pressed hard. Her skin was slimy with the cold sweat of shock. "Steady! Stop it! Listen to me. Get your head down. . . . Wait, there's a blanket. . . ." He scrambled for the bundle on hands and knees.

"No. Don't touch me, Sinclair." The strength of her voice froze him. "I . . . I've got to have water. Water."

"Yes, there's water." He ripped open the airline bag, found Alison Burnie's little canteen, and unscrewed the stopper.

"No. Water. Please, Sinclair—*water to wash.*"

The red tide began to flow again, the blood thunder in his ears.

No! If you crack now, she'll die here. Swallow your vomit and use your head.

"Colleague, do you read me . . . ? Do you read me? I promise I'll bring you water to wash as soon as I can. I promise that. But the others aren't here yet and I can't leave. You've got to drink and you've got to get warm."

"Don't touch me, Sinclair. I know what I'm saying. I read you. I read you. I read you. . . ."

Five ampules. Morphine sulphate. Two of thirty

milligrams, three of fifteen. Fifteen would only bounce. Thirty now, and fifteen in an hour or when she became restless.

Control yourself. . . . Don't spill the bloody stuff or break the bloody needle in her leg. . . . They trained you for these capers.

"All right, Diagulski. It's time for a fix, junkie. Lie still—and afterward I'll go for water."

The injection took effect more quickly than he expected. He busied himself with frantic scavenging on the floor for fuel—charred ends of branches, charcoal, twigs in the newer ash heaps.

Near one heap which had been used recently, he found a small store of mulga brush and a log that had barely burned through. He kindled a fire almost as tiny as the one on which Elewee boiled the quart pot . . . how long ago? This morning? Or last year?

By the time the reluctant flames were licking around the quart pot, Diagulski's eyes were closed. He knelt beside her, felt for her pulse. Fast and irregular, but less feeble than he had feared. She began to slump sideways.

Out! Praise God for that! With another fifteen milligrams in an hour, she might stay out until morning.

Inch by inch he eased the girl's limp body from the butt of stalagmite onto Mountfort's blanket. He wrapped it around her closely. Lacking anything that might serve as a splint, he could do no more than align her broken shin, which had been smashed just above the ankle.

He calculated that he would require two Ritalin tablets, and when he had swallowed them composed himself to wait until the stimulant took effect.

By one o'clock in the morning, George had made three return trips between the cave and the shacks without seeing or hearing anything of Burnie or his riders. He was reasonably sure, now, that they would not come back to the encampment before daylight. He was moving with almost reckless confidence, on a galvanic high from the two pep pills.

It was a pitiable pile of booty to have cost so much effort, but he was satisfied that it could be vitally important if he had to hold out against a determined attack. At the end of the second trip he had accumulated between three and four gallons of discolored water in the rusty drum from Mountfort's hut, topped up from another container in the hut where the dead men lay; two tattered blankets wrapped around an assortment of clothing; a rag-stoppered wine flagon three parts full of kerosene; three cans of meat; and the two little calico bags of tea and sugar.

On the third trip he collected fuel—casewood smashed from the crudely improvised furniture in the shanties, and lengths of more solid wood from the hearths. The stuff was maddeningly difficult to carry, even when bound with strips of hessian ripped from the door screens. But he persisted, for when the time came—*if* the time came—quick fire would tip the balance.

A fourth trip? No. Any minute now those blasted pills were going to dump him, hard. His hands were beginning to shake again and his stomach was knotting with tension.

Get on with it while there was mileage left, and hold to the priorities.

Smoke. However slowly Roger Huskisson had hastened, it was conceivable that aircraft of one kind or another would overfly the country around Elumkuranji sometime tomorrow, but doubtful indeed that they would spot bark huts against a low cliff in a maze of small canyons—unless he could put up smoke.

After hauling the last load from the ladder head, George rested briefly, back propped against a rock. He did not dare to sit down. Then, moving very slowly and deliberately, he set about building his beacon pyre on a flat slab of limestone projecting from the ledge a few feet beyond the cave mouth. He worked mainly by touch and used the flashlight sparingly. First, a handful of rags saturated with kerosene from the wine flagon. Second, shavings whittled from the casewood, and brush overlaid with an open lattice of heavier kindling and sticks. Finally, the most threadbare blanket, also treated with kerosene but sparingly.

When the pile was completed he was sure that it would fire quickly, but how much smoke it would make and for how long were imponderables.

In action, only incompetents chewed over imponderables. . . . Next?

If Burnie or any of his men came looking for Mountfort, they would have to use the pole ladder— so would any men who might have occupied caves or overhangs further along the ledge and wanted to pick up gear before dispersing. He must locate a protected position from which he could use Mountfort's rifle to cover the close approach—the stretch of ledge between the ladder head and the entrance to this cave.

No. Not until daylight. Scrub that for the time being. Next?

Check Diagulski's condition. If there was nothing to do for her, get rest without falling asleep.

The problem of sleep . . . more Ritalin? No. The timing would be bad. It was quite on the cards that he'd get the low just when he needed a high. The first two or three hours after daybreak would be the likely critical period. If the gang had realized he'd tricked them and abandoned the wild-goose chase after Alison Burnie's riderless horse, they'd be on their guard against a trap and move with caution when they came back.

Or would they come back? In Burnie's shoes, he knew what he would do. He'd tell his riders: "Blow. Scatter. Catch up with the rest of the tribe on walkabout upriver. If a police party rounds you up, stand on one leg, let the friendly neighborhood flies crawl into your eyes, and look stupid. There's no one who can identify you with the Wandonning raid or any other raid."

Except the woman.

Ben Burnie would have to find out if Mountfort had done the job he'd been left behind to do—otherwise he must kill her himself. Whatever orders he gave the gang, Ben Burnie would have to return. And he, George Galbraith, had the problem of staying awake to welcome him, whenever he chose to come.

It was a problem beyond solution. George sat down just inside the cave mouth with the rifle beside him, knees drawn up, and head thrown back, luxuriating in the nerve-shredding agony of an amphetamine hangover that should make sleep impossible.

He woke when the sun was an hour high.

"Sinclair."

Blurred, muzzy, far away in a morphine daze. . . . He had given her a third injection after splinting her leg, now badly swollen and discolored, and sponging her vulva and thighs with diluted antiseptic.

"Here, colleague, and planning to stay. Is the leg hurting?"

"Don't . . . don't think so. Where are they?"

"Gone with the wind. Unless you mean the police —they're on their way."

"You . . . alone, Sinclair?"

"So far, but don't worry."

"You came alone?"

"Rather—hadn't much choice actually. But it worked like a charm—a one-man Entebbe to snatch the hostage. Your old colleague Sinclair is smart, and never you forget it."

Her eyes were coming into focus and wide open. They were too bright. He could sense her sudden, struggling tension. What had he said?

"The next job is to get some more drink into you. Hot tea. I remember you don't take sugar, but you'll take it this time. Give me a few minutes to brew up."

"You . . . you know about me, don't you, Sinclair? You always . . . find out."

Too bright! Her forehead was dry and burning.

Know about what?

"Look, Diagulski-as-a-term-of-endearment, I know everything about you that I want to know or need to know and I love you. Do you read me on that? Loud and clear enough? Now behave yourself and pipe

down. If you stop talking nonsense, I might even let
you hold my hand until the water boils."

Know about what?

The valley was lifeless, except for two crows wheeling
over the saucer of scrub like fragments of fire-
blackened paper caught in an updraft. And, of course,
the flies.

Lying flat on the beacon slab, moving to and from
that vantage point on his belly as slowly as a snail,
George swept the visible terrain time after time with
the binoculars. He was edgy because the huts were
hidden by a bulge in the cliff and could be approached free of his surveillance by routes other than
the ravine.

Once, soon after midday, he heard—or thought he
heard—the sound of an aircraft motor. But the heat-
hazed sky was empty and the distant humming, real
or imagined, dwindled into silence.

Two hours later, rags of cloud began to gather
about Elumkuranji's bulbous crown. To the physical
misery of waiting, grilling slowly on the rock slab, and
trying to stay alert, was added the torture of collapsing confidence—the depression of exhaustion sliding
toward a pit of despair.

For God's sake, Huskisson should have sent out
spotter aircraft after three days! Surely he couldn't
have ignored the note! It had explained clearly his
plan to improvise a smoke marker if he failed to
make headway with a hostile Burnie family and was
forced to bolt into the bush.

No, oh no! Roger Huskisson and his emu hunters
were too bloody dim to follow a boy scout's paper
chase, the devil rot their flat feet and moronic brains!
Rain clouds were already forming. By nightfall they
would have closed in over the hills.

At three o'clock in the afternoon, George abandoned his observation post and went back into the
cave. Since Diagulski had first regained consciousness, he had checked her condition hourly and had
twice forced her to drink sweetened tea. Afterward
she seemed to sleep. But this time her fever was

higher. She was tossing and muttering incomprehensibly.

There were two ampules of morphine left in the panic pouch—one of fifteen milligrams, one of thirty. George pressed the heels of his hands into weary, inflamed eyes and made his decision. Go for broke with the larger dose.

The longer he could suppress pain, hold back coherent recollection, the better her chances would be. It was layman's logic—yet another inescapable gamble.

He cradled her in his arms until she had quietened. As he lowered her head very gently when her eyes had closed, he heard the clatter of a helicopter coming in at cliff-top level from the northwest.

By the time the kerosene-soaked blanket burst into flames and spewed outward a fat, choking cloud of black smoke, the machine had passed the cave mouth and was gaining altitude half a mile beyond it.

George stood raging on the lip of the ledge, waving his arms and shrieking senseless curses. He did not see Ben Burnie leave the cover of the mulga clump a hundred yards away and move forward to bring him into the field of the telescopic sight. The 30.30 carbine slug slammed with sledgehammer force into his right thigh six inches above the knee and pitched him headlong onto naked rock just as the chopper pilot throttled back, hovered, and turned to land.

CHAPTER 26

"TEN minutes only, sergeant, and do not tire him," said Staff Nurse Felina Peredes, trying to look sternly authoritarian—which is difficult for a nubile Filipino girl aged twenty-one. "The doctor has instructed me. In ten minutes Mr. Sinclair Galbraith must have his medication. Mr. Sinclair Galbraith, you have a visitor."

George, whose waking hours since recovering consciousness in the Port Epsom Base Hospital had mostly been spent in staring at a slightly mildewed ceiling, swiveled his head and glared balefully at Roger Huskisson. "About bloody time, brother," he muttered. "Where have you been?"

Huskisson's mouth hardened. "Busy," he said crisply. "Too busy to waste time on cantankerous casualties. How do you feel?"

"If you're not careful, I'll tell you in detail. When Flatface sticks her needle in my backside in ten minutes, she'll make my day."

The old policeman's expression softened. "They've told you we're getting you out on an ambulance plane tomorrow, I expect? The neurosurgeon chap in Perth, Sorenson, is supposed to be a hotshot at cobbling up sciatic nerves and the like. We'd have moved you sooner but the local witch doctors thought it inadvisable. How about your head?"

George's eyes swung back to the ceiling. "Can't remember a thing that happened after I left the homestead, sergeant. A classical posttraumatic amnesia. Consistent with severe concussion and a hairline skull fracture. The Gunfighter told me so."

"The Gunfighter?"

"That pink, scrubbed infant with the drooping moustaches who seems to boss this pesthouse. He looked it up in his book."

Huskisson smiled broadly. "How distressing for you, old chap! And what a damned nuisance for the police, too. It's completely pointless trying to get statements from cases of posttraumatic amnesia. The poor devils can't remember a thing."

George began to say something, but then gritted his teeth and waited until another wave of pain in his back and leg broke and receded. When he spoke, his voice was a little unsteady.

"What's new on the . . . other casualties, Huskisson?"

Huskisson's tone was gentle. "You can stop badgering the matron and the Gunfighter, lad. Tamara Diagulski's out of the woods. And that's a personal assurance, not official soothing syrup. In a month or two when her leg has knitted up, she'll be back to normal. The Perth doctors said it was a fairly straight-forward repair job."

George was again studying the pattern of mold on the ceiling.

"Those bloody animals smashed it deliberately, didn't they?"

"Yes. After she'd tried to run away."

"I'm not worried about her leg—nor her other physical injuries for that matter."

"I think," Huskisson said, putting his words together with care, "that for your own peace of mind, Galbraith, you ought to spend a little time recapping what we know about Diagulski. She's not a schoolgirl. She's a woman of thirty or more, highly intelligent, physically and mentally tough, and she's proved herself in a job that would have burned out many men. She couldn't have done that unless she'd been a pragmatic realist. I don't see her as the sort of woman to let pack rape deform her emotionally. She's too strong a character."

"Yes," George said at last. "Point taken. Thanks, Huskisson—and I apologize for being a twitchy bastard. This damned leg is putting me off form. What's the news about Wrightson?"

A shrug—almost indifferent. "Out of the picture—indefinitely and perhaps permanently. A stroke. Extensive paralysis. He can't speak."

George closed his eyes. Poor sod, he thought. Even if you couldn't like him, or share his vision of the power and the glory, you had to admire his ruthless drive, his passionate determination to beat the odds. The blow dealt by an inscrutable Providence, through rupturing a few tiny blood vessels in his brain, and in a fraction of a second transplanting him from the bullring to the vegetable patch, was capricious malice of the type for which inscrutable Providence is well known.

George tensed his body to withstand another surge of pain. Huskisson watched until the spasm passed, his lined face impassive with sympathy. He had his own scars and memories of their healing.

"Well," he said, "I can offer you a bit of Job's comfort. If Ben had been carrying an Armalite instead of a carbine, you wouldn't have a leg to complain about."

"So they had an Armalite, did they?"

"They had seven in one dump near the beef road —with enough Russian-made burp guns to outfit a commando company and enough plastic explosives to flatten Port Hedland. Young Max must have convinced the cultural attachés that he was a good investment. You have grateful admirers in high places, Galbraith."

George grinned feebly. "That's a new experience for me, old boy. I've always found high places more apt to bitch than admire when something uncomfortable gets turned up. How many of the gang have you got in the bag?"

Huskisson managed to look blank.

"One, if you don't count the Canberra arrests and Ted."

"Oh."

For once in his life, George was genuinely moved to tact. No wonder Huskisson had lost weight and looked bone tired. Emu shooters at work! Tread gently.

"And who's the one? Anybody I know?"

"Ben."

George pursed his lips in a silent whistle. "I'd call that a reasonable score. Ben was the man of action— the field commander. The rest of the gang don't matter much now. And you *must* count the Canberra arrests. Young Max was only the back-room boy, the bright revolutionary tutored and manipulated by the Canberra commies, but he played a key role in organizing the diamond sales and the arms buying. Without him the campaign against Wrightson wouldn't have got far, and Black Power action wouldn't have been sparked off elsewhere. Now that the Canberra cell is out of circulation, has any further trouble occurred?"

Huskisson shook his head. "Not so far."

"Then you can't complain, can you? Still, I'm surprised that Ben wasn't smart enough to get away. I'd have put money on his being one of the last to be caught."

"We can hardly take credit for it," Huskisson said.

"Why not?"

"It'll take too long to tell now."

"Cut it for encoding," George said, closing his eyes. "Flatface is poised to swoop."

"Yes. Why do you call that girl Flatface?"

"Because she's got a flat face. Don't waste time. Get on with it."

"Very well. Four days after we picked you and Diagulski off that ledge, we got surface vehicles into Silent Reach homestead and set up a forward communications post for police parties on the ground. I'd got into the homestead forty-eight hours behind you, by chopper, with Wilf Fischer, a droopy Native Affairs body, and Rawlings—our Darwin man. We got nowhere, except to be told you'd come and gone. Until the missionaries from Barramundi Bay arrived. A redheaded priest and a nun in riding pants, a wide-awake hat, and wimple, a Sister Mary Antony, made the trip from the mission to protect the family from the excesses of the brutal constabulary. Your idea, I believe, Galbraith?"

"Sorry—an idea that wasn't necessary as things turned out," George said.

"Wrong. As things turned out, it was very necessary. If the equestrian nun hadn't persuaded Alison Burnie that Jesus Christ had told her personally that He was firmly against bombers and kidnappers, however noble their motives, we wouldn't have got aircraft over the Elumkuranji country for another twenty-four hours, maybe longer. We were concentrating the search further west."

George blinked and swallowed. "Go on."

"When you and Diagulski were out of it, I pulled back here and the state police took over ground operations. They set up their post away from the house because the old people and the missionaries were being bloody difficult. Three days later, Fischer was walking up to the homestead on some errand or other when he copped an Armalite bullet through his hat. Enter Ben."

"But . . . but for God's sake, *why?* The man could have been out of the country by then!"

"Ask the headshrinkers, Galbraith. Why did a man of his intelligence believe terrorism and sabotage could help the cause of aborigines? He must always have been unbalanced. In the end he went completely round the bend."

Staff Nurse Felina Percedes sounded as nubile as she looked.

"I'm sorry, Sergeant Huskisson, but you must leave now. Doctor gave me very strict instructions. Mr. Sinclair Galbraith is not well enough for longer visits."

"We'll be finished in a couple of minutes, nurse."

"I'm sorry, sergeant. I have to obey orders."

Huskisson started to rise.

"Just a minute, sergeant! Nurse Peredes—"

"Yes, Mr. Sinclair Galbraith?"

"I wish to speak to the doctor immediately, on a matter of great importance."

She frowned dubiously. "Very well, Mr. Sinclair Galbraith. Now, if you'll follow me, sergeant . . ."

"No," said George loudly. "What I have to say to the doctor about this hospital and its standards of professional care must be said in the presence of the police."

The girl's eyes registered amazement. "But . . . but—"

"Be off with you, young woman. Hurry, Nurse Peredes!"

She turned and ran. George lowered his head onto the pillow weakly.

"Get on with the story, Huskisson, while the enemy's diverted. A shoot-out, was it?"

Huskisson had trouble with his voice level. "No. They staked out the house and called in extra men. Ben had the priest and the nun tied up in one of the bedrooms and threatened to shoot them if the police rushed the house or used tear gas. He used Alison as a go-between. He demanded a helicopter to fly him, with the nun as hostage, to an unspecified destination. He'd read his PLO do-it-yourself handbook pretty carefully, I'd guess."

"Ho-hum," George said. "You don't exactly surprise me. Who got him—a sniper?"

The old policeman's face was stony. "No. Ben was fool enough to forget one thing. There was a double-barreled shotgun in the house, ordinarily kept under old Ellie's bed, and he hadn't bothered to tie up old Max. On the second day of the standoff, Max let him have it with both barrels, point blank."

George lay very still, looking at the ceiling again. He did not speak until he heard the clipping of the Gunfighter's shoes approaching at speed along polished vinyl. Then: "I wonder what it takes to do that to your own son, Huskisson—even in those circumstances. Madness—or sanity?"

Huskisson had started to reply when the Gunfighter came into the room, professionally brisk, jovial—and wary.

"Now, Mr. Sinclair Galbraith, what's all this about a statement to the police—scaring the cottontails off poor Nurse Peredes?"

This time Huskisson stood up. Flatface, round-eyed, hovered in the doorway.

"For the love of Pete, Dr. Paladin," George said with exaggerated peevishness, "just call me either Sinclair or Galbraith, will you? I had my hyphen-ectomy years ago. Yes, I want to make a statement, not to the police but in the presence of the police. I wish to state that this institution, despite the deplorable nature of the community it serves, is highly efficient and has a commendably competent staff. Can I say fairer than that?"

The Gunfighter flushed and swallowed. He looked very young and much confounded, even when stroking his sinister moustaches.

"Er . . . no. Quite. Of course not. That's very generous of you. How are we feeling this afternoon? Headache troubling you at all?"

"Intolerable, Dr. Boone," said George.

"Well, we can certainly do something about that. Nurse Peredes—"

"Has my medication at hand. That's precisely what I mean. Cheerio, Huskisson. Jolly decent of you to have dropped in."

"Sergeant," said the Gunfighter, "if you'll . . . perhaps a word on the way out?"

"Just a minute, doctor," Huskisson snapped. "To continue what I was saying, Galbraith—the old gentleman we've been discussing flatly and indignantly denies any blood relationship with the deceased. He seems to mean it. I'll see you before you go tomorrow —and in Perth in a day or two. I'm being relieved."

On the way down the corridor, the Gunfighter cleared his throat for a proper ventilation of professional indignation.

"I had thought, Sergeant Huskisson, that I made myself clear on the phone. I agreed to your visit on condition that the patient was not to be excited. You told me he was a personal friend. Normally we would admit only close relatives."

"He is a personal friend—"

"In addition to a severe leg wound, he is suffering a partial amnesia as the result of extensive head injuries. He was unconscious for more than a week. It was unethical of you to subject him to a police interrogation. You saw the result—"

"I did not subject him to a police interrogation. He asked for news of a family in which we have a mutual interest. To set his mind at rest, I told him what I could."

The Gunfighter gulped.

"Nevertheless, he was excited and disturbed—erratic, irrational. As a police officer—"

"You listen to me, young man," Huskisson barked, in the vein of a man who has come to the end of his patience, "I've known your patient a good deal longer than you have. I've never known him to be other than erratic. As for irrational—he never has been that and he certainly isn't now. He simply has a sense of humor which makes pompous people uncomfortable. Good day to you."

Slipping down, down, into the warm, woolly depths of Staff Nurse Peredes's medication, George could hear echoing in his head the sound of old Max Burnie's bellowing laughter: *"Suffering mother of Jesus! Did you say Hamilton Wrightson?"*

And Oscar Salinger's fluting, uneasy whine: *"For Christ's sake, how would I remember a thing like when they met? It was thirty years ago, before you was born."*

No, Oscar Salinger wouldn't want to remember Ham Wrightson's youthful indiscretions, especially his affair with a pretty aboriginal nurse at Broome Hospital so many years ago. He wouldn't want to remember why Wrightson had fallen out with Max Burnie, the young soldier back from a prisoner-of-war camp who had fallen in love with the girl, and married her, and made his remote cattle station into a refuge for her people. . . .

CHAPTER 27

IN spite of the bafflement and irritation that had been building up to the point of exhaustion over weeks, George Galbraith had to concede that Mr. Richard K. Smith, described on his engraved card as Liaison Officer, Department of the Prime Minister, handled a touchy assignment with considerable aplomb —not perhaps with quite the panache of a top-ranking Home Office man but with a very nicely calculated proportion of "you-know-that-I-know-that-you-know-old-man" to the obligatory double-talk.

George was secretly too alarmed and puzzled by his situation to indulge in the fractiousness natural to him. He acknowledged inquiries about his health and comfort civilly, accepted assurances of the authorities' gratitude for valuable information with a self-deprecating smile and modest disclaimers, and voiced appreciation for excellent medical attention in somewhat more subtle terms than he had employed with the Gunfighter.

When the set piece was finished, inner turmoil impelled him to speed up the tempo of play.

"Now that the niceties are over with, Mr. Smith," he said pleasantly, "would you be a good chap and tell me what the hell this visitation is all about?"

To his credit the young man did not miss a beat.

"Of course. With the niceties over I was coming to that. If you wouldn't mind answering a question or two, you might help me."

"Answering would be enlightened self-interest, I take it?"

"Quite. Tell me, were you thinking of taking up permanent residence in this country, Mr. Galbraith?"

George appeared to give the matter deep thought.

"It's possible, but I should say unlikely. It depends upon personal considerations that I've not yet been able to resolve. Would you be suggesting, by any chance, that I'd be well advised *not* to take up residence in Australia?"

Mr. Richard K. Smith burst out laughing. "By jove, you are a tartar, aren't you, Mr. Galbraith. I assure you the decision's entirely yours. Let's look at the facts. We have a problem. You have a problem. The problems are interwoven. The law requires that reports be lodged with the coroner on the deaths of three men in the Kimberley Division—two aborigines and a European. The deaths were not the result of police action against suspected criminals resisting arrest. The circumstances under which they received their fatal injuries are not known. There's a certain awkwardness, don't you agree?"

"Good God!" George said, barely audible. "Are you serious?"

"Naturally I am. The Silent Reach affair and the sabotage of the Halley's Circle mine attracted very wide publicity in the media. There have been other incidents of violence involving natives as well. Both politically and legally the issues are very much alive, Mr. Galbraith."

"At least I've been able to read the newspapers—for which I presume I must thank you."

"Not at all—and I notice you have a television."

George felt his face smile obediently. "Then I'm correct in concluding that the whole business is, politically and legally, a very sensitive area, Mr. Smith."

The liaison officer inclined his head. "Very sensitive indeed. So far we've been able to contain any newspaper speculation about a connection between the Canberra student arrests and violence in the far North West. The lunatic fringe is at present quite obsessed with visiting the sins committed against aboriginal people by our forefathers upon their children unto the third and fourth generation. Historically absurd, but—"

"The sins aren't as historical as all that, Mr. Smith," George interposed drily. "I suppose you haven't been to Port Epsom lately?"

"That's rather away from the point, don't you think?" suggested the liaison officer. "You must appreciate why it's to your advantage to avoid interrogation by the West Australian police."

"Ah," George said. "And it's to the advantage of Canberra if I don't talk to the newspapers and disclose that the troubles on Silent Reach are connected with a diamond strike. It would be too messy politically. It might give too much ammunition to the aboriginal lobby for land rights, and to those silly, sentimental folk who might sympathize with Max Burnie's fight to keep white exploiters from corrupting his wife's people . . ."

"Really," Smith interposed frigidly, "you're going too far, Mr. Galbraith."

George ignored him and went on: "That explains my . . . what would you call it? . . . protective detention in a Commonwealth repatriation hospital. It explains why I am still officially on the critically ill list when I'm as fit as a flea, apart from a leg in a brace and the occasional headache. It explains why I have no access to an outside telephone and why I receive no personal messages—even from my client firm, Conwright. By God, you Canberra characters have really grown up, haven't you? You're getting to be positively bloody Russian! When are you going to shunt me off to a loony bin to keep me quiet?"

The young man from the prime minister's department sounded even more frigid. "Don't be facetious," he said. "If you're wise you'll keep away from the Silent Reach business in the future."

George smiled unpleasantly. "I'd be happy to cooperate, Mr. Smith," he said. "Frankly, my experience of Australia has been unfortunate, but as I told you there are certain personal difficulties."

"Such as?"

"The reaction of Miss Tamara Diagulski, who presumably is also being kept under wraps—and with whom I've been unable to communicate."

For the first time, the young man from the prime minister's department looked acutely uncomfortable. He spoke carefully after a long pause. "Two things, Mr. Galbraith. I've read your file and I'm aware that it would be useless to try a red herring under your nose. So I can only hope you'll believe me when I say that all I know is that Miss Diagulski has been discharged from the hospital and is convalescing in the country. She has made sworn statements to the police, and I suppose she'll be required to give evidence if and when other members of the Silent Reach gang are arrested and charged. I have not been briefed on her and I have not read her file. I'm sorry."

George decided that the young man was telling the truth. That, in its context, alarmed him.

"Odd," he said, "to divide the responsibility, don't you think?"

Smith made a wry face and misquoted: "In my masters' house, there are many mansions."

"Which letteth not their right hands know what their left hands doeth," George capped recklessly. "Very well. Inform your many-mansioned masters that I won't feel disposed to oblige them until I've been given the opportunity to discuss our respective positions with Miss Diagulski, fully and in private. That's not negotiable. Any need to repeat?"

"No," said the young man from the prime minister's department unhappily.

"That seems to complete the agenda then, Mr. Smith."

"If you take the . . . er . . . list of sanctions for non-cooperation as read, yes."

"You mean the list of penalties," George corrected him. "Yes. Good. By the way, are we bugged in this room?"

"Good Lord, no!" Smith seemed genuinely startled.

George raised a waggish forefinger. "Naughty chap! What's the good of sophisticated technology if you don't make use of it? How were you to know I wouldn't be indiscreet?"

The young man rose abruptly.

"If second thoughts modify your attitude, Mr. Galbraith," he said primly, "the telephone number on the back of my card will get me at any time. Ask the nurse to call me. We will be in touch."

George waited until his visitor had had time to mutter confidentialities to the medical superintendent and leave the building. Then he pressed a finger on his bedside bell.

Exactly one hour later, a taxi deposited him at the portico of the Golden Galleon. His brace was hurting, his leg was cramping, and his head was aching, but he felt much invigorated by his brush with the authoritarian Dr. Hansen Dockerman. He had lectured the hospital chief in his coldest, most precise Cantabrigian voice—about wrongful detention, writs of *habeas corpus*, falsification of medical records, suits for damages, the Australian Medical Association, and the Council for Civil Liberties.

In surprisingly short order, George signed a standard self-discharge indemnity form with firmness close to a flourish, and limped defiantly off.

Of course, reception at the Golden Galleon remembered Mr. George Galbraith of Conwright—and, of course, George realized that reception didn't. Certainly Mr. Galbraith could be accommodated in a suite with a view of Perth Water. How long would he be requiring it?

Mr. Galbraith confided that he wished he bloody well knew and dragged himself to the elevator, followed by a cabin boy bearing luggage now reduced to a single suitcase. The trusty airline bag had not caught up with him.

A pleasantly warm breeze was blowing up from the river. George switched off the air conditioning, opened the windows, and stood with his miserable memories before lying down on the bed and taking the telephone on his chest.

Yes, this was the office of the managing director of Conwright Holdings. Who was calling, please? Oh, yes, Mr. Galbraith. Mr. George Galbraith. No, Miss Weatherley was not in the office. Dr. Margan would be tied up in a board meeting until five o'clock. There would be no chance of making an appointment to see him today. Of course, Dr. Margan would be given a message. Of great urgency . . . great personal urgency? Certainly. Mr. Galbraith would call at five o'clock and wait until Dr. Margan was free. What? The company's solicitors? Wrigley, Russell, and Slim. Yes, in the directory. Not at all. Mr. Galbraith was most welcome.

In his natural habitat the emaciated, sun-blackened Doc Margan, even in nothing but shorts, boots, and a hat, was an impressive personality. Here, in Hamilton Wrightson's scruffy office, wearing a blue business suit and a yellow tie below his jouncing Adam's apple, he was almost ludicrously insignificant—a gangling, dried-out bushman come to town for the Royal Agricultural Show. Long afterward, George was to recall Margan's greeting with rather wistful affection.

"God strike me pink, George, what *is* this? You're supposed to be in a coma."

"Who said so?"

"The hospital. Well, if not in a coma, well and truly out of circulation. Jesus, man, I've been leaving skid marks on my underpants about you. Scrambled brains and no memory. No visitors."

"We'll get around to that, Doc. Where's Diagulski?"

The expression of incredulity, surprise, and pleasure faded from Margan's face. It set into an old, stained, leather mask.

"Sit down."

"Big of you," said George viciously. "Well?"

Margan's lips hardly moved. "I don't know. I only wish to Christ I did. So do we all."

George felt the constriction of panic around his heart.

"Tell, Doc. What happened?" The demand was whispered, almost inaudible.

Margan drew a long, painful breath. "We flew her down here to the hospital, the day after the army chopper brought the pair of you out to Port Epsom. They wouldn't clear you for the trip because you were raving. All considered, she was lucky. Apart from her smashed leg, she was just lacerated and bruised and her tits were bitten. A couple of days after they shipped you down to have your own leg fixed, she asked to be discharged from the hospital. She wanted to go home to her flat in Subie. She said the hospital was depressing her. Mentally she seemed normal—a damned sight more normal than we should have believed."

"Who was with her in her flat?"

"We had a day nurse until the cast was off her leg. She's always lived on her own."

"Visitors?"

"Of course. Weatherley and she are friends, and Weatherley was there in the evenings. Several people from the office went out, too, and three of the field boys who were down on leave."

"Any outside visitors?"

Doc Margan hesitated. "I suppose so. She'd played a bit of club tennis and—"

"All right, all right, all right," George cut in harshly. "You know all about her private life but you say you don't know where she is."

"Give me a chance, man! Ten days ago, she telephoned Wrightson's home and asked to visit him. She went to the house and sat with him for half an hour but, as you know, the old man knows what's going on but he can't talk. It must have been pretty awful for them both. Next morning she came into the office to see me. She looked a bit pale and washed out and she was limping, but not too badly. As I told you, she seemed normal. We spoke about Wrightson and this and that, including you. I tried to talk her into taking a cruise or a holiday somewhere, on the company. I even pressed it a bit—too hard maybe. She was sitting where you are. Suddenly she stood up and said: 'It's no good, Doc. I'm no use to Ham anymore and I'm no use to you or the company. I've got my resignation here. I realize it seems a pretty rotten thing to do, but it's got to be effective from now. It's out of my hands anyway.' "

George leaned forward, gimlet-eyed. "She said it was out of her hands anyway. Were those her words?"

"Yes. I don't think I took much notice then, but I remember that's what she said."

"And after that?"

Margan still looked bewildered at the recollection.

"Christ, it was so completely out of the blue! I started to get up and yell at her, but she chopped me off. Diagulski could always chop a man off in mid-yell. Then she came around the desk and grabbed me and kissed me hard between the eyes and she said: 'Goodbye, Doc. Don't worry. I'll be all right.' Nobody's sighted her since."

The thin man at Ham Wrightson's desk, George perceived dimly, was very close to tears. After a while he asked: "Can you buy me a drink, Doc? Ham used to keep a bottle of Glenlivet in the cupboard."

Margan got up, went to the cabinet, and poured two whiskies without speaking. George held the glass to the light and smiled faintly. "My first since . . . How much do you really want to know if Diagulski's all right?"

Doc Margan's stare was icy.

"I wouldn't risk that line of talk if I were you."

George lifted his hands. "Okay. But if you're willing to help me, I can find out."

"You can *what?*"

"I can find out. It's up to you."

"Then speak your mind."

"Very well. But not here. This room puts me off my stroke. The whole damned business started here. Come back to the pub with me. I need a few minutes to sort my mind."

Doc Margan looked doubtfully at the level of whisky George Galbraith poured into his glass.

"Look, are you sure you ought to be knocking back big ones with that crack in your skull—"

"Shut up, Doc," George said. "Your petticoat's hanging. You said you wanted to help me find Diagulski. Does that go as far as telling me the truth?"

"Now see here—"

"I am seeing here. I know Frenchman's Bay is big. I need to know how big."

The thin man froze, dropped his eyes to his own glass, and put it down carefully without drinking. George waited.

"I hadn't heard that particular cat was out of the bag, Galbraith," he muttered uncertainly.

"But you knew the Silent Reach cat was out of the bag, didn't you?"

"Yes, thanks to the discovery of young Nathan Ebbet's body and a specimen of crystal the cops found in his pocket. The forensic lab didn't have any trouble identifying it as diamond. After that, the hunt was on. Some bright bastard in Canberra who'd read your reports to Ham put two and two together. It didn't take long for the Commonwealth demons to shake out the people young Max had sold his carbonado to. There aren't many buyers for black-market industrial diamonds in this country."

"The Burnie gang speared Nathan Ebbet because he'd made a diamond strike on the Beechover River —is that the story?" George asked.

"No, Ebbet didn't make a diamond strike. He was working much too far upriver. He happened to pick up one diamond that was being used as a *gimiri* stone —a sort of sacred talisman carried by medicine men.

He found it while he was robbing an aboriginal burial cave of stone artifacts to flog to a Perth curio dealer. The police theory is that a party of Kimberley natives, or maybe one of the true desert clans to the south, caught the poor, stupid young bugger at his grave robbing and killed him to avenge the sacrilege."

George sipped his drink. "Okay. Now answer the real question, Doc. How big is the Frenchman's Bay strike?"

Margan made a gesture of resignation.

"Never take a mining man's word," he said, "but I believe that if the Frenchman's Bay sands together with the Oakover gravels on Silent Reach upstream were fully explored and exploited, they would produce more carbonado and boart than now comes from the mouth of the Orange River in South Africa. If all of southwest Africa went the way that Angola's gone, they could make good a very considerable percentage of the shortfall of supply to western European industry."

George finished his whisky without speaking. Margan watched him somberly and held his own silence.

"Who made the Frenchman's Bay strike, Doc?"

"I did—five years ago, after Ham bought up the beach-sand company's stock when the bubble burst. He had a hunch about Frenchman's Bay. He wanted the leases kept alive. He sent me in to drill a few wildcat holes and organize a maintenance crew after the dredge closed down. More or less by accident, I discovered that the lower levels of the river sand carried boart. Boart's easy to miss. There's a hell of a lot of dirt around every carat of industrial diamond that ends up on a drill or a grinding stone."

"So the gins on the Silent Reach tin claims would probably tell you," George said. "And you've been working on Frenchman's Bay under the hat ever since?"

"Off and on, and very much under the hat."

"Why sit on it for five years?"

"Ham sat on the Millswyn iron-ore strike for ten years, until the time was right. Your answer comes in two parts—politics and money. If all of southwest Africa goes communist, Frenchman's Bay isn't just a big thing strategically—it's bloody gigantic. But whatever happens, it'll take two or three hundred million dollars to get the field off the ground as a producer. Spring tides in the Beechover estuary run forty feet."

"If the show's as big as you say, surely a few hundred million dollars is pocket money to a multinational company like the Diamond Corporation."

Margan's laugh was short and equivocal. "If you'd known Ham better, you'd know how he felt about multinationals. He had a bee in his bonnet about plowing mining profits back into regional development. He was determined to keep overall control of Frenchman's Bay. Years ago he'd had to sell his iron-ore leases at Mount Millswyn to a foreign-owned mining consortium for a lump sum and royalties. He didn't have the capital at that time to exploit the deposits himself. But today it's a different story. Conwright's profitable enough for him to pick and choose his own partners. That's why he was trying to swing a deal with a bunch of big-time London financiers, who operate independently and are not tied up with the multinationals."

"Using the good offices of the British high commissioner—very much under the lap," George muttered. "Well, that's the name of the game. Resources diplomacy . . ."

Margan shrugged. "I guess the Brits would want to get in on the ground floor of a big diamond strike."

"Wouldn't all-Australian mining concerns, or even the Australian government itself, have been interested to come in on the ground floor?"

This time Margan's laugh was entirely unequivocal.

"What all-Australian mining concern? If you exclude piss-farting scratchers like Excon, there's no such animal as an all-Australian mining concern. As for governments—federal and state alike—Ham had a bee about them, too. He reckoned the multinational miners buy and sell them in this country like share scrip. No, he wanted outside money that would give him independence from the cartels."

George passed a hand across his throbbing eyes. He felt he hadn't the interest nor energy to explore Hamilton Wrightson's dreams.

"Thanks, Doc," he said. "I've got the picture. This time tomorrow, I'll know where Diagulski is and, God willing, how she is. I've got to put myself away now. But before you go, there's one question that's got nothing to do directly with our present problem. What happens to Conwright and Frenchman's Bay now that Wrightson's laid aside?"

"God knows," Margan said wearily, hoisting his skeletal body upright. "I don't, and neither does that tight-assed bunch of stooges I spent three hours with in the boardroom this afternoon. Ham had absolute financial control. In the end, I suppose, it'll depend on his will, or whoever's legally appointed to administer his affairs."

"I see," George said softly. "You've got your worries, Doc."

"No. I'll sit in Ham's seat and fix a few oddments like your consultant's fee. Mostly I'll do nothing until the dust settles. Then I'll get the hell out. Maybe it'd be different if Diagulski was around."

CHAPTER 28

MR. RICHARD SMITH was in conference. Would the caller care to leave a message? Mr. Smith would call back.

Yes, of course the message would be given verbatim.

One moment please. What was the text? Mr. George Sinclair Galbraith . . . yes, the name was clear . . . needs to confer with Miss . . . how was that spelled? . . . D-I-A-G-U-L-S-K-I . . . to confer urgently concerning a proposed statement to the press on Beechover River and mineral deposits at present being worked by aboriginal miners. Stop. Sworn statements

covering this subject exhaustively have been lodged
with the legal firm of Wrigley, Russell, and Slim, solicitors to Conwright Holdings, to meet unforeseen
contingencies. Stop. Essential that a private meeting
between Mr. Galbraith and Miss Diagulski be arranged
today. Ends. Did Mr. Galbraith wish that read back?

Mr. Galbraith did, listened, and said, "Thank you.
Mr. Smith might prefer to cast his eye over the text
while he's still in conference. You have an awfully
nice voice, my dear. Bye!"

It took longer than George expected. Reception did
not ring to announce the arrival of Mr. Richard K.
Smith until after lunch. The morning had been so
painful that George tended to believe that Dr. Hansen Dockerman's case against self-discharge from the
hospital had more validity than appeared at the time.
But his real torment arose from the stubborn silence
of the bedside telephone.

The young man from the prime minister's department entered abruptly and at first bidding. His previous ease of bearing and manner was no longer evident.
He was pale, perspiring, and his tie was awry. A nerve
jumped in one cheek.

"How nice to see you so soon, Mr. Smith," George
said, waving a hand. "Sit down. Forgive me for not
getting up. I'm enduring a touch of the miseries."

When Mr. Smith spoke, it was in a strangled voice.
"I have been dealing with that message of yours since
I received it at eight thirty this morning, Galbraith.
Your preposterous attempt at blackmail is intolerable.
From a man with your intelligence background, it's
unethical, unprofessional, damned close to treacher-
ous!"

George closed his eyes wearily. "Mr. Smith," he
said, "you should really remember the precepts in-
stilled into you during your training. Effective nego-
tiators do not lose their tempers under any circumstances. Now let us examine what you said. You have
not been dealing with my message since eight thirty—
your many-mansioned masters in Canberra have been
dealing with it. As for blackmail, you are well aware

that you and I live in an age of blackmail—and thrive on it. Your attempt yesterday to induce me to agree to leave the country was the most arrant blackmail. And your present manner leads me to conclude that my own preposterous attempt at blackmail has been successful."

A light of sheer triumph shone out of Mr. Smith's eyes. He snapped open his briefcase, took out a sheet of official-looking paper, and thrust it at George like a dueling pistol.

"Read that, Mr. Galbraith, and you may revise your conclusion."

With a prodigious effort of will George held the smile on his lips from the beginning to the bitter end.

(1)

INFORM GEORGE GALBRAITH THAT ISRAELI NATIONAL TAMARA DIAGULSKI EMPLANED MELBOURNE INTERNATIONAL AIRPORT QUANTAS FLIGHT 11/3 DESTINATION ATHENS UNDER SURVEILLANCE OF OFFICERS OF DEPARTMENT OF IMMIGRATION. AFTER QUESTIONING BY SECURITY DIAGULSKI ADMITTED OBTAINING AND TRANSMITTING CONFIDENTIAL INFORMATION OF EXPLORATION AND DEVELOPMENT OF AUSTRALIAN MINERAL RESOURCES TO ISRAELI ECONOMIC AGENCIES. HER ACTIVITIES HAVE EXTENDED OVER A NUMBER OF YEARS BUT ATTORNEY GENERAL HAS DECIDED NOT TO PREFER CHARGES IN LIGHT OF CURRENT SITUATION.

(2)

THAT CONFIRMATION OF THE FOREGOING MAY BE OBTAINED FROM OFFICE OF BRITISH HIGH COMMISSIONER.

(3)

THAT TWO WEEKS FROM TODAY SUBPOENAS WILL BE SERVED ON HIM TO GIVE EVIDENCE AT CORONER'S INQUIRY INTO SILENT REACH AND ELUMKURANJI FATALITIES, BUT ACTION TO ASSURE HIS APPEARANCE OR IF NECESSARY NONAPPEARANCE IN CORONER'S COURT WILL BE TAKEN IMMEDIATELY IF LEAKS TO THE PRESS OCCUR.

Still smiling, but quite blindly, George held out his hand.

"Where's the rest of it, old boy?"

"Not authorized," snapped the man from the department of the prime minister.

"Nothing about . . . er . . . sanctions . . . if it suddenly came over me to be indiscreet in, say, London or New York?"

Smith intended to register more sorrow than anger and he succeeded, although George, hovering on the brink of blackout, did not notice the niceties of his facial control. "I told you I've read your file, Mr. Galbraith. I don't think even you would be reckless enough to try that."

"Probably not, probably not. But pass a message to the appropriate dignitary in your organization. Tell him that if he ever decides to put the finger on me, I'd advise him to give the contract to a top-ranking professional. I doubt that he can muster a single field agent with enough know-how to rub out a crippled midget in a football riot."

But even the gallantry of the rally didn't help. George Galbraith knew when he was beaten into impotence.

The dope was beginning to work when she came in— a little, middle-aged woman with an apple-shaped face and a withered apple-blossom mouth.

"I'm sorry if I've disturbed you, Mr. Galbraith, but I thought you would like to have it immediately."

George fought his way up through the clouds, groaning inwardly.

"Hullo, Miss Weatherley. It's nice to see you again. Sorry, I'm hardly at my best. What did you think I would like to have?"

"It's this—an enclosure in a letter with a Haifa postmark addressed to me. I've just collected the office mail from the box."

George focused his eyes with difficulty. . . . Square envelope, addressed only "SINCLAIR."

His heart seemed to explode.

"Mr. Galbraith!"

"No, no, no. I'm all right, perfectly all right. Excuse me. . . ."

Dearest of Colleagues,
I know that by now you—being you—will know. I think this is the most difficult letter I have ever had to write because I love you even more than I loved you when you rode off to find Mary Dalziel. But love and luck don't always go side by side in life. I wish I had words to tell you all that I have in my heart, but I haven't. Yet I must try to tell you what I have in my mind. We played for different teams, but we are not and never will be enemies, even in the rottenest of ever-changing worlds. I did not harm Ham Wrightson, although perhaps I would have seen it as my duty to do so in other circumstances. I admit that. Nevertheless I admired him for what he was trying to do, which in its own way was very much what my own people are trying to do. Because of that, I was able to lose myself in my work for him.
As for you, my darling, what's in my mind is harder to explain. I still cannot run away—even to the happiness you and your dear body could bring me.
I must continue my work and I will never marry. I am, if you like, programmed.
When the 1967 war began, I had gone to Israel from Australia after my foster parents died. I was nineteen years old and working on a kibbutz near the Syrian border which Palestinian irregulars overran on the second day. I received from them the same kind of wounds that Peter Mountfort and his senseless savages inflicted on me in the cave under Elumkuranji.
In my mind I was, and am still, able to cope with the reality. I have received wounds in a certain sort of war and I know that they are not dishonorable. But even the most honorable of wounds can cripple and I must face up to the fact that my emotional attitude to sexual love is not normal.
You, dearest of colleagues, made me whole again

because you were gentle and normal and you so clearly regarded me as specially deserving of gentleness and normalness.

I can't write any more—finish what I want to say. You will understand, and not grieve for us too much. Sometimes try to hear what happens when the dew falls in the desert, Sinclair. Do you remember?

The letter was unsigned.